# BRITISH FICTION IN THE 1930s

*Also by James Gindin*

THE ENGLISH CLIMATE: An Excursion into a Biography of
  John Galsworthy
HARVEST OF A QUIET EYE: The Novel of Compassion
JOHN GALSWORTHY'S LIFE AND ART: An Alien's Fortress
POSTWAR BRITISH FICTION: New Accents and Attitudes
WILLIAM GOLDING

# British Fiction in the 1930s

## The Dispiriting Decade

James Gindin

*Professor of English*
*University of Michigan, Ann Arbor*

### St. Martin's Press

First published in Great Britain 1992 by
THE MACMILLAN PRESS LTD
Houndmills, Basingstoke, Hampshire RG21 2XS
and London
Companies and representatives
throughout the world

A catalogue record for this book is available
from the British Library.

ISBN 0–333–51976–0

Printed in Great Britain by
Billing and Sons Ltd, Worcester

---

First published in the United States of America 1992 by
Scholarly and Reference Division,
ST. MARTIN'S PRESS, INC.,
175 Fifth Avenue,
New York, N.Y. 10010

ISBN 0–312–07477–8

Library of Congress Cataloging-in-Publication Data
Gindin, James Jack, 1926–
British fiction in the 1930s: the dispiriting decade / James
Gindin.
p.   cm.
Includes bibliographical references and index.
ISBN 0–312–07477–8
1. English fiction—20th century—History and criticism.
2. Literature and society—Great Britain—History—20th century.
3. Social problems in literature.   I. Title.
PR888.S62G56   1992
823'.91209355—dc20                                        91–46126
                                                              CIP

To Joan

# Contents

# Acknowledgements

This study has been aided considerably by libraries and librarians. I am grateful to the University of Sussex and its large collection of social and historical material from the 1930s, to the Bodleian Library at Oxford for its holdings of little-known novels and manuscripts, to King's College Library at Cambridge and its archivist Michael Halls, and to the University of Durham Library. I should also like to thank the University of Michigan Library for its holdings, its helpful retrievals, and its use of inter-library loan. Paul Beavers has been particularly helpful in finding material and introducing me to new computer systems. The University of Michigan has provided me with considerable aid in other ways as well. I began reading, talking and working toward this study while on a Summer Research Fellowship and Travel Grant from the Horace H. Rackham School of Graduate Studies at the University of Michigan, and the reading and writing accelerated while on a later sabbatical leave. Successive chairmen of the Department of English, John Knott and Robert Weisbuch, have been unfailingly generous and encouraging. Not only have they both made whatever arrangements they could, but they have been interested in the subject, listened willingly and provided intelligent challenge. I am also grateful for the computer knowledge and skills of E. Karen Clark, Sue Gibson, and particularly Rebecca Sizemore in preparation of this work for the publisher.

As one who learns through reading, writing and talking with others who read and write, I have been fortunate in finding numbers of people in both Britain and America who have provided insight, information, or both. Some are those who were themselves writing or reading in the thirties; some lent or found books for me I would not otherwise have discovered; others are friends or fellow teachers, some able to furnish me with information and perspectives I didn't have, some eager to discuss their own responses to fiction we both know; still others on the following list are past or present students whose questions or scepticism about my thought and interpretations have led me to reconsideration and sometimes revision. I should like to express my gratitude for one thing or another to all of the following: Professor and Mrs W. H. G. Armytage, Simon Baddeley, Richard W. Bailey, Alan Custance Baker, John Bowen, Kenneth Buthlay, David Cook, Nicholas Delbanco, Kay Dick, Lisa D'Innocenzo, Kathleen Farrell, Donald Hall, Christopher Heywood, the late David Holman, the late Dorothy Ivens, Heather Jordan, Katherine Kelly, the late Dame Rosamond Lehmann, Neil Nehring, Warren Olin-Ammentorp, Norman Page, the late Earl Schulze, Sir Stephen Spender, Robert Super, the late Dame Rebecca West, John Whitley, Ralph G. Williams, the late Sir Angus Wilson, and John Wilson.

My gratitude to my wife, Joan, to whom this book is dedicated, is singular. For more than thirty-five years, as we have read and talked, we have come back often to fiction we read in the first year of our marriage, in Cambridge, that of Rosamond Lehmann. Hers were the first novels we asked a bookseller to find for us, since all of them were not then generally available. In the ensuing years, others included in this book, L. P. Hartley, Storm Jameson and Nicholas Blake, were my wife's discoveries before I read them. As parts of our continuing conversation, the historical and academic frameworks were mine (and I am solely responsible for all the generalisations herein), the focus on particular fictions my wife's, although the discourse of long marriages tends to blur the genesis of discovery. Therefore, I would like to thank Joan, not only for her astringent and committed readings of my prose (she is, as always, a helpful and demanding editor), but also for all the creative, carefully articulated enthusiasms and insights about writing and life she has made part of my language over the years.

# 1
# The Ambiguities of Commitment

More than that of most decades, British literature of the 1930s is insistently topical, both in reference to a world outside literature and in its sense of immediacy. In part an inheritance from an earlier literary modernism that wanted to deny, question or reconstruct its connections with the past, and in part a response to an external world that seemed to be breaking down, literature for most audiences conveyed an obligation to deal with the immediate and contemporary. The writing had a tone of urgency – not always an implicit message that something need be done now, but at least a recognition that the conditions of experience had drastically changed. Historical complacency was impossible for any thoughtful writer, as were assurances that some permanent perspective could tie past, present and future together. The Jarrow march of the unemployed, the searing divisions of class and region, the attraction of intellectuals to communism and fascism, wars in China, Africa and Spain, and the apparent sterile stasis of the British government were all reflected in literature and journalism of panic, fracture and despair, in the decade's language of social and international concern.

Another language also existed about Britain in the thirties that had little currency among intellectuals. National unity, benevolent control, and a muted version of the glories of Empire still emanated from the public celebrations of the 1935 Silver Jubilee of King George V. Such a reassuring portrait of Britain might best be seen from considerable distance, as for example in America's *Time* magazine, still – during that decade likely to take its patterns of social experience from the myth of an older Britain as guidelines for those in America – as if Britain were the wise patriarchal sibling. (The opposite popular voice in America might be represented by Colonel Robert McCormick's *Chicago Tribune* which urged isolation and avoidance of the corrupt royal society

1

of Britain until after the Japanese bombed Pearl Harbor in 1941.) A
randomly selected issue of *Time* (random in its accidental survival
in a second-hand shop fifty years later), that of 23 September 1935,
assumes an audience as knowledgeable about social issues within
Britain as within America and accustomed to British dominance in
international affairs. The Britishness of that particular issue of *Time*
is overwhelming in both the extent of coverage and the language
of respect for the establishment. Despite the quick chronicle in
'The Weekly Newsmagazine' of such American fractures as Huey
Long's funeral, Father Coughlin's unsuccessful and ultimately false
attempt to accommodate his social ideas to those of President
Roosevelt, reports about conflict within the social agencies of the
New Deal, and a Weather Bureau failure to predict and government
failure to ameliorate the consequences of a hurricane in the Florida
Keys (protest led by Ernest Hemingway), these stories together
take less than one-fifth the space of the single cover story on the
newly appointed British Foreign Secretary, Sir Samuel Hoare, and
his attempts to quell fears of international crisis in Geneva. *Time*
summarises Sir Samuel's career, praises his knowledge and calm,
reports that he 'at once dwarfed' Anthony Eden, and expresses
confidence in his gentle capacity (in contrast to the ineffectuality
and undependability of the Czechoslovakian Dr Benes) to restrain
Mussolini's adventures in Ethiopia in the interests of world peace.
Throughout the long account, *Time* is certain that the British aristocrat (columns are spent on his pedigree and the artifacts in his
Cadogan Gardens town house), now that he is finally involved,
will straighten out the messes others have made. The caption under
his cover picture reads: 'When he says collective responsibility he
means collective responsibility', and *Time* undercuts its tone of
authority with none of the irony the redundant caption might
suggest for others. The British focus continues to dominate the
magazine. Other material can be treated with tolerant and knowing irony, like a report of the Prince of Wales's travels around
the Mediterranean, Geneva and Budapest with Mrs Simpson, or
an extended account of 'Old George' Lansbury's threatened resignation as Labour Party leader because his anti-imperialist and
'Christian Socialist' principles are outmoded in 1935. *Time* assumes
its readers knowledgeable about the National Government and
Ramsay Macdonald's presumed defection from the Labour Party.
The science pages begin with a long account of the British scientist's
attempt to refute Darwin's work at a convention in Norwich; the

pages summarising the week in religion contain Frank Buchman's efforts to convert Norway, Denmark and Switzerland to his campaign of Moral Rearmament. The cinema column begins with a review of *The Thirty-Nine Steps* and an account of John Buchan; the first book reviewed is A. J. Cronin's *The Stars Look Down*.

Although some of the incidents and details in *Time*'s account are reflected in British literature and journalism, appropriately little of the perspective and the reassurances are evident in literary historical reconstructions of the decade. In addition, literary works, particularly ones as topical as most of those from the thirties, change in time as they are read differently through changing events and other fictions. A definition now of what the literary thirties were can be different from definitions at the time or in the immediate aftermath. For a number of years, the most frequent reconstructions of the decade's climate have focused on what has been called the 'Auden Generation'.[1] Centring on a group of poets and novelists young in the thirties – Auden, Spender, MacNeice, Day Lewis, Isherwood, Graham Greene and Orwell – all highly conscious of social strains and dilemmas, committed to public statement and experimentation with various literary forms, the Auden Generation has, with good reason, become the critically canonical formulation of the decade. I have no wish to overturn or bash this canon – it is appropriate and self-justifying – or to position myself critically through a simple negative alternative. Rather, I see some consideration of the Auden Generation as a starting point, a cogent and forceful definition that provides a coherent beginning for literary reconstruction. But the definition needs extension, particularly considering some of the period's important and involving fiction, often read then and since. The *Time* magazine account is almost a cartoon of the decade, but some of the implications of attitudes associated with it (although not its complacency about Britain) are visible, in other contexts, in the fiction.[2] Contexts change in time; shapes from the past alter into different forms contingent on language and retrospections from a more proximate past and the present. History, as it is constantly rewritten, is always in danger of hardening into the perspectives once used cogently to explain a part of it.

My intention in this book is to try to broaden and resurrect a general critical commentary of the British literary thirties through a treatment of both the content and form of some of its fiction of social representation. I am not the first to expand and qualify Samuel Hynes's 1976 formulation of the Auden Generation. Two

much more recent books, those by Frank Kermode and Valentine
Cunningham, implicitly and explicitly extend that definition as
well.[3] Cunningham's comprehensive work adds essays, polemics
and journalistic accounts of historical events. Kermode readjusts
historical understanding of middle-class transgressions and worthy, self-critical motives within the Auden Generation itself. I shall
try to shape a greater complexity of middle-class social attitudes
through their fictional representations in what I hope to illustrate
is a representative variety of literary forms.

One of the immediately noticeable elements in the definition
of the Auden Generation is its focus on newness (itself a time-
sanctioned way of defining generations), its emergence within a
set of young, distinguishable, unique writers. In some senses, of
course, the consciousness of newness outlines a generation, its
articulated differences from earlier generations. The Auden Generation was acutely conscious of its newness, full of the language of
demands for social change and new frontiers. Intensely responsive
to the atmosphere of social crisis, the writers sought to extend the
boundaries of the literary treatment of class and sexual issues, as
well as to respond directly to the problems they perceived. But
the definition of a literary decade based solely on the writers first
emerging during that decade simplifies ahistorically what a lot of
thoughtful and talented people were reading and writing. A fuller
account of the literary culture of the thirties requires consideration
of writers who were responsive and changing beyond the age
of thirty-five. If literary generations are to be defined by close
proximity in age and a flourishing emergence within a span of
no more than ten years (various commentators have talked of
generations as changing every three or four years, the span of
a university education), the historical study of a decade needs to
acknowledge a number of simultaneous generations all treating and
responding to some version of the same external events.

For the young Auden Generation, the problems and events of the
thirties called for some form of apocalyptic transformation. Many
others, too, whatever their politics, viewed incidents as manifestations of extreme crisis that would require total transformation
to solve. The event need not have been political. As Valentine
Cunningham points out, when the vast Victorian exhibition hall,
the Crystal Palace, burned in 1936, 'it was widely taken as an
apt emblem for the times: a sort of Reichstag Fire for Britain,
mirror image of what was happening in Madrid'.[4] Apocalypse

seemed imminent and necessary for the Auden Generation, even though many of its best writers finally backed away from the implications of totalitarian forms of political apocalypse in the world of the thirties. The backing away and the edging of the apocalyptic with irony became more pronounced in retrospect, as in Auden's almost immediately subsequent uneasiness about what he had in 'Spain, 1937' called 'the necessary murder'. Conversions or serious considerations of conversions to communism or the Roman Catholic Church, as in the work of Graham Greene, were frequent, testimony to the appeal of total transformation. Many of the poems debated the issues of a journey to some total and newly apprehended truth. Older writers, and particularly writers of fiction, however, while responsive to the same sense of cultural crisis, were often less attracted to the totality of apocalypse, both in its tangible manifestations of the world of the thirties and in its metaphorical necessity. Although Frank Kermode, the most learned, imaginative and sympathetic critic of a generation just slightly subsequent to the Auden Generation, has argued that the form of fiction itself satisfies a reader's desire for apocalypse in its endings or conclusions,[5] the length, variety and social irresolution of much of the thirties' actual fiction works against any overwhelming simulacrum of or interest in apocalypse. Fiction is likely to be a longer, more attenuated, perhaps safer form than poetry.

In her late essay called 'The Leaning Tower' (originally a talk given to the Workers' Educational Association in Brighton in May 1940), Virginia Woolf criticised, despite her admiration for their honesty and probity, the younger writers of the Auden Generation for too easily succumbing to abstract political, psychological and genealogical determinism in their ideas of what a writer should be. She also mocked equally, with somewhat less sympathy for the young, the visionary and potentially apocalyptic artist for whom the 'writer is a heavenly apparition that slides across the sky, grazes the earth, and vanishes'.[6] Another writer and critic just slightly older than the Auden Generation, Robert Graves, whose *Goodbye to All That* (1929) was one of the first significant memoirs from the First World War, derogated the thirties' fascination with apocalypse even more sharply in his account of the interwar period from 1918 to 1939 he called *The Long Week-end*. In a preface written for a reissue of the book in the survivors' security of 1950, Graves maintained that Britain now was 'well rid of its nastier internal dissensions and its neurotic sense of imminent catastrophe. You feel that the worst has now happened, that it was deserved, that the British as a whole have since behaved better than at any period of their history, and that though it is hard to decide whether one should view the cutting-away of so much national top-hamper with admiration or resentment, they may even, after all, have a future'.[7] Graves's criticism, however, is too easily dismissive, particularly when it degenerates into personal and inaccurately reductive attacks on members of the Auden Generation: 'Auden was a synthetic writer and perhaps never wrote an original line: but modern literature was so extensive that his communistic use of contemporary work was not at first suspected. He wrote satirically of existing British society and rather vaguely drew the moral that only the teachings of Marx and Freud and George Groddeck could reform it; Spender wrote poor-little-rich-boy poems, full of genuine pity for the exploited poor, and for himself; and Day Lewis's sentiments were those of a simple-minded Red'.[8]

The writers of the Auden Generation added to their focus on total transformation a more politically naïve interest in the heroic, the figure who might propel the transformation. They were close enough to the slaughter of the First World War to reject connection with any conventionally articulated heroism of the recent past. But they were, until after the experience in Spain, young enough and sufficiently removed from the actual conditions of war not to be sceptical about the elevated conditions of heroism itself. Dramatisation of the heroic figure with any degree of complexity presented problems, as in Auden and Isherwood's 1936–7 play, *The Ascent of F6*, which concentrated on the mountain climber whose monomania destroys both his world and himself, but which evaporates in empty rhetoric and psychological jargon. In contrast, their earlier dramatic collaboration, *The Dog Beneath the Skin* (1935–6), a brassy, cabaret-like parody of the conventional country-house hero on a quest, is still startling and effective theatre. The good heroic figures worked better, for Auden and others, in the context of poetry where they could be represented, abstracted, removed in time, like the figures of old unconventional Norse Gods, or in space, like the figure of the airman. No image was more common for the writers of the Auden Generation than the heroic airman who, combining range, comprehensive sight, totally new technology, activity and distance might point the way for human redemption. Often seen as a bird as well, connected with various examples of powerful classical birds, the airman gloried in his new and distinctively contemporary power. The power was not simply abstract; it was also the power over the ordinary dull and undiscerning people who were frequently dehumanised into masses or puppets. The glory in exceptional power, in new technological, moral and visionary supermen, was defended on the basis of the overwhelming need to transform the corrupt, complacent and static past. In strictly British social and political terms, writers of the Auden Generation thought there was 'no Parliamentary solution to the problems of Britain'.[9] In more global terms, the airman became the figure whose power and mission could not be limited by old, earthbound, sterile national divisions. The form of the novel, unless it is converted to parable, is less hospitable to the heroic. Novelists of the Auden Generation, Greene and Orwell, for example, were likely to undercut the potential hero, like Greene's whiskey priests or seedy saints.

Orwell is particularly difficult to discuss in this context, since his disillusion with totalitarian transformation combined with his painful, almost physical, attraction to it, and his work exudes a romanticised envy for a proletarian simplicity he felt he could not incorporate. His attempts to express his contradictory world in stringent, direct language led to forms like the report or the parable that, as he used them, simplified his ideas and his experience. His forms were direct, easily accessible; his uses of metonymy were vague and uncontrolled. Although he advocated and wrote a clear, unambiguous prose, the representations of his social and political perspectives and the ambiguities of his commitments were sufficient to warrant a number of different and contradictory posthumous glorifications by other writers. Orwell can be and has been read as staunch conservative, non-ideological leftist, closet totalitarian welcoming the pain of his self-destruction, and simple man of common sense avoiding all cant or political propaganda. A recent book by John Rodden, *The Politics of Literary Reputation: The Making and Claiming of 'St. George' Orwell* (OUP, 1989), develops some of the different legends (sometimes the same writer creating different legends of him at different times) others have made of Orwell since his death in 1950. Orwell was also horrified by what fascinated other members of the Auden Generation – new technology. Both in form and in content, new kinds of communication like radio and cinema, as well as new modes of danger like bombs, infuse their work. From the point of view of subsequent generations of writers almost innured to television, automation and computers in fact and myth, the thirties concern with technology seems a slightly naîve and excessive enthusiasm. On a 1988 television programme commemorating the centenary of T. S. Eliot's birth, Stephen Spender poked fun at himself for the days when he wrote poetry about pylons, although he more often and seriously now defends his generation in the thirties against charges of 'moral bankruptcy' by asserting that their choice 'was not for a vague abstraction (political conscience) over *patria*, but for the horizontal world of the whole of humanity viewed as one in the classless substratum of the oppressed and the proletariat – the International – as against the vertical segmented *patria* of England'.[10]

Explicit attempts to counter moral bankruptcy seem a more definitive and significant characteristic of the Auden Generation than does enthusiasm about technology. Conscious of themselves not only as writers of a particular time of crisis, but also as didactic, the members of the Auden Generation expressed themselves as moral voices directly challenging the corruptions and emptiness of their time. They wrote short instructive parables with messages underlined, manifestoes, orations and other moral injunctions to their fellows. Their voices were those of the demanding and concerned schoolmaster, which some of them initially were. Aware that they were highly educated, middle-class writers reacting against what they saw as the stabilities and sterilities in their own backgrounds, the writers of the Auden Generation tried to reach a large audience. The schoolmaster's voice was, in part, a device to bridge the distance between themselves and an audience they knew could not, by class and education, identify closely with them. The attempt to be simple and popular was full of contradictions, for their topical references were often contorted and their style abrupt and opaque in their desire also to avoid the literarily familiar, old-fashioned and complacent. The moralism was clear, the conjunction of their interests and focus with those of the wider audience they sought often much less so. They also were primarily poets trying to include an audience that might have a residual memory of ballads and hymns but was not much accustomed to reading contemporary poetry. Slightly older writers of fiction, however, were often less interested in parable than in the condition-of-England novel. For them moral injunction, repeated over the space of the novel, could become simplified hectoring, alienating audiences of whatever class or education. While many of the novelists to be treated here were moral in their own, sometimes more complicated ways, they avoided the language of injunction and the didactic schoolmaster's voice.

The stance of the schoolmaster was important for the Auden Generation in other ways as well. Upper-middle class, classically educated, and at school during the First World War, the writers spent a good deal of their literary energy excoriating the public schools they thought had largely imprisoned and formed them. Although, from the retrospective outside, contemporary social commentators can legitimately write that, for that generation, 'there was, significantly, some evidence of the softening of the hard lines between the "hearty" and the "aesthete" at the public schools, and somewhat less insistence on the absolute primacy of games',[11] the writers themselves endowed their experience in public schools, set as social islands in the midst of chaos, with a crucially formative influence. To their reaction against the ethos of their schools, they attributed their initial devotion to the aesthetic (in defiance of the old boys and the games), their cliquishness, their scholarship, their commitments outside of class and nation, and their sometime use (clearer in retrospect than at the time because of the restrictive laws that also helped to determine their behaviour) of homosexuality as part of what they intended as liberating sexual experimentation. But they carried the language and concerns of the public schools with them. Even Henry Green (one of the novelists to be discussed here), only tangentially to be connected with the Auden Generation and seldom writing his fiction as if determined by the school he did not hate, spent most of his 1940 autobiography, *Pack My Bag*, recounting experience at the school he would not name (Eton) and left in the mid-twenties.

The Auden Generation's explanations of themselves were likely to be schoolmasterly as well. They traced influences of family and school, devoured Freudian and Marxist accounts of personal, social and historical experience. Although they were not necessarily ideological Marxists (and among themselves demonstrated a range of current reading and knowledge), they tended to explain themselves and others in inflexible chains of cause and effect, in terms of social and historical necessity. The account of cause and effect was likely to be carefully logical, meticulous, an assemblage of topical details that demonstrated society's corrupt stasis. All this was to be swept away by change, by the future, by the heroic airman or other transforming figure. Frank Kermode is acute in duplicating a characteristic language and semantic leap in his summary of the committed Marxist Christopher Caudwell's last definition of transforming love:

> Trying to tell us the truth about love, he says it isn't what the movies suggest, nor is it what Freud thinks it is, or we should have a whole set of words to distinguish between sexual love, the love of friends, the love of one's children, the love of one's fellow humans. Sexuality is important because, via genetics, it creates consciousness, creates individuals; but even deeper than sex there is a primitive economics, which seems to be for Caudwell the deepest level of love. It emerges at different periods in the distorted forms imposed by economic history: chivalrous love in the feudal, passionate love in the bourgeois eras. In the present age, in the time of the death throes of capitalism, human relations lack even the distorted strength they had under feudalism; affection is conditioned by the cash economy, tenderness dies (a touch of D. H. Lawrence here), and love is displaced on to Fascist dictators. True social consciousness is repressed. Communism alone can restore direct contact with that primitive economic base and bring back love into human societies.[12]

Caudwell's lines of historically determined change are to be transformed by visionary wish activated into will.

Caudwell represents the extreme of unambiguous commitment within the Auden Generation. A prodigious talent, he published advanced aeronautical engineering reports, detective fiction, sociological accounts, and influential historical and literary criticism, all within less than ten years of the thirties. But his function as visionary historian came to seem hollow to most middle-class intellectuals by the time his posthumous *Studies in a Dying Culture* was published in 1938. The book was reviewed in the *New Statesman* by E. M. Forster who by 1938, through his earlier fiction and his essays, had, almost against himself, become a kind of authoritative middle-class literary voice in the context of the general intellectuals' disillusion with communism in Spain and elsewhere. In the review, Forster gave Caudwell credit for his genuine concern with all classes and people, his moral intentions and honest extensions of love. Forster then delicately disentangled the inflexibility of Caudwell's reasoning about cause and effect, concluding with a characteristically gnomic note of caution: 'Beware of the long run'.[13] Sensible and immediate as the advice seems, Forster's comment can also be interpreted as a warning against the immediacy and topicality of Caudwell's proposed revolutionary and transformative solutions. The 'long run' may be read as the short run or the lethal quick fix, after all, and for Forster the only constant legacy and alternative to despair may be in the decade's language of social concern as an individual defence against the tyranny of totality.

Virginia Woolf's criticism of the Auden Generation's social perspective uses more personal language and the metaphors of fiction to make an historical point similar to Forster's. For Woolf, the writers of the Auden Generation have built a 'leaning tower':

> All those writers too are acutely tower-conscious: conscious of their middle-class birth; of their expensive educations. Then when we come to the top of the tower how strange the view looks – not altogether upside down, but slanting, sidelong. That too is characteristic of the leaning-tower writers; they do not look any class straight in the face . . . Then what do we feel next, raised in imagination on top of the tower? First discomfort; next self-pity for that discomfort; which pity soon turns to anger – to anger against the builder, against society, for making us uncomfortable. . . . And yet – here is another tendency – how can you altogether abuse a society that is giving you, after all, a very fine view and some sort of security? You cannot abuse that society whole heartedly while you continue to profit by that society. And so very naturally you abuse society in the person of some retired admiral or spinster or armament manufacturer; and by abusing them hope to escape whipping yourself. The bleat of the scapegoat sounds loud in their work, and the whimper of the schoolboy crying "Please, Sir, it was the other fellow, not me." Anger; pity; scapegoat beating, excuse finding – these are all very natural tendencies; if we were in their position we should tend to do the same. But we are not in their position, we have not had eleven years of expensive education. We have only been climbing an imaginary tower. We can cease to imagine. We can come down.[14]

Samuel Hynes, the definer of the Auden Generation, calls Woolf's essay the generation's 'obituary' and complains that Woolf's own forms of unacknowledged determinism have fixed her criticism into historical myth.[15] If so, which is not the way I read the essay or her fiction, the myth is wider, more vital and more understanding than 'obituary' can suggest. Throughout the essay, Woolf cites the extenuating facts of the Auden Generation's vulnerability to the events of the thirties and claims that had she been their age in their circumstances she'd have become the same. She praises their difficult honesty with themselves and their conscientious attention to ameliorating abrasions of class they cannot resolve. She claims that their work and teaching will lead to the probability of a merging of classes in the post-war world (it is an ancillary amazement, confirmed in the metaphors of *Between the Acts*, to find Woolf in 1940 envisioning any kind of post-war world) that will itself be able to write fiction of 'no private ground' but of 'the common ground'.[16] For Woolf, the Auden Generation will live as teachers rather than as writers of fiction. Her critical characterisation underlines their shortcomings as particularly damaging to the novel form: their failure to apprehend human emotion, their incapacity to create character, and the lack of recognition that all towers are imaginary.

The Auden Generation saw the Spanish Civil War as unequivocally the central event of the decade. As it began in 1936, they regarded it as the extreme struggle between forces of good and evil, the polar battle between the necessitarian dogmas of Communism and Fascism. That it took place outside of Britain also satisfied the conscious internationalism of their viewpoint, the honesty of their humane concern, and their conviction that what was going on in Spain was an image of an imminent Armageddon. They could retain the symbol and the displacement through their foreknowledge of the fact that the British government of the thirties would do nothing decisive. In addition, they knew enough about Spain to recognise a frightening religious intensity in the culture, a quality so far from the bourgeois compromises of Britain that Spain could serve as the locus for the universal struggle soon to arrive. Others, just slightly older, saw Spain differently, in a focus that concentrated on Spain's neutrality and lack of involvement in the First World War. Some, like the American Hemingway, regarded that neutrality as immunity from the corruption that the First World War had revealed in the rest of Europe, the religious intensity as a primitive purity Europe had lost over centuries of bourgeois conflicts. Others, like Rose Macaulay, saw the primitivism as itself corrupt and barbaric, a lethal immunity from the complexities of civilisation. Robert Graves, who lived there between the wars, thought that Spain had escaped the First World War 'only by accident' because their military rulers had inclined towards Germany and their industrialists and commercial leaders towards France. In the twenties and early thirties, he thought that the Spanish would 'one day have to pay for their neutrality, which had been at the expense of national honour'.[17] Some of the members of the Auden Generation, like Auden himself, recognised the differences between Spain's past and the rest of Europe. But for Auden, in 'Spain, 1937', the religious intensity, the barbarity, and the Inquisition were 'yesterday', ironically and totally different from the global 'struggle' representing Spain 'today'.

Writers of the Auden Generation debated their own individual commitments, agonised genuinely over what they could or should do, and many of those who participated actively, like the poet John Cornford, the poet Julian Bell (Virginia Woolf's nephew) and Christopher Caudwell, were killed. Whether they committed themselves physically to the Spanish war or not, members of the Auden Generation recognised a psychic commitment, the opportunity to assuage their guilts concerning their favoured births and expensive educations by joining a common cause. Julian Symons, a survivor of the period, has convincingly developed what for many was the 'wish to submit themselves to this dread authority'.[18] After the experience of the war itself, its disasters and defeats, the compromises and betrayals within what they had thought the righteous cause of international communism, their guilts switched to an even more painful recognition of how mistaken and naive their choices, both physically and intellectually, had been. They had desired the possibility of unselfish and total transformation, which the age seemed to welcome and require. The Auden Generation's fascination with heroism, never in itself simply conventional or naïve, had both an intellectual warrant and a painful willingness to sacrifice self for a vision of the common good, its own form of a global religious intensity. Or, to put it in terms that Kermode applies to Caudwell and others, the desire to transgress established conventions and extend the boundaries of human love. Crucial about the actual experience of Spain for the Auden Generation was its erosion of their confidence, of the force of their characteristic language, and its painful lessons about the ambiguities of commitment. The experience was far less crucial for the world of corruption and compromise they sought to redeem, the world that, in the thirties, had long since lost or had never had faith in social transformation.

More than the Auden Generation is necessary for this study of
the thirties fiction of social representation. The continuities implicit
in most fictional forms and the proliferation of the condition-of-
England – or to describe with more particular accuracy the condition-
of-Britain novel – requires treatment of other writers as well. Yet in
many ways language, themes and attitudes are identical. The simultaneous necessity for and fear of violence that is visible throughout
the work of the Auden Generation is either explicit or a central part
of the linguistic subtext in the work of almost every writer of the
period. Derived from a memory of the First World War or a fear of
the Second, or both, the language of battles seems overwhelming.
J. B. Priestley's *English Journey* (1934) is full of English scenes that
recall the misery and violence of the trenches; bombing metaphors
infuse Elizabeth Bowen's *The Death of the Heart* (1938), explosions
of emotion and sensitivity. Images of social and emotional violence
crowd the fiction of writers as different in subject matter and social
location as Rosamond Lehmann and Lewis Grassic Gibbon. All
these authors, like those of 'the Auden Generation', constantly
suggest a perspective that fears encirclement and destruction, as if,
physically or metaphorically, to be surrounded or to be threatened
is to be destroyed. Both socially and psychologically, the writers
of the thirties, almost universally, convey a fear of invasion. A
recent article on popular culture (noticed widely enough to earn
respectful refutation from Valentine Cunningham) makes the point
that fiction in the thirties had little of the panic and fear of invasion
of the popular fiction before 1914, that 'Fascism was treated as an
internal disease rather than as external military danger'.[19] But the
refutation doesn't go far enough. The article pays no attention to
the language and imagery of any writers. What, for many, changed
between pre-1914 and pre-1939 is the degree of explicitly expressed
panic (emotions are expressed in ways more muted or understated,
although no less frightening, when made familiar by the repetition
within such a short span of historical time), as well as the jingoism
and the definition of the 'home' threatened by invasion. In pre-1914
popular fiction, home was literal, the Englishman's castle and the
repository of virtue. But the serious fiction of the thirties extended
the signification of home. The fear of encirclement or invasion, as
well as of the socially or politically static, led writers to want, both
metaphorically and physically in so far as they were able, to keep
moving. In this sense technology mattered, and all the writing is
full of modern means of transport, communication and journeys.

Many of the best novels are also accounts of travel, gestures against the fears of both insularity and destruction that home represents. Settings are often outside Britain, or, when within Britain, far from the point of origin. The fiction is full of landscapes and provinces as settings, facts and metaphors. Geography signifies. The fiction contains a good deal of both conflict and assimilation between the representations of London and the provinces. No single set of values, attitudes or even kinds of representation can apply. The serious fiction of the thirties demonstrates a literary extension of concepts of place, an extension aided considerably by technological change. For the middle classes, travel on limited funds was more possible and desirable than it had been. Geography was an important part of literary consciousness, and its use expressed the restlessness, lack of security, curiosity, sense of imminent change, and fears of destruction that characterised the literary decade.

The fiction of the thirties, like the writing of the Auden Generation, reveals an increasing interest in the human body, just as it shows an interest in bodies of land and water. Physical experience was valuable both in itself and as a representation for all experience when danger and destruction threatened. Frequently, the physical experience in the fiction is sexual experience. Sex and love have always been themes of imaginative literature, and sexual relationships used constantly as the most intense and meaningful of individual relationships, with implications for family and society, are significant representations in almost all bourgeois fiction. In thirties fiction, the treatment of sexuality in terms of human feelings, emotions and psychological responses is particularly noteworthy. It is as if almost every novelist, in his or her own way, followed D. H. Lawrence in examining or analysing the importance of the physical response to sexual experience rather than using sexuality as simply an emblem of the revolt against family, convention, or the past, as did some of the Edwardian novelists and those of the twenties. In part, of course, the interest in the variety and meaning of sexual experience can be attributed to the growing interest in Freud (Freud often read simply as an analyst liberating sexuality) and others dealing with psychology. In addition, fiction of the thirties shows, from various points of view, an increasing interest in homosexuality. The First World War, with young men imprisoned for months in the mud of the trenches, with no other outlet for impulses of love and sex and little possibility for belief in the virtues of postponement, had led to an increased consciousness of homosexuality that worked its way into serious literature. For members of the Auden Generation, public school boys who were young and felt guilty for just having missed the pain of war, the psychological connection with homosexuality, however one acted, was acute. As Valentine Cunningham summarises, in explaining why a number of young members of the Auden Generation took German lovers: 'It was all a way of being, so to say, in the First War by proxy, a participation in a murky underground substitute for the uniformed world of the military father and elder brother, a wasteland place that was legally and physically dangerous, where one's pacifist conscience could be appeased in a parody of the Christmas Day 1914 fraternisation with the enemy, and one's guilt over missing the War could be assuaged in submission to the father and elder-brother as chastiser'.[20] For other, sometimes older writers, the connection between homosexuality and psychic pasts was less intense, apprehended less clearly or shrouded by greater silence or guilt. In addition, in the thirties, young writers, both in fiction and in experience, deliberately experimented with homosexuality as a broadening of sexual knowledge in a more liberated age without any anticipation of this as a life-long commitment or definition (and, for some, it was not). Although, because of their youth, the writers of the Auden Generation were sometimes more explicit than other writers, the consciousness of the possibilities, languages, dangers and ambivalences of human sexuality was common to the decade.

With a constant sense of imminent danger, a major theme in thirties fiction, as in the work of the Auden Generation, is that of betrayal. In social, political, religious, personal or sexual terms, referring to both individuals and societies, the pain of betrayal, of disastrously broken promise or expectation, reverberates through all the literature. The thirties felt betrayed, violated by the difference between expectation and experience. Unlike much of the fiction in the fifties and sixties, for example, in which betrayal is irrelevant because nothing was ever expected, and nihilism can be cheerful, the fiction of the thirties, like that of Elizabeth Bowen, Rosamond Lehmann, J. B. Priestley, or L. P. Hartley, radiates the pain of betrayal. This does not mean that the fiction is suffused with self-pity. Most often, in good fiction, it is not, for a subtext of self-pity can drown a novel, and many of the writers of the thirties were as rigorous in avoiding sentimentality or self-pity as were those of the twenties. Still, the pain of the betrayal, justified through the text, makes a strong impact on the contemporary reader. As might be expected in a decade so concerned with what seemed to be a dissolution of society as it had been understood, a great deal of the betrayal in thirties fiction is localised in terms of social class. In a decade of economic deprivation in which social and educational inequities lingered from a system that writers saw increasingly as never having been justifiable, a consciousness of class issues was part of every novel that dealt with British society. To some extent, of course, that issue is not new, for Victorian and Edwardian novelists were generally far from complacent about the inequities of British society. But the pain increased in the thirties, as did the attempt of the middle-class educated writer to develop masks, personae, submerged guilts, changed voices or names, in order to participate in the experience of other, often voiceless classes. Orwell's emotion of proletarian envy is an extreme although not an unusual example. Sometimes, the fiction was the writer's transcription of an honest attempt to change or become part of a deprived and mostly silent other class, sometimes itself, as fiction, a substitute or simulacrum for a transposition in class the writer could not manage outside his or her imagination. Of course, these attempts were full of contradictions or illusions, and the good writers of the thirties knew this as part of the pain and betrayal they chronicled, the ambiguities of class and commitment they expressed. Writers sometimes sought to dissolve the fissures of class in love, physical, political, even international. But, like Henry Green, they also realised that, in trying to dissolve the divisions of the exterior world, they were sometimes dissolving themselves. In the fictive imagination, they knew one might not emerge from a process of deliberate submerging. In addition, the social problems of the decade were too acute to permit, for most of the writers, the consolation and feeling of triumph in the creation of art itself that characterised some of the best writers of the previous decade. The novelists of the thirties, for the most part, simultaneously questioned and were attracted to the primacy or special value of art and the artist, the work itself as the imaginative transformation of experience. Instead of defending art as a privileged sanctuary, most of them, like Rebecca West and Storm Jameson, felt the need to deal with the ambiguities of class and society, the pain of social, political and sexual fractures, within whatever representatively non-transcendent forms they could.

In terms of form, most of the serious, able, reflective novelists of the thirties to be discussed here avoided the parable or other form that could yield a single message. Their use of form was often less compressed, their treatments of experience sufficiently complex to require looser, more adaptable forms. They were less conscious of their newness than the modernists a short generation earlier had been, and saw themselves, like Rosamond Lehmann, as in a tradition of the growth of the novel as a voice of the emerging bourgeoisie of the eighteenth and nineteenth centuries, trying to articulate and assimilate its view of its world. Although they recognised other literary origins (and often used them or mixed them), they were not about to abandon the social concerns, the explicit or implicit statement about the condition of Britain or the awareness of the complexities of class that the bourgeois form suggests. Formally, as thematically, they often tried to incorporate the past as well as to demonstrate the changes and deepening severity of problems that rendered the past alone inadequate. Some like J. B. Priestley used the picaresque or the mock picaresque, ways of satisfying the interest in both range of social statement and travel or journey, the map of contemporary Britain; some, like Storm Jameson, depended on the chronicle, a loose form that could incorporate both changes in time and the representations of geopolitical diversity; others, like Henry Green, worked through tighter and more compressed metaphor, although he represented diversity and social complexity through the comedy, intricacy and language of the metaphors themselves. None of these writers is apocalyptic, or dependent on abstract statement about the nature of the human being. Implicit in all their work is some suggestion of untransformed historical continuity and change, as well as a texture of social and characterological detail. Their forms often allow a mixture of journalistic reporting and fictional detail, a mixture of different kinds of discourse that novelists have always used and literary critics have come more frequently to analyse and appreciate.[21] And the details are as likely to convey social meaning through various patterns of metonymic representation as they are through developed metaphor. In both formal and thematic terms, the suggestively social elements in much of the fiction of the thirties are not always resolved.

In part, the difference between the Auden Generation and the writers of the fiction of the thirties is the difference between a definition derived from poetry and one derived from prose. When they grant primacy or greater value to a definition derived from poetry, critics sometimes depend on the old critical and cultural tradition that good poetry, in its compression and succinctness, reaches a depth both resonant and revealing which the looser and more popular forms of fiction can only more clumsily approach. The more intense and consistently significant language of poetry is granted an intellectual and historical status denied the formulations of prose. The poets of the Auden Generation, historically knowledgeable, linguistically intense and well able to use their classical educations, can sustain and illustrate this distinction, although, for the most part, they did not themselves make such a narrowly high-minded and evaluative judgement. Besides, a number of them, like Isherwood and Orwell, were novelists. The work of the Auden Generation, mostly poetry but some fiction, sustained the linguistic intensity, the capacity for total transformation, the sense of possible apocalypse, and the sweeping historical statement in a way different from the qualifications of both history and metaphor common to many other writers of fiction. Transforming intensity is much more difficult to conclude from the length and texture of historical and social reference in most of the fiction of the thirties. Even in prose, the question is one of the intensity of social language and metaphor. Orwell, for example, could write about cricket that: 'It is not a twentieth-century game, and nearly all modern-minded people dislike it. The Nazis for instance . . .'[22] The kind of novelist under discussion here might dislike cricket just as much, but, if using it as detail or example, could not (unless satirising a character or perspective) allow so historically or metaphorically sweeping or falsely connected a statement to remain unchallenged.

Although often influenced by older forms of the bourgeois novel, and interested in one way or another in conveying the condition of Britain, most of the novelists to be treated here did not deny the innovations of a preceding generation of modernists in fiction. To call them formally conservative would be to overstate the case. Besides, what we now describe as modernism, both thematically and technically in fiction, was a gradual and uneven series of changes in fiction, taking place over half a century, not the sudden thunder-clap that many of the novelists themselves, in their anxiety to separate themselves from their progenitors, thought it was about the time of the First World War. In 1924, separating herself and her generation completely from Arnold Bennett and his, Virginia Woolf could still write that, since human nature had changed in 1910, fiction needed to change entirely in order to represent interior experience adequately. She called *The Years*, the novel published in 1937, her Arnold Bennett novel – a designation that carried more respect than irony. Both *The Years* and *Between the Acts* were expansions, not retreats, from her versions of modernism, and they also illustrate a talent changing during that decade. For other writers, too, mostly younger than Woolf, fiction incorporated much of the scepticism concerning coherence, the fragmentation, the avoidance of explicit or underlined transitions, the linguistic and metaphorical extensions, the lack of assurance that one could know or value the external world, and some of the interiority we have come to associate with literary modernism.

The voices of the Auden Generation were male, treating women with various degrees of sympathy and sensitivity. The novelists of the Auden Generation most often discussed seem more exclusively male: Isherwood's women are specimens, seen from a distance; Graham Greene's are seedy or sanctified, often both; Orwell's depiction is most damaging, the woman flawed and unreliable, except occasionally as mother. Women's voices in addition to Woolf's partially compel this study, the voices of Winifred Holtby, Rosamond Lehmann, Elizabeth Bowen, Rebecca West and Rose Macaulay, not just because of the critical consciousness of feminism in the last twenty years (although that has done a great deal to bring these writers and others back into serious public attention), but because so much of the concerned literary, social and historical insight of the decade came from women who had always been sceptical of heroic transformation. The particular selections are to some extent arbitrary, sometimes compromises between the contradictory requirements of extensiveness and coherent focus. A further question, relevant for any consideration of fiction in the thirties, is the wavering line between serious and popular fiction. The question is particularly acute in a decade in which middle-class authors, conscious of their origins, often sought to represent experience among all the divided classes more accurately, but generally found journeys in physical space easier to accomplish than journeys in class. Connected questions are those of wide popular appeal and authentic lower-class voices (relatively few in an age in which good educations were still more segregated than they later became and sheer economic survival consumed so much more of human time and energy for those born into the lower classes). Again, choices are finally arbitrary. Despite its authentic working-class voice, its convincing representation of the industrial slums of Salford, and its appeal among all literate classes during the thirties, Walter Greenwood's *Love on the Dole* will not be discussed because its patterns seem too predictable and its language too consistently simple and flat. Similar although less judgemental points might be developed about the proletarian fiction and rhetoric of Lewis Jones and Edward Upward. Although these voices received and deserved respect and attention, the full, complex, condition-of-Britain novel remained primarily a middle-class form. I will, however, discuss some fine fiction that has also achieved an audience, perhaps thought to be less characteristic at the time, like that in the abbreviated careers of Patrick Hamilton and Lewis Grassic Gibbon, the latter a proletarian Scot, because of the Britains and the languages they effectively and unusually depict. I will not, however, discuss here the fiction of the transformative right in Britain, that of Henry Williamson and Wyndham Lewis, which went far beyond the passion for order and tradition that characterised Evelyn Waugh and many others. Although in their attraction to Hitler and Nazism, writers like Williamson and Lewis had a public and represented social attitudes that existed in Britain in the thirties, their fiction now seems so obsessed with social and racial theories as to nullify the particularities of the social observations. Their works, like Lewis's *Apes of God* and much of Williamson's *Chronicles of Ancient Sunlight* radiate contempt for all people, and their imagined transformations seem barbaric, anti-social and destructive. That choice, like the rest of my omissions and selections, is arbitrary, too.

Reverberations of the First World War dominate the fiction of the thirties. The chaos, mud, gas, horror and destruction in the trenches had changed everything. Any sense of cultural, historical or public security was gone, betrayed by meaningless disaster. In this sense, the response to the aftermath of the First World War was different from that after the Second, when many turned around surprised to find they had survived relatively intact. Some survivors of the despair of the thirties were even angry at what they saw as the triviality and complacence in the literary ethos of the fifties, those articulate voices that had not expected to be there.[23] But shock, pain, the betrayal of the First World War, and despair dominated the thirties. Writers were sceptical about any contemporary coherence and needed to recall or invent stable pasts. Then, the expectation of another war encouraged the imagination of apocalypse, at its most intense and graphic in the Auden Generation, but a premonition of defeat and disaster everywhere. They saw the coming war as far more an unmitigated disaster than it, for many people, turned out to be. Henry Green, for example, was hardly unique in beginning his autobiography, published in 1940 (although written in 1938 and 1939), by saying that he 'was born a mouthbreather with a silver spoon', 'too late' for the First World War, but not for the Second, in which 'surely it would be asking much to pretend one had a chance to live'.[24] The factual and imagined memory useful for fiction was dominated by the First World War, casting backward through it a dimmer memory that, however sharply realised, was idyll, innocence or myth. Not until the thirties was the First World War fully part of the general literary consciousness, for the shocked survivors took some time to write and the shocked public an equivalent amount of historical time to read. The first serious and probing play about the First World War to acquire a large, involved audience, R. C. Sherriff's *Journey's End*, began its run in December 1928. Searching memoirs from the war's literary survivors began to appear: Siegfried Sassoon's first volume of *Memoirs of a Fox-Hunting Man* and Edmund Blunden's *Undertones of War* in 1928, Robert Graves in the year following. In the re-creations of fiction, the shock and horror of the war did not fully penetrate literary consciousness until the impact of works by survivors like Ford Madox Ford in *Parade's End* (the final novel of the four was published in 1928), Remarque in *All Quiet on the Western Front* (published in German in 1928 and translated into English in 1929) and Frederic Manning in *Her Privates We* (1930), later republished with the manuscript language restored as *The Middle Parts of Fortune*. And, in addition, Richard Aldington's *Death of a Hero* (1929), the novel which, by virtue of its achieved content, its form, the representative implications of its title and focus, and the fact that its author continued to write fiction throughout the thirties, this study appropriately begins.

## NOTES

1.    The term, so far as I know, was first used in the title of Samuel Hynes's well-known book, *The Auden Generation*, published by Bodley Head in Britain in 1976 and by Viking in New York in 1977.

2.    By 1940, *Time* and *Life* had manifestly much less confidence in the British. According to Raymond E. Lee, the American military attaché in London throughout 1940 and 1941, who was always strongly opposed to what he saw as the 'defeatism' of Ambassador Joseph P. Kennedy, both *Time* and *Life* sensationally exaggerated the Blitz of 1940. The Luce publications, full of dire forecasts for Britain, consistently escalated the tonnage of bombs, the assumption that

all London was burning, and the likelihood of invasion from the Continent. In September 1940 Lee thought the weekly magazines 'pretty bad trash' (James Leutze (ed.), *The London Journals of General Raymond E. Lee* [Boston, Toronto: Little, Brown, 1971] pp. 68–9). Lee quoted Churchill in 1941 as saying '*Life* and *Time* had been somewhat opposed to him' (p. 437). Lee also had a sense of British class more complicated than and different from *Time*'s edgy veneration for the aristocracy. In late 1941, back in America, he wrote: 'Ultra Anglophile Americans are probably the best Nazi propagandists in the United States. Several charming ladies who married Britishers and became snobs of the first water are now back here in Washington doing as much harm as the German–American Bund, with their acquired accents and impatience and intolerance for their native country.' (pp. 434–5)

3.  Frank Kermode, *History and Value* (Oxford: Clarendon Press, 1988). Valentine Cunningham, *British Writers of the Thirties* (Oxford: Oxford University Press, 1988).
4.  Cunningham, *British Writers of the Thirties*, p. 42.
5.  See Frank Kermode, *The Sense of an Ending: Studies in the Theory of Fiction* (New York: Oxford University Press, 1967).
6.  Virginia Woolf, 'The Leaning Tower', in *Collected Essays*, vol. II (London: Hogarth Press, 1966) p. 163.
7.  Robert Graves and Alan Hodge, *The Long Week-end: A Social History of Great Britain (1918–1939)*, 2nd edn (London: Faber & Faber, 1950) p. 7.
8.  Ibid., p. 300.
9.  Julian Symons, *The Thirties: A Dream Revolved* (London: Faber & Faber, 1975) p. 22.
10.  Stephen Spender, *Journals 1939–1983*, John Goldsmith (ed.)(London, Boston: Faber & Faber, 1985) Entry of 24 November 1979, pp. 386–7.
11.  John Stevenson, *British Society, 1914–45* (Harmondsworth, Middlesex: Penguin, 1984) p. 437.
12.  Kermode, *History and Value*, p. 40.
13.  E. M. Forster, 'The Long Run', *New Statesman*, 16 (10 December 1938) pp. 971–2.
14.  Woolf, 'The Leaning Tower', p. 171.
15.  Hynes, *The Auden Generation*, p. 392.
16.  Woolf, 'The Leaning Tower', p. 181.
17.  Graves and Hodge, *The Long Weekend*, p. 12.
18.  Symons, *The Thirties*, p. 122.
19.  Martin Ceadal, 'Popular Fiction and the Next War, 1918–39', in Frank Gloversmith (ed.), *Class Culture and Social Change* (Sussex: The Harvester Press, 1980) p. 162.
20.  Cunningham, *British Writers of the Thirties*, p. 55.
21.  See, for example, Kermode, *History and Value*, p. 111.
22.  *Times Literary Supplement*, 26 June 1987.
23.  For an expression of anger, see Symons, *The Thirties*, p. 129.
24.  Henry Green, *Pack My Bag* (London: Hogarth Press, 1940) p. 5.

# PART I

# The Language of Social Reference

# 2

# Richard Aldington's Excoriation of the Past

Richard Aldington's *Death of a Hero* (1929) is distinguished from other works written by survivors of the trenches in France that suddenly claimed public attention, after what seemed a necessary decade for recuperation, in the mocking fury and anger of its language. Other works described equally the physical misery, shared loss and pointless waste of the trenches; other works, too, inscribed the self-slaughter of a generation in terms of historical cause. Aldington combined these depictions and attitudes with a relentless excoriation of previous generations in popular and deliberately vulgar terms. As an early Imagist in his poetry, he had been associated for nearly twenty years with modernism and its need to formulate a complete and linguistically violent break with the past. His jazzy, derisive language is visible throughout *Death of a Hero*, even in passages that simply describe the 1890 courtship of the parents of the war victim:

> So it wasn't hard for George Augustus to swank. He took the Hartlys – even Isabel – in completely . . . He gave them copies of the Non-conformist tract he had published at fifteen. He gave Ma Hartly a fourteen-pound tin of that expensive (2s. 3d. a pound) tea she had always pined for since they had left Ceylon. He bought fantastic things for Isabel – a coral brooch, a copy of the *Pilgrim's Progress* bound in wood from the door of Bunyan's parish church, a turkey, a year's subscription to the *Family Herald Supplement*, a new shawl, boxes of 1s. 6d. a pound chocolates, and took her for drives in an open landau smelling of horse-piss and oats . . . One night, a sweet rural night, with a lemon moon over the sweet, breast-round, soft English country, with the nightingales jug-jugging and twit-twitting like mad in the leafy lanes, George Augustus kissed Isabel by a stile, and – manly fellow – asked her to marry him.

The language, still in 1929, conveyed to a large public the same kind of modernity and reversal of literary gentility that was conveyed by Aldington's former friend T. S. Eliot in his description of a sunset 'like a patient etherised upon a table', in addition to the more directly borrowed 'jug-jugging' and 'twit-twitting'.

Aldington's spleen characterises the social and historical representations of almost all his figures of earlier generations. In *The Colonel's Daughter* (1931), the novel that follows *Death of a Hero*, the father of the contemporary victim, female this time, is the Victorian Army officer who had 'jabbed the butt of a pig-sticker into himself and broke two ribs; he came a purler at polo and broke an arm; a Fuzzy-Wuzzy nicked him in the ham with a spear, and brother Boer broke his omoplate with a well-aimed Mauser bullet'. These experiences, for him, justify his attitude in 1914 when 'he pranced about the streets of Bath on an invisible high horse, while the unseen spurs jingled more evidently than ever'. He defers only to the commercial, newly rich village squire who 'had absorbed at least three estates which had been intended for the nurture and comfort of warriors, defenders of the Throne, and he had done it all on grease'. The old village gossip was 'one hundred and eighty pounds of monogamous and matriarchal flab, possessed of an unknown but apparently limitless reserve of oleaginous spite'. The angry language extends historically. Names like John Knox and Oscar Wilde are used as pejorative adverbs. Frequently, Aldington's spleen centres on easily recognisable portraits of contemporaries. *Death of a Hero* contains a long section on literary journalism in London just before the war. The journalism is 'accurately defined as the most degrading form of that degrading vice, mental prostitution', and its practitioners are introduced as 'abject morons'. The principals include: the grossly fat womaniser, Herr Shobbe, who panders to the wealthy to support his 'literary review, one of those "advanced" reviews beloved by the English, which move rapidly forward with a crab-like motion' [Ford]; Mr Waldo Tubbe, the American High Tory 'who leaned so very far to the extreme Right that without knowing it he sometimes tumbled into the verge of the extreme left' [Eliot]; Mr Upjohn, the 'extremely vain' egotist who hears no one and 'since he was destitute of any intrinsic and spontaneous originality, he strove much to be original and invented a new school of painting every season' [Pound]; Mr Bobbe, a 'narrow-chested little man with spiteful blue eyes and a malevolent class-hatred. He exercised his malevolence with comparative impunity by trading upon his working-class origin and his indigestion, of which he had been dying for twenty years . . . He was the Thersites of the day, or rather that would have been the only excuse for him . . . His vanity and class-consciousness made him yearn for affairs with upper-class women, although he was obviously a homosexual type' [D. H. Lawrence]. Such villification is seldom clever, pointed or shaped to the historical and social context of the novel. Quicker gratuitous derogations abound, like a literary survey of England in the 1890s: 'Hardy a rural atheistic scandal, not yet discovered to be an intolerable bore; Oscar prancing negligently, O so clever, O so lad-di-dah'. Contemporaries, too, are reduced, as in a contextually irrelevant slap at J. B. Priestley, who, like Ethel M. Dell, is 'simple' and lowbrow.

Whatever Aldington's motives or design in the splenetic individual portraits, they often trivialise the fiction, especially when read through the distance of time. They are a patternless *Dunciad*, increasingly irrelevant and lacking Pope's sharp wit. Aldington persisted in personal excoriation, devoting much of a whole satirical work, *Stepping Heavenward* (1931) to a vitriolic personal attack on his one-time friend and always strong influence, T. S. Eliot.[1] Even after the 1930s, when Aldington stopped writing novels, the tone continued and antagonised others. He achieved considerable distance and intelligence in biographies of the Duke of Wellington and D. H. Lawrence (quite a different and deeper portrait than that in *Death of a Hero*), but his biographical investigation of T. E. Lawrence, published in 1955, angrily proclaimed that the subject was nothing other than a fraud and liar. Reactions to the work generated a much more extensive and political antagonism toward Aldington than did any of his earlier portraits, including the Eliot.

Nevertheless, Aldington's fiction voices much deeper and less personal excoriations. In seven novels written between 1929 and 1939, he both depicts and represents the generation of the victims of the First World War. And Aldington's fiction works on the antagonism between generations, with axioms like 'Youth is so much more valuable than experience; it is also far more intelligent' and 'even the greatest minds degenerate annually'. The war that victimised a whole generation gives the theme a particular force and cogency, as the narrator of *Death of a Hero*, a rare survivor of the trenches, sees clearly. He recognises that future generations, his 'magnanimous nephews' (he cannot even imagine a more direct continuity), may well excoriate him in turn, but 'they must see we *did* struggle, we did fight against the humbug and the squelching of life and the worn-out formulae'. As the novels move in generations treated and historical time depicted, the point of view remains that of the 'young' generation, born anytime between the early 1890s of the victim and narrator in *Death of a Hero* to the 1916, the second generation of war victims, of the young central character of *Rejected Guest* (1939). Most often the material, the embodiment of particular experience, is that of the 1930s, the decade during which Aldington wrote his fiction. But the targets treated with unforgiving anger are invariably those older generations that, either in welcoming the struggle others enacted or in the confidence that 'we're far too civilised for war', caused the total destruction of 1914–18.

*Death of a Hero* is, as Aldington states in an introduction, both a 'jazz novel' in its contemporaneity and a 'threnody' in its focus on mourning George Winterbourne, the young victim killed after more than two years in France in November 1918. To reinforce the representation of a generation, the novel of George is narrated by his distant friend and wartime contemporary, Christopher Ridgeway, who begins his retrospectively told prologue with the end of the war and George's death as 'the last spasms of Europe's severed arteries'. The cause is traced back two generations to the mid-Victorians, a generation so concerned with purity and religiosity that all sex must be repressed and England preserved from 'filthy vile foreigners', a generation that encouraged 'angel-in-the-house, idiot-in-the-world cant'. Victorian cant, surviving until 1914, made the war a national principle, full of 'Delusion' and 'Delerium', unable to recognise that English nationalism sought to destroy the Prussian power and alliances it had itself created, while the Prussians were full of an equally debilitating brutality, denial and hatred. Although, for Aldington, art could provide sensible alternatives to 'Victorian Cant', 'The great English middle-class mass, that dreadful squat pillar of the nation, will only tolerate art and literature that are fifty years out of date, eviscerated, de-testiculated, bowdlerized, humbuggered, slip-slopped, subject to their anglicized Jehovah'. As such imagery underlines, the Victorian world was ruthless in its suppression of the physical, the body. The next generation, that of George's parents, in revolt from their elders, tried to express themselves physically. But George's father was 'an inadequate sentimentalist . . . incompetent, selfishly unselfish (ie, always patting himself on the back for "renouncing" something he was afraid to do or be or take)' who, when he realises that his wife has often been unfaithful, declaims 'that his "religious convictions forbade" him to divorce her'. His wife, in her long 'unsanitary' skirts with her long 'unsanitary' hair, is with her twenty-second lover, a young man named Sam Browne, 'an adult Boy Scout, a Public School fag in shining armour – the armour of obtuseness', when she receives the telegram announcing that George has been killed. Forcing herself on Sam Browne, she is 'not only a sadist, but a necrophilous one'. For Aldington, both parents are 'grotesques', initially victims of their parents, but themselves excoriated as causes of further religious cant and physical cruelty.

George is more intelligent than his parents, and, although his childhood is happy only in one short scene of 'release, an ecstasy', when a maid-servant takes him to her family's home for the hop-picking in Kent, 'the tenderness of the rough women hop-pickers, the taste of the smoky picnic tea and heavy soggy cake', he grows up more sensible and expressive about his sexuality than is either parent. He acquires both a wife and a mistress in the early days of the war, both 'clean', non exclusive relationships in the modern world in rebellion against sanctified monogamy. The wife is physi-cally direct, although a bit hard, she 'could be quite Stonehengey at times'; the mistress is a further stage, directly sexual but with a sort of 'physical indifference' that 'had something Lethean about it', as physical and spiritual cannot be separated. Yet the differ-ences between them are obliterated by the war, and, by 1918, both women have other men and neither is more than distantly and momentarily distressed at the news of George's death. The war had suddenly catapulted George into another dimension of the body, the crawling, wet, filthy, bloody, constant pain of the war. The most effective scenes in the novel are those of men in the trenches, the constant agony, the physical pain and filth, the darkness, the world around visible only at dawn 'over a desolate flat landscape, seamed with irregular trenches and infinitely pitted and scarred with shell-holes, thorny with wire, littered with debris'. The soldiers do not hate the Germans. Rather, their 'enemies were the sneaks and the unscrupulous; the false ideals, the unintelligent ideas imposed on them, the humbug, the hypocrisy, the stupidity'. Part of the false ideas that Aldington dramatises are ideas of class difference, visible and isolating everywhere in the military except at the front. In the novel, class structure is less the cause than past generations' denial of and incompetence with the human body, a violation so deep that the older generation can sanctimoniously

send the younger into a world of total physical destruction, one
that denies all promise of life or health. The earlier modernistic
liberations are trivial, and the younger generation feels itself pun-
ished for the mild gestures toward physical freedom it expressed.
The narrator, Christopher Ridgeway, the survivor, finds that slight
impulse toward freedom for George entirely betrayed. Christopher,
involved because he has been in the war and accidentally survived,
feels guilty. His 'threnody', the novel, is 'an atonement, a desperate
effort to wipe off the blood-guiltiness'. He wonders if George, the
victim, unable to express his body cleanly, dissatisfied with his
commitments on his last leave, and not having lived long enough
to become fully conscious of his historical location, really committed
suicide.

A different language for the body denied is applied to Georgie,
the young woman of George's generation who is the central character of *The Colonel's Daughter*. After the war, Georgie is still living
with her parents, retired from the military Colonial Service, on a
pension in a country village. Her father objects fiercely to rice-
powder or lipstick, for they are the marks of 'a London street-
woman'. Georgie must keep her hair unsanitary, long, wound in
an 'uncomely bun' that is squashed by a school straw hat. Her
parents have kept her, like her clothes, young and uneducated,
and 'this meant in fact a perpetual servitude *in statu pupillari*, with
the result that with the body of a woman Georgie had the mind,
habits and feelings of a child of sixteen'. The body, 'essentially
*healthy*', is encased in the paraphernalia of a moribund society. Yet
Georgie begins to know some of the rebellious young of her own
generation, 'frantically talking Russian Ballet, Josephine Baker,
Riviera, motoring', while her elders talk only of the Girl Guides, the
church and various forms of sport. The anger of the young focuses
on economics and class, as well as on sex, for Georgie, in coming
to know a local gypsy-like family, a rural proletariat, realises the
force of the comment: 'It was just like the War, where a man got
a shilling a day and discomfort for fighting in the front line, and
two pounds a day plus field and fuel allowances for remembering
the General liked Oxford marmalade for breakfast'. The voice of
Aldington emerges through an older 'bookish' local socialist who
objects both to the obsolete society of Georgie's parents and to the
more intelligent purveyors of doom, 'mere Manicheanism'. Georgie
also awakens to her desire for sex through her observations of her
half-envious, half-helpful maid-servant. But at a crucial moment,

although he understands, the older socialist excites expectations in
Georgie that he then evades. The discerning within this society are
seen as socially, economically and sexually impotent. On the other
hand, a possible suitor, a young distant relative on leave from the
Colonial Service, is seen as the next generation of her father. Vital
because he is young, he also excites expectations in Georgie, and
she hastily assents to the fact that her growing interest in art is
not to include 'those Cubist chaps . . . They may be all right for
foreigners . . . but you'll never get English people to tolerate that
sort of thing. We may not be a very brainy people or very *artistic*
and all that sort of thing, but we've got too much healthy common
sense to be taken in by such stuff.' He soon betrays Georgie for
her more overtly sexual and artistic friend (lucky enough to be an
orphan) who would not tolerate his insularity about 'those Cubist
chaps'. And Georgie, who keeps creating fantasies of another war
in which she 'would give herself unflinchingly and unsparingly in
the national cause, and work the flesh from her bones to give of
her best to wounded heroes and return them fresh and fit once
more to a man's real work in the firing-line', then to single out
a fantasy hero for herself, can find no appropriate language or
action for the expression of her physical self. When her father dies,
her responsibility to her mother and the house, the world that
nurtured and circumscribed her, leaves her no alternative. She is a
physical being stranded in a limited, repressive world, preserving
a virtue 'she does not want'. Aldington's language at the end is a
1930s language of deprivation and despair, of atrophy that leaves
the once 'Stately Homes of England' as 'hunchy little cottages,
silent and infelicitous in the rainy dawn'. And the contemporary
daughter is seen only as 'Poor Georgie'.

Not all significant members of Aldington's contemporary post-
war generation are victims, for Tony Clarendon, the central character of his next novel *All Men Are Enemies* (1933), is a well-born, fortunate exception. Aldington calls *All Men Are Enemies* a 'Romance',
not a novel. He frames the story with Tony's quick visit to the
country stately home where he grew up to find it, some years after
the war, kept up artificially by parvenu money from London while
the surrounding village decays with trade and wages going down,
unemployment going up, the village discontent despite the 'new
station . . . squalid brick and varnished deal construction, looking
like an abortive Swiss chalet which had never been anything
but shabby'. After the frame, Aldington returns to Tony's early

years before the war. His wealthy, upper-class parents are a less
inhibiting version of the Victorian generation. Still, they are caught
up in a science versus religion dichotomy whose abstractions are
ultimately life-denying, other terms for a D. H. Lawrence Victorian
mind/body conflict that leads to atrophy. Tony's father is a scientist
and 'conscientious atheist' who 'could not help feeling a faint
contempt for someone who had no scientific instincts' and was
convinced that 'if you looked at things with your two eyes you
were unscientific and liable to illusion, but if you covered one eye
with a shade and put a microscope between the other eye and the
object, then you were infallible'. His mother, whose family was
artistic and evangelical, had been influenced by Christina Rossetti
and Holman Hunt, and loved Italian painters 'mixed up with an
adoration for German Romantic music, a cult of Wordsworth, and
a touching faith in the social theories of William Morris . . . these
saints were all included in a gentle Christian hierarchy, presided
over by God, who was indistinguishable from Jesus Christ, and
who was preparing a crystal age millenium just round the corner.' The conflict in Tony's background isolates him intellectually
and from his schoolfellows, but he has no occasion for bitterness
or anger and is not emotionally inhibited, for he has a warm
and satisfactory short affair with a slightly older visiting cousin.
Rather, the anger, before 1914, is given to the local schoolmaster
who inveighs against the Industrial Revolution with 'little children worked in the mines like pit ponies', talks of the people 'in
chains, chains of ignorance, poverty, labour and hopelessness',
and advocates socialistic revolution. Tony, as teenager, objects,
in the name of a more individualistic and romantic conception
of experience, that the schoolmaster would 'hand us over to the
mediocrity of committees, who will plant us in garden suburbs with
the right brand of sterilized milk and the plays of Bernard Shaw'.
The schoolmaster jeers at Tony as a member of the 'old Squirearchy'
and a snob. Tony is sceptical about all theories, like Aldington
himself who later in the thirties, wrote that he felt the need to be
out of England, even out of Europe, since 'there was no place for me
among the intellectual fanatics who were busy labelling themselves
leftists and rightists, and who constantly summoned one to stand
and deliver on one silly side or another'.[2] Tony is placed at an
earlier historical stage of protest against English society. When
his mother dies, he goes to the emotionally and artistically wider
world of the Continent, to taste the 'essentially sacred nature' of

the 'fresh brook trout, sweet smelling bread, good butter and white wine of Bordeaux', and to study architecture through the Classical and Renaissance masterpieces of Italy. What is outside England is not the insularity of Empire that he was taught to regard as 'abroad' when at school. Tony's journey can satisfy body and spirit simultaneously, as he could not in England. The journey and a growing sense of expanded geography and sensitivity is capsulised in an idyllic love affair with a young Austrian woman named Katha on an island in the Mediterranean in the spring of 1914.

But 1914 shatters the idyll and all Europe, and the years of war are done quickly in jeering snatches from popular songs. Tony begins 1919 with nightmares of finding everyone he has known dead in the trenches, and his language has changed to characterise peers, cabinet ministers, diplomats, newspaper owners, 'all the wealth, power, and glory', as just a 'Pack of swine'. Tony, who had fought the war neither believing nor disbelieving in any pretended principles, fought because that was what people of his genera-tion did, finds the principled retrospective arguments over the war, from the victors, defeated or pacifists, hollow and fraudulent postures. The upper-class business world he is expected to join seems irrelevant and insensitive; his wartime mistress, Margaret, once an 'Aphrodite', now seems predatory and possessive, anxious to join the society; crowds in London are described as: 'Human bodies, anonymous, indifferent, wedged all round, making an intolerable prison of living walls'. Aldington's language becomes a protest against physical entrapment. Unable to locate or learn of Katha in the welter of post-war confusion, Tony resigns himself, with something close to despair, to the life of modern business and marriage to Margaret. Questions of race and class constantly obtrude into Tony's post-war life and the texture of Aldington's language as they did not in the world before the war. As European culture seems shattered, the language and references excoriate outsiders: 'Trouville – no more France than the Mayfair mansion of a German Jew millionaire is England'; North Africans display 'the Semitic mind . . . uncreative, like the Jews, but without Jewish intelligence'; 'I've long said that Jew empire of Disraeli's was a mistake' (this quotation may not be from Aldington's point of view); Paris has become a 'heterogeneous and unpleasing multi-tude of freaks and pretenders – men-women and women-men, charlatans, pimps, amateur prostitutes, Negroes, numerous wops and Middle-European Jews with American passports'. For the most part, this racial attitude fades from Aldington's fiction after 1933, although an occasional unmodified remark appears irrelevantly as late as 1939 in *Rejected Guest*.

Far more often than race, questions of economics and class infuse the language and texture of *All Men Are Enemies*. Talk of the miners, the angry and discontented workers, the removed, greedy and insensitive upper classes, and the possibilities of revolution all build toward the impending 1926 General Strike. Tony sees the potential revolution as cultural as well as economic and muses about Titian's *Bacchus and Ariadne* in the National Gallery. He thinks of Titian as angry and upset by the throngs of 'desensitized barbarians' looking at his picture and thinks that 'a new Titian . . . would be insulted by sterile universitaires and smelly-souled journalists'. Yet, for Tony, Titian is still the important European artifact, more healthy and physical than his mother's pre-Raphaelites who 'represented the etiolation of the English soul, cut off from reality by dividends'. The General Strike turns out to be the damp squib of a revolution, a ten-day lark for the upper and middle classes running trains and buses, and random disgruntlement among the working classes who lacked the 'guts' for machine guns and 'bred from the stupid optimism and narrow-minded scientific dogmatism of the last century, were too many to be civilized, and therefore would probably retrograde further into a washed and mediocre barbarism'. Tony resolves that he is finished with England. He resigns his job, leaves Margaret with all his property (telling her that the next war is certain, even if only that of 'men against their own machines'), and sets off to walk the Continent. He stops at Chartres where 'the usurer, the impresario, and the parasite had no place of honour'. He drifts further south, into Italy, and finds Katha on their Mediterranean island. He restores her to physical and psychic health (she in a sundered Austria had been more deprived and violated than he) and their idyll resumes, as the fiction flows into romance. None of the social, racial or economic issues that form the body of the fiction are resolved, just presented in sharp, striking terms before the fiction drifts into idyll.

Aldington's later novels, more entirely embedded in the thirties, excoriate idylls as impossible and self-deceptive. In *Women Must Work* (1934), only a short preface conveys standard images of Victorian inhibition (a school that teaches young women nothing other than gentility, although it at least 'had never heard of the team spirit', a nurse who forbids any contact with mud, and the dull ambience of respectable religiosity) in the background of Etta Morison, who, at nineteen in 1913, is determined to leave her safe, south coast middle-class town for life in London. As she laboriously learns shorthand and typing to earn her living in the only way open to her and becomes an intelligent, skilful office manager, Etta represents the younger generation. She acknowledges her own sexual desires, although not without guilts assimilated from the older culture. She berates herself for inviting expectations from a lecherous boss; she denies giving herself to the man she loves because he is the nephew of an older upper-class suffragist who later employs her. Etta thinks sex in the circumstances might show aggression and ingratitude in class terms. In London, she finds the new world she instinctively craves through the formulations of art, the paintings and plays she sees, the ballet, and music, with images like Mozart as the 'Kappelmeister of some heaven where there were no Christians'. The war that shatters so much gives Etta independence, for her office skills are now in demand in government departments and she is no longer dependent on crude commercial employers or upper-class benefactresses. She also yearns for a freer life, and Aldington develops expansive imagery for her aspirations. Widening geography holds her imagination, for one could still in 1934 write of 'castles in Spain' seemingly immune from the modern world. Some of the imagery seems borrowed from D. H. Lawrence, like that of a woman whose 'patriotism had the ferocity of Huitzilopochtli demanding blood sacrifice'. The narrative voice gives expansive form to Etta's desires and inserts short essays about human impulses always seeking healthy life: 'Three hundred generations ago men gathered cowrie shells because their sexual shape made them life-givers'. Elaborate preparations for her long-delayed first consummated love with the benefactress's nephew, Ralph, about to come to London on leave from the trenches, are conveyed in the legendary terms of the coming of the sun-god, or the long preparations of Penelope for the return of Odysseus.

The elaborate and legendary are disappointed, punctured and excoriated by the narrative voice. The plot intervenes when Etta's sole instance of feeling responsibility to her family (her younger brother has just been reported missing in action) causes her to postpone the expected week with Ralph. He is furious, suddenly, from his own deprivations in France, callous and unwilling to wait another few days. They part and Etta feels betrayed. More cynical now, she loses her virginity to a seductive older lawyer in his aesthetically furnished *pied-à-terre* amidst long talks about Madame du Barry, art and erotic poetry. Although the language of the affair is more artistic, evasive and removed than physical, Etta does become pregnant. She then imagines the lawyer in a kind of primitive vision 'striding in from haymaking or ploughing, sunburned and earth-scented, sitting down to eat the food she had prepared'. She is surprised and frightened by his lack of interest in the primitive and his cool assumption that he (who has no intention of leaving his wife) will just arrange for an abortion. He has always, like almost all Aldington's males of his generation, including George in *Death of a Hero*, wanted to practice contraception carefully so that, in an overpopulated world, people 'will for their own sakes come to breed more eugenically'. Etta refuses the abortion angrily. Having saved considerable money as she was promoted to more demanding government jobs during the war just ending, she decides to live her vision of healthy motherhood, to buy and work a small farm. The new stereotype is satirised as a disaster. Etta is far less competent at farming than she was among the offices and machines of London; the child is difficult, fractious, an unwilling participant in the healthy rural myth; the nearby rural people are mean, hostile, suspicious, one farmer even unwilling to discuss in front of a woman the economically necessary mating of one of Etta's cows with his bull.

By this point in the novel, Aldington has abandoned all his legendary or cosmic imagery. The language, like the theme, centres on issues of power, social and economic or the emotional power of one character over another in a world of commerce clotted with social reference. Etta must compete and manipulate to regain her status. She must learn what to tell people and what not to, must use social contacts for economic gain, itself a conversion of the independent woman from freedom to manipulation. She achieves considerable success in administering an advertising agency, 'which seemed like a Wells's dream of the future without the interest and hope of Wells's enthusiasm. It was like the temple of a queer, ugly, inhuman god, the abstract Yahweh of Business, whose praises were hourly clicked by choirs of typists'. Advertising, from Aldington's point of view, is now triumphant: 'The G. B. Shaws and the Arnold Bennetts of the future won't worry about plays and novels – they'll be sitting in the Creative Department of this office'. Etta can even overcome her class scruples by buying the weekend small country property of her benefactress, now reduced to near poverty. She

can see but not ameliorate Ralph's pitiable regret for what he lost
through anger. She marries a devoted younger artist, who is 'aston-
ishingly malleable', exercising her power sexually and economically
in giving him the commercial jobs he needs to preserve his own
illusion of independence. For Aldington, this is what independence
for a woman in the world of the 1930s requires. The narrative voice
sympathises with Etta and the texture of excoriation diminishes.
She has even lost her child's love, for the child is much fonder
of her artist stepfather than she is of Etta. In the final scene, Etta
refuses to follow their country-weekend custom of dancing on the
lawn to gramophone music coming through the open window (Etta
had earlier valued that immediate post-war symbol of liberation)
because, 'as she exclaimed in a high hysterical voice', the lawn has
too many dead leaves. Her own sense of power, in the darkening
climate of the novel, has turned to control and deny others, as she
was denied at the beginning. Aldington's excoriation shrivels into
grim, silent inhibition.

The last of Aldington's novels, *Rejected Guest*, is framed synop-
tically by the two wars. The wars, for Aldington, differ in that in
the Second World War, bastardy no longer matters, 'It is simply
biology without culture'. Wars are always periods of 'sexual sanity',
circumstances overcoming moral inhibition, but the emphasis on
bastardy, the social consequence of war, is no longer seen in the
historical tradition of a violation of appropriate lineage. The novel
begins with the birth of David Norris in 1916, a bastard, the product
of a wartime affair between an upper-class young officer and a
young woman in a country town whose family has fallen into
the lower-middle class. Pride, circumstance, class division and the
officer's fear of the reaction of his own father prevented disclosure
of the pregnancy until after the officer went to France, where he was
killed. David knows nothing of his father or his father's family. He
is raised substantially by his mother's parents, especially when after
some years his mother marries again and produces a respectable
family in a town where her past is unknown. David's grandparents
illustrate another of Aldington's late Victorian dichotomies. His
grandfather, now reduced to a rent-collector for a housing cor-
poration, had become very moral after a rakish tour as a doctor
on board a ship that went around the world. He 'felt the need of
strong moral principles on account of that sea tour and because
he wanted to show the world that a man can live with almost
puritanical strictness simply because he doesn't believe in God'.

Morally, he matches his wife, a clergyman's daughter, once 'a young woman with strong moral principles and no money, whose dowry consisted of a lot of untearable bed-linen and unwearable underclothes all hand-made, a set of English poets and serious novelists, and a few trinkets'. Their polarity intersects in their morality and concern for David. Their representative Victorian qualities are handled comically, juxtaposed in a revelation of mutual incompetence, and they are not excoriated with the bitterness Aldington applied to Victorians in his earlier fiction. The grandparents protect David, a delicate child, moving him to a religious school when the children at his state school jeer at him as 'bastard'. He is attracted at first to his grandmother's religion, later to his grandfather's science. When they die, David takes the money his grandfather left to secure his future as a rent-collector to try to study science in London. Not well prepared either academically or for living a spartan existence in the morally threatening world of London (he narrowly avoids what would be a crippling entanglement in his first sexual experience), David is placed in the dingy, chaotic mid-thirties world of poverty, fraudulent posturers, pompous and indifferent professors, and depressing political and class agitation. Aldington has little sympathy with the politics. Among the science students 'were acrimonious Leftists for the nonce, because they had no money and other people had'. The rightist students 'had no desire to work at anything, but wanted lots of money to spend'. Both envied those who 'had motor bikes and pillions – you can get off with a girl so much better in the country'. Only David cared for science. The Arts students were more articulate, but politics determined the required reading: for Rightists, 'Percy Wyndham Lewis, Roy Campbell, and Count Potocki de Montalk'; for 'sacristans', Gerard Manley Hopkins and T. S. Eliot; for Leftists, 'the Moscow news', and 'no poetry but that of Auden, Spender, and Day Lewis, and unfortunate young men who had gone to the Spanish War'. Aldington also satirises various schemes of social credit and economic organisation, including 'the farmers of Alberta, who have the singular distinction of being the only white men in the Empire to pay local wizards to make rain in times of drought'.

Through a series of accidents, David finds his aristocratic grandfather, his father's father, still alive although feeble. Through their reunion and David's conversations with a high-living and iconoclastic old friend of his father's, Martindale, Aldington outlines the enormous rift between rich and poor in the thirties, the entirely separate world of chauffered cars, oak panels, dances and long dinners. The distances are seen as unbridgeable, two worlds with the insulated rich feeding on the work and service of the debilitated poor, their resentment activated only by inchoate, empty rhetoric and meaningless gesture. Because his grandfather wants David educated as a gentleman before he commits his fortune to him, he sends him, with a huge allowance, to spend a year with Martindale on the French Riviera. Martindale would wean David from his 'vicious habits of asceticism' and hard work, encourage him to be a poet, to write one presumable masterpiece and live on his reputation for the next sixty years. David learns well, although Martindale keeps cautioning him against marriage because 'nothing could be more inappropriate, more ill-mannered, than procreation on your part . . . You belong to the race of people with more aspiration than common sense, more goodwill than reason, more sensitiveness than strength, more brains than brawn, more emotion than knowledge, who are doomed to extinction'. David acquires a mistress, a siren-like beauty whom Martindale warns him against, and they spend weeks idyllically cruising the Mediterranean. They vow eternal fidelity. They return to shore to find David's grandfather dead (intestate, the year's trial not yet over) and the escapist Riviera culture frightened of Munich and talking war. David would evade the war entirely, cruise the Mediterranean in love forever, but his mistress is escaping to America and, seeing David penniless, breaks off the affair. David only gradually faces the impossibility of immunity from the war, which others have been telling him for months. Even an old patrician historian, who has lived for years as if he could retreat to his favourite Renaissance poets, now says: 'It is too late to go back, and to go on as we are must lead to destruction. There is no way out'. No matter what David's class or lineage, claimed or unclaimed, he is necessarily involved in a war about which he has no choice. Even the entirely amoral and sybaritic Martindale cannot countenance the Nazis and knows he must work to oppose them and defend what he thinks of as civilisation: 'In comparison to the people who are now getting on top in the world gorillas are sane, sweet disciples of Matthew Arnold'. David is again, as he was when the novel opened, divested of lineage by war. This time, however, the bastardy is irrelevant, since the question is lineage at all rather than appropriate lineage. Races, classes and cultures are subsumed in the threat to humanity the Nazis represent.

In his introduction to the novel, Aldington called the First World War the 'Futile' war, and the Second the 'Serious' war. The difference between the two was the difference between outrageous folly and survival. He added the note that America would have to explain or understand the Second World War since 'there won't be much of Europe left to comment on it'. Yet the novel itself in its specifications of the unbridgeable worlds of London class and the follies of escapist geography around the Mediterranean, explains how one war slid into the next well enough. The victims of the Futile war could blame their progenitors and justify Aldington's rage, his characterisations of the late Victorian generations; the victims of the Serious war were so total and general, in such an historically precarious position, that all blame was irrelevant. Aldington's excoriations sink into the language of despair, of recognition that all the issues of body, politics and economics that had filled the texture of the decade, and of his novels, had little meaning in the face of the overwhelming question of survival. *Rejected Guest* was Aldington's last novel about society. In 1941, he wrote: 'For more than ten years I had been engaged on a series of more or less satirical novels, giving my views of the period which was called 'post-war' but was in fact merely a long armistice. After listening to Mr Chamberlain's speech over the radio on the morning of 3 September 1939, I threw the novel I was writing into the waste basket. It would be absurd to denounce calamity; ignoble to satirize a people fighting for their existence'.[3] Despair is silent, and words themselves create the vitality and possibility of meaning. Before the point of silence, however, in his novels and in the long, 'serious', tactile descriptions of London and the Riviera in *Rejected Guest*, Aldington's excoriatory language conveyed a great deal of the social texture and complexity of the 1930s.

## NOTES

1. A full account of both the influence of *The Waste Land* on Aldington, and the relationship between Aldington and Eliot, derived through letters and other published sources, is available in Fred D. Crawford, *Mixing Memory and Desire* (University Park, Pa.: Pennsylvania State University Press, 1982).
2. Richard Aldington, *Life for Life's Sake: A Book of Reminiscences* (New York: Viking Press, 1941) p. 400.
3. Ibid., pp. 5–6.

# 3

# The Fabric of J. B. Priestley's Indigenous Social Voices

In the Indian summer of 1935, about when the issue of *Time* that concentrated on praise of Sir Samuel Hoare's diplomatic skill, Moral Rearmament, and the fiction of A. J. Cronin appeared, J. B. Priestley (1894–1984) was in New York on his second visit to America. At the height of his popularity in England – *The Good Companions* was his first successful novel in 1929 and had been followed by *Angel Pavement* (1930) and the travel ramble of *English Journey* (1934); his plays also achieved a wide English public, particularly *Dangerous Corner* in 1932, *Laburnum Grove* in 1933, and *Eden End* in 1934 – Priestley had come to New York to supervise the production of *Eden End* because he thought New York productions of three of his previous plays had been badly done. At first he was exhilarated by the energy of New York, as he had been on his first visit. But he found that, for days, the people he met would talk of nothing except the heavyweight championship fight in which Joe Louis knocked out Max Baer. Walking the streets in his heavy suits and starched shirts in the hot weather, and reading whatever news from Europe he could, Priestley became despondent. As his recent biographer, Vincent Brome, records his impressions, they bear no resemblance to those of the writers of *Time* magazine:

Slowly a sense of frustration combined with the heat and exhaustion to reinforce his darkest mood. New York became a jungle of steel, concrete and gasoline vapour, and even Central Park with its thinly covered volcanic rock made the birds and the grass artificial products of a landscape gardener who had lost his connection with nature. The continual torrent of news, pounded out by newspapers which were available day and night, was consistently depressing. Threats of war, which finally burst into reality one year later in Spain, were consistently headlined, and the League of Nations, which had lost its credibility, became an easy target for newspaper chauvinism. The excitement of Roosevelt's New Deal was in the air, new shows were being launched, and old dance bands resurrected. People were full of a brittle excitement but Priestley formed the impression that underneath "nobody felt secure". The cataclysm of 1929 still haunted the city and not all Roosevelt's New Deal had yet reassured New Yorkers.[1]

Reassurance, like that of *Time* magazine, about a sanely manageable political world, from the point of view of either Britain or America, was outside the ken of a social chronicler as observant and concerned as J. B. Priestley. He was less shrewd about American popular taste, for *Eden End* ran fewer than the three weeks he took to cast the play.

Neither forecasting nor America was Priestley's strength. Rather, as in his appeal to 'nature' implicit in his comment on Central Park, his strength was external physical description, his sense of the unique or indigenous place, particularly in England. His descriptions invariably combine the physical or natural with the social. *The Good Companions*, for example, begins its tour of England with a description of the Pennine Range, 'the knobbly backbone of England', and follows with an account of hills and fells among which the wool trade of Yorkshire and the cotton trade of Lancashire are set. The geography is connected with customs and taste, with the way people look and speak, unchanged through centuries, before he focuses on the end of the twenties when trade had been bad for a decade, which justifies his central cloth-capped figure, Jess Oakroyd, in leaving home to join a vaudeville troupe that tours England. Each spot in the tour is placed imagistically and geographically: the West Country with 'grey stone villages, their walls flushing to a delicate pink in the sunlight . . . parish churches that have rung in and rung out Tudor, Stuart, and Hanoverian kings'; the Fen country with its lonely farms and omnipresent railroad tracks raised above the 'plain of dried marshes' where the 'vague sadness of a prairie has fallen'. Similarly, in *English Journey*, Priestley's narrative tour is simultaneously an examination of differing regional economic conditions during the worst of the slump, the masses of unemployed in the North East shipyards and the new small industries out the Great Western Road from London, and a description of the influences of constant differences in regional landscape, his interest, for example, in the contrast between his native Yorkshire and the soft, old southern landscapes with different historical associations, 'the lovely thickness of life, as different now from ordinary existence as plum pudding is from porridge'. *They Walk in the City: The Lovers in the Stone Forest* (1936) contrasts the hills and moors around a West Riding textile town with the dismal streets and poisoned chemicals in an impoverished London where his lovers seek their fortunes and each other. Priestley is particularly effective in describing spots of temporary urban refuge like the ornate movie palaces, the warm shabby cafes that serve as offices, and the convenient and almost affordable elegance of Lyons Corner Houses. *Angel Pavement* includes the splendour of cosmopolitan Woolworth stores 'at once larger and shallower' than older shops, as well as an extended description of a 'kind of Babylonian' teashop that 'was golden, tropical, belonging to some high midsummer of confectionery'. The sugary images are applied to the chocolate and gold of the adjacent cinema, conveying both the pretense of the palace and its appeal to the poor young clerk who would live within its fantasies.

Geographical and social simultaneously, place often represents class as well. In each of the northern industrial towns, the homes of the nineteenth-century entrepreneurs command the heights of hills and the workingmen's row cottages, back to back, line the ridges down to the mills in the valleys and alongside the streams. Frequently class is part of a geographical contrast like that in *English Journey* between historically more prosperous Lancashire, its centre in Manchester, which once claimed the best newspaper and orchestra in the country, as well as fine theatre, a city 'more critical than creative', and the harder, bleaker world of Yorkshire, lower in class. From the Yorkshire point of view, Lancastrians are 'inclined to be frivolous and spendthrift', whereas Yorkshire people are 'quieter, less sociable and less given to pleasure, more self-sufficient and more conceited'. *Angel Pavement* begins with a description of the grubby lane called Angel Pavement near the London docks before gradually focusing on the declining inherited business of Twigg & Dersingham, dealers in wood finishing supplies, veneers and inlays, and the social class and background of each of the few still connected with the firm. The plot is propelled when an adventurous new supplier from the Baltic, Golspie, arrives to resurrect and command the firm. At first, the outsider's efforts seem successful and his changes attractive, but without the questionably valuable moorings of past and class those changes are finally disastrous for each of the workers and Golspie's irresponsible departure destroys the firm. Priestley is inclined to introduce or set early within each of his novels a full geographical, social and historical account of the subject, like the economic and social history of Haliford, the West Riding textile town in which *They Walk in the City* begins, which is traced back to its industrial ascent in the 1850s, its prosperity during the Franco-Prussian war, its temporary salvation during the First World War, and its slide downhill because of world competition ever since.

In his graphic historical settings, as in his constant dependence on the language of the material fabric of experience, Priestley's fiction and perspective often resemble those of Arnold Bennett. The admiration for and use of Bennett are conscious. In *English Journey*, Priestley begins his account of Bennett's territory of the Potteries with respectful recall of Bennett's fiction and then wonders why none of the people he meets talk of Bennett who described them so well. In 1932, Priestley assumed Bennett's old job as weekly book critic for the *Evening Standard*, a culturally authoritative forum for the criticism of popular and avant-garde fiction. Although, for Bennett's last few years (he died in 1931), the relationship between the two had been difficult and contradictory,[2] Priestley, into the late 1970s, kept complaining that Bennett had never received the Nobel Prize he deserved. Perhaps the closest link between the two is the fact that both, Priestley the lineal descendant of Bennett, were seen antagonistically by the avant-garde in the twenties. For Virginia Woolf, they were materialists, 'the tradesmen of letters'.[3] While neither ever denied the materialism of his focus, and both thought that verbal recall of the material fabric of experience gave fiction a richer texture, the judgement against the materialist is more social and metaphysical snobbery than literary criticism.

Priestley's texture of social reference derives from older literature and art as well as from direct observation of experience. The landscapes and cityscapes of *English Journey* are often seen in terms of painting: the visible signs of unemployment in Salisbury are even more 'pitiful' in the still existent echoes of Constable's light; the look of local prosperity and controlled industry in Coventry suggest Vermeer in domestic buildings and Canaletto in general design. While, for Priestley, Bath may seem touristy and arid, as he wonders who lives 'behind those perfect facades', the countryside as he moves toward a bustling Bristol is still 'hearty' Fielding country. In *They Walk in the City*, the parting of the lovers in Haliford, which requires their search for each other in the chaos of London, is determined when the young man locks himself in his bathroom and accidentally breaks the key, a long, carefully engineered scene, balanced by a later similar scene for the girl, which parodies all the locked-room detective fiction of the thirties. Literature and art figure even more centrally in some of Priestley's plays, particularly those in which, given the form's necessary abbreviation in verbal texture, class backgrounds and relationships are less extensively developed than they are in the novels. *Time and the Conways* (1937) uses Meredith to isolate what was thought socially 'clever' a generation earlier. More significantly, the central themes in the play are explicitly drawn from Blake with appropriate quotations – the prophetic or reforming Blake of 'We shall build Jerusalem in England's green and pleasant land' for the false confidence of the first 1919 scene and the deep ambivalence of 'Joy and woe are woven fine', only half understood by the character who quotes it in the sadder recognition of the 1937 scene. In a later play, *The Linden Tree*, which looks back at the thirties from the perspective of 1947, Priestley represents the distillation of history, the sad recall of the older world that collapsed in 1914, through the playing of Elgar's Cello Concerto. The figure from the thirties is an aging, humane professor, urged by his university and most of his family to retire. But he refuses, loyal both to the sound of Elgar and the fabric of his own reduced historical and temporal experience. He remains at work because life has 'a pinched look, frayed cuffs and down-at-heel shoes – whereas coffins have satin linings'.

Priestley's fiction of the thirties, however, has not the static resolution or stances of the plays. The fiction is always in motion, most often contingent on a physical journey. Like the eighteenth-century fiction he venerated so highly, Priestley's form is often picaresque. In *The Good Companions*, Jess Oakroyd joins the vaudeville troupe as a stage carpenter. They tour England, have 'adventures', and stay at grubby inns or digs, a structure that permits both approval of the ordinary and satire of the pretentious, like public schoolmasters and Oxford dons. For Jess, as for the wealthy Miss Trant and the poor dressmaker who also join the troupe, life is the movement, the picaresque process of travelling, escaping from isolation and insularity. The only conclusion, after the year of the tour, is what 'good companions' all of them have been. *English Journey* follows a similar formal pattern, although the content focuses more on deprived lives and industrial squalor. Priestley gives the work a

long consciously eighteenth-century-sounding subtitle: 'Being a
Rambling But Truthful Account of What One Man Saw and Heard
and Felt and Thought During a Journey Through England During
the Autumn of the Year 1933'. *They Walk in the City* echoes the picaresque once it leaves Haliford for London. Priestley begins with two
shop-girl sisters in Haliford. The older, Nellie, is a social snob who
grades men by occupation and is eager to rise as far as she can. The
younger, Rose, deeper and more sensitive, who becomes one of
the lovers in the novel, sets out for an unknown London when she
thinks she's been deserted by her potential boyfriend. Although,
in both worlds, ads for jobs request 'the experienced, keen, efficient and public school preferred' and slang like 'swank-pot' is
universal, the London world is more changeable and linguistically
diverse, requirements for the picaresque. As Rose's journey begins,
Priestley comments directly: 'We all know Nellie's England, but
we have a lot to learn about Rose's'. Priestley's sense of form,
particularly in *English Journey*, was widely imitated during the
1930s; the photographer Bill Brandt, for example, attributing much
of his well-known photographic documentary, *The English at Home*
(1936), to Priestley's influence. Critics have also pointed out how
much Orwell's *The Road to Wigan Pier* owes to Priestley's *English
Journey*, although Orwell, who thought Priestley's work boring and
superficial, did not acknowledge the influence.[4]

In so far as Orwell sought to provide penetrating commentary on English working-class life, attempted to uncover a previously inarticulate working-class soul, he had some reason for refus-
ing to sanction any connection between his work and Priestley's.
Priestley's depictions of the working classes sometimes seem per-
formances, viewed from a distance, like scenes in vaudeville or in
the British music-hall comedy he so much admired. In an incident
in *The Good Companions* in which Jess Oakroyd needs to confront the
police, Priestley converts Jess's working-class fear of authority into
a comic music-hall turn of paranoia that is inconsistent with both his
character and the function of the police in the novel. *They Walk in
the City* uses show tunes effectively to characterise a contemporary
class attitude, but Priestley overloads his device with an essay
explaining why show tunes can be revelatory social phenomena.
As in other novels, some of the philosophising about the 'mystery'
or the 'core' of 'life' heavily underlines superficiality. When the
young clerk in *Angel Pavement* goes to the cinema palace with
Golspie's attractive and sophisticated daughter, and is described as

experiencing 'a golden immortality, a balcony seat high above Time and Change', the comment seems both empty and condescending to the character. More frequently Priestley's satire works because it sticks firmly to the external, the look and feel of things. The satire of the pretentious Dersingham's initial dinner party in *Angel Pavement* is an example, done entirely in terms of their snobbish class mannerisms, looks and tricks of speech without content. Even though the characters hear a great crash from the kitchen and see a brown stain appearing from under the kitchen door, their remarks are vapidly evasive and only the outsider, Golspie, is capable of saying that the dinner is ruined. It is a music-hall scene, a set piece.

In the plays, as in the novels, the antidote to the set scene or social stasis is not to probe the stasis more deeply but to move to another venue, to extend oneself by enacting other roles in the continuous vaudeville of England itself. In *Eden End*, neither his son on leave from a dull colonial post in Nigeria nor his self-sacrificing daughter who has stayed at home can help the aging doctor in a northern town in 1912 when he recognises how meaningless the conventional stability of his life has been. His third child, the rebellious and not very successful touring company actress, along with her boozy actor husband, is at least more generous, more able to talk with her father because she has seen and played so many pockets of similar isolation. Home, the conventional suburban home, in *Laburnum Grove* is probably based on lies and a financial scam. This discovery sends sponging in-laws and children scattering to their own travels, and leaves the couple who established the home happy in the uncertainty (the police have not quite enough evidence to prosecute) they generated themselves. Priestley subtitles *Laburnum Grove* an 'immoral comedy' and claimed that when working on the play in 1933 he 'was very suspicious about our financial system, if only because the banks appeared to flourish when industry was failing'.[5] In the 1930s, both as limitation and as the voice of an unpretentious common sense, much of Priestley's fiction and drama revolved as a series of music-hall turns, a form in which the variety and the motion conveyed the value of the experience. He did not, however, during the thirties, endow the tradition of vaudeville itself with nostalgic value, as he did in 1965 when he returned to the territory of *The Good Companions* and wrote *Lost Empires*, a fiction of the year 1913–14 on the variety stage in which the title is both the theatre and the England it represents.

Priestley was deliberate in concentrating on externals, especially during the 1930s. In his blunt, common sense voice, he often asserted that he had little in common with modernists and he invariably rejected Virginia Woolf's claim that fiction should convey interior experience. As late as 1960, in *Man and Western Literature*, his most wide-ranging critical work, he thought that literature now 'is over-introverted, often so deeply concerned with the inner world, with the most mysterious recesses of personality and so little concerned with the outer world'. He asserted his preference for Tolstoy and Balzac to the 'grey, thin' and introverted work of Henry James. Priestley did not fall into the critical simplicity of claiming that Balzac's work was more realistic than that of James; rather, his contrast was a preference for the more energetic, extroverted, external life available to the common man and woman. Attractive as this hearty externality seems, Priestley's work in the thirties also illustrates a less attractive side of the bluff English-man who focused and sometimes judged on external appearances. The work is full of statements of appearance that assume various forms of racial, sexual and ethnic determinism. When, in one of the London adventures in *They Walk in the City*, Rose is tempo-rarily imprisoned in a whore house, the sinister black chauffeur is described as a 'man-animal', and Priestley comments about a 'deep racial gulf between them'. In *English Journey*, the mixed races around the docks of Liverpool look like 'some profound anthropo-logical experiment'. Priestley writes of a woman there who had four children by four different men, 'probably all of a different race', and who 'deserves a subsidy from some anthropological research fund'. His most barbed remarks concern the lazy Irish lower classes who he thinks are violent and willing to accept slum conditions no Englishman would, not even the 'vulgar' in Birmingham who have 'the wrong kind of vulgarity, the decayed anaemic kind'. In a way Priestley anticipated objections from reviewers to the anti-Irish bias and the English insularity visible in the book.[6] Within the book itself he wrote: 'I wish I had been born early enough to have been called A Little Englander. It was a term of sneering abuse, but I should be delighted to accept it as a description of myself'. Signs of Jews are everywhere in *English Journey* from the showy avatars of the fur trade to the sad men in beards who cluster outside synagogues. Priestley distinguishes the ponderous German Jews who had 'outlandish names' in his native Bradford before the First World War from the Polish and Russian Jews of Leeds at the same time who spoke Yiddish and still display 'traces of that restless glitter which is the gift of the Jew'. He notices Jews wherever he goes: 'There are lots of Jews in Sunderland and on the way we passed a large synagogue which looked as strangely out of place as a herd of camels would have done'. A passing man in London in *Angel Pavement* is 'a neat dark Jewy sort of chap', and Jews on the streets generally exude a volatile and vulgar energy. Yet, often as he notes them, Priestley conveys none of the animosity toward Jews that he does toward the Irish. As early as 1933, he wishes his native Bradford would absorb more German-Jewish refugees, as it did before the First World War. And, by 1937, in the play *I Have Been Here Before*, he makes one of his central characters, a man whose insights can transcend time, a German-Jewish refuge. When another would banish him because of his strange and discomfiting perceptions, the voice of the play, as metaphor and as dramatic fact, insists that solid Yorkshire welcome and value him.

Despite his spots of bigotry and insularity, and his judgements that can rely too heavily on external appearances, Priestley's England ideally would combine warm, generous, responsive natures with cogent and practical social action. Early in *They Walk in the City*, he establishes Rose as his prototypical heroine. He calls her a healthy, thriving, handsome lass 'by nature', despite an environment of bad food, overheated rooms, dreadful medicine and 'ignorance, swinishness, savagery'. In Rose, he comments: 'Nature had found a way to circumvent the idiocy of half-civilised Man'. Rose also needs to find something socially worthy to do. London offers little possibility, certainly not the modern trading company her boyfriend (dispossessed heir to a declining Yorkshire wool business) works for where 'nothing it bought seemed worth buying and nothing it sold worth selling'. London is full of malaise: on a cold, foggy morning, most people 'looked disappointed and rather angry, as if they had just discovered that life had been cheating them for years, that all the gold in the forest was turning into dead leaves'. Useful social function, for almost all Priestley's young characters in 1936, is missing. In the world of *The Good Companions* in the late 1920s, an older man like Jess, a good carpenter, has a useful function for the theatrical troupe. But that becomes increasingly difficult in the world of the thirties which leaves the young only fantasy for pleasure.

Priestley is never puritanical or denying about physical pleasure. He begins his *English Journey* luxuriating in a new motor coach, 'voluptuous, sybaritic, of doubtful morality . . . how the ancient Persian monarchs would have travelled had they known the trick of it'. He can sympathise with the upper classes now also devoid of function: 'It is the decaying landed county folk, with their rattling old cars, their draughty country houses, their antique bathrooms and cold tubs, who are the Spartans of our time'. As he travels around England, he appreciates the working factories he sees, is fascinated by the intricacy of machinery and the skill of the men who handle it. What depresses him is the society with too many once thriving factories closed, too many people forced to live on dwindling inherited shares and promises of paper money, too many sullen unemployed. He regrets the decline of music-hall and participatory popular entertainment. Yet he never sees the films or any imaginative re-enactment of experience as depravity: 'patrons of cheap popular amusements, the cinema and the wireless and so on, have largely come from a class of persons that before did nothing in its leisure but gossip and yawn and kick the cat and twiddle its thumbs'. Priestley, in the thirties, held little veneration for the pre-1914 past, for the music-hall had always been the imaginative escape, not the reality of experience. He also, in *English Journey*, appreciates the skill displayed at a football match in Nottingham, despite his simultaneous aversion to the fierce partisanship and yelling crowds. Amusement as well as work requires a civilised understanding of function to satisfy the complex physical and sensuous nature of the human being.

For Priestley, nature and function together need to be satisfied in a tangible role within a community. And, in the thirties, community was overwhelmed by economic deprivation. Clearly, political reform and change were necessary, but, unlike many of his contemporaries, particularly those of the Auden Generation, Priestley was always sceptical about political theories, about what he saw as abstract or unnatural importations of doctrine into the visible English scene. In the twenties when many intellectuals, desperate for forms of social order, venerated Mussolini's Fascism, Priestley apparently once screamed at Shaw that Mussolini was 'a fraud, a mountebank, a megaphone. He doesn't amount to anything more than a black-shirted bullfrog croaking away in the mud'.[7] His fiction of the thirties links communism and fascism as equally violent dangers for the English. In *They Walk in the City*, the two lovers are separated and hurt when accidentally caught in a demonstration/anti-demonstration fascist/communist rally in Trafalgar Square. They don't realise what fascism or communism represent; they are simply inundated in the chaos of a mob scene. The clerk in *Angel Pavement* finds Hyde Park political speakers equally irrelevant, although his friend complains that his rejection of political evangelists shows he has no class consciousness. The evangelists, like the preachings of Golspie on enterprise in business, or the sexual freedoms of his daughter, are seen in the novel as alien teases, political or sexual lures that may trap the naïve English man or woman. *English Journey* is more specific in its condemnation of social doctrines. At one point, in Bristol, Priestley attends a meeting in which the fascist speaker is drowned out by communist appeals to the 'masses' from the audience. He finds both sides equally dreary, equally without knowledge of the issues facing local factories. In a Cotswold village, he meets a man who romanticises farming and would force a re-established peasantry. But Priestley thinks actual 'peasants' are 'ignorant, stupid, mean', and realises the Cotswolds were once a prosperous textile centre, deserted when the industry demanded coal. Like Newcastle, where he finds the blackest poverty, and where he thinks T. S. Eliot might have visited to write of a 'real' rather than a 'metaphysical' wasteland, the Cotswolds reveal signs of waste and economic mismanagement. Priestley concludes that Britain needs 'a rational economic system, not altogether removed from austerity', although the doctrinal alternatives are highly suspect. His scepticism about system, in hints and suggestions, seems connected with his experience during the First World War. Although he seldom speaks of it directly, he writes as if those who can accept allegiance to an abstract, orderly, totalitarian system are more naïve and younger than he. At one point his anger emerges. He attends the reunion dinner of his old battalion, from which he was transferred when injured just before much of the battalion was decimated on the Somme in 1916:

I have had playmates, I have had companions, but all, all are gone; and they were killed by greed and muddle and monstrous cross-purposes, by old men gobbling and roaring in clubs, by diplomats working underground like monocled moles, by journalists wanting a good story, by hysterical women waving flags, by grumbling debenture-holders, by strong silent be-ribboned asses, by fear or apathy or downright lack of imagination.

The horror of the First World War constantly in the background lingered in Priestley's distrust of all officialdom and all causes throughout the thirties. Although his comments are frequently concerned with social responsibilities to a community, he never follows an officially sanctioned line or a political party. He was president of the International PEN for eighteen months in 1936–7, and, like Galsworthy and Wells before him, he saw clearly the implications for writers and intellectuals of both fascism and communism and would sanction no connection with either. Although his social ideas toward the end of the thirties were more left than right, he achieved his widest audience in his BBC broadcasts commenting on social and wartime issues after the nine o'clock news (fairly regular between June and October 1940, less frequent thereafter), just at the time when Britain, alone, represented opposition to both signers of the Nazi–Soviet pact. He became a popular political voice, not connected with the government (he disagreed with Churchill on many social and economic issues), but one that could articulate communal sense and interest in reform apart from the context of any continental form of social order. He chaired a 1941 committee to suggest post-war social reforms that was organised and financed by Edward Hulton, the publisher of *Picture Post*. The committee was described as 'a sort of Leftist Brains Trust with progressive political views'.[8] Although twice urged by the Labour party to run for Parliament in by-elections, Priestley refused, although as the war continued he did develop into an articulate supporter of the Labour government elected in 1945. A frequently quoted speech appears in *The Linden Tree* in defence of the post-war Labour welfare state through the history professor (who is contrasted to both his daughter who is married to a French Catholic aristocrat and his daughter who is a ruthlessly Puritanical doctor, 'Thomas Aquinas and Lenin' – the third daughter, the approved symbolic Cordelia, plays Elgar's Cello Concerto) in the rhetoric of Priestley's popular political voice:

> Call us drab and dismal, if you like, and tell us we don't know how to cook our food or wear our clothes – but for Heaven's sake recognise that we're trying to do something extraordinary and wonderful as it's difficult – to have a revolution for once without the Terror, without looting mobs and secret police, sudden arrests, mass suicides and executions, without setting in motion that vast pendulum of violence which can decimate

three generations before it comes to a standstill. We're fighting in the last ditch of civilisation. If we win through, everybody wins through.

Later in the play, the professor repeats that England is 'trying to do a wonderful thing here' but 'somehow not in a wonderful way', as if, by 1947, Priestley felt that the need to be 'not altogether removed from austerity' might be less important than the fabric of physical well-being. In the 1950s and 1960s, much of Priestley's public political voice was involved in a running argument with Evelyn Waugh over the cultural significance of country houses and landed families, and in a series of articles in the *New Statesman* on the folly of nuclear war regarded as one of the principal instruments that initiated the Campaign for Nuclear Disarmament (CND),[9] Although the CND became, for a time, a popular policy within the Labour party, Priestley still avoided explicit political connection. He refused the barony Harold Wilson offered, fearing the honour might require him to echo the party line.[10]

In his serious fiction of the thirties, Priestley's social voices retain their independent commentary, their refusal to follow dogma, party stance or orderly global abstraction. The observations match the picaresque form, the running commentary that allows for a wide range of popular voices, some superficial, some not. Priestley, however, is not always content to rely on the inconclusive implications of the picaresque, to trust his recognition that the range of observations and voices cannot be easily assimilated. More than any other quality, this lack of trust, this pasting on of a falsely simplified conclusion, makes Priestley sometimes vulnerable to the charge of superficiality. In his acknowledged pot-boilers (like Bennett and other later writers, Priestley distinguished between his pot-boilers and his serious comedy), novels like *Faraway* (1932) and *Wonder Hero* (1933), the charge matters little and the novels have long since faded from historical or critical consideration. The charge matters more for the serious social fiction like *The Good Companions*, *Angel Pavement*, and *They Walk in the City*. *The Good Companions* perhaps suffers most from heavy adumbrations that suggest some unexplained but possible universal meaning for the picaresque. Chapters begin or end with heavy spectral links, details repeated or a pattern of coincidence insisted upon, as if some significant fate beyond our ken has brought these characters together. Yet that fate is nowhere made tangible or credible, as if Priestley wants to suggest confidence in a reassuring pattern for experience for which he takes no intellectual responsibility. He occasionally interrupts the picaresque to explain why he wants to dismiss or incorporate a character, not as a post-modern sign of the arbitrary quality of literary form, but as if the author would like to reassure the reader with the comfort of some truth beyond the form. The characters are wrapped up neatly, assigned to fortuitous fates with little justification in terms of the novel, brought on stage in a music-hall finale as if all the pains and problems of their experience have not mattered. They are, after all, 'good companions', but that concept as conclusion sentimentalises the pain and dislocation of their experience and re-enactments articulated throughout the novel. Priestley's devices create a cast of optimism that seems unearned in contrast to the travelling process of theatre depicted so graphically and energetically. The conclusion trivialises the substance. *Angel Pavement* is a deeper and better novel than *The Good Companions*, yet here, too, the voice of the end, manifested through the plot, palliates the version of London experience presented. The young clerk, gulled and inadequate in an eroding world, is led to understandable despair, then suddenly rescued by his landlord and landlady, as well as by a temporary typist he had scorned. Psychologically, this seems false, as if Priestley, although generous, is violating all his own observations by letting his character off the hook. The novel needs something of the relentless and unassuageable materialism of Bennett's *The Old Wives' Tale*. Then, too, the alien destroyer, Golspie, glides off to South America, that repository for the unknown and unknowable so useful in Victorian and Edwardian fiction. Whereas Evelyn Waugh, in *A Handful of Dust* (1934) uses consignment to South America in bitter parody, for Priestley South America is a means of attenuation, a way of suggesting that what Golspie represents is a strange visitation that struck Central Europe in the past, England now, some odd place on the other side of the world next. It matches the shallowness of the apparently destroyed characters' unearned reconciliations. *They Walk in the City* uses South America in a different, funnier and more appropriate way for Priestley's fiction. In a passage satirising all the 'unhealthy' and useless cosmetics advertisers implore people to buy, Priestley comments that the young shop-girls 'fear' none of the effects of cosmetics or economics but only 'dark sinister foreigners who would lure them into luxurious flats, give them dope, and then in some mysterious fashion ship them off to South America'. Here, however, Priestley recognises that fear is also attraction, and the novel, perhaps Priestley's best, remains, despite a melodramatic hint at the end of a chapter or two, true to its terms of endorsing 'nature' in a world that combines dingy, thwarted reality with attractive artifice and fantasy. Even the populist rhetoric of young health and independence that Priestley gives Rose and her young man as they return to Haliford at the end of the novel seems earned because it does not violate the values of their painful experience and will not change the London world.

In the plays of the thirties, Priestley sought to deepen his work through various theories about the operation of time. In a 1946 prefatory note he wrote for a reissue of *Three Time Plays* from the thirties, Priestley claimed that each of the plays rejected an 'ordinary conception of Time'. *Dangerous Corner* (1932), Priestley's first success on the London stage, divided time to 'produce two alternative series of events'. The second, *Time and the Conways* (1937), influenced by the theories of J. W. Dunne, illustrates that each of us, as observers, has a different 'peephole' into a series of events through time. One character can, therefore, dream or create the 'glimpse of the future' into the life of others. For the third play, *I Have Been Here Before*, Priestley cites Ouspensky's theory concerning the fact that our knowledge of repetitious patterns of experience can enable us to anticipate the future and, therefore, control or change a predetermined series of events. Both *Time and the Conways* and *I Have Been Here Before* also exude Jungian theory concerning the collective unconscious which alters time. Priestley concludes, in his preface, that the three plays represent 'Split Time, Serial Time, and Circular Time'.[11] But the theories of time consciousness, alluded to vaguely, are not central to the meaning or force of the plays. In *Dangerous Corner*, a set of middle class characters who know each other well gather for cocktails. A chance trivial remark about a cigarette box leads, through more than two acts, to the disclosure of past shootings, infidelities, drugs and financial dishonesty among the group. Toward the end of the play, Priestley returns to the beginning and has the characters repeat opening lines. The remark about the cigarette box is passed over with something equally trivial and the characters remain in their comfortable illusions and deceptions. The 'Split Time' is a gimmick in a play about the accidental discovery of buried truths, about a 'dangerous corner' in human interchange, not about time. Similarly, extraneous time theory does not impede the force or meaning

of *Time and the Conways*, then and now (to judge by the frequency
of its productions) regarded as one of Priestley's best plays. Its first
act establishes a middle-class family of mother and six children, the
two sons having survived the First World War, full of plans and
promises for a better and happier world in the euphoria of 1919.
Act II is set, with the same characters, in 1937, introduced as if a
dream of the novelist daughter on her birthday. The promise of
1919 has turned sour for all of them: the novelist daughter is writing
journalistic interviews with film stars and has just spent ten years
in a love affair with a married man who would not leave his wife;
the sensitive, accommodating son is a shabby town clerk; his charismatic brother, an officer during the war who planned business
success selling motor cars, is dishonest, a self-pitying example of
faded charm; their sister, the social reformer initially at Girton, has
dried into a dogmatic and prissy schoolmistress; another sister, the
pretty one, has married the initially lower-class business success she
once scorned, and he bullies her. That act ends with a few phrases
about 'peepholes' of time, and the third act returns to 1919 where
the audience, now knowing the future of the characters, can pick up
the social and psychological causes of 1937 implicit in the dynamics
of 1919. The play works on the contrast between the worlds of
1919 and 1937, both the changes and the psychic constancy that
have shifted the Blakean attempt to 'build Jerusalem' into a saga
of mostly 'woe'. The time theory means nothing more than an
ordinary historical sense of the serial, a description of the society
and some of its causes in this 'bad patch', the 1930s. In *I Have Been
Here Before*, discussion of time theory does obtrude more into the
play's substance with the outsider arriving at the inn, finding no
room, and announcing that this must be the 'wrong year'. But
room is found, and the other characters set in motion around issues
of possible expulsion of the alien and possible adultery between
two other characters. The 'spirals' of time create foreknowledge,
which enables the characters to change, to avoid the disasters
that expulsion or adultery represent. 'Foreknowledge' is really a
matter of deepening understanding and social change, intelligent
anticipations not contingent on theories of the repetition of time.

Priestley's theories are less than the substance of the plays themselves. The theories seem to combine pop versions of mysterious
scepticism about linear time and history with modernist conceptions of subjective time and theories of relativity. Whereas consciously modernist writers, like Woolf, Eliot and Lawrence, were

strongly influenced by new philosophical and scientific conceptions of time, Priestley, calling himself anti-modernist, was fascinated by more sensational, spine-tingling, popular echoes of play with linear sequences of time. 'Play' is the operative word, as, even in drama without theories, Priestley injects lines that superficially play with time. In *Eden End*, for example, the doctor in 1912, who has just delivered a baby and is momentarily optimistic, remarks: 'When he grows up – sometime in the Nineteen Thirties – he simply won't understand the muddle we lived in'. For a 1934 audience the line may have reverberated with irony, but it has little connection now with a play that still works as a 1930s' treatment of the illusion of 1912's stability and contentment.

Priestley's plays, like his novels, work best through the substance of their social depiction. When he attempted a symbolic structure, his work became essayistic and dull, sometimes fey. A 1936 play called *Bees on the Boat Deck*, subtitled 'a farcical tragedy', which Priestley described as 'an attempt to write political satire in terms of farcical comedy',[12] concerns blowing up a ship, which is society. A series of characters who represent political perspectives, fascist, communist and others, deliver speeches and dash about the decks as if in a bedroom farce. They are opposed by the simple engineer, although the owners decide at the end to blow up the useless ship anyhow. Despite a production staged by Richardson and Olivier, the play found little audience in 1936 and has seldom been revived. Much of Priestley's work, however, survives abstractions and theories, his own or those critics have applied. As John Bayley has recently written: 'Even Ouspensky, Jung and Gurdjieff could not spoil the good moments in *Laburnum Grove* or *An Inspector Calls* [1947]'.[13] The 'good moments' artistically are often bad moments historically, points of pain and deprivation in the attrition of an older England through the First World War and the two decades that followed. In describing his world, particularly that of the thirties, Priestley does not temporise or simplify despite his residual faith in a healthy human 'nature'. The life of the fiction inheres in the bleakness, cogency and vitality with which he describes social representations like the grubby tobacconist, the damp, fetid clothes, the appeal of the revelatory detective or adventure story, and the aimless revolt of the young in *Angel Pavement*, or the seedy music-halls and Bloomsbury hotel rooms, the warmth of greasy cafes, and the lures of orientalised cultural artifice in *They Walk in the City*. No conclusion emerges from the observations of the fiction, the voices simply record the fabrics of thirties experience. When Priestley adds a conclusion, the voice seems superimposed. At the end of *English Journey*, his account of his own rambles mediated by fiction as little as consciously possible, Priestley's voice concludes. He thinks that 'Modern England is rapidly Blackpooling itself' and is now 'lacking in character, in zest, gusto, flavour, bite, drive, originality, and that this is a serious weakness'. He thinks the young energetic and concerned, but they are 'not politically-minded', not as their nineteenth-century grandfathers were. Alien political importations violate freedom and don't work. *English Journey* finishes with the plea for a flexible indigenous politics, a recognition of nature and locality in a 'little England' that may find a way out of the 'dark bog of greedy industrialism' into the natural sunlight.

## NOTES

1.  Vincent Brome, *J. B. Priestley* (London: Hamish Hamilton, 1988) pp. 162–3.
2.  Ibid., pp. 125–6. This account is slightly suspect in that Brome, sometimes vague on dates, does not seem to realise that Bennett died in 1931. Brome writes as if the relationship involved mutual jealousy in 1932 when Priestley began his column for the *Evening Standard*.
3.  Anne Olivier Bell (ed.) assisted by Andrew McNeillie, *The Diary of Virginia Woolf* (London: Hogarth Press, 1980) entry of 8 September 1930, p. 318.
4.  Cunningham, *British Writers of the Thirties*, p. 239. For more of Orwell's denigration of Priestley's work, see Brome, *J. B. Priestley*, pp. 128–9.
5.  *The Plays of J. B. Priestley*, vol. I (London: Heinemann, 1948) p. ix.
6.  Brome, *J. B. Priestley*, p. 153.
7.  Ibid., p. 104.
8.  Ibid., p. 255.
9.  Ibid., p. 398.
10. Anthony Burgess, 'Northern, burly, populist and radical', *TLS*, 21–27 October 1988.
11. J. B. Priestley, *Three Time Plays* (London: Pan Books, 1947) pp. vii–x.
12. *The Plays of J. B. Priestley*, vol. II, p. x.
13. John Bayley, 'Phantom Jacks', *London Review of Books*, 5 January 1989.

# 4

# Moments of Intense Social Visualisation: Winifred Holtby, Lewis Grassic Gibbon, Patrick Hamilton

One response to fiction maintains that an author re-creates a given time and place with insight, then is unable to accommodate change or loses the talent when he or she applies it somewhere or sometime else. An example is the career of H. E. Bates. During the 1930s, Bates wrote fine fiction, principally short stories, about the repressed male confronting and respecting female sexuality in specific settings that were graphically documentary. As his sympathies expanded and his observations of class intensified, he gained both a popular audience and greater critical approval with his stories about Flying Officer X at the beginning of the Second World War. The moment was less a moment of talent than of the time and place of subject, for, after the war, he produced his most searching novels, like *A Moment in Time* (1964), which brilliantly chronicled a young woman's growing understanding of class and sexuality in the midst of the warm, frightening spring and summer of 1940, a 'sanguine' moment that 'like Churchill, fit both optimistic and bloody at the same time'. Another excellent novel, *The Triple Echo* (1968), is set in the same time-frame, and, on a slightly less searching level, *Love for Lydia* (1952), set in 1929–32, deals with the obsession of a middle class young man in a Midlands town for a young woman of the enervated aristocracy in the Great House, although it gains its force from the historical observations about dances, taxis, economics and social customs. Bates continued to write about the contemporary world after the Second World War. Those fictions are increasingly superficial and cantankerous, grumbles about the post-war world at the level of the television sitcom. It is as if Bates's discerning imagination was fixed at 1943, although he continued to observe and write into the 1970s.

This chapter will deal more particularly with three other writers who had shorter careers and whose moments and vision, themselves perhaps more complex and intense than Bates's, were mostly confined to the 1930s. In addition, the moments of social visualisation in the fiction of Winifred Holtby, Lewis Grassic Gibbon and Patrick Hamilton were intensely local and showed some signs of dissipating into international abstractions in which the authors genuinely and visibly believed. The inability to resolve in fiction an implicit contradiction between feelings and belief is also, itself, part of the literary climate of the 1930s. For two of the writers, resolution through time, even through the span of the thirties, was sadly impossible, for both Winifred Holtby and Lewis Grassic Gibbon died in their own thirties in 1935. The intense moment was virtually all they had, yet these moments were the product of considerable thought and complexity, were far from automatic responses to origin or environment.

Winifred Holtby, after service in the Women's Auxiliary Army Corps during the First World War, began publishing fiction with *Anderby Wold* in 1923. The novel contains many of the themes that characterise Holtby's fiction: the strong, independent woman who both exudes a 'flame of vitality' and is practical in her capacity to hold family and farm together; the attractions of a more diverse world outside the community; the struggles for power and social control between like-minded women; the weakness of the deeply loved men. The 'flame of vitality' is represented in Mary Robson, a young woman who has inherited the shell of a destitute farm from her feckless father and married the much older gentle, silent farmer, John, who could help finance the stock, work and restore the farm to prosperity. Mary is a force in the farming community, protectress of her servants and others, dreaming herself the 'mistress of bountiful acres', while she acknowledges that the farm is still in a mediate position, the large house 'cold and clammy' with weather stains and decaying tiles, the way to the market and her charities 'down a fog muffled road'. She fences off the weather as she steadily and practically extends the warmth and protection of her cooking and household, trying to extend her domain to the poor, nearby tourist town where 'the straight shower-washed streets shone like polished metal above the dancing grey and silver of the sea' and 'blank flat-chested boarding houses with lace-veiled windows lay swept and garnished, ready for the transitory influx of summer visitors'. Conflict and relationship between women is represented in two ways: Mary's grim struggles with Sarah Bannister, John's older sister and the wife of a prosperous farmer, who thinks Mary pushing the gentle John beyond his capacities; Mary's jealousy of her wealthier town cousin, Ursula, who 'from her scarlet toque to her high-heeled shoes . . . looked about as appropriate in that Victorian gathering as Dodo in a Cranford parlour', plays golf and is about to have a baby, while Mary has been unable to conceive. The outsider is a young red-haired radical writer from Oxford, David Rossitur, whom Mary succours after an accident in a storm. Although she has read his book beforehand, and they argue about society as he recovers, Holtby gives him no language or social fabric of his own. When not a series of abstract quotations, his talk sounds silly: 'if I stay here any longer, I shall like you both so much that I shan't be able to hate you. As it is, every time you are nice to me, I have to recite little pieces of Marx to myself to convince me what an abomination you really are'. The plot becomes melodramatic: Rossitur and Mary in unacknowledged love, John dead of a stroke, Rossitur propelling an agricultural strike he didn't intend through workers misunderstanding his words, strike turning to arson, Rossitur finally killed by a loyal workman who loves Mary and mistakenly thinks Rossitur responsible for the fire. Mary at the end has only the bright, vivid colours of the fire. The whole last half of the novel has no language other than images of flame or fire, rather an overstated version of the images that counter Coketown in Dickens' *Hard Times*. Mary never manages control over flame. Her own language of control, her elaborately structured domesticity, farm management and social concern, is inadequate for the fires, within and without, that Holtby sees consuming the modern world.

As she worked as an international journalist and wrote poetry, essays, short stories and a critical book on Virginia Woolf, Holtby also wrote five novels that expanded her fictional sense of geography and history over the next decade. *The Crowded Street* (1924), for example, goes back to 1900 to place the repressed small-city middle-class heroine with a snobbish dominating mother in the antiseptic world of tennis clubs and formal, heavily chaperoned receptions that focus more on trivial mating gossip than on chastity.

Sexuality is possible only for the protagonist's sister who, working on a farm during the First World War, rebels disastrously into a primitive culture. Only after many years is the protagonist able to escape into the world of jobs in contemporary London. The language at the end is stock and flat, with none of the artifacts or words of the pretentious middle-class repression or the primitive farm. Another novel, *The Land of Green Ginger* (1927), is consciously international. It begins with a woman, in 1896, setting off for colonial South Africa and marriage in defiance of her background: 'She was Saint Paul, setting forth toward Rome. She was Sir Walter Raleigh seeking El Dorado'. Some years later her daughter, Joanna, at the age of eight, returns to England an orphan to live with her maiden aunts. Yet she retains her mother's visions of Sir Walter Raleigh, and the difference between the language and social artifacts of her respectable aunts and the ardent talk and vision of Joanna's two school friends, a Russian-Jewess and the daughter of a Chinese custom's official, lends excitement and promise to the theme of a young girl growing up. But the First World War, a hasty marriage, the gassing of her husband, trying with two children to manage a hard, rocky farm (one incident about the death of a favoured pig seems lifted, in both theme and treatment, from Hardy's *Jude the Obscure*), and fascinated by the mystical talk of an itinerant Finno-Hungarian exile, provide a mixture of cultural tags and language that both antagonises the inert, xenophobic English villagers and overwhelms the novel. The second half of the novel is full of essays about travel and the spirit, as if Holtby is reaching for a language and a location that can allow her character to thrive. Joanna returns to South Africa to run a boarding house and nourish her children on 'gloriously silly' versions of the language that sustained her own childhood: 'I'd want to send hundreds and hundreds of cables to all sorts of people in all parts of the world. Just imagine inquiring after the Shah of Persia's kittens! Is there a Shah now, and has he kittens? Or sending Valentines to Mussolini, and Christmas greetings to Trotsky and to the agent of the British American Tobacco Company in Hankow? Is there one?'

Winifred Holtby's moment of intense and coherent visualisation of a fictional world emerged in *South Riding: An English Landscape*, published posthumously in 1936. A brilliant re-creation of a farming community and market town in the Yorkshire South Riding in the early 1930s, the novel is organised under headings that reflect the documentary journalist's attempt to impose

order on contemporary social chaos. The headings, like 'Educa
tion', 'Finance', 'Public Health', 'Public Assistance', of the eight
books that comprise the novel are like the agenda at a meeting
of the county council. Within these headings, experience over-
laps, for the principal characters go through the whole novel,
their stories extended into the various areas over which society
attempts to exercise control. Language is more complicated than
it was in Mary Robson's domestic control in *Anderby Wold*. In the
world of *South Riding*, even a farmer's servant has three languages:
'Like most of her generation and locality, Elsie was trilingual.
She talked B.B.C. English to her employer, Cinema American to
her companions, and Yorkshire dialect to old milkmen'. Along
with the cinema, old social customs still exist: the public con-
certs, the pubs that become music-halls, the spontaneously vulgar dancing on the village greens. Through all the narratives of
individual characterisation, the pain and loss of the First World
War are omnipresent, a world living with a constant sense that
it can never be what it was at the same time that it constantly
discusses change or debates the necessity for new roads that will
both cut off old farms and encourage new industry and settlement.
Political categories are also mixed. The principal local socialist
most admires the tough resiliency and vitality of the conservative
farmers. The young Liberal headmistress of the local high school,
Sarah Burton, and the strong, wise, Tory alderman, Mrs Beddows,
speak the same language on many necessary reforms in both the
society (like the need for a maternity hospital) and education.
Both are strong feminists, eager to help a bright, indigent teen-
age girl stay in school instead of dropping out to care for her
younger siblings after her mother dies worn out by repeated
child-bearing, or anxious to do what each can for the confused
adolescent daughter of Carne, once the wealthiest local farmer
who plundered much of his land and stock to please his aristocratic
wife, a belle of past Hunt Club balls who is now in a mental
institution.

Sarah Burton and Mrs Beddows are given Holtby's 'flame of
vitality', a constant sense of sympathy and activity in regard to
their community and their relationships. The flame, like Mary
Robson's, is also sexual. Sarah imposes her repressed sensuality
on her descriptions of the landscape she sees on her first long bus
ride through the community, and her desire to release herself is
always behind the efficiency, sympathy and control of her public

statements. She theoretically endorses a 'free love' she never has the chance to practice. Mrs Beddows, conventionally married for many years at the price of her feelings, invariably sympathises with those less in control than she. As the Depression exacerbates the public and private problems within the community, the plot rushes to melodrama. Carne loses his farm entirely and, just as he is about to make love to Sarah, suffers a fatal heart attack. Mrs Beddows defends Sarah in the subsequent public revelations, as they each realise the other has long loved Carne, despite the fact that both see him as 'reactionary, unimaginative, selfish, arrogant, prejudiced', as socially irresponsible. Yet the new social ideas, in which Holtby voices belief and which are reflected in Utopian suggestions, don't apply to the community and are unable to satisfy the flame of Holtby's strong, intelligent women. Holtby adds an epilogue that takes place on the day of King George V's Silver Jubilee (6 May 1935) when Sarah's triumphs concerning her new school buildings and her relationship with Mrs Beddows are balanced by her sense of defeat with the young women she tried to help and her betrayal of her lost love for Carne. A letter from an ailing communist friend is no help; his language is irrelevant, brave and sanitised. The moment Holtby depicts so brilliantly is the moment of intense and irresolvable social strain, the old community's erosion that is balanced by the irrelevance of the sensible new communal ideas in which Holtby so logically believes.

The intensely local and brilliantly achieved moment in Lewis Grassic Gibbon's trilogy, *A Scots Quair* (which consists of *Sunset Song*, 1932, *Cloud Howe*, 1933, and *Grey Granite*, 1934), comes historically earlier than it does in Holtby's work, emerges in the imagistic and linguistic evocation of the relatively recent north-eastern Scottish past in *Sunset Song*. Whereas Holtby's headings in *South Riding* are schematic issues in the new world, Grassic Gibbon's headings in *Sunset Song*, his impositions of rhythm and order, are timeless representations of the agricultural and human worlds: 'Ploughing', 'Drilling', 'Seed-time', 'Harvest'. They are both the land itself and the principal character, Chris Guthrie, as she grows to womanhood on the poor farm between the drought of the hot summer of 1911 and the bleak clearing of the cold January after the First World War. Grassic Gibbon invents a language that combines English with some old Scots words (a language that suggests a modern version of what rural Scots dialect might be without having an authentic locus in time or place), a combination that reflects Chris's own sensibilities, 'the English words so sharp and clean and true – for a while, for a while, till they slid so smooth from your throat you knew they could never say anything that was worth the saying at all' and, both in past and present, the 'Scots words to tell your heart, how they wrung it and held it, the toil of their days and unendingly their fight'. Some have thought Grassic Gibbon's lilting style 'affectation', but a growing number of critics and readers have valued the style as mostly English, with some old Scots vocabulary and 'the rhythms and cadences of Scots spoken speech'.[1]

Grassic Gibbon's style is capacious enough to combine Scottish history and legend with a language of irreverent common sense, beginning with Norman days 'when gryphons and suchlike beasts still roamed the Scottish countryside and folk would waken in their beds to hear the children screaming' and continuing through a drunken Boswell and the conflict between the Jacobite French-worshipping gentry and the Jacobin 'poison of the French Revolution'. The language and perspective are consistently anti-clerical and anti-religious, from the prophetic harangues attached to John Knox to the popular prejudices like 'only coarse creatures like Catholics wanted a kirk to look like a grocer's calendar'. The narrowly religious voice is that of Chris's brutal father, usually silent, who refers all things to 'Jehovah'. When his eldest son, Will, at sixteen, grooming a reluctant horse, echoes what he thinks is his father's voice and, hitting the horse with the brush, calls out 'Come over, Jehovah!', his father beats him until his face is bloody for taking his 'Maker's name in vain'. The local non-believer is Long Rob of the Mill, thought by the community to have learned his atheism 'from the books of Ingersoll though God knows if the creature's logic was as poor as his watches he was but a sorry prop to lean on'. The Scots rhythm is conveyed emotionally and historically in passages like the following account of a sermon delivered by visiting preacher, a 'poor old brute from Banff' who 'seemed fair sucked dry:'

> So hardly a soul paid heed to his reading, except Chris and her father, she thought it fine; for he told of the long dead beasts of the Scottish lands in the times when jungle flowered its forests across the Howe and a red sun rose on the steaming earth that the feet of man had still to tread; and he pictured the dark, slow tribes that came drifting across the low lands of the northern seas, the great bear watched them come, and they hunted and

fished and loved and died. God's children in the morn of time;
and he brought the first voyagers sailing the sounding coasts,
they brought the heathen idols of the great Stone Rings, the
Golden Age was over and past and lust and cruelty trod the
world; and he told of the rising of Christ, a pin-point of the
cosmic light far off in Palestine, the light that crept and wavered
and did not die, the light that would yet shine as the sun on all
the world, nor least the dark howes and hills of Scotland.

Almost all his listeners are immune to his rhythmic evocation of a
geographical and legendary past, for the quotation is immediately
followed by the iconoclastic voice of the parishioners: 'So what
could you make of that, except that he thought Kinraddie a right
coarse place since the jungles had all dried up? And his prayers
were as short as you please, he'd hardly a thing to say of the King or
the Royal Family at all'. Long Rob of the Mill, a different iconoclast,
remarks of another visiting minister who tries to please everyone
by preaching a sermon on the 'Song of Solomon': 'Well, preaching
like that's a fine way of having your bit pleasure by proxy, right in
the stalls of the kirk, I prefer to take mine more private-like'.

The central vehicle of both the language and the landscape is the
consciousness of Chris herself. Her mother, worn out and unable
to tolerate repeated child-bearings, commits suicide (this, as in
Holtby, represents the thirties' most unequivocal condemnation
of the older world); the younger brothers are sent to relatives
in town; Will and his girlfriend emigrate to Canada; the tyranny
of the farm ends when Chris's splenetic father dies of a stroke,
leaving Chris the farm and all his money. She could, she thinks,
go to the college in Aberdeen. But the land has worked deeply
into her consciousness. At her crucial moments, she walks to the
Standing Stones, set high near the loch by the ancient crofters,
which function as her church. She realises: 'Sea and sky and the
folk who wrote and fought and were learned, teaching and saying
and praying, they lasted but as breath, a mist of fog in the hills, but
the land was forever, it moved and changed below you, but was
forever, you were close to it and it to you, not at a bleak remove
it held you and hurted you. And she had thought to leave it all!'
The land is also represented in the time of her 'drilling', her sexual
awakening, and she falls in love with a young farmer named Ewan
Tavendale. They marry, a community celebration that combines
English and Scottish songs, old and new, a language of unity,

and Chris has a son, born just as war begins in 1914. The kind of Lawrentian love/hate relationship that develops between Chris and Ewan presages a destruction only averted by Ewan's joining the army. When he returns on leave from training camp, before going to France, he is so coldly distant and rapacious, in ways so like her father, that Chris emotionally turns from him. She keeps the stony farm going through the war that virtually decimates the community. Long Rob of the Mill, atheist and conscientious objector, is jailed when he refuses conscription. After his sentence, he returns to his mill, but sees the farming community broken by the war and, in despair, joins the disaster of his generation in France. Just before he leaves, in a rhapsody of land and love (as atheist and pacifist, his only focus, like that of Chris, has been the land), he and Chris make love 'below the rounded breast of the haystacks, the dusky red of the harvest night, this harvest gathered to herself at last, reaped and garnered and hers in her heart and body'. The scene is the climax of both plot and lyrical, rhythmic prose, Chris 'kissing him, she sought with lips and limbs and blood to die with him then'. It is also the end of the independent Scottish farming community. Ewan is shot in France as a deserter before a battle; Long Rob of the Mill, rushed to the front as a replacement in the last German offensive, is killed as he heroically covers the retreat of his unit.

*Cloud Howe* follows Chris to the borough of Segget, a larger village community of spinners and weavers, near a city. She marries Robert Colquohoun, a minister (the son of the 'poor old brute' from *Sunset Song*) who had been gassed in the war and believes in using the church as an instrument of social and economic reform. The headings of the novel are the clouds that obscure the clear purpose of reform, successively thickening through the novel from 'Cirrus' to 'Cumulus' to 'Stratus' to 'Nimbus'. Segget is permeated with a sense of the past war, a defeatism that Robert would alter through intelligent organisation. Chris is more sceptical, seeing the villagers in their divisions of class and status: 'They gossip and claik and are good and bad, and both together, and mixed up and down. This League of the willing folk of Segget – who'll join it or know what you want or you mean'. Although Chris tries to retain her lyrical, rural sense of language, she finds it increasingly difficult to be understood in class-conscious Segget. Their iconoclasms are more judgemental, meant more to put down others, than were the iconoclasms that characterised the farmers in *Sunset Song*. Grassic

Gibbon's language, too, although it contains many of the rhapsodic echoes of *Sunset Song*, particularly when the subject is Chris's feelings, also contains more of the hectoring 'you', the injunctions delivered in the second person that suggest the author knows better than we or the characters. These are applied particularly to Chris's child, young Ewan. Occasionally, too, a common word seems forced into the Scots, like the insistence that 'fey', whatever its origins, is usable only in a Scottish context. *Cloud Howe* reaches its climax in scenes that surround the 1926 General Strike, the national defeat of the workmen whom Robert has organised in Segget, a near riot that also leads to Chris's miscarriage, the loss of the only child she and Robert had conceived. As the subsequent nimbus clouds gather, the increasing weakness of Robert's gassed lungs, Chris's worries about young Ewan, her distances from land and emotion, the Labour government of 1929 and Ramsay Macdonald's subsequent betrayal of his party to the National Government, and unemployment and economic privation after 1931, Segget seems as dead as the farming community was in 1919. A more quiet, defeated Robert dies while delivering a sermon on the need to receive 'a stark, sure creed that will cut like a knife, a surgeon's knife through the doubt and disease – men with unclouded eyes may yet find it'.

*Grey Granite* dispenses with clouds entirely in favour of meta-phors for the stark and sure. The phrase of the title had been connected with young Ewan in *Cloud Howe*, an indication of his growing interest in the certainties of geology and science. He is, as *Grey Granite* begins in the large city called Duncairn (Grassic Gibbon adds a prefatory note that some have identified his city as Dundee, some as Aberdeen, some even as Edinburgh, but he insists that it is fictional), eighteen years old, interested in hard, necessary doctrines and living with Chris, who now runs a boarding house in the city. Headings for the novel's sections are those of geological substrata: 'Epidote', 'Sphene', 'Apatite', and 'Zircon'. The prose is gritty and granitic in the hard, dirty world of 1932. The boarding house is a collection of characters hanging on to once respectable white-collar jobs, angry at their diminishing circumstances and significance in society. Young men, like Ewan, find work in industry as inadequately paid apprentices, although, once their term is over, they are fired in favour of the cheaper labour of new apprentices (a practice that also propels the plot of Walter Greenwood's *Love on the Dole*). The urban language reflects the bitterness in a nasty iconoclasm that skewers anything deviant or outside the industrial slum. When Ewan condemns the Scots Nationalist candidate for writing 'Synthetic Scots' and asks if that means he can't 'write the real stuff', a voice of his contemporaries responds, 'sounds more epileptic than synthetic to me'. The once hopeful chances of emigration to the New World are dismissed in a view of America derived from films and the myths of Hollywood – an older woman wonders if she made a mistake not migrating, 'to think she might now have been out in New York with big Jews chasing her in motor-cars and offering to buy her her undies free'. Chris and Ewan are themselves appalled by the reductive vulgarity of the working classes. At one point, when Ewan and his girlfriend, Ellen Johns, pass a 'pleb' beating his wife as she tries to haul him home from a pub, they recognise that they are unable to do anything to help. Ellen, with comic bitterness, says that they might have 'stopped and sang him some William Morris!'

The language of the novel is increasingly Ellen's. She is educated, English, and her words are the rigid abstractions of what she calls 'International Socialism'. Although she will, on occasion, walk the nearby Scottish moors with Ewan, both their love-making and their conversation reduce to the granite of abstraction. The relationship changes through time. Ellen becomes more Scots, more willing to submit to Ewan's past, to 'this queer Scotland that had felt so alien, the dark, queer songs of lust and desire, of men and women and this daftness of love, dear daftness in soft Scotch speech, on Scotch lips – daftness like this that she felt for Ewan, and it didn't matter what he thought or did'. But Ewan becomes increasingly hard and abstract, loyal to the Communists in a strike that he knows will be a disaster for the workmen. Arrested and brutalised, Ewan is radicalised into a dedicated Communist, ranging the world for his examples of the victimised and 'one with them all, a long wail of sobbing mouths and wrung flesh'. He is released from prison through the corrupt efforts of one of Chris's capitalistic lodgers, whom Chris later marries in gratitude. But the marriage doesn't work, just as Ellen can find no way to connect with the now militant and intransigent Ewan. Ellen leaves the Party and returns to an amorphous England; Chris with no 'faith', thinking Ewan's 'just another dark cloud', returns to the farm in despair. Ewan cannot bring past or emotion together with conviction, just as Grassic Gibbon, in the final novel of the trilogy, can no longer invent or discover a language that can convey both past and present, both emotion and conviction, a unified sense of a social and particular life within time.

Readers and critics have noted, almost since the publication of *Grey Granite* (James Leslie Mitchell, the writer for whom Lewis Grassic Gibbon was a pseudonym, died only three months after the novel was published), the decline in both the use of Scots and fictional energy in the final novel of the trilogy. Generally regarded as the most imaginative proletarian novelist of the decade, the 'most distinguished case' of a writer able to combine authentic working-class life with linguistic and imaginative vision,[2] Grassic Gibbon's inability to sustain the linguistic level of his achievement has been the focus of considerable sympathetic critical commentary. Most literary and historical critics have tended to agree with John Lucas, the editor of a 1978 volume entitled *The 1930s: A Challenge to Orthodoxy*, who, in his introduction, talks of the stone-like prose in *Grey Granite* as Grassic Gibbon's enervating realisation that the language and ideas of international communism were unsatisfactory, that the novel does not finally suggest the vision of an ultimately triumphant proletarian imperative for the politically committed. Yet, in another essay in the same volume, Roy Johnson chronicles Grassic Gibbon's increasing commitment to class warfare throughout the trilogy. Johnson quotes Hugh MacDiarmid (Grassic Gibbon's close friend, and the famous literary Scots Nationalist and sometime Communist who lived until 1972) as saying the 'principal criticism to be levelled against' Grassic Gibbon is his 'theoretical inadequacy – this anti-intellectualism and Left-Wing infantilism'.[3] Although Johnson acknowledges that MacDiarmid's judgements and opinions changed frequently, he suggests a Grassic Gibbon whose inadequacy was insufficient commitment to the language and assumptions of the new international order.

Mitchell himself (he used J. Leslie Mitchell for most of the seventeen books he wrote, works of journalism, exploration and archeology, as well as novels, in his short career; he used Lewis Grassic Gibbon only for the trilogy and a late work of collaboration with MacDiarmid, *Scottish Scene*) was always interested in communism, addressing meetings and appearing on a communist platform before he was seventeen.[4] Yet his principal biographer, Ian S. Munro, regards his commitment to another set of abstractions as far longer and more significant than his communism. Mitchell called himself a 'Diffusionist', part of a set of late nineteenth-century ideas about evolution that were anti-Darwinian and anti-progressive, and held that the decay of the modern world could be blamed on 'the unfortunate accident of civilisation'.[5] In 1933, Mitchell published a novel, *Image and Superscription*, based on Diffusionist beliefs, which fit better than do the beliefs of international communists the whole imaginative perspective of *Sunset Song*. For Mitchell, Diffusionism and communism shared the conviction that 'all great literature is propaganda'.[6] Nevertheless, as MacDiarmid indicated, proletarian politics were always important for Mitchell. MacDiarmid thought, at various times, that Mitchell's 'adherence to Trotsky kept him out of the Party',[7] and that his beliefs in a 'golden age in the distant past . . . in a state of primitive communism' separated him from many communists of the 1930s.[8] Linguists are likely to offer another reason for the decline visible in *Grey Granite*. They point out that the invention of a rural or pastoral language has some authority in old dialectical Scottish speech, but that there is no urban equivalent, or, rather, perhaps, that a similar urban voice, the 'patter', was until very recently regarded as debased, incapable of feeling and useless for literature. Grassic Gibbon paid no attention to the patter, either because he didn't know it or thought his audience would not acknowledge its existence.[9] For the reader interested in social forms of definition, however, the linguist's answer seems, by itself, too simple. Rather, the increasing anglicisation and abstraction of Grassic Gibbon's language toward the end of the trilogy suggests something of a recognition that the healing of social fractures he so deeply desired could not be accomplished in the world he observed so acutely through the international forms of reconciliation in which he believed. He had the pre-lapsarian nostalgia common to many communists, as well as the willingness to force the issue, but he lacked the imagination of any future Utopia. His moment of unity, and his linguistic and imaginative achievement, was the depiction of the world fractured in 1914. Even more intensely than the vision of Winifred Holtby, Grassic Gibbon's version of the thirties is trapped in an inexpungeable despair.

Alone of the novelists treated in this chapter, Patrick Hamilton physically survived the 1930s (he died at the age of fifty-eight in 1962). But his moments of intense social visualisation, invariably urban, all take place in the thirties or during the 1943 stasis of the Second World War in fiction published no later than 1947. Most of Hamilton's work deals with characters who are obsessed. In his best-known and highly successful plays, *Rope* (1929), drawn from the earlier Loeb–Leopold murder case, and

*Gaslight* (1938, called *Angel Street* when produced in America in 1941, although the later film restored the title of *Gaslight*), the obsession, dramatised in shocking terms, is criminal. Although Hamilton, who worked for a time as an actor in his youth, wrote other carefully crafted plays, none achieved the success or the emotional force of the evil that characterised *Rope* and *Gaslight*. Hamilton regarded his fiction as better than his plays, examining more deeply and less sensationally the psychopathology of obsession.[10] In his early decline, after 1947, he returned to the criminal and the sensational. His trilogy about the adventures of a rogue figure, Ernest Ralph Gorse, which consists of *The West Pier* (1951), *Mr Stimpson and Mr Gorse* (1953), and *Unknown Assailant* (1955), dissipates into a litany of all Gorse's sinister larks in defrauding or violating each of the series of women who are attracted to him. Although the first novel was praised by Graham Greene as the best novel written about Brighton (Gorse's career begins with picking up female victims on Brighton's West Pier) and a *TLS* reviewer praised Hamilton's capacity for expressing the modish banality, the 'significant cliche',[11] the settings and language are more repetitious than resonant, and the trilogy lapses into language that simply and unsympathetically excoriates the imaginative poverty of the bourgeoisie. As character, Gorse becomes increasingly manipulative and criminal, with occasional suggestions, never explored, that his desire to hurt others, part of him since childhood, originates in feelings of sexual inadequacy. As psychopathology, the novels simplify and sensationalise. In contrast, the meaningful depth and concentration in Hamilton's fiction, achieved both through his examination of obsessed characters and his re-creation of the constricted world in which they are placed, occurs unevenly in the work that includes the trilogy, *Twenty Thousand Streets Under the Sky: A London Trilogy* (1935, consisting of *The Midnight Bell: Bob*, 1929, *The Siege of Pleasure: Jenny*, 1932, and *The Plains of Cement: Ella*, 1935), the novel *Hangover Square: The Man with Two Minds* (1941), and the novel *Slaves of Solitude* (1947).

Hamilton's effective sense of place is less a geographical entity than a severe compression, a crystallisation of urban space into metaphor. His metaphors frequently resemble those of Dickens, as in the *Slaves of Solitude*, set at the nadir of constricted experience in 1943, which opens with a Dickensian image of the large city:

London, the crouching monster, like every other monster has to breathe, and breathe it does in its own obscure, malignant way. Its vital oxygen is composed of suburban working men and women of all kinds, who every morning are sucked up through an infinitely complicated respiratory apparatus of trains and termini into the mighty congested lungs, held there for a number of hours, and then, in the evening, exhaled violently through the same channels.

Dickensian notes continue in the description of the rooms and lounge in the boarding house west of London where the central character, secretary to a publisher, Miss Roach, lives, in the type characterisations of the others, and in the crowds moving toward the cinema to become part of 'the lurid, packed, smoke-hazed, rustling audience'. In *Twenty Thousand Streets Under the Sky*, the voice of the first novel, Bob, a waiter in the London pub, The Midnight Bell, is explicitly and consciously Dickensian. Trying to be a writer, Bob describes London and the pub through Dickens' fiction and regards Dickens himself as 'the greatest exemplar of what industry might create from nothing'. In his introduction to a later edition of *Hangover Square*, J. B. Priestley (a constant advocate for Hamilton's fiction for over forty years), emphasises another Dickensian element in Hamilton's fiction: 'He [Hamilton] is above all the novelist of the *homeless*. Instead of a specific society, which most novelists require, he takes us into a kind of No-Man's-Land of shabby hotels, dingy boarding-houses and all those saloon bars where the homeless can meet'.[12] Hamilton's London is the contemporary crowded public space, the intense mirror of the society. In contrast, in the fiction set in London, Brighton is the illusion of escape or holiday (perhaps one of the reasons *The West Pier*, set entirely in Brighton, loses fictional force), the place where the obsessed Bob in *The Midnight Bell* imagines he might take the prostitute Jenny for a Christmas holiday although he recognises that she is 'an erotic and deadly drug now utterly indispensable alike to his spiritual and nervous system', or where the similarly obsessed George, the homeless central character of *Hangover Square*, might escape his pub companions, who 'all loved Chamberlain and fascism and Hitler', just as the war is about to begin in 1939.

The centre of experience in all these novels is a congested London within which obsession takes place, what J. B. Priestley, in another of his introductions to Hamilton's work calls 'the brick and concrete

jungle of lower middle-class London life'.[13] Obsession feeds within
the constrictions of urban space. Working within the banality of
the pub, listening to the same conversations among the same
people night after night, like that of the former medical student
who has spent time in prison for having once done what he calls
'The Illegal Operation', Bob uses the cinema where his 'soul was
filled with adoration' as his only outlet. When Jenny, an attractive
and agreeable prostitute enters the pub, Bob sees her as someone
to serve and rescue. In one sense, he can understand the story of
the Salvation Army boy bilked of his money by a prostitute because
he wanted to save her soul and 'they ain't got none'; in another
sense, however, Bob follows a more sophisticated version of the
same pattern, giving Jenny hard-earned money she promises to
repay, but never does, understanding when she fails to show up
for carefully arranged dates, and, finally defeated by his addiction
to Jenny, forced to abandon his plans to become a writer. The
middle novel, *The Siege of Pleasure*, is the voice of Jenny, as she
wanders from house to house and man to man after squandering
the money Bob has given her. This novel is the weakest of the
three, both in probing character and in re-creating a visible world,
for Jenny is less obsessed than endlessly eager to please, willing
to follow any passing emotion without a shred of responsibility.
Although as determined and unchangeable as the other characters,
the origins of the determinism, from Hamilton's point of view, are
too shallow and amoral to be interesting, and the fiction loses
energy. The fiction recovers in the final novel, *The Plains of Cement*,
through the voice of Ella, the pleasant, intensely loyal, physically
unattractive barmaid who is quietly and obsessively in love with
Bob. Again, the banal, circular, repetitious language in the pub
helps to carry the novel, the men who want to call Ella 'puss'
or a 'tease', and 'squeeze' her, which gives her the 'creeps', all
the language of deprived and unintelligent courtship. Similarly,
in emotional situations with her mother and her mother's second
husband, Ella and others can only converse in cliches given capital
letters: 'Solid Gold', 'Have a Good Cry', or there'll be 'A Little
Something Coming' when he dies. Hamilton sees his characters
from a considerable distance, occasionally making comments like:
'So uncanny, grotesquely adjusted, and obscurely motivated are
the parasitisms and coalitions formed by the small fish in the weird
teeming aquarium of the metropolis'. The distance from Ella is
far greater than it was from Bob in the first novel, Ella made

'uncomprehending of social causation'. Hamilton has the same
sense of his obsessed characters not understanding themselves
that Arnold Bennett did in his fiction, though less of Bennett's
sympathy. The novel effectively yields a social or communal entity,
seen from a distance, rather than individual or psychological depth.
The entity has political implications as well. Hamilton was, his
brother explained in a biography, always anti-Fascist, opposed to
Mussolini and Kipling equally, and more defined through what
he thought of as a tradition of English poetry than through the
influences of continental modernism. In 1933–4, however, just
when he was working on *The Plains of Cement*, he experienced a
'religious conversion' to Marxism, which satisfied his 'passionate
longing for a firm and final belief'.[14] In the trilogy, however, the
communistic solidarity is limited to the English proletarians who
cluster in the pub. Seldom good or evil, or crazy, part of their
obsession is a beleaguered, defensive Englishness. The prostitutes
in the pub are appalled at any suggestion of bi-racial cohabita-
tion. Bob is frequently anti-Semitic in talking of Jewish 'criminal
elements', a point of view Hamilton never mediates as he describes
the vulgarity and dishonest ostentation of the Jews. Ella makes
similarly insular remarks, and describes the surrounding area as
'the criminal patches and Belgian penury of Charlotte and Whitfield
Streets'. Hamilton's provincialism is less the warm locus of Priestley
than the bitter, concentrated, survival of a national and racial
identity.

The echoes of communism and the politics of *Hangover Square*,
set in the winter, spring and summer of 1939, are less insular and
transposed more confidently and effectively into metaphor. In this
novel, the central character, George, is obsessively in love with a
former actress named Netta who generally ignores or humiliates
him and travels with a sinister and violent man named Peter.
George is constantly at Netta's or in the Earl's Court pub where
Netta, Peter and their friends gather and sponge off George for
drinks. At times, George's mind 'clicks', and he imagines killing Netta and Peter, and retiring to the semi-rural sanctuary of
Maidenhead where he was once happy. But he soon clicks off
again and resumes his willing victimisation, unable to recall his
visions of honest violence. George is also made a representative
of Englishness in the post-Munich world, as he recognises how
*'indecent'* it is that Netta loved 'Adolf, and Musso and Neville all
grinning together, and all that aeroplane-taking and cheering on

balconies'. Peter, first seen as only silent and brutal, described by George as having the 'sneering chin' of Velasquez's portrait of King Philip IV, becomes more the overt bully and fascist. After he and Netta make love in the back of a car while George sits in front with the driver (George has never been allowed to sleep with the presumably chaste Netta), George realises that Peter has been in prison for fascist activities. Barred by birth from the aristocracy he longed for, Peter has transferred his class resentment to allegiance with the Nazis. George also recognises that Netta is 'sexually stimulated' by the 'boots, the swastikas, the shirts', by 'violence and brutality', and that 'the pageant and panorama of fascism on the Continent' is her 'principal disinterested aesthetic pleasure'. As his knowledge becomes more certain, and as the Nazi–Soviet pact of the summer of 1939 seems to eliminate political choice, George's two 'brain clicks' come together. Just as war begins in 1939, George, the ordinary Englishman, kills Peter and Netta with a golf club (golf is the only thing George has ever been good at) and goes to Maidenhead to commit suicide. In this, Hamilton's most metaphorically resonant novel, he visualises intensely, politically and psychologically, the moment of complete despair at the end of the thirties.

The same metaphorical and social intensity characterises the position of England in 1943 in *Slaves of Solitude* (published in the United States as *Riverside*). With a job that barely requires her (little use for a publisher's reader in wartime when the paper shortage and military necessity dictated much of what was published) and dependent on the sterile routines of the boarding house for food and security, Miss Roach, the representative of a sensitive although beleaguered England during the lull in the war, is lonely and isolated. The types in the boarding house represent past class issues, clinging to trivial and known forms of order to insure survival. The boarding-house bully, Mr Thwaites, teases Miss Roach about her 'Russian friends' and the belief in 'equality' that will destroy the structured order of the English class system. In fact, Miss Roach's only outside friend is a German woman, apparently even more isolated, and Miss Roach succeeds in getting her the single vacancy in the boarding house. Once there, the German woman becomes Mr Thwaites' ally, joining him in teasing Miss Roach as the 'English Miss', too prudish and delicate to understand the modern world. Miss Roach, at first, wonders if she herself is hyper-sensitive, as she finds the teasing about English class 'nauseatingly Ribbentropish'.

As time goes on, as the German woman, first seen as 'timid'
and 'ingratiating' (assumed to be a 'good German' because she
is living in England), betrays Miss Roach with her new American friends, and as both the German woman and Mr Thwaites
become more aggressive in verbally assaulting Miss Roach, the latter, with considerable justice, begins to see them both as examples
of 'Teutonic arrogance' which 'had developed into plain, good-old,
familiar, Jew-exterminating, torturing, jack-booted, whip-carrying,
concentration-camp Nazidom . . . the spiritual odours which had
prevailed in Germany since 1933, and still prevailed'. Almost obses-
sionally, the German woman and Mr Thwaites bait Miss Roach,
calling her insufficiently 'cosmopolitan' because she will not agree
that the Germans are as much victims of the war, that 'petty
pilferer', as the English are. The baiting becomes viciously personal
and, when Mr Thwaites stands face to face and falsely accuses her
of seducing the young boy she tutors, she pushes him away. He
falls and, although apparently unhurt, suffers a stroke and dies a
few days later. Miss Roach feels enormously guilty, even requiring
the assurance of the doctor that her push had nothing to do with
his death.

The alternative to the Nazism within the structure of old England is represented by the Americans who begin to crowd the
pubs and towns along the Thames west of London. As they pre-
pare for the invasion of the Continent, they are generous and
irresponsible. One evening, when Miss Roach and the German
woman have been drinking with Americans and others, they all
decide to try to find dinner somewhere: 'No imaginable combination of peace-time circumstances could have brought about such
a composition of characters as now filled the car and sat on each
other's knees . . . The war, amongst the innumerable guises it had
assumed, had taken on the character of the inventor and propri-
etor of some awful low, cosmopolitan night-club'. Miss Roach is
fascinated by the Americans. She even falls in love with one of
them and considers his offer to join him after the war and help
run his laundry business in Wilkes Barre. But she soon discovers he has made the same offer to a number of other women –
it is part of his charm. She realises what Hamilton underlines,
that the American's principal characteristic is 'his inconsequence:'
'He was not only inconsequent, as most human beings are, in
drink: he was chronically and inveterately inconsequent'. Although
Miss Roach can escape the boarding-house world through the

help of an old actor who silently watched the boarding-house baiting, and can treat herself to a holiday at Claridge's, time is still only the silent lull in the midst of the war. Hamilton ends the novel with a paragraph in which Miss Roach knows nothing 'of the future, . . . of the February blitz shortly to descend on London, . . . of flying bombs, . . . of rockets, . . . of the Ardennes bulge, . . . of the Atom Bomb'.

In some respects, Hamilton's social depiction of England changed from the insular defence of the proletariat in 1935 to the firm revulsion against Nazism and class structures visible in the ordinary Englishwoman in 1943. He became less puritanically judgemental about sex, visible in the differences between the excoriated amorality of prostitutes, the only alternative to the virginal, in *Twenty Thousand Streets Under the Sky*, and the appreciation of human and sexual contact as a way out of isolation in *Slaves of Solitude*. In other respects, however, the changes are less than they seem. English social life in Hamilton's terms is always constricted, turned in on itself, more comfortable within a rigid social code even though Nazism is a brutal and criminal perversion of all codes, a rot at the depths of the psyche, and communism is at best unreliable. For Hamilton, communism was certainly always preferable to Nazism. He never, in his fiction, equated the two and in life his brother maintained that the 'basis' of his consistent attraction to 'Marxist-Leninist-Stalinist' thought was always 'love'.[15] But the bitter, reductive language and categories of Hamilton's thought always held something of the shapes of his constricted 1930s, of his search for some final, determining, unrealised explanation. Although his 1943 demanded acceptance of the 'cosmopolitan' and 'inconsequent', of attitudes important in defeating Nazism, he was equivocal and uncomfortable, as if he needed the firmly provincial and consequent to survive. He could accept the 'inconsequent' only in drink, his personal resolution. And he maintained all his life that Germans were 'racially evil'.[16] Despite his brilliant re-creation of the English urban world of 1943, and the awareness of changing social perspectives, much of Hamilton's social imagination seems fixed at 1939, that moment in which the beleaguered urban English, violated by the aggressive brutality of one alien social system and betrayed by the false promise of a sustaining love from another, yet emotionally attracted to both, could feel only the constriction of despair in their shrinking world.

# NOTES

1.  Ivor Brown, introduction to Lewis Grassic Gibbon, *A Scots Quair* (London: Jarrolds, 1946) p. 8. This 1946 edition was the first in which the separately published novels were printed as the intended trilogy.
2.  Cunningham, *British Writers of the Thirties*, p. 313.
3.  John Lucas (ed.), *The 1930s: A Challenge to Orthodoxy* (Brighton, Sussex/Totowa, New Jersey: Harvester Press/Barnes & Noble, 1978).
4.  Ian S. Munro, *Leslie Mitchell: Lewis Grassic Gibbon* (Edinburgh: Oliver & Boyd, 1966) p. 24.
5.  Ibid., p. 70.
6.  Ibid., p. 106.
7.  Ibid., p. 134.
8.  Ibid., p. 173.
9.  I am indebted to Professor Richard W. Bailey of the University of Michigan for this quick summary of a linguistic position.
10. Bruce Hamilton, *The Light Went Out: The Life of Patrick Hamilton* (London: Constable, 1972) p. 57.
11. *TLS*, 7 September 1951.
12. J. B. Priestley, introduction to Patrick Hamilton, *Hangover Square* (London: Constable, 1972) pp. x xi.
13. J. B. Priestley, introduction to Patrick Hamilton, *Twenty Thousand Streets Under the Sky: A London Trilogy* (London: Constable, 1935) p. 8.
14. Hamilton, *The Light Went Out*, p. 81.
15. Ibid., p. 155
16. Ibid., p. 177.

# PART II

# Social and Historical Metaphor

# 5

# Rosamond Lehmann's Social and Historical Landscapes

In the fiction considered thus far, much of the social representation has been referential, a texture for experience drawn from the author's version of the external world. Although individual voices and perspectives shape the worlds communicated, as they do in all fiction, the sense of social history recalled exists outside the fiction, which functions as commentary. The chapters that follow focus on fiction the genesis of which seems more literary and interior. This fiction is more dependent on metaphor that combines or does not distinguish between private and public experience. Often, individual and sexual experience is intrinsically related to the social and historical, the language of each realm becoming a way of understanding the other. This method, often encouraged by the techniques, the confidence in an individual shaping consciousness, and the attempt to articulate interior experience directly in fiction which we sometimes too loosely associate with the modernism of a generation earlier than the thirties, is responsible for some of the decade's best fiction, its most cogent and involving metaphors that combine individual and historical experience, as seen in novels like those of Rosamond Lehmann, Elizabeth Bowen, Henry Green and, retrospectively, L. P. Hartley.

Rosamond Lehmann's first novel, *Dusty Answer* (1927), the only one to achieve the popularity accorded a voice of a new generation, conveyed the intensity of a young woman's experience growing up and at Cambridge in the early twenties. Some reviewers questioned and savoured what they thought was shocking immorality; other reviewers and literary friends made more significant claims, comparing her fiction to that of Virginia Woolf, D. H. Lawrence or, in several instances, in its combination of passion and a response to the conventional that fears and welcomes social isolation, to Tolstoy's *Anna Karenina*.[1] Yet Lehmann's women are never set in Tolstoy's social or moral world, their isolation never public or moral tragedy. They are Lehmann's own contemporaries, born into the security of the English intellectual and artistic upper class at the end of the nineteenth or beginning of the twentieth century. Rosamond Lehmann herself, several times in print, cited self-mockingly the fact that she was born during a thunderstorm on the day of Queen Victoria's funeral, 3 February 1901, which, in *The Swan in the Evening* (1967), 'seemed' to give her 'an unexpectedly distinguished *cachet*: almost the reflection of a royal nimbus'. Although the use of the royal name or event was never taken seriously or with sanctity, and had no connection with an author's politics, writers like Lehmann, Virginia Woolf and others still relied on it as a form of historical definition, an echo of past social unity.

The social unity of the past is reflected in the families through and against which Lehmann's young women protagonists define themselves. Judith Earle in *Dusty Answer* is given the once-famous father, now remote and dying, and the much younger mother who manages capably the large, settled home along the river, characteristic of much of the fiction. Judith is an only child, dependent for friends on a group of cousins (unrelated to her) who together visit their grandmother at the adjacent country house. Later novels, like *Invitation to the Waltz* (1932), bring both generations into one family, two or three daughters (the three reflects Lehmann's own family) followed by an independent and spoiled son. The protagonist is always the second daughter, the process of growth often coming through definitions of sibling and family relationships. Even in *The Ballad and the Source* (1944), in which the second daughter's, Rebecca's, learning comes from voices outside the family, the dynamics of family and siblings are important. Qualities 'are enhanced by establishment of their origin and continuity; a clue, a dignity is given to idiosyncrasy of temperament. Even disabilities – fatness, lack of inches, straight hair, tone deafness, failure to spell or do sums . . . touched with the mystery of a recurrent phenomenon'.

In most of the novels, particularly *Invitation to the Waltz*, the continuation of the same family in *The Weather in the Streets* (1936) and *The Echoing Grove* (1953), the contrast and rivalry between the two older daughters is one of the crucial ways in which the second daughter establishes her identity. In *Invitation to the Waltz*, set in

1920 or 1921, when both are teenagers, Kate, the elder daughter, is also the voice of social convention. Both are, for example, aware that their gentle father is an atheist, 'irritated' at the sight of clergymen, while their mother conceals 'her beliefs, if any, assuming a curiously formal and reverent manner'. As Olivia, the younger, sees it, Kate 'looked pure the day the curate came to tea, and stonily refused to respond when one caught her eye and winked; and said afterwards nothing disgusted her more than vulgarity'. When the dull Oxford man their mother has unearthed to escort them to the dance at the neighbouring social Great House turns out to think dancing only remotely pleasurable because he has decided to take Holy Orders, the sisters are differently disappointed. Neither the devout Kate's 'eye, the clear, proud, challenging eye of a beauty, nor Olivia's, melting and sympathetic, should swerve him from godly thoughts'. At the dance itself, Kate finds and attracts the one young man who interests her, whereas Olivia, the central consciousness, goes through experiences in which she is neglected, victimised, momentarily appreciated, patronised and defeated. Ten years later, in *The Weather in the Streets*, the rivalry is more conscious and explicit. Summoned to her father's bedside from her life as a divorced young woman in London, Olivia is jealous that Kate, in a 'suitable' marriage to a doctor and with four young children, has been summoned days before. Kate sees Olivia as 'touchy', 'her immediate reaction was a sort of defiant irony, exceedingly boring', not as capable of nursing their father as is Kate, now that her own 'dreadfully nervy phase', when she first came back from Paris, is well in the past. Olivia still loves Paris and smokes too much. On the train from London, Olivia meets, for the first time in ten years, Rollo, the only surviving son of the Great House at which the dance in *Invitation to the Waltz* took place. Her affair with the married Rollo, its substance and its consequences, is the major focus of the novel, and Kate rarely appears after the opening scenes. Yet Kate's disapproval, her satisfaction that she is fulfilling an expected social role, echo in Olivia's mind throughout the novel. She feels at times less competent, at other times a superiority in her vulnerability to the intensity and the irresolvable pains of her love.

The sisters in *The Echoing Grove*, Madeleine and Dinah, are established as rivals. Dinah's long affair with Rickie, Madeleine's husband, during the 1930s, is central to both lives. The novel opens after the Second World War and Rickie's death, the two sisters attempting to reconcile after not having spoken throughout the thirties. Long narratives of the past establish that, even before Rickie, the two sisters had been politely rivalrous, each wondering what the other had obtained as psychological inheritance, Dinah, the younger, thinking Madeleine conventional and superficial, Madeleine thinking Dinah 'secretive' and 'cold'. Rickie and Madeleine have had three children, one now dead in the war, Rickie and Dinah an illegitimate child born dead. As conscious voices other than Dinah's narrate the past, Lehmann shows that both sisters, in different ways, have experienced the pains of abandonment and betrayal, have known the intensity, failures and inconsolabilities of love, and can feel the force of the line quoted from William Blake, 'Go love without the help of anything on earth'. Both have taken conscious risks for love against convention and lost. In this most complex and psychologically subtle of Lehmann's novels, they seem, by the end, two sides of the same woman, far more alike than different.[2]

The shift from themes of rivalry to those of what women share reflects Lehmann's focus, throughout the novels, on women's intense need to articulate an interior self. In *Dusty Answer*, Judith, at first, wants each of the family of cousins to like her better than anyone else, their lives to 'revolve intimately round her', at the same time she wants to know these 'strange other creatures'. Only gradually does she realise that she is as mysterious as they, that she must find her own identity, recognising that as an incipient writer she is always an outsider. For Lehmann, feeling herself the outsider was both personal, endemic in any writer, and generational, true for all those like herself 'who remember the pre-1914 sheltered Edwardian world'.[3] The family provides the initial locus for identity, but, in the fiction, Olivia, separating herself from what she sees as sterile conventionality, must symbolically run toward a more mysterious landscape of greater emotional possibility. Only in *The Weather in the Streets* does she recognise how much colouration she takes from others, how difficult identity is to find: '*We* don't know what we look like. We're not just ourselves – we're just a tiny nut of self, and the rest a complicated mass of unknown quantities – according to who's looking at us'. The focus on identity and its complexities continues through all Lehmann's fiction. In her last novel, *A Sea-Grape Tree* (1976), in which Rebecca, sixteen years after the conclusion of *The Ballad and the Source*, on a lush tropical island in the Caribbean, calling herself 'Anonyma', must deal with her own 'discarded self' and 'establish an identity, tense with the efforts at all costs to conceal it'.

Rebecca discovers herself through her communications with a mysterious past and her love for Johnny, who has been living, in escape from the world, on the island ever since he, a pilot, was maimed during the First World War. Although at first she is attracted only to someone else who, after painful experience, 'never gives himself away', and she feels only that 'my laceratingly unacceptable identity no longer troubled me', she and Johnny love intensely. At the end of the novel, Rebecca feels she must leave the evasion of the island to have their baby in England. Johnny, recovering gradually from his partial paralysis (he is able to swim, not walk) promises to join her. This is potentially the only illegitimate child born alive to one of Lehmann's intense protagonists. But the potential ending seems a possibility achievable only imaginatively or historically, an extension of identity only in the strength to survive despair with which the more psychologically complex of the earlier novels end.[4] The achievement of identity through love is more precarious in all the earlier fiction. In *Dusty Answer*, Judith's sexuality is barely formed. She experiences intense vicarious attractions to both men and women, and, when she finally makes love, she chooses Roddy, the cousin most enigmatic and 'indifferent' to her, hardly aware that he is homosexual. She avoids the advances of the dull, reliable cousin Martin, as well as those of the sardonic and self-exculpating cousin, Julian. In Lehmann's second novel, *A Note in Music* (1930), Grace Fairfax feels trapped with a pompous husband in a northern town. Her only baby was born dead eight years earlier, and the respectable marriage is no substitute for the constantly recognised loss of 'spirit' in the 'mud-flats of her daily life'. By the time of *The Weather in the Streets*, Olivia is able to love Rollo intensely, but feels love her only identity: 'In this time there was no sequence, no development. Each time was new, was different, existing without relation to before and after; all times were one and the same'. Outside time and weather, she is betrayed, for no love lasts and intensity violates continuity. Intensity alone is madness in *The Ballad and the Source*. Dinah in *The Echoing Grove*, like Olivia, finds her intense love betrayed, although she realises finally that Rickie's betrayal originated in a despair he could not survive, although she, the stronger and a woman, can survive deeper, childless despair. Rickie 'had decided to resign', which Dinah realises is not 'indifference'. The central women,

Grace, Olivia, Dinah, finally Madeleine as well, survive without self-pity. They try to behave well in conventional terms and don't always succeed. Nevertheless, they recognise, as Lehmann's men seldom do, their own emotional responsibilities for an intensity never matched and always betrayed.

Female identity over time, in Lehmann's fiction, requires both intense connection with another and separation from the conventional world, is never just love or self. This is visible not only in the plots and themes, but in the language, metaphors and landscapes through which Lehmann's world is so brilliantly and colourfully conveyed. The writer, for Lehmann, is both inside and outside. As she writes at the beginning of 'The Red-Haired Miss Daintreys', a wartime short story published in her only volume of stories, *The Gipsy's Baby* (1946), the writer is central to the work, close to her own experience: 'Writers should stay more patiently at the centre and suffer themselves to be worked upon'. Not always consciously, the writer becomes a 'kind of screen . . . or . . . a kind of preserving jar in which float fragments of people and landscapes, snatches of sound. It is a detached condition. It has nothing of the obsessed egotism of daydreaming, and only a ghost of its savage self-indulgence'. The story itself dramatises her own family, on holiday, observing an affectionate bourgeois family with four six-foot tall red-haired daughters. The Daintreys exaggerate and externalise attitudes and relationships only dimly half-perceived in the author's own. All the representations of the Daintreys' vivid singularity, dependence on each other, and class position have more muted, half-seen echoes and contrasts within the author's family. The story follows the Daintreys through the First World War and disasters afterwards, provides external justification for the conclusion that applies to the bourgeois family generally: 'Product of an expanding age, the mould is broken that shaped and turned those out. Forced up too rapidly, the power in them, so lavish and imposing as it seemed, sank down as rapidly and faded out'.

Inside and outside also press closely together in Lehmann's language and landscapes. Olivia, in *Invitation to the Waltz*, mixes her emotional projections with the exterior serene winter landscape on her birthday: 'a luminous quality glowing secretly behind the white veil of air . . . serene and wan, as if it had begun to draw slowly out of exhaustion into the crystalline purity and delicacy of convalescence, replenishing itself in peace after the agony of trees, the driven cloud-wrecks, the howl, the roar of the whirling dark'. She sees herself and others, in part, through clothes, like the badly cut flame-coloured silk she wears to the dance or, in *The Weather in the Streets*, the lady of the Great House, Rollo's mother, 'full-rigged, confined in an ample severity of black'. Lehmann's women characterise and are characterised through the colour and shape of clothes, both the revealing statement of an inner consciousness and the observable external statement. *The Ballad and the Source*, in particular, dwells on the colours each woman wears or changes to, like Sybil Jardine's mysterious and ubiquitous blue cloak. Crimsons, greens of various shades, sun-splashed yellows, serviceable browns, screaming magentas – all describe and suggest in Lehmann's personal and social landscapes. Frequently, the colours clash or contrast sharply, as Rollo indicates distance when he loves 'dark ladies in white dresses'. Lehmann's prose, whether coloured or not, suggests and encloses contradiction in its use of the dense, oxymoronic phrase, a character explained in 'rigid screaming silence'. The language and oxymorons reflect a changing world in which cause and effect clash, often violently. In *The Echoing Grove*, the child conceived in Rickie and Madeleine's angry embrace of false reconciliation, an embrace depicted as 'brief, violent, anonymous', turns out to be 'the flower of the flock . . . from her first hour a laughing matter, a child of fortune'. Most frequently, from the point of view of Lehmann's protagonists, sexuality and childbirth are seen as antagonistic or contradictory, as are fathers and lovers. In the external world of social class, extreme contrasts are equally proximate and searing. In 'The Gipsy's Baby', another of the wartime short stories, the front door of the house opens to the lawn that sweeps graciously to the river while the back door reveals that other world that 'ever beckoned, threatened, grimaced, teeming with shouts and animal yells and whipping tops and hopscotch, with tradesman's horses and carts, and the bell of the muffin man and words chalked up on palings, just beyond our garden wall'. Both worlds are apparent in Lehmann's perspective, socially, emotionally and intellectually. She herself wrote, in *A Letter to a Sister* (1932), that she would want to be 'precise, a scientist', as she would also want to discover Shakespeare's private journal in some old trunk.

The women in love want to exist entirely within the singularity of their own emotion, but they are aware of both interiors and exteriors, of the interaction of self and not-self. The landscapes they see are, simultaneously, projections of their own emotions and perceptions of a densely textured outside world. Grace Fairfax can look out the window in her northern town and see the street lamps as 'a row of blurred incandescent chrysanthemums', but she also sees that 'beneath their light the wet tram-lines gleamed sleek and serpentine'. When the attractive young man she knows she cannot have announces he may go to Ceylon, she sees 'sun beating on burning sands, and sapphire seas lapping the coral reefs . . . intensest sunlight always, filling the fierce blue sky, the thirsty land from end to end; no clouds, no shadows at all'. *The Weather in the Streets* is full of landscape as well as weather and streets. On the first weekend Olivia and Rollo go into the country, Olivia notices 'the tree trunks' silvery shafts wired with gold and copper, violet transparency in between the boughs . . . a line of washing in a cottage garden – such colours, scarlet, mustard, sky-blue shifts, petticoats – all worn under grey and black clothes, I expect – extraordinary . . . red brick Queen Anne houses on the outskirts of old villages'. They drive 'through sandy roads among the pines, past astonishing brick and stucco residences with towers, turrets, gables, battlements, balconies – every marine-Swiss-baronial fantasy' to the elegant sea-side hotel where they make love. The next day, however, is different, 'sodden' in an 'infinite thick soup of rain', the car breaking down and repaired while Olivia looks at 'a shed of pink corrugated iron, telegraph wires, some chicken coops and a new yellow stucco bungalow'. Love is more difficult in the airless, damp room in the hotel with 'stuffed birds and fish in cases and pampas in giant vases, and dark-brown and olive paint . . . a smell of . . . dust and beer and cheese, and old carpets and polish'. Later, in an odd May frost, 'full-sailing, torch-loaded chestnuts were caught, islanded in the pale blue-green Arctic fields of the sky', Olivia realises the jealousy she thought she was above, 'jealousy coming like a bank of poison gas out of a clear sky, corrupting the face of the earth'. After an idyllic holiday with Rollo among the lakes, flowers and mountains of Austria, Olivia returns, alone and pregnant, to London in a 'scorched irritable airless' August. Main roads are empty, 'only in the by-streets, where mews and slum just touch', are 'groups of children . . . London's strident August undergrowth, existing like cactuses in waterless stone'. She wanders, ill, feeling as if she's living 'in a third-class waiting-room at a disused terminus among stains and smells, odds and ends of refuse and decay'. When she realises, after her abortion, that their love cannot survive, she concludes: 'We don't live by lakes and under clipped chestnuts, but in the streets where the eyes, ambushed, come out on stalks as we pass; in the illicit rooms where eyes are glued to keyholes'.

In *Invitation to the Waltz*, *The Weather in the Streets*, and *The Echoing Grove*, the landscapes the women describe are compounded of natural, visible, psychological and social phenomena. In *The Ballad and the Source*, however, the landscapes seem more mystical, suffused with the suggestive blue of the unknown. The prose sounds animistic, as if sensitive to spirits not locatable in the natural world. The ballads of the title are the long narratives from various voices from the past that reveal to young Rebecca the complicated history of corruption, failure and resentment in the family of Sybil Jardine that has gone from elegance to madness to the severe and tenacious competence that eliminates love in three generations. Mrs Jardine, the progenitor, is seen as 'savage', 'unearthly', an 'enchantress' of considerable charm, or an 'Enchantress Queen in an antique ballad of revenge'. Rebecca, the 'preserving jar in which float fragments' in this novel, is fascinated with Mrs Jardine who talks not only of ballads but of the 'source': 'The fount of life – the source, the quick spring that rises in illimitable depths of darkness and flows through every living thing from generation to generation'. The source is ahistorical, beyond physically perceptible landscape, and, although the source is often 'vitiated, choked' by history and circumstance, as intense love is 'betrayed – murdered', fidelity to the source is equated with the 'truth' which Mrs Jardine says women must try to live. *The Ballad and the Source* ends in the midst of the First World War, all influence of Mrs Jardine destructive, mad or irrelevant within her own family. The only legacy of her 'truth' or source is half-consciously within the clear-sighted outsider, Rebecca. Sixteen years later, in *A Sea-Grape Tree*, Rebecca, on the tropical island, discovers that Mrs Jardine, referred to by her earlier name of Sybil Anstey and now dead, had lived on the island for her last few years and influenced Johnny toward partial recovery and the avoidance of despair, encouraging what she had called his 'untapped creative potential', at which subsidiary characters laugh. Rebecca, however, does not, and Johnny still has the ubiquitous blue cloak. In bed alone one night, Rebecca holds a long and enigmatic conversation with a voice designated as Sybil Anstey. The conversation includes recall of the past, more history of betrayals and jealousy, and Sybil's urging Rebecca to leave her 'luminous cocoon', her 'sceptical

defenses' and her 'intellectual nihilism', and 'wake up' to her deep
love for Johnny. Within the text itself, I cannot determine whether
the episode is dream or conversation with a supernatural voice,
just as Rebecca herself is unsure whether to follow or exorcise
the spirit she has encountered. Yet Rebecca then begins her affair
with Johnny, and Lehmann wrote, in 1985, that the enigmatic
(the voice of Sybil will not 'foretell') conversation 'was intended
to be a telepathic one'.[5] In *The Swan in the Evening*, Lehmann
wrote that she began holding telepathic conversations with her
daughter, Sally, sometime after Sally died suddenly in Java in 1958
of poliomyelitis. She had always identified most closely with Sally,
had claimed that only thoughts of her daughter at one point had
saved her from 'the temptation to despair', and was distraught at
her death. Compelling as reasons to explain these conversations
as projections from her own interior psyche might be, Lehmann
consistently maintained that they were actual conversations with
Sally's spirit. Lehmann first published an account of her mystical
experiences in 1962, then expanded them in *The Swan in the Evening*.
Yet she always said that she was not conventionally religious,
not a believer. She wrote, late in life, to Gillian Tindall: 'Like
Jung, I didn't – I don't – believe: I know'.[6] Hints of Lehmann's
interest in telepathic knowledge antedate Sally's death. A number
of letters from 1951–3 exist in her correspondence now at King's
College Library, Cambridge, that ask questions or request accounts
of the telepathic experiences of others, and, in one short scene
in *The Echoing Grove*, Dinah had thought herself in telepathic
communication with Rickie, whom she had not seen in years, just
before he died. In all these instances, telepathy, for Lehmann, is
contingent on intense, overwhelming love.

The images of landscape, geography, seasons and weather, the
images that mediate between or combine self and other, almost all
emerge from the accounts and perspectives of women. Women,
like Olivia, see a place 'a long, long way off . . . and then in one
particular weather', and the men do not know what they're talking
about. Grace, in *A Note in Music*, when she visits her native south
on a chaste holiday from her husband, responds to the hollyhocks
in a fancy 'that their round heads were notes of music painted upon
an outspread scroll; chords and scales splashed down in tones
of rose and crimson upon the green keyboard of the espalier',
knowing her husband would think her mad if she articulated
the feeling. Her framework is constantly geographical, which her

husband never notices. Perhaps the only exception is Rickie in *The Echoing Grove* who, not long before his death, sees the smile of an attractive anonymous young woman as 'the forgotten taste of an unthreatened vernal intimacy'. Yet the image is abstracted, never particularised in prose or person. Lehmann's men are invariably less sensitive to and able to describe the weather and the landscape than women are, less able to articulate the boundaries of self and not-self. The best men in almost all of Lehmann's fiction are amiable, generous, well-mannered and superficially competent, but they don't articulate depths or sensitivities. Particularly in the early fiction, the women and the narrative voice, on the surface, resent and excoriate the men. Young Judith Earle expects men to be incomprehensible and indifferent, and she finds them dull and unattractive when they're not. At Girton, she often feels lonely and isolated; when she visits a man's college, she finds his room 'untidy and rather dirty, with something forlorn and pathetic and faintly animal about it, like all masculine rooms'. Returning to Cambridge after she has finished her degree, planning to meet her close woman friend who never appears, Judith attaches betrayals to Cambridge itself: 'Under its politeness, it had disliked and distrusted her and all other females'. Despite an active social life at Cambridge, Lehmann felt that her years (1920–23) marked a particularly sexist period in Cambridge culture. She wrote her mother about the male protest when a woman was granted a *'titular* degree', which 'seems to me more like d—d cheek than a concession'. The women at Newnham College had locked themselves in against a protesting mob who 'smashed the lovely memorial gates and did 700 pounds worth of damage – and *that* is the superior sex!!!'[7] The women in *A Note in Music* see both the dull and the attractive as examples of 'masculine indifference'. The one attractive, generous man, his thoughts revealed only in the last few pages of the novel when he muses about the man he will join overseas, recalls Grace as the only woman who might have loved him. Standing on the creaking ship, 'he watched the great bows plunging majestically; spinning out of their prodigious iron austerity delicate ruffles, ephemeral films of foam; white laces, ruffles of foam over a dark breast; blown over a swelling breast . . . a vanishing breast'. *The Ballad and the Source* presents even less from a male point of view. The novel is full of Mrs Jardine's objections to male control of society, stating 'Englishmen dislike women: that is the blunt truth of it'. She is also a strong advocate of education for women, one of the heart as well as the head: 'How long, I wonder, will ignorance spell purity and knowledge shame?'

*The Weather in the Streets* and *The Echoing Grove*, the novels most concerned in presence or retrospect with the 1930s, yield a more complicated version of 'masculine indifference'. In *The Weather in the Streets*, in which Olivia, when in love, narrates in the first person (before and after are subjects of third person narration), she recognises men and their inadequacies in more profound ways. Rollo is not just generous and amiable, he is seen as 'magnanimous', able to understand others without judging. He never tries to inflate himself and tells Olivia from the beginning that he is unreliable. Although he loves her, he often says that he won't leave his wife, a commitment he alters only for a moment among the chestnut trees above the lake in Austria, a moment quickly reversed (without telling Olivia) when he gets a letter from his wife announcing that she is pregnant. His inadequacy is the lack of depth or intensity in his emotional commitment. He could live within a permanently adulterous triangle, always willing to take all the blame himself, trying to make things easier for others, but never intensely suffering or singular. He is often a good lover, although, like the later Johnny in *A Sea-Grape Tree*, he has 'the capacity of men for falling fast asleep at crucial moments' and he doesn't like being as 'irresponsible' as he is. Olivia is attracted to Rollo's self-revelations, even when he betrays her: 'quite matter-of-fact, laconic, almost – not exactly – evasive; as if he wanted to dismiss himself, shrug off the responsibility of being himself'. After his return to his wife, Olivia's lonely, painful abortion (which Rollo never knows about), and his own motor accident, Rollo is able to talk of their love as 'such lovely times', as 'fun', and to hope gently that they might see each other again. When Olivia protests, he says: 'Let's not be final and desperate, darling'. On the surface, Rickie in *The Echoing Grove* is much like Rollo, although Rickie is given more of a voice, his suffering made more interior. Outwardly as 'magnanimous' and non-judgemental as Rollo, Rickie has moments of fantasy in which he sees himself as victim, torn between responsibilities to the two rivalrous sisters he loves, 'stripped, raked by their deadly cross-fire'. After he leaves Dinah in despair, he returns to Madeleine just in time to go to a dinner party in a taxi 'in close sad separation'. At the dinner party, where he drinks a lot, he charms and attracts the new

American wife of his best friend in order to hide from himself. He knows that his resignation is a 'self-defensive impoverishment of self'. All the discerning women see that he is 'less concerned than most to provide adequate safeguards against pain to himself. Women would love him for that, but on the other hand...'. The pain is turned inward into drink and an ulcer. Living in London at the Admiralty during the Second World War, while Madeleine is living with the children in the country, he is able to articulate his pain and his deficiencies directly, to experience release, in a long narrative of the night he spends with the compassionate American woman. In the narrative, Rickie's pain and despair at his own incurable emotional irresponsibility, are unrelentingly dramatised, as are the pain and despair of Dinah and Madeleine in earlier narratives as they warily approach each other. When the novel was published, John Lehmann wrote his sister: 'You know you make all other novelists writing today seem inarticulate or phony. I mean that, it's not flattery . . . It is terrific; and terrible; because such writing could only come out of the most terrible suffering. It is one of the most unmitigatedly painful books I have ever read: the almost total absence of that enveloping aura of the poetry of natural beauty which I have always loved so much in your writing, makes it seem like an inferno'.[8] Three days after the night with the American woman, Rickie, only forty-two years old, dies as his neglected ulcer haemorrhages. She is killed by a flying bomb shortly thereafter.

Both Rollo and Rickie are not held accountable for their emotional irresponsibility. They, unlike the women who can love intensely outside of or apart from time, are always within time, always representative of that generation of male survivors maimed by the First World War. Rollo is the only surviving son of the Great House, his older brother, who was publicly 'a good chap', killed in the war. He thinks 'any one dead is automatically superior to any one alive'. His brother had been 'shocked' by the war, had 'believed in God'. But Rollo, barely surviving, is 'never shocked' and feels he can live only 'privately'. This is less a defence than an axiom, the only response of a generation. Rickie, just too young for the First World War, is part of the same socially maimed generation. The estate he was to inherit in Norfolk had had to be broken up and sold, his share reduced to the 'small Jacobean dower house' where his mother 'once barbed with ostentatious unreproach' has been permitted 'piously, rheumatically to fade, fret, potter'. Although

the sale enabled Rickie to secure a well-paid job in a relative's ship-
ping firm in the City, he feels that, in his generation, 'everybody
is inadequate' and suffers from a 'withered heart'. For Rickie, the
First World War created a permanent homelessness, 'the root of
this loss or intermittence of personal identity'. Only by working
day and night at the Admiralty during the Second World War,
'this *passive urgency*', can he find release. To understand Rickie and
themselves, Dinah and Madeleine must participate symbolically
in the killing and maiming the First World War represented. At
the beginning of the novel, frightened and horrified, they shoot a
rat the dog has maimed before they can start to understand. The
disaster of the First World War pervades all Lehmann's fiction.
Mrs Jardine's only male descendant, Malcolm, is killed in 1917,
and Johnny in *A Sea-Grape Tree*, still bitterly 'unpleasant' about
any public issue since August 1914, says 'the heart of the world
is broken'. The attitude is apparent in Lehmann's earliest fiction.
Near the beginning of *Dusty Answer*, just at the end of the First
World War and the promise of the cousins' return to the house next
door, Judith looks out her window at 'rain-wet branches . . . a long
dark-golden evening . . . tree-tops quiet . . . no leaf upon them:
yet in that liquid mauve air', and she thinks 'wars and rumours
of wars receded, dwindling into a little shadow beyond the edge
of the enchanted world'. But she goes next door and learns that
'everybody's favourite' cousin, Charlie, has been killed in the
war. She realises that she must 'forget' him, that her adolescent
feeling for him was 'a romantic illusion, a beautiful plaything of
the imagination', but she also sees that next door 'all the colours
were drained away; only white spring flowers in the border shone
up with a glimmer as of phosphorous'. The landscape of the world
is permanently altered. Lehmann always verified the importance
of the First World War. As late as 1983, in an article in the journal
of the Society of Authors, she wrote that, as a young woman,
'I had it lodged in my subconscious mind that the wonderful
unknown young man whom I should have married had been
killed in France, along with all the other wonderful young men;
so that any other suitor – and quite a few uprose – would be a
secondary substitute, a kind of simulacrum'.[9] The brooding death
that hangs over the inadequate simulacrum, at least until the
release through another death in the Second World War, dominates
all Lehmann's depictions of males, makes them representations of
historical metaphor.

Although crucial, the influence of the First World War on Lehmann's fiction is far from the only significant historical representation. History pervades the fiction. *A Note in Music* carries an epigraph from Walter Savage Landor: 'But the present, like a note in music, is nothing but as it appertains to what is past and what is to come'. Both Lehmann's family past and her education were saturated with nineteenth century intellectual and literary history. Her father was an editor of *Punch* and a Liberal MP. A great-grandfather wrote a defence of Darwinian thought entitled *The Vestiges of Creation*, but, since he lived in Scotland with his wife and eleven children, his authorship was not acknowledged until a posthumous reprinting in 1884, some thirty years later.[10] Her father's parents were friendly with Browning, George Eliot, Dickens, Wilkie Collins, Hawthorne and Emerson. Lehmann's own novels contain frequent literary reference. The consciousness of the adolescent protagonists is full of E. Nesbit and Dickens as ways of both explaining themselves and describing others. The attractive male is seen by the woman as Steerforth, 'the fatally lovable betrayer' in *David Copperfield*.[11] Rollo, however, sees the world more in terms of *Tristram Shandy* and Michael Arlen's *The Green Hat*. The texture of literary reference expands in the later work, for *The Echoing Grove* uses Hardy and Forster on the 'developed heart', William Blake and T. S. Eliot. In the autobiographical *The Swan in the Evening*, Lehmann claims that, long before her interest in telepathy, she had been haunted by Ralph Hodgson's imagery. She had initially known the Victorian novelists like Meredith (whose sonnets are the source for the title *Dusty Answer*, as well as numerous references) better than she knew her own contemporaries. The most significant reference, however, as for many others of her generation and later, is that of T. S. Eliot: on time (both the coexistence of present and past and the intense, impossible desire to escape time), on the fragility of the individual ('human kind/Cannot bear very much reality'), and on the attempts of art in 'that sublime, unhopeful, consoling cluster of poems', *Four Quartets*.

The literary references suggest a complexity of response to experience that does not nullify the appeal to the clear sight of truthful perception that Mrs Jardine makes in *The Ballad and the Source*. Rather, Lehmann's protagonists attempt to see and feel with as much intensity and clarity as they can. Fog is the barrier to the apprehension of Lehmann's landscapes, fog that can be meteorological, moral, conventional or emotional. Lehmann described herself as inhibited by one fog or another, once even suggesting that the whole period of her writing *Dusty Answer* was shrouded in the 'haze' of her unhappy first marriage in the North of England, the novel itself an attempt to clarify.[12] In the fiction, public or social fog, which emanates in the horrors of the First World War, covers more of the landscapes, rural and urban, as time moves into the 1930s. Fog particularly permeates *The Weather in the Streets*, the one novel that, both in composition and in setting, is confined to the decade. The novel opens in London, Olivia's 'crammed dolls'-house sitting-room . . . dense with the fog's penetration, with yesterday's cigarettes', colour drained from the setting and the streets. Summoned to her dying father, Olivia, on the train, leaves 'lentil, saffron, fawn' behind, goes through the 'grubby jaeger shroud . . . over the first suburbs' toward the 'luminous essence, a soft indirect suffusion from the yet undeclared sun' of her country past. The country, too, has 'a fog-breathing motionless dusk . . . looming black, extinct, monstrous', as well as the 'amorphous emotional fog' of her familial past. Although she and Rollo can sometimes escape temporarily into love or the myths of clear, sun- and cloud-coloured landscapes, she invariably returns to the gritty London fogs of contemporary streets. The same grittiness and landscape characterises the geography of *A Note in Music*. The drab encrustations of northern social life are made parallel to February when 'the wind-carved snow-wreaths still lie on the brown moors, old drifts heap the ditches. Should the rain unbind the earth for one day, an iron frost will lock it once again on the morrow'. In contrast, Grace recalls old southern Februarys with 'mild blue watery air, with the ploughed earth mysterious in the dark fields . . . over the river, stark branches swim in fresh mists of green'. Although a few of the descriptions of northern life, like those of the musical hall reviews, the dancing palace that suggests 'the repressed and dismal lasciviousness of British Non-conformist imaginations', the brave postures of the prostitute, and the tawdry excitement of the country fair, share the vulgar energy of Priestley's northern cityscapes (although the implicit attitudes are markedly different), most of Lehmann's urban North is the dark barren stone of structure and the noisy, glistening steel of tram-lines in the rain. London and the North, weather and geography, characterise an England that, in Lehmann's historical terms, is at its most intense during the decade of the thirties.

Issues of class and politics are part of the daily grit of thirties life, its pervasive texture. Lehmann, of course, had always noted differences in class, the ragged children in their games, silences or derision visible and audible just outside the back door of the country house. She had also depicted working-class people and servants with complex and discerning sympathy, although Lehmann could also be snobbish, as in the characterisation of the scholarship girl trying to work assiduously beyond her capacity in *Dusty Answer*. But nowhere is the material of class more omnipresent than in *The Weather in the Streets*. Olivia's first marriage is a descent in class. She recalls sharply 'the smutty window . . . the smell of geyser, of cheese going stale in the cupboard . . . nails always dirty, breaking . . . figures on the stairs . . . shunned at the door of the communal, dread, shameful W.C.' of her first marriage. After her divorce, with a woman friend in London, 'drifting about for inexpensive meals . . . always the cheapest seats in movies', Bohemian parties that are drink-sodden and unclean among scattered bits of broken-down furniture, and the recognition of others' 'lives passing up and down outside with steps and voices of futile purpose and forlorn commotion', she is always aware of class. She is edgy about the class ascent that Rollo would represent, thinking herself an undeserving interloper. She is self-conscious, as she would not have been ten years earlier, in describing Rollo's family: 'In prime condition they all looked: no boils or blackheads here, no corns, callouses, chilblains or bunions. No struggle about underclothes and stockings. Birthright of leisure and privilege, of deputed washing, mending . . . Can they sniff out the alien upon this hearth?' Although Lehmann recognised the connection between class and politics in the thirties, the novel contains little explicit politics. Lehmann's kind of commitment, in public speeches and scripts for broadcasts she wrote and delivered in the late 1930s, was far more visible after 1936, when the principal issue was fascism, than it had been earlier in the decade when class attention was more specifically economic. She spoke at a large 1938 rally of writers against fascism. She always defended the artist, as in a speech objecting to the 'smarty left dismissal' of Virginia Woolf ('Nobody was ever less arrogant, spoilt or vulgar') and to judgements of art by the values of 'class war or political consciousness'. In another speech, late in the thirties, in 'these days of class war', she thought anti-fascism the most important cause: the worst scenario imaginable would be to see 'our children grow up defeated: morally, physically, intellectually warped and stunted'.[13] In some of the later novels, explicit politics is material for only minor characters or a quick satirical reference: 'Mrs. Jardine behaved toward her as a sovereign might toward a Communist M.P. at a royal garden party'; a woman in a story assuages her class guilt by thinking: 'She had friends with revolutionary ideas, and belonged to the Left Book Club'. Politics is given a more sympathetic structure in the retrospective view of the thirties that constitutes much of the fabric of *The Echoing Grove*. After Dinah's love is betrayed by Rickie, and after her short self-hating affair with a parasitic Bohemian, she marries a kind, intelligent, politically committed Jew from the East End. They are 'very happy' for a year or two, until he is killed fighting Fascism with the International Brigade in Spain. He is part of her history, but, unlike Rickie, not deeply part of her interior emotional life or central to the novel. Far deeper than this man is the recognition Dinah and Madeleine retrospectively share, that the decade propelled 'a new attitude towards sex . . . a new gender may be evolving – psychically new – a sort a hybrid' and this attitude is 'much more fundamental than the obvious social economic one'. They see 'bourgeois' love as no longer meaningful or possible, Rickie as well as themselves betrayed in 'one of the minor fun-fairs of our late blasted civilization'. For Lehmann, the war in Spain, painful and disastrous as it was, was only part of the public and private strain, collapse and atrophy of the 1930s.

The texture of Lehmann's response to the outer world became more tactile and deeper as the world moved from 1930 through 1945. Earlier, in *Dusty Answer*, the outside world is quick reference to the Scottish shooting season and 'Bilious obese old Jews and puffy, pallid Americans . . . and ancient invalids . . . in bathchairs with their glum attendants' who, as tourists, crowd the best summer landscapes in France. But the social focus soon changes. In *A Note in Music*, Grace recognises that older forms of social responsibility, charities and committee work, were 'no use at all', but that she might supply a small 'revivifying drop in the unpalatable ocean' by allowing her pregnant maid to stay on, have the baby, and raise it as a single mother while working for Grace. She realises that an earlier generation and many in her own class and time would not do the same. *Invitation to the Waltz*, set back in time in the perspective of the adolescent, sees the newer women's world only in the attraction of daring advertisements that convey sexuality through drawings of clothes. *The Weather in the Streets*, however, is immersed within the social world of the thirties. Among the upper classes, the conflict between generations over diet, health, style and treatment of servants is severe and irresolvable. In the deprivation of all classes, none able to sustain what life they had, money is a constant subject of conversation and concern. Everyone in the upper classes constantly notices and responds, in one way or another, to the visible excitements and horrors of lower-class life: the celebrity boxer at a Bohemian party; the grubby urchins playing silently in the streets; the militarised pleasure-boat outing on the river, watched by silent couples on the banks who 'ate out of paper bags' – 'Like a picture by Rousseau, they looked . . . the bourgeoisie under the aspect of eternity'. The most prominent indications of social change and deprivation in the novel concern women's sexuality. Since sexuality and childbirth are seen as almost mutually exclusive, the worst of the young women, insulated from the world and entirely attached to her parents' generation, spends her life cooing mindlessly over her babies: 'If *only* they'd stay wee and cuddly and *never* grow up. Personally I think up to a month old is the sweetest time of all'. She is asexual and judges other women harshly. Olivia is at the opposite pole. Pregnant and abandoned by Rollo in the sterile heat of London, she must break the 'seals of arduous secrecy, of solitary endurance', her integrity, to find someone willing to perform an abortion. The process of the abortion itself is protracted (she is given an injection in the fetid, hidden space behind an elegant medical address, then sent home to lose the baby painfully, unattended), expensive (she must sell the jewelry Rollo has given her) and horrifying. When she first consults the abortionist, he asks what she thinks of his bronzes, 'female figures, semi-nude, with drapery, holding torches aloft . . . "Nice, aren't they? Empire."'. She finds the figures, like the abortionist, 'repulsive', but replies simply 'It's not a period I know much about.' When the novel first appeared in England in 1936, the publishers omitted a few paragraphs describing the painful loss of the child. The American publishers first suggested that the whole episode of Olivia's pregnancy and abortion be deleted, but finally followed the English. Only the French translation used the whole text.[14]

When time between the two wars is seen retrospectively in *The Echoing Grove*, some of the intense horror and inflexibility has abated. Not all inns, like 'The Wreath of May', reveal 'mongrel

chickens pecking in the damp grass', 'thick sagging beams' damp
with the smell of mice, bad food and surly, resentful service. Inns,
like landscapes and characters, are more mixed, various. The social
world that first condescendingly sees the American woman as a
type ('over here we tend to think Americans a bit solemn, much
as we love them') comes, through time, to recognise her as wise
about human sexuality and disorder. More centrally, the parallel
to Olivia's abortion is, in *The Echoing Grove*, Dinah's loss of the child
she wanted with Rickie. Dinah's child is born dead in the midst of a
rare crippling snowstorm in Devon, where she'd planned to raise
the child. All communication, save with the somewhat unreliable
woman who tends her, is cut off. Rickie, driving down to Devon
with a vague promise, is unable to reach her in time. For Dinah,
the pain, the betrayal of love, and the psychological despair, are
just as intense as they are for Olivia, and they are located within
the dispiriting decade. But the exterior deprivations that contribute
to Dinah's despair are seen retrospectively as accidental, random
possibilities that intensify pain. Olivia's, on the other hand, from
the point of view enclosed by the decade itself, are inescapable,
almost deliberate products of a complete social breakdown without
hope or consolation.

Yet Olivia did, in Lehmann's fiction, lead to Dinah, as, historically, the release and survival of the forties followed the despair
of the thirties. That historical movement, which combines the
themes of both women's sexuality and exterior social change, can
perhaps best be described through metaphor. In all Lehmann's
early landscapes, the river or the lake is significant and resonant,
a repository of human energy. Judith, in *Dusty Answer*, expresses
herself and her unfocused sexuality most completely when boating
or swimming, particularly swimming, the release and immersion
of the self into the water without the clothes of convention or
suppression. Even when a landscape attractively revelatory for
Judith's emotions contains no water it is described almost as if
it does: 'Into the deep blue translucent shell of night. The air
parted lightly as the car plunged through it, washing away in
waves that smelt of roses and syringia and all green leaves'.
Subsequent novels, like *A Note in Music*, use particular lake or river
scenes to express a sexuality thwarted by the parched ambience
of society, working the imagery into the development of plot or
theme. Increasingly, however, in *The Weather in the Streets*, the
world is dry and the magical excitement of swimming can seldom

be sustained Olivia and Rollo's attempt to return to the paradise of their single summer swimming scene with Olivia's friends, the only public acknowledgement of their love, is a disaster in an empty cottage in a sere, brittle autumn. The catastrophes of London in August are entirely without water, the landscapes of arid despair. The sexual and the social are simultaneously and equally paralysed.

In the remarkable short stories Lehmann wrote during the Second World War, located in the consciousness of the female protagonist alone with her children in the country while the war is going on, the metaphors compress and convey both historical and personal meaning almost entirely. In 'A Dream of Winter', set in the frozen winter of 1939/40, the winter of the phony war, 'a mineral landscape: iron, ice and stone. Powdered with a wraith of spectral blue, the chalky frost-fog stood', a 'bee man' comes to take the swarm that, for years, had been buried in their country house. The weather makes the job almost impossible, as the bee man burrows ever more deeply through the 'unfructifying salt stones of the sea'. The woman, ill in bed with the dry fever of flu, has little confidence that the bees or honey can ever be found: 'Life doesn't arrange stories with happy endings any more, see? *Never again*'. But the woman is wrong. The bee man finds honey and life in a wetness buried more deeply than he had imagined, and, although the children think the honey has a terrible taste, they see that the injured bird they have put before the fire has unexpectedly revived and flown away. The weather begins to change, as the woman feels she will recover. 'When the Waters Came' is metaphor virtually without situation. Set in the same frozen winter, among 'the catastrophes of British plumbing' and the nearby peacock 'sheathed totally in ice . . . stiff in its crystal case, with a gemmed crest, and all the blue iridescence gleaming through', the freeze is both the sterile beginning of war and the paralysis of healthy sexuality. Lehmann conveys the combination of historical and sexual directly: 'The war sprawled everywhere inert: like a child too big to get born it would die in the womb and be shovelled underground, disgracefully, as monsters are, and, after a while, with returning health and a change of scene, we would forget that we conceived it'. But the thaw is wet, the active war, the release of the woman's guilts and paralyses into the 'ever more enormous clogged mudshoes' her boots have become. She cannot tell the children whether they all will be 'saved' or 'drowned', but they recognise the release from frozen historical paralysis, despair, into historical movement that indicates both change and continuity.

Seen retrospectively, the release into the Second World War is fatal for that generation of responsive men maimed in the First. Rickie dies, as does his older son, in the pain of social and historical expiation. Yet Rickie, in the 'deep water' of his last night with the American woman, experiences a release from silence, a capacity to articulate his fears and suffering. Similarly, in *A Sea-Grape Tree*, Johnny experiences release with Rebecca, particularly in a scene in which they nearly make love while swimming. Although his promise to return to England may exist only in imagination (and, as the notes for the possible sequel indicate, he would have died in 1939 anyhow), the release achieves, at least temporarily, the dissolution of the dry bitterness through which he had survived the First World War. For the women who survive, however, painful as the Second World War is, the release, a rhythm accidental and unplanned, has more of integrity, understanding and consolation (as in the art of T. S. Eliot) than they would have expected. Both historically and personally, restoration or reconciliation, would be words too strong and positive to account for all the pains of breakdown, failure, disillusion and death. And the healthy child born out of love, the continuity of the woman's integrity, is still, in the fiction, never achieved. Yet the Second World War at least enabled some clear-sighted, sentient women of a new vulnerable generation, to survive the social and psychological aridity of the English 1930s without encasing themselves in the total dryness of despair.

## NOTES

1. Letter from Jacques Emile Blanche to Rosamond Lehmann, 16 November 1930, and letter from Harriet Cohen to Rosamond Lehmann, 16 July 1936. King's College Library, Cambridge.

2. Gillian Tindall, *Rosamond Lehmann: An Appreciation* (London: Chatto & Windus, The Hogarth Press, 1985) p. 192. Although perceptive comments on Lehmann's fiction exist in reviews and scattered articles, Tindall's is the only good fully developed critical book I have seen. Tindall also interviewed Lehmann on a number of occasions. She calls Dinah and Madeleine 'two aspects of their creator's personality'. This, as biographical statement, is more difficult to credit than the sense of the characters as two aspects

of a generalised contemporary woman. I think that, by the end of the novel, the two characters generate equal sympathy, but Dinah still seems closer to what one can surmise of the author's sense of her own experience. As Tindall says, the fact that Lehmann wrote so directly of her own feelings does not warrant a reading of particular characters in terms of biographical models. Lehmann also said very little of her older sister in print, although she often wrote and talked of her younger sister, Beatrix, the actress, political activist, and an early 'Christ for animals' [*A Letter to a Sister*, New York: Harcourt Brace, 1932, p. 14] and her brother, the writer and editor, John. About her older sister, Helen, I have seen just a caption to a picture published in *Rosamond Lehmann's Album* which regrets that, in maturity, the older sister was not as close as were the three younger siblings.

3.  *Rosamond Lehmann's Album*, With an Introduction and Postscript by Rosamond Lehmann (London: Chatto & Windus, 1985) p. 11.
4.  In the early 1980s, in the introduction to the Virago reprint of *A Sea-Grape Tree*, Janet Watts wrote that the novel 'requires a sequel'. Lehmann agreed, and, in her postscript to *Rosamond Lehmann's Album*, citing her diminishing energy, sketched in several pages 'a rough idea of this book I shall never write'. Rebecca returned to England. Johnny did not follow. After delaying and continuously promising for years, he dies suddenly of a heart attack in 1939. Rebecca, concerned with other characters and other plots from the island, operates helpfully in England before and during the war. The postscript sketches resolutions for these sub-plots, but never mentions Rebecca's pregnancy or baby. The only illegitimate baby born alive, and seen as thriving, is that of Maisie, the blunt, unloved, dissident granddaughter of Sybil Anstey Jardine. Maisie has denied the past and become a practical and intelligent doctor. Ibid., pp. 107–9.
5.  Ibid., p. 107.
6.  Tindall, *Rosamond Lehmann: An Appreciation*, p. 201.
7.  Letter from Rosamond Lehmann to Alice Lehmann, 23 October 1921, King's College Library.
8.  Letter from John Lehmann to Rosamond Lehmann, 10 April 1953, King's College Library.
9.  See Tindall, *Rosamond Lehmann: An Appreciation*, p. 32.
10. Rudolf Chambers Lehmann, *Memories of Half a Century* (London: Smith, Elder, 1908) p. 8.
11. Tindall, *Rosamond Lehmann: An Appreciation*, p. 86.
12. Galley proof of essay in *John O' London*, 13 April 1953. King's College Library, Cambridge.
13. Rosamond Lehmann papers, King's College Library, Cambridge.
14. Tindall, *Rosamond Lehmann: An Appreciation*, pp. 76–7.

# 6

# Houses and Cultural Betrayal in Elizabeth Bowen's Fiction

In 1924 in 'Mr Bennett and Mrs Brown', Virginia Woolf used one of Arnold Bennett's elaborate descriptions of houses as her principal example of an outdated convention in her argument for a new fictional focus on the interiority of human character. She charged that Bennett 'is trying to hypnotise us into the belief that, because he has made a house, there must be a person living there'. Although she acknowledged the skill of Bennett, Wells and Galsworthy – 'To give them their due, they have made that house much better, worth living in' – she thought them materialists, unable or unwilling to represent deeper qualities of human nature: 'But if you hold that novels in the first place are about people, and only in the second about the houses they live in, that is the wrong way to set about it'.[1] For Bennett, the 'first place' and the 'second place' were not so easy to separate; nor were they for the later Woolf, who, apart from the brilliantly and successfully propagandistic focus on the newness of her generation and her techniques, exploited, in her own fiction, the representative function of the houses people constructed and used. For later novelists as well, those modernistic writers who, like Elizabeth Bowen, respected Woolf and her achievements enormously, the house, present or past, and the people who lived or had lived there were always connected in complicated ways. Houses and locations represent, explain and oppose the people in Bowen's fictional world; Bowen's houses, her human and cultural constructions, signify.

The residential structure as cultural artifact dominates Bowen's early novels, those of the late 1920s and early 1930s. Her first novel, a repository for British travellers at a North Italian resort,

108

is entitled *The Hotel* (1927). Her second novel, *The Last September* (1929), develops the house as cultural artifact from the past much more completely and personally. She uses her own inheritance of an eighteenth-century manor house in Ireland, the structure of her family as part of the Anglo-Protestant Ascendancy since the time of Cromwell, a house she owned and maintained from her father's death in 1930 until increasing taxes and the problems of maintenance forced her to sell in 1959. Yet Bowen, living as a child mostly in England with her mother (who died in 1912, when Bowen was thirteen), then at school, then married and shaping her career in England during the twenties, seldom lived in the decaying manor house. Even after she inherited it, she spent only parts of summers or other long vacations there. As she wrote retrospectively, in a preface for a 1952 Knopf reprint of *The Last September*, writing the novel itself, at Oxford in 1928, required a 'Proustian' effort to recall her own unconscious, to create the world she had lived through in Ireland in the waning of the Ascendancy in September of 1920. She felt herself 'captured by the mysterious, the imperious hauntedness of a period not understood in its own time'. Simultaneously, she felt part of a new generation, those who had been adolescents during the First World War and the beginnings of Irish rebellion, severed from the past: 'To the core, we were neither zealots or rebels. "There's been enough of that!" we felt. "Stop it: *we* want to live!"' In the novel, the young protagonist, Lois, niece of the owners (in the fiction, almost all Bowen's protagonists are nieces or other distant relatives, often literal orphans, outside the direct line of descent), feels estranged both from an imagined past and from the society around, the violence of Irish protest building toward the independence achieved in 1922: 'I might as well be in some kind of cocoon'. As she goes through the ceremonial rounds of the Ascendancy, the dances and tennis parties, she wonders what she is and whether what she does, within a culture that had always stressed the importance of behaviour, matters or not. When one of her older generation of relatives tries to reach her in terms of a common past, she is politely silent, 'reticence as to a lack rather than as to a superabundance that produced her embarrassment'. Although seen as culturally but not socially or economically deprived, she thinks herself more complex than the older generation, but can explain her complexity only in self-consciously comic and simplified genetic terms: 'for she must

be: double as many people having gone into the making of her'.
The incipient young writer, she also perceives the estrangement of
her elders in Ireland from any Irish tradition. In so far as the elders
are literary, they argue about many writers, but Lois notices that
the most sensitive and articulate of them is, like Virginia Woolf,
within a literary tradition that has no connection with Ireland or
the Troubles: 'nowadays she argued about Galsworthy'.

The English manor house in Ireland is described as massive
but extraneous. From Lois' point of view, the house is isolated,
'pressing down low in apprehension, hiding its face', and 'had
that excluded, irrelevant sad look outsides of houses do take
on in the dark'. The house is 'compassed about': inside, by
useless old furniture, 'mirrors vacant and startling, books read
and forgotten . . . the procession of elephants that throughout
peaceful years had not broken file'; outside, by gun-searching
Irishmen, who may have been former servants and whom the
members of the household do their best not to notice. Bowen
satirises the attitudes of the English. They hire neighbouring Irish
children to retrieve the tennis balls hit into the copious shrubbery,
thinking themselves generous because they pay a halfpenny for
each retrieval. One character talks of being brought up on Irish
songs and dances, taught that the simple Irish peasants loved
being servants. She adds in a tone of the complacently obvious
that 'of course we had none of us ever been in Ireland'. They
are also delighted to hear that an Irish party, having raided
a neighbouring manor house looking for arms, incompetently
steal only old boots, although they leave 'a quite unnecessary
message behind with a skull and crossbones'. When they discuss
the impending war, one young woman is described as 'relieving
the tenseness tactfully' by suggesting that it might be a 'rag' if the
Irish 'tried to fire in at the windows while we were dancing'. Lois is
courted by a young English soldier, a frequent visitor at the dances
and tennis parties, stationed at the local garrison. He is socially
not quite adequate, even if social standards for military personnel
have declined since the slaughters in the trenches of France. Love
is not a question in a country where 'sex seems irrelevant'. When
Lois asserts that she has no sexual feeling for the young soldier,
the lady of the house says that Lois can have no conception of
love or marriage. Lois' only reply is that she reads, and her aunt
replies that, at Lois' age, she was reading Schiller, whereas 'girls
nowadays do nothing but lend each other these biological books'.

Love is discussed only in thin, astringent prose, devoid of feeling. For most of the novel, the language for both the English and their estrangement in Ireland is light, comic, full of *non sequitur*, almost an anticipation of the more extensively developed language of Henry Green in *Loving*, in which the Anglo-Irish world is enclosed by metaphor.

Bowen's language, however, changes at the end of the novel when Lois' suitor is killed on patrol and the manor house is dramatically shocked into a serious questioning of itself. The inhabitants recognise that a young man has died defending them, but that his death is meaningless. 'Heroism' is false, and the novel ends with 'the first wave of a silence that was to be ultimate'. Lois has learned little about her past, her present or her feelings. For Bowen, too, the value of the tradition, the house and the past are questionable, at this point in her career simply a series of trivial ceremonies unconnected to either present experience or the life of literary and historical imagination. Yet Lois' search for meaning in the tradition of the past is significant. Bowen herself, in her attempts to keep her house and its ceremonies alive as long as she could, as well as in her later fiction, sometimes directly, sometimes transposed into other terms, continued to try to find meaning in the always acknowledged as outdated traditions of her past. The values of the past and the house were not nearly so apparent to others, even those who, like Virginia Woolf, shared sympathetic views of a past culture and were admiring readers of the fiction. When, in 1934, Bowen finally persuaded Woolf and her husband to visit Bowen's Court, Woolf wrote her sister, Vanessa Bell, that she had not been impressed: 'all the villages are hideous, built entirely of slate in the year 1850: so Elizabeth's house was merely a great stone box, but full of Italian mantelpieces and decayed 18th Century furniture, and carpets all in holes however they insisted upon keeping up a ramshackle kind of state, dressing for dinner and so on'.[2] Two years later, giving Lady Ottoline Morrell advice on travel in Ireland, she wrote that 'Elizabeth Bowen is not I think in the best part'.[3]

Houses, although not situated in Ireland or confined to the past, represent and dominate in Bowen's most accomplished fiction in the middle and late 1930s. *The House in Paris* (1935) begins with the young observer, eleven-year-old Henrietta, taken on a taxi ride from the railroad station, through a grey, early morning Paris, shutters blocking off cafes and shops, a 'cardboard city' in which 'there might have been no sky', past residential streets where 'doors had grim iron patterns across their glass; dust-grey shutters . . . almost all bolted fast', to the house where she is to wait and be cared for by an old family friend before being taken to an evening train to join her family in the south of France. The house itself, on a street that seems 'though charged with meaning, to lead nowhere', is forbidding, silent, high and narrow, 'its cream front was a strip marbled with fine dark cracks'. Inside, the rooms are isolated from each other, connected only by a hall with no visible windows, the hall papered in a 'stuffy red matt . . . with stripes so artfully shadowed as to appear bars'. For Henrietta, who had anticipated the open and inviting Paris she had seen only in pictures of the Trocadero, the house is 'antagonistic, as though it had been invented to put her out'. Both in its description and in its owner, Mme Fisher, the mother of Henrietta's custodian, who is slowly dying in an upstairs room, the house evokes suggestions of sinister houses within the Gothic tradition.[4] On that day, another child, Leopold, a few years younger than Henrietta, is also waiting in the house for a visit from his mother whom he has not seen since infancy. The situation is seen as sinister as well. Mme Fisher had in the past maintained her house as a residence for young well-bred English and American women studying in art schools or attending lectures at the Sorbonne, not so much a finishing school as an introduction to the cosmopolitan life of Paris in the early 1920s. Leopold had been the product of a love affair between Karen, a young Englishwoman engaged to a kind and bland Englishman, and Max, a talented and unstable young Jewish banker who had been engaged to Mme Fisher's plain daughter, Naomi, now the caretaker. In her controlling and cryptic representation of cosmopolitanism, in her propelling Max to suicide after he reveals his sexual encounter with Karen, and her delight 'in some terrible way' in the fractures of sexual morality, Mme Fisher is seen as culturally sinister. She is the 'witch' in control of the disastrous cultural assimilation her house represents. Although his mother never arrives, Leopold may be rescued by her kind English husband who takes him from the dark house to show him an illuminated, night-time Paris. They also deliver Henrietta to the train station to continue her appropriate familial journey. The house, enclosing only the dying Mme Fisher and the poor, servile Naomi, is left a sterile monument to the debasement of moral value and authentic tradition.

*The Death of the Heart* (1938) is dependent on three separate houses. Dimly in the background, presented only in retrospect, is the family country house where, as seen by Matchett, the servant who, along with the furniture, is the only survivor from it, secure young ladies could grow up 'with bows on flowing horsetails, supping upstairs with their governess, making toast, telling stories, telling each other's fortunes with apple peel'. Mr and Mrs Quayne, with their son Thomas, then a student at Oxford, had lived there. But Mr Quayne fell in love with a woman who had only a flatlet in London. When the woman became pregnant, Mrs Quayne insisted that her husband leave the house he loved and shaped to support his mistress and new child in a series of back apartments and seedy hotels along the Mediterranean. None of the older generation lives very long, as if the cultural and sexual fracture has been lethal, and in the time of the novel, the rootless child Portia, sixteen, lives with her half-brother Thomas and his wife, Anna. Thomas and Anna, representative of the new post-war generation, have created a large, elegant London townhouse in a terrace overlooking Regent's Park. Yet, as Matchett sees it, the new townhouse, like the expensive day school to which Portia is sent, is inadequate for a young woman: 'In this airy vivacious house, all mirrors and polish, there was no place where shadows lodged, no point where feeling could thicken. The rooms were set for strangers' intimacy, or else for exhausted solitary retreat'. The house also lacks 'the religious element' old country houses had. Portia, the innocent, is confused and hurt by all the 'strangers' intimacy', the violations of her privacy, her diary and her emotional life by Anna and Anna's friends, the parasitic and unreliable Eddie and the remote novelist St Quentin, the insubstantial and polyglot emotional life of the modern world. A third house also becomes central to the novel when Portia is sent for weeks to the South Coast home of Anna's old governess, Mrs Heccomb and her two step-children, Daphne and Dicky, a cottage directly on the sea called Waikiki. Full of wind, noise, the smell of seaweed, and constant activity in ramshackle disorder, a 'fount of spontaneous living', Waikiki illustrates comically done differences in class in Bowen's world. Portia is surprised to find that everyone eats in the 'lounge', at his or her own time or pace, that the smell and clutter of Daphne's cosmetics crowd the small, thin-walled house, and that Dicky has for months delayed fixing the broken front door pull. Daphne, Dicky and their friends make frequent excursions to the cinema and cafes along the seafront; they take day trips to the coastal town of Boulogne to 'enlarge their ideas'. The young men wear 'plus fours, pullovers, felt hats precisely dinted at the top, and ribbed stockings that made their calves look massive', while the women wear 'berets, scarves with dogs' heads and natty check overcoats'. At the cafe, one of the young men loudly imitates Donald Duck, and 'making a snatch at Daphne's celluloid comb, he endeavoured to second the orchestra on it'. Portia learns that morality at Waikiki is different from morality at Regent's Park. At the latter, comment on behaviour is open and she resents the reading of her diary or impositions on emotional privacy; at Waikiki, her comment on the behaviour of others, like noticing that Eddie, visiting her, has held Daphne's hand throughout the cinema, is regarded as vulgar and childish. Neither 1930s world, neither house, is, for Portia, understandable or helpful. She could acquire appropriate guidance only in the old country house that no longer exists.

Bowen does not treat her country houses, her cultural artifacts, with nostalgia. As structures, they were designed to civilise, to tame the animal, and they denied or suppressed young women as frequently as they helped them. Portia comes to understand through Matchett that old Mrs Quayne, in her insistence on banishing her errant husband and keeping the house he loved to herself, had been as culpable in violating one meaning of tradition, in denying life, as Mr Quayne had in his errant love. Mrs Quayne, like Mrs Kerr in *The Hotel* or Mme Fisher, is manipulative, one of Bowen's many older women who represent a tradition through intimidating and selfish forms of control. Sometimes the matrons violate their own traditions, as in *Friends and Relations* (1931) in which adultery in the controlling past generation is suppressed and so re-enacted in the present. The characters understand little about the illicit love. The only explanations are deliberately trivial, comic forms that recognise their own inadequacy, like 'it must have been something prenatal. Perhaps . . . [she] had been to an unpleasant play'. The young can be malicious as well, like the unattractive cousin named Theodora Thirdman who helps propel the adultery in a combination of malice, jealousy and the excitement of vicarious disruptions of convention. Whether knowing or innocent, Bowen's young women are unformulated, unincorporated into a system of civilised behaviour. As Bowen comments on Theodora: 'She had to confess inexperience; her personality was still too much for her, like a punt-pole'. Fringe young women in other novels, whether dissident or adaptable, often literally orphans as in *To the North* (1932), are shipped from one relative or code of behaviour to another for the momentary convenience of the older generation.

Portia is both Bowen's principal example of the unformulated orphan attempting to adapt to the modern world[5] and the fullest illustration of how the difficulties of incorporating tradition have intensified in the 1930s. Anna, herself sharp, vulnerable and feeling displaced in having had two miscarriages instead of children, sees Portia in terms of social distance:

> But, after all, death runs in that family. What is she, after all? The child of an aberration, the child of a panic, the child of an old chap's pitiful sexuality. Conceived among lost hairpins and snapshots of doggies in a Notting Hill Gate flatlet. At the same time she has inherited everything: she marches about this house like the Race itself. They rally as if she were the Young Pretender.

Portia, of course, does not see her lineage in such terms. She recalls that her father saw their life on the Continent as aberrant and arranged for Thomas to care for her after his death in what he'd told Portia would be a resumption of 'ordinary life'. Portia realises that 'if he and I met again I should have to tell him that there is no ordinary life'. Bowen explains Portia's innocence directly: 'Innocence so constantly finds itself in a false position that inwardly innocent people learn to be disingenuous. Finding no language in which to speak in their own terms, they resign themselves to being translated imperfectly'. Portia cannot keep the civilised room Anna decorates for her in order, and she loses or forgets her keys. Most frequently, she is seen as the uncivilised 'animal', although she no longer requires the overt symbol, as does eleven-year-old Henrietta in carrying her plush monkey with her. Eddie, too, himself unformulated, originally from the provincial working class and acting as if he is no older or more responsible than Portia, sees them as two animals, himself the 'wild' one, and is described by Bowen as brilliant, unstable, parasitic, with 'a proletarian, animal, quick grace'. His flat still shows 'the bleakness of college rooms – the unadult taste, the lack of tactile feeling bred by large, stark objects, tables and cupboards, that one does not possess'. He can shift his allegiances from Anna to Portia and back in a moment, telling Portia he loves her, although betraying her by holding Daphne's hand, by his verbal play with Anna, and by telling Portia falsely that Anna is his mistress. Eddie is presented as loving and hating simultaneously, unable to bring the 'wild animal' of his feelings into any form of civilised focus.

The civilised in *The Death of the Heart* are perched on the edge of Regent's Park, conscious of the Zoo and the animals contained within, as if they can acknowledge and contain the animal within themselves. Valentine Cunningham has used Bowen (*The House in Paris* also contains numerous references to zoos and animals) as one of his illustrations of a general phenomenon of the thirties, the widespread interest in the architecture, design and construction of zoos.[6] Despite their interest, the civilised near Regent's Park are, literally and historically, formless and incoherent in understanding or containing the animal. Thomas has no confidence in his admittedly bourgeois advertising agency or social functions, and he thinks that English history is both sad and 'shady': 'Bunk, misfires and graft from the very start'. He says that 'Anna and I live the only way we can, and it quite likely may not stand up to examination'. When Major Brutt ('Makes of men date, like makes of cars; Major Brutt was a 1914–18 model'), whom Thomas and Anna cannot help to 'relocate' since he has returned, displaced by history, from the Colonies, tells Thomas that he feels 'out of touch', Thomas wonders 'in touch with what?': 'What do you think there is, then?' Anna, too, feels misplaced. She had, before her marriage, been an interior decorator, although 'only in a very small way – she had feared to commit herself, in case she should not succeed'. She had married to have children, although she no longer wants them and her version of civilised behaviour makes her recoil from her friends' pity. Thomas' civilisation is inadequate as well. He feels a passion for Anna 'that nothing in their language could be allowed to express, that nothing could satisfy'. Anna is intellectually close to the ineffectual and civilised St Quentin, who betrays Portia by telling her that her diary, her words, are public knowledge, a betrayal that Bowen calls 'the end of an inner life'. The structure of contemporary civilisation is eroding in a texture of betrayal, inadequacy and loss.

When Portia runs away in anger and despair, she seeks Major Brutt, staying in a cheap, airless room at the top of the Karachi Hotel in the Cromwell Road. He, betrayed himself, urges her return, and Matchett comes to collect her. Only Major Brutt and Matchett do not betray Portia, but they are relics from an ineffectual past, able to connect with Portia emotionally but unable to help her in the present. Although Thomas and Anna, shocked by the drama of Portia's desertion, resolve to try to understand her better, there is little hope that they can change or that the losses of time, history and coherent cultural artifacts can be reversed. The novel and its periodicity are as much the stories of Anna and Thomas, their representative decline and inadequacies, the limitations of the house off Regent's Park, as they are the story of Portia and her adolescent consciousness. *The Death of the Heart* is not, in form or substance, a novel of education. Not only is Bowen lethal about the irrelevance of Portia and her friends' education within the novel, but, as Hermione Lee has shown, Bowen frequently expressed considerable scepticism about the social or intellectual efficacy of education.[7] For Bowen, sensitivity and intelligence seemed inborn, culture and attitudes the products of time and a complicated, non-linear chain of inheritance. The structure and value of that culture, however flawed its origins, was, like the old country houses, collapsing throughout the 1930s. Architectural and interior-decorating metaphors carry an even greater proportion of the fiction in some of the stories from the thirties like, 'The Disinherited'. Two restless women's journey to a party at 'Lord Thingummy's' country house, which becomes a Bohemian orgy of bad drink, stupid talk and meaningless sex, is done through extensive description of social and architectural detail, crowded, decaying shops along the way, 'synthetic panelling' in the road-house where they stop. 'Lord Thingummy's' is worse, an 'immense facade . . . between high white-shuttered windows pilasters soared out of sight above an unlit fanlight like patterns of black ice'. One of the women is taken into a room where 'Italianate ceilings and sheeted icebergs of furniture sprang into cold existence', but cannot even see the 'grand saloon' because the lightbulbs 'are all gone; he's poor as a rat'. The Lord himself is apparently absent.

Unlike her houses, done in such profuse detail, Bowen's exterior landscapes are likely to be symbolic sketches, useful only to establish the tone and themes of the fiction. Frequently, the novels begin with landscape or weather as setting, *The Last September* in a 'yellow theatrical sunshine' that Lois would like to 'freeze . . . and keep'. The house is so bounded by itself that, when she looks out, she can see only 'some intolerable trees and a strip of gold field hot on the skyline'; she imagines that 'somewhere, there was a sunset in which the mountains lay like glass'. *Friends and Relations* begins with a 'wedding rain' so thick it veils 'trees and gardens' and darkens 'the canvas of the marquee', an augury for the marriage that will re-enact the social fractures of the past. Similarly, in *The House in Paris*, Max and Karen's single idyll takes place in the pouring rain on the English South Coast. Often, the landscape is abstracted, drained, only a setting, as in *To the North*, with its disastrously anti-social love affair, in a world in which 'the downs in their circle lay colourless under the sky' and human impulse, at most, is 'a blue bloom of morning powdered with light'. Landscape and weather open each of the three sections of *The Death of the Heart*: 'The World' begins with 'that morning's ice, no more than a brittle film' as Anna and St Quentin walk in the frozen 'bronze cold' of Regent's Park; 'The Flesh', beginning in the Park as Portia is about to go to Waikiki, has a few crocuses in early spring and an almost unseen sunset, 'with mysterious white light . . . the curtain of darkness is suspended, as though for some unprecedented event'; at the start of the final section, 'The Devil', the house itself absorbs exterior nature, is 'lanced through by dazzling spokes of sun, which moved unseen, hotly, over the waxed floors . . . the house offered that ideal mould for living into which life so seldom pours itself'. Unlike the fiction of Rosamond Lehmann, in which colourful, vibrant, particularised landscapes reflect both inner natures and exterior perceptions, reflect the relationships between self and not-self, Bowen's natural landscapes are astringent, thematic and symbolic. They are settings for, not the complicated fabric of, human and emotional experience.

In the sense that perception of landscape is a mirror of the connection between inner and outer, the relationships of the self, the contrast between Lehmann's and Bowen's characteristic depiction of landscape is also a contrast between their characteristic versions of female sexuality and connections with others. Lehmann's young women, even in her earliest fiction and if only imaginatively, are participants, responding to all the emotions of connection, all the pleasures and pains, they are able to feel. In Bowen's fiction, sexuality is treated with more distance. Many of her young protagonists, especially in the early fiction, seem pre-adolescent, curious about sexuality but almost without feeling. Lois, in *The*

*Last September*, is presumably twenty years old, old enough to be
the object of the young soldier's love even though she herself
feels nothing. She is curious about love and marriage, but 'one
of the things Lois chiefly wanted to know about marriage was
– how long it took one, sleeping with the same person every
night, to outlive the temptation to talk well into the morning?
There would be nothing illicit about nocturnal talking, as there
had been at school'. This kind of comedy, like a drained landscape,
creates considerable distance. Bowen's wit often keeps sexuality at
a distance, even in the midst of affairs actual or contemplated. In
*The House in Paris*, Karen, anxiously weighing her illicit attraction
to Max, can still respond with approval of the probity of a young
Irish woman who, talking of the Irish and the English, explains:
'The relation between the two races remains a mixture of showing
off and suspicion, nearly as bad as sex'. Accounts of sex or love
are abstracted. *Friends and Relations*, for example, is complete in
diagramming the social causes and consequences of the past
adultery, but the emotions themselves are almost entirely absent.
Bowen shows or tells us little more than that years later, having
broken the fabric of both families, the controlling matron felt she
had 'to account for that stupefying cessation of love, positive as
the passion itself and like a flood not arrestable, coming down
on them both when they were entirely for each other at last, in
Paris'. Similarly, in *To the North*, Emmeline, in an illicit love affair
with the socially suspect Markie, in which neither really wants to
marry the other although the affair is intense enough to lead to
their melodramatic deaths when, going north, she near-sightedly
and recklessly drives them into another car, the particular feelings
of sexuality are confined to a few abstracted lines like: 'The
passionless entirety of her surrender, the volition of her entire
wish to be his had sent her a good way past him: involuntarily, the
manner of her abandonment had avenged her innocence'. What
generates the force of the novel is Emmeline's attraction to the
energetic, commercial, vulgar Markie, a social violation in terms
of the family from which she, the orphan relative, feels displaced.
She sees her women friends and relations discontented in dull,
respectable marriages, and 'thought idly, free will was a mistake,
but did not know what this meant'. Markie is the disastrous
alternative, and she sees herself and the relationship as if he is
leading her 'into a theatre . . . reluctant, she was made free of a
mock-heroic landscape with no distances, baroque thunder-clouds

behind canvas crags'. Similarly, in *The House in Paris*, Karen's
attraction to Max, the mercurial and commercial Jew, is a deliberate
violation of her class, and she only agrees to go to bed with him (the
single time that produces Leopold) when she thinks, mistakenly,
that he wants to marry her no more than she wants to marry him.
She thinks that women not seeking husbands 'have no reason
to see love socially'. They can express the 'vulgarity, inborn like
original sin', that 'unfolds with the woman nature'. Their love
depends on different backgrounds, exists only in compulsion
when 'they were free of themselves'. Karen has a stable family,
a kind, firm mother, and her planned (and later enacted) 'marriage to Ray would have that touch of inbreeding that makes
a marriage so promising'. The affair with Max is presented as
social revolution in the chaos of the modern world: 'With Ray
I shall be so safe. I wish the Revolution would come soon'.
For many of the writers of the 1930s, those of both the Auden
Generation and others, love is a form of social transgression.[8]

The *Death of the Heart* buries the intense, socially transgressive
love even further. Anna has experienced her single inappropriate
affair and betrayal in the past, so far removed and covered that
she seldom thinks or cares about it, and Thomas has no language
whatever to express what he feels. The social tradition itself has
decayed so far, the past value become so frail and irrelevant for
members of their generation, that transgression itself carries little
meaning. For Bowen, as for Lehmann, the end of the 1930s both
conveys and represents the intensity of betrayal. For Lehmann,
that betrayal is deeply emotional, the destruction of the promise
of love and intense relationship between the self and whatever of
society remains. Female sexuality is a kind of release. For Bowen,
sexuality is more often a relationship of power than release, and the
betrayal is almost entirely social, the erosion of the cultural artifact
that alone, positively or negatively, can give meaning to the self.
Bowen herself, in reviewing Lehmann's 1936 novel, *The Weather
in the Streets*, which she praised enthusiastically, expressed something of the contrast when she particularly appreciated Lehmann's
capacity to deal with emotion: 'She attempts to make no relation
– necessarily a false relation – between emotion, with its colossal,
unmoving subjective landscape, and outside life with its flickering
continuity of action and fact'.[9] In Lehmann's work, that relation is
not necessarily false; rather, her 'subjective landscape' changes,
experiences and reacts to 'outside life'. The statement is more

accurate for Bowen's fiction in which the 'unmoving subjective landscape' is protected from, often buried by, the 'flickering' disorder of 'outside life'.

Lehmann's fiction provides a contrast with Bowen's in terms of the incorporation of another kind of traditional artifact, the recall of literary tradition as part of one's own version of experience. For Lehmann, as for Woolf and many other writers of the period, the whole development of nineteenth-century English fiction, the tradition of education and romantic self-fashioning, is significant. A novel like Woolf's *Orlando*, for example, is dependent on this tradition for its transgressions and reversals. Bowen, however, seems often outside, unconnected to much of the English literary or industrial nineteenth century. She does include a few references, like the young protagonist of *The Hotel* reading Hardy's *Jude the Obscure*, as if it is axiomatic that the nineteenth century has been obliterated. But Bowen's Meredith is virtually only the trivia of a single reference to a woman beautiful 'in the Meredith tradition' in *Friends and Relations*, and her few Dickens references recall only obvious comic stereotypes. Although she wrote a guide to *English Novelists* (1945) and clearly knew them well (she was appreciative and discerning on the Brontës and Mrs Gaskell, enthusiastic about Trollope although too restrictive in seeing him primarily in terms of the comic escape from the relentless horrors of the Second World War, and rather dismissed George Eliot[10]), she made little reference to them in her fiction, her own reconstructions of experience. Similarly, although she knew and appreciated the fiction of her own age well, she seldom referred to it, and unlike almost all her contemporaries, used only a single reference to T. S. Eliot's *The Waste Land*.[11] Other writers, however, are central and explicit in her fiction. Bowen often recalls Proust, both as the sensitive catalyst for memory and consciousness explicit in the 1952 preface to *The Last September* and in quick comic reference, like that to a literate but emotionally feeble minor character in *To the North* who regards the orphan thrust into his charge as illustrating 'the disheartening density of Proust . . . superimposed for him on a clear page of Wodehouse'. A more frequent literary origin for Bowen's work is the fiction of Henry James with which her work is saturated. References to James abound, plots parallel those of many of his novels, dramatic revelations operate in similar ways, the social world of the novel is often carefully anatomised by the outsider, and the language frequently combines sensitivity and abstraction (phrases like 'the unintimacy of their silence') in a Jamesian manner.[12] Many of Bowen's contemporaries reviewed her work as that of James's most significant descendant. Jane Austen is also a constant presence in Bowen's fiction, as if the reach back to the late eighteenth or early nineteenth century is significant for Bowen's sensibility, the time and tone of the high point of the Anglo-Irish Protestant Ascendancy. One of Bowen's short stories from the thirties, 'The Needlecase', calls its eroding and violated country house 'a disheartened edition of Mansfield Park', Austen's most securely eighteenth-century setting. Both Bowen's authorial voice and the voices of her characters (like Anna in calling her governess 'Poor Miss Taylor' from Austen's *Emma* and feeling relieved when the governess marries a widower) sometimes refer directly or obliquely to Austen when introducing accounts of class, as if no one so well understood the subtle and minute vibrations of British class. The wit and sharpness of Austen is in Bowen's style as well, and Bowen once praised Antonia White's *Frost in May* for a style 'as precise, clear and unweighty as Jane Austen's'.[13] Bowen's focus on the implications of social tradition is the appropriate descendant, in different ways, of both Austen and James. Her style, too, less a twentieth-century artifact than that of many of her contemporaries, combines the sensitivity and weight of James, sometimes somewhat uneasily, with the wit and 'unweighty' quality of Austen.

By the end of the 1930s, Bowen's artifacts of cultural tradition seemed close to obliteration, the dominant social voice of the fiction moving toward Anna and Thomas's despair. Yet Bowen's evocations of the thirties are unlike those of many of her contemporaries, just as her uses of literature are different from theirs. The novels all contain criticism of the English and Anglo-Irish upper classes, the owners and builders of the houses, but the criticism and rebellion come from within, and perspectives of other classes are seldom noticed or articulated. Servants remain servants, taking their identity from their loyalty to the people they serve, as if a distinction between masters and servants is part of an inevitable order of being. The inhabitants of Waikiki, although attached through a former servant, represent a different class, a more active, uncivilised, guiltlessly amoral life, a lower order of being that is generally treated comically. Looking at all Bowen's fiction, this representation is more a function of the South Coast (as opposed to the country or the town house), an influence of place than of class. The South Coast, open to the sea, a portal to the Continent, represents, for Bowen, a more open, vulgar sense of life, in some of the stories like 'A Queer Heart' and 'Ivy Gripped the Steps', a form of rebellion represented by its amusements, flowers and architecture. In the latter story, one from the forties, the south Coast house has been strangled, physically and emotionally, by its own overgrowth of untamed ivy, 'desuetude and decay'. Apart from the South Coast, Bowen's physical world of the thirties includes almost nothing of industrial decay, the unemployed or life in London that is not cushioned by the privileges of class. There is little of Lehmann's 'weather in the streets'. The buildings described represent current and former upper-class bastions, like the decaying Karachi Hotel with its 'public rooms . . . lofty and large in a diluted way . . . extensive vacuity, nothing so nobly positive as space', 'the homes of a class doomed from the start . . . without grace', which 'builders must have built to enclose fog'. The 'fog' is a declining British imperialism, more visible in Bowen's version of the thirties than is any strictly national social perspective. She also uses the language of imperialism, a word like 'nigger' without any self-consciousness, rancour or apparent sense of what it might suggest.

Bowen's thirties world is nationally much less insulated than that of some of her contemporaries, full of the cultural influences of Europe and issues of ethnicity and race, as if cultural, moral and racial autonomy and integrity are breaking down in an unassimilable cosmopolitanism throughout Europe. Echoes of race and racial judgement remain: Henrietta sees that Leopold 'looked either French or Jewish' at first sight, Max 'looked either French or Jewish, perhaps both', his face 'flinching and sensitive . . . intellect, feeling, force were written all over him'; Karen's mother, when she first hears of the possible connection with Max, warns Karen that Max is after her background and money because 'No Jew is unastute'. Despite these and other echoes of racial thinking and regret at the breakdown of order in the modern world, Bowen expressed no sympathy whatever with the Nazi and fascist attempts to restore intransigent and debased forms of cultural order to a depraved modern world. In practice, she joined her contemporaries in anti-fascist activities in England during the late thirties, and she often insisted that good writers and sentient commentators must write with sympathy and discernment from outside their own nationality, race or class.[14] Bowen's focus is directed toward the cultural entity, changing or eroding through history. Specific political comment on the fabric of thirties' issues is rare, comic or trivial, like Leopold's statement that Italy is a better place to live than France because 'it has got a king still'. Whereas in Rosamond Lehmann's streets one hears the radio proclaim the news of Mussolini's cruel, imperialistic invasion of Abyssinia, only Bowen's world of Waikiki mentions Mussolini and that in one young man's jocular derision of another's bragging posture, Mussolini as an icon in Chaplin's film.

Bowen pokes fun at other specific political and social perspectives in the thirties world. For example, in an age of increasingly easy travel and concern with a more diverse Europe, many of Bowen's British contemporaries, already knowledgeable about France and Italy, went to the Balkans, anxious to understand the complicated strains of nationality and culture which presumably generated the horror of the First World War, the beginnings of the destruction of all European culture, as in Rebecca West's *Black Lamb and Grey Falcon*. But, for Bowen, the Balkans are matter for chaotic comedy in the midst of the unassuageable cultural and emotional tragedy of *To the North*. To try to establish the financial and occupational independence of the modern young woman, Emmeline – with a partner – runs a small select travel agency quite different from Cook's. Full of social snobbery and aristocratic incompetence, she sends her equally snobbish clients to various Balkan destinations since they already know Paris and Rome. Her (and her partner's) ignorance, in spite of their file of train schedules, is matched only by chaos in the Balkans, all cheerfully accepted, although in at least one instance 'a client who having bribed and fought her way to Belgrade on the wrong ticket found her hotel room full of roses ordered by Emmeline'. Travel in the Balkans is like the Anglo-Irish ignorance of the Irish rebellion around them, a comic set-piece.

Bowen's world changed violently in 1940 as the fabricated structures, like her own house in a terrace off Regent's Park, were badly damaged by bombs. In her brilliant novel about the Second World War, *The Heat of the Day* (1948), her most deeply socially representative novel, although it has sometimes been criticised as further from the ideal of a Jamesian seamlessness than *The House in Paris* or *The Death of the Heart*, the cultural artifacts, like many of the houses, have been destroyed. The destruction comes both from the outside, the Nazis, and from within: 'The grind and scream of battles, mechanised advances excoriating flesh and country, tearing through nerves and tearing up trees, were indoor-plotted; this was a war of dry cerebration inside windowless walls'. The protagonist, Stella Rodney, like Bowen herself remaining in London and working for a government ministry throughout the war, has lost or given up her houses, stored her furniture, and lives in a furnished flat that, 'decorated in the last year of peace, still marked the point at which fashion in the matter had stood still'. Her structures have been reduced to mirrors, photographs, and a few tiny artifacts from her former life. She has long been substantially alone, parents dead, two older brothers killed in the First World War, a short, early marriage that had collapsed before her husband, gassed in the war, died. Hers is the generation 'come to be made to feel it had muffed the catch'. She has been left with a son, Roderick, now twenty and in training in the Second World War's military. The only structure besides Stella's flat that is shown unimpaired is Holme Dene, the pretentious suburban middle-class house that has bred her lover, Robert Kelway, who unknown to Stella is a Nazi spy. When Robert takes Stella to visit his mother, called 'Muttikins', at Holme Dene, she sees first the notice that says 'Caution: Concealed Drive', then recognises the huge gables on the 'blood red' structure that 'combined half-timbering with bow and french windows and two or three balconies'. Inside, she finds imitation oak beams, screens and shelters of different heights among the arches and intricate passages, and is shown Robert's bedroom kept as a shrine to some sixty school photographs and 'glass cases of coins, birds' eggs, fossils and butterflies'. Stella is not shown all the upstairs rooms, many blocked off to save fuel during the war, passages in the patterns of the swastika, 'planned with a sort of playful circumlocution' and full of stored, useless impediments, 'being flock-packed with matter – repressions, doubts, fears, subterfuges and fibs'. The house has been on the market for many years, ever since the long-dead Kelway father first bought it as a gesture of bourgeois confidence, but it has not sold, and when finally an offer is made, 'Muttikins' feels too threatened to sell. She represents life-denying order, full of compulsive trivial regulations for her children and grandchildren. Her integrity is her insistence on finding three pence to pay Stella to post a parcel for her back in London. Stella sees the house and family as a 'moral' violation: 'You could not account for this family headed by Mrs Kelway by simply saying that it was middle-class, because that left you asking, middle of what? She saw the Kelways suspended in the middle of nothing. She could envision them so suspended when there *was* nothing more'. Later in the novel, she also recognises Holme Dene as a fount of hate, one so suppressed and intense it could create a traitor like Robert.

No house, no private structure, represents an England worthy of survival. Rather, a valuable and loosely coherent England is represented, during the depressing autumn, 1942, interval between the bombings of London and direct military action, the 'lightless middle of the tunnel', in the outdoor Sunday concert with which the novel begins. At first, the 'tarnished bosky theatre . . . held a feeling of sequestration, of emptiness the music had not had time to fill'. But the music gradually 'entered senses, nerves and fancies that had been parched' and strolling lovers are able to appreciate something that is not just themselves. Harrison, the loyal government investigator – who eventually shows Stella that Robert is a spy – presented as classless, is able to approach Louie, the cockney woman, with the same honesty and uncertainty he later approaches Stella. Personally shadowy and complex, not particularly attractive, Harrison is publicly honest and knowledgeable. He is attracted to the suggestiveness of Louie's mouth, although he knows that 'Halted and voluble, this could but be a mouth that blurted rather than spoke, a mouth incontinent and at the same time artless'. Speech is the sign of class, and the values of 1942 are unspoken. For Louie, cheerfully and resiliently amoral about sex, since her husband, Tom, is fighting overseas and her parents had been killed in a bombing raid on the South Coast to which they had retired, speech is an irrelevant distraction: 'She had found all men to be one way funny like Tom – no sooner were their lips unstuck from your own than they began to utter morality'. Louie, connected to Stella only through Harrison's interest and one long nocturnal walk, during which they talk about what they feel as equal non-innocents in a world in which morality is no guide to survival, is, by the end of the novel, pregnant with a soldier's illegitimate child she will bear, name Tom, and raise, when she hears the news that Tom has been killed. The worthy England that can survive requires the assimilation of classes and nations (the father of Louie's child, conceived in 1944, could be a Czech or American soldier). England survives in 'the bloodstream of the crowds, the curious animal psychic oneness, the human

lava flow'. Similarly, in the novel, Bowen describes a great deal
more of 'the weather in the streets' than she did in her earlier
fiction. Although war limits landscape, as so much of Stella's life
is confined to her flat without 'apprehension of time' and people
travel on blacked-out trains, Bowen spends fictional space on the
specific look, feel and words of public England during the war. She
includes a long description of a village street, complete with shop
windows, shabby clothes, old architectural bits and the placards
of rationing, shortages and public appeal; she treats extensively,
in retrospect, the 1940 Blitz, the fires, relationships, activity and
fatigue of those days in which 'the night behind and the night
to come met across every noon in an arch of strain'. Almost
Bennett-like in the precisions of exterior verisimilitude, Bowen
uses the newspapers for summaries of daily life in England, as
well as for the impact of global news, carefully charted to match the
attitudes and responses of the public English during the war.

Complexity and individuality in the central male characters are
constantly sacrificed to public representation. For Harrison, the
thorny, honest investigator, whom Stella gradually respects but
never loves, to whom she is prepared to offer herself only once
in the humiliation of her recognition of her mistaken judgement,
the public representation is clearly sufficient. For Robert, however,
whom Stella has presumably loved for two years, since they met
during the Blitz after Robert had returned wounded from Dunkirk,
this is perhaps less aesthetically convincing. When Stella first tells
Robert of her suspicions about his loyalty, he asks her to marry
him, as if to silence her: 'He fixed his eyes on her face – though
somehow not, it appeared, on *her*. Nor did those eyes appear to
her to be his – they were black-blue, anarchical, foreign'. Later,
when he is forced to confess his public betrayal to Stella and she
mentions her belief in 'freedom', Robert is scornful: 'Freedom
to be what? – the muddled, mediocre, damned . . . Freedom?
what a slaves' yammer'. He announces his belief in 'order' as
overwhelming, more important than just 'control:' 'It's a very
much bigger thing to be under orders'. When Stella says that,
even if one accepted that, the Nazis are 'horrible – specious,
unthinkable, grotesque', Robert responds, in a statement that is
the obverse of Louie's pleasure in her coming child: 'And, in birth,
remember, anything is grotesque'. Significantly, Robert, about to
be captured, falls or jumps from Stella's roof to his death as the
news arrives of the Allied landings in North Africa, the turning

point of the war. All this is credible as Bowen's diagnosis of and aversion to the Nazism inside Britain, but it is difficult, in the context of the novel, to accept the fiction that one so discerning as Stella, even in the midst of experience so isolating and enclosed as that of the war, could have shared his bed and his life for two years. One other male representation, which occupies much less space and emotion in the novel, is handled with greater clarity and conviction. Roderick is depicted as composed, quiet, amiably distant from Stella and the politics of her generation. He, without any expectation, inherits, through a distant relative of the father he cannot remember, a run-down country house in Ireland. He had never been there, Stella only once on her short honeymoon during which Roderick was conceived. When the relative dies, Stella does not even tell Roderick to allow him to try to attend the funeral. She goes herself, learning, to her amazement, that Roderick is the heir. She thinks he will be uninterested and sell the unprofitable legacy as soon as he can, but Roderick is another generation, 'all for the authoritarianism of home life; the last thing they wished was Liberty Hall'. Roderick immediately assumes the distant, non-linear family responsibilities he has so accidentally inherited, wants to protect the relative's widow, asks Stella to find out the particulars of the estate, and is determined to live and farm in neutral Ireland after the war. Roderick is not seen as an innocent in Bowen's world in which there are no longer 'innocent secrets'; rather, he is a new generation which, born into a world of cosmopolitan chaos, may authentically find, represent, and be able to sustain the values of a distant, perhaps obsolescent past.

Like many of her contemporaries, socially paralysed in a form of despair at the end of the thirties, Bowen felt the war and 1940, however painful and full of further loss, as a release. For Rosamond Lehmann, the war was a baby, perhaps to be miscarried, but at least the possibility of a difficult birth and a renewal of life. Bowen, always more distant emotionally, with a less motherly sensibility, saw the release in more general terms, 'the human lava-flow'. For both, and for many other writers equally dedicated to what England in 1940 represented for them, Nazism was the principal enemy, the cruel, inhuman order, the obliteration of human impulse and diversity. Both recognised, too, the possibility of betrayal, having lived twenty adult years within a texture of many social and cultural betrayals. When *The Heat of the Day* was published, Lehmann, as always full of enthusiastic admiration and respect for Bowen's fiction, said that she was bothered 'a little' because she was unable to see why Bowen's English betrayer was a Nazi rather than a communist and, in 1942, 'therefore pro-Russian, pro-Ally, rather than pro-enemy'.[15] This seems not just the recognition that Lehmann and Bowen both knew and were close to more writers who did or would betray British secrets to the Russians than would to the Nazis – probably neither was close to any British Nazi. Rather, and less literally, Lehmann saw, as did many of her contemporary writers and intellectuals, communists as betrayers because Stalinism, actions in Spain, and purge trials were cruel betrayals of social forms, humane values, and devolutions of class in which these writers believed. Communists betrayed the social change they presumably represented. For Bowen, however, social value was never represented by anything close to communism, not in myth, theory or debased actuality. But Nazism presumably represented a return to forms of social and racial order that Bowen implicitly respected, however strongly she satirised their contemporary inapplicability and irrelevance. The inhuman betrayal of the Nazis was the cruel, vulgar and violent betrayal of Bowen's sense of social order and hierarchy, a grotesque parody of social values about which Bowen deeply cared.

Much as Bowen appreciated the fiction of Lehmann, Henry Green and others, she was not in sympathy with the political focus in other contemporary writers. She had little in common with the Auden Generation.[16] When Virginia Woolf gave her 1940 Brighton lecture, 'The Leaning Tower', dramatising the inadequate social perspective of the young, committed writers of the thirties, she sent Bowen a copy of the talk. Bowen responded in immediate and exaggerated agreement:

> The leaning tower metaphor seemed to me perfect. I'd never thought *into* those young men's positions before, and your leaning tower, with the sense at once of unnatural angle and panic, made it (their position) suddenly comprehensible. The element of *fuss* about their work is explained, though not, I think, excused – and you don't excuse it. I didn't think you over-severe – did you think you were? – only deadly accurate. The quotations were damning.[17]

Bowen's respect for the working classes and the theme of class assimilation, expressed in *The Heat of the Day*, apparently did not survive the 1940s. She had little sympathy with a perspective like Priestley's, even in its more complex versions, that the Second World War and the subsequent Labour government reflected and institutionalised a healthy, socially more beneficial and responsible, sense of relationships in Britain that made class origin or behaviour less significant. Bowen had no interest in the welfare state or what it represented. Not long after the war, she wrote her close friend and frequent correspondent, William Plomer:

> I have adored England since 1940 because of the stylishness Mr. Churchill gave it, but I've always felt "when Mr. Churchill goes, I go." I can't stick all these little middle-class Labour wets with their Old London School of Economics ties & their women. Scratch one of these cuties and you find the governess. Or so I have always found.[18]

While racial or religious remarks do not appear in Bowen's later work (the effect of the Nazis was, in that sense, permanent), her sense of English class, particularly as it adopted a moral posture, returned to that of the 1930s.

As social representations, Bowen's next two novels, *A World of Love* (1955) and *The Little Girls* (1964), return to her earlier territory with, whatever their individual virtues, less force as expressions of a past culture. The pre-First World War Anglo-Irish culture is the background of *A World of Love*, though its applications to contemporary experience are dim and problematic, ceremonial and fantastic echoes that afford no relevant pattern for emotional or moral experience. In *The Little Girls*, three women in their early sixties dig up a box of apparently significant mementoes they buried while at school half a century earlier, before the First World War. But the novel, interesting though it is as a psychological study of the women, shows only the irrelevance of the past cultural tokens to both their fifty years and the consequences of their search. The most interesting of Bowen's late novels is the final one, *Eva Trout* (1968). In this sprawling novel, set in the random contemporary world, the outsize, rootless character, Eva, represents an awkward sense of life, unable to find any social or cultural form, rather like a bizarre exaggeration of Theodora Thirdman's 'punt-pole'. The world surrounding Eva is also puzzling, full of minute and trivial forms, conventions, that bear no relation to all that is chaotic, unpredictable, full of bizarre

incident and violent Life still exists, but the world has no place for
it. Cultural assimilation is reduction, shrivelling, but expressing
life is chaotic and violent. Morality has come to seem a luxury
the characters cannot even imagine. Eva has a child whom she
loves, a deaf mute, almost an icon for a future world without
language. Any kind of transmission to the next generation, any
sort of motherhood in the work of this novelist who never really
depicted motherhood or linear succession, seems impossible. In a
melodramatic conclusion, the child, unable to hear or understand
what he thinks is a toy to greet Eva after long absence, shoots her
dead. The novel can be read as a 1970s fable of post-modernism;
it might also be read, as Bowen wrote William Plomer, in the
context that she 'easily could begin to believe an entire book
has been a hallucination'.[19] Yet it is neither of these: *Eva Trout*
is the long, bizarre, comic statement that, for Bowen, cultural
betrayal is now complete, endemic and universal. No houses
finally exist. In terms of both historical depth and intensity, her
finest writing is that of the thirties and forties, the symptomatic and
socially representative fiction of her particular versions of cultural
coherence and betrayal.

## NOTES

1.  Virginia Woolf, 'Mr Bennett and Mrs Brown', *The Captain's Death
    Bed and Other Essays* (New York: Harcourt, Brace, Jovanovich, 1950)
    pp. 109, 112–13.
2.  Nigel Nicolson and Joanne Trautmann (eds), *The Letters of Virginia
    Woolf*, vol. 5 originally published in England as *The Sickle Side of the
    Moon* (New York and London: Harcourt, Brace, Jovanovich, 1979)
    letter of 3 May 1934 to Vanessa Bell, p. 300.
3.  Nigel Nicolson and Joanne Trautmann (eds), *The Letters of Virginia
    Woolf*, vol. 6, originally published in England as *Leave the Letters Till
    We're Dead* (New York and London: Harcourt, Brace, Jovanovich,
    1980) letter of 7 June 1936 to Lady Ottoline Morrell, p. 45.
4.  See Hermione Lee, *Elizabeth Bowen: An Estimation* (London and
    Totawa, N.J.: Vision and Barnes & Noble, 1981) pp. 80–81 for a
    thorough discussion of the connection of the house to the Gothic
    fictional tradition.
5.  In a generally excellent essay on Bowen, James Hall overstates the
    impulse toward adaptability in Bowen's protagonists by applying
    it to all the novels and generalising: 'Over and over she shows the
    purposelessness, ineffectiveness, eccentricity, and insanity remain-
    ing in the less adaptable'. James Hall, *The Lunatic Giant in the*

*Drawing Room* (Bloomington and London: Indiana University Press, 1968) p. 19. Although Hall's statement is revealing for *The Death of the Heart*, I think it less true for earlier novels, particularly *To the North*.

6. Cunningham, *British Writers of the Thirties*, p. 87.
7. Lee, *Elizabeth Bowen: An Estimation*, p. 29.
8. For a full account of this theme in the thirties and earlier, see Kermode, *History and Value*.
9. Elizabeth Bowen, *New Statesman*, 11 July 1936, reprinted in Hermione Lee (ed.), *The Mulberry Tree: Writings of Elizabeth Bowen* (London: Virago, 1986) p. 141.
10. For this and much more fully developed indications of Bowen's literary appreciations, see Lee, *Elizabeth Bowen: An Estimation*, pp. 213–39.
11. Allan E. Austin, *Elizabeth Bowen* (New York: Twayne Publishers, 1971) p. 17.
12. Hermione Lee, throughout *Elizabeth Bowen: An Estimation*, presents an exhaustive and convincing account of many of the specific parallels to James's fiction.
13. Elizabeth Bowen, review of Antonia White's *Frost in May*, in *The Mulberry Tree*, p. 115.
14. Heather Bryant Jordan's chapter, 'The Map of Europe', in *Elizabeth Bowen and the Landscape of War* (Ann Arbor: University of Michigan Press, 1992) contains the most comprehensive discussion I know of the complexities of Bowen's understanding and treatment of national and racial issues during the thirties.
15. Victoria Glendinning, *Elizabeth Bowen: Portrait of a Writer* (London: Weidenfeld & Nicolson, 1977) p. 151.
16. Lee, *Elizabeth Bowen: An Estimation*, p. 224.
17. Hermione Lee (ed.), *Selected Letters of Elizabeth Bowen* (London: Virago, 1986) letter of 1 July 1940 to Virginia Woolf, p. 215.
18. Elizabeth Bowen, letter to William Plomer, University of Durham Library, reprinted in *The Mulberry Tree*, p. 204.
19. Ibid., letter of 27 February 1968, p. 210.

# 7

# Henry Green's Particular Visionary Gerunds

Much of the serious comic fiction written between the two world wars, like that of Aldous Huxley or Evelyn Waugh, depicts the contemporary world as a metallic construction of artifice and posture, a series of sharp edges without coherence or love. Consciously characterising what the authors regard as a wasteland, they create a valueless contemporary world and deepen the comedy with a frenetic, futile search for value and stability. Values echo from a recalled or imagined past, but such recall, like Tony Last's country house in *A Handful of Dust*, only magnifies the impossibility of recovery and the comically seen difference between a stable past and the chaotic, vacant present. Transformation is possible in the fiction of Huxley and Waugh, particularly in their later work, but is only achieved through altered states of human consciousness or reassertions of old religions, through attitudes or institutions seen as unlikely to influence the contemporary social world. Henry Green's fiction, in contrast, is silent about the values of the contemporary world, and his comically rendered depictions depend little on an historical version of experience that can substantiate theories of decline. They suggest no transformations, however unlikely. Waugh's Tony Last ends bitterly, reading the irrelevancies of Dickens to uncomprehending natives in the Brazilian jungle. Henry Green, in *Living*, his 1929 novel set entirely among workmen in a Birmingham factory, also has a character dedicated to reading and rereading Dickens. But Green's old workman, released after fifty-seven years, simply gives it up: 'And, somehow, he said, he had lost the taste for Dickens, times were different now to when that man lived – it was funny he said that he should wait till he was this age to grow restless'. Green is never scathing about the institutions and artifacts of the contemporary world he re-creates. A young woman in *Living* is momentarily transported to worlds other and more interesting than hers by her weekly trips to the cinema. People of all classes enjoy the new picture palaces: 'supported by each other's feeling, away away, Europe and America, mass on mass their feeling united supported, renewed their sky'. Green characterises but does not derogate the mass emotions that Huxley and Waugh treat as a symptom of the wasteland. In *Living*, two of the workmen manage to get to the home Aston Villa football matches every other Saturday, 'transfixed with passion' as '30,000 people waved and shrieked and swayed and clamoured' at the players who 'took no notice of the crowd'. Rather than the search for stability in the fiction of Huxley and Waugh, Green's fiction shows the conflicts and inconsistencies of the contemporary world unresolved, explored deeply without judgement or search, in the static, continuing terrain of his metaphors.

Green's stable point is the focus of the metaphors themselves. Although this focus is not consistently achieved in his first novel, published in 1926 before his twenty-first birthday, *Blindness* demonstrates his early recognition of the kind of intense, limited point of view from which he moulded his fictional world. *Blindness* begins with the diary of an intelligent, literary seventeen-year-old at school. After about twenty-five pages, he is suddenly blinded when a small boy outside throws a rock that shatters the window of the train in which the student is going home on holiday. The novel deals with his attempts to adjust, to realise experience fully even though deprived of sight. This is both a conscious experiment in perspective and an implicit statement that by shutting off sight, one human perspective, one can become more sensitive to feeling, to deeper, more sensuously apprehended areas of human capacity. Particularly in a series of scenes with a young woman his age, although of another class, the daughter of a poor rural clergyman, Green develops the boy's sensitivities to speech, touch, the feel of landscape and emotion. He learns to feel sexual attraction (although it is chaste) on their long country walks, and recognises that, as a writer, he wants to describe sensation that lies behind sight. He plans to write 'such amazing tales, rich with intricate plot. Life will be clotted and I will dissect, choosing little bits to analyse'. The prose itself is sensuous, rich, an adequate vehicle to convey his sense of feeling in a world in which, he and the young woman agree, class is blindness and justice does not exist. Other perspectives in the novel are examples of more conventional typology: the protective point of view of his stepmother (his mother, then his father, had died long before) who would use her money to shield him from life; the dim, hierarchical perspective of his nanny who disapproves of his walking out with a woman of another class.

Green's subsequent novels also work through uniquely developed and deliberate limitations of perspective and subject matter. *Caught* (1943) is based entirely on Green's experience in a fire-fighting brigade during the Blitz. He announces at the beginning that 'in this book only 1940 in London is real'. Although the novel includes the theme of a child abducted and returned, the ties between generations lost or blurred, as well as a description of the apparatus of fire-fighting, the prose pays most attention to the smells, sounds and physical feel of London. When part of a building is saved from fire, 'the small room was breathless with curtains, knick-knacks, dark wallpaper and carpet. Every particle was clean but had gone dark from the years'. As in much of Green's fiction, when confronted with feelings or disasters, class issues and hierarchies dissolve. Those fighting fires 'knew now, for the first time, the sense of impotence which goes with authority, the feeling that those he commanded did not care'. Asked by Terry Southern, in an interview for *The Paris Review*, whether thoughts of character or situation began his fiction, Green replied, 'Situation every time', and added that he felt he needed to 'get everything' into the first twenty pages.[1]

In Green's fiction, sexuality is the most important of human feelings and the principal means of dissolving the blindnesses of class. Although his 1940 autobiography, *Pack My Bag*, takes place at school, and he claims that the school was fascistic, gym class particularly so, he does not emphasise the description or significance of the unnamed Eton as what he calls the 'humane concentration camp'. Rather, Green focuses on private feelings and experiences, descriptions of fishing while on holiday: 'There is no excitement apart from sex so keen as the approach to a favoured place in good conditions'; or lovers on the river, arms round each other, who would stop 'to see what luck you had'. He recounts that his family's country house became a convalescent centre for wounded officers during the First World War. When some of the officers married servants, 'I had no idea this was possible'. Green began, through his naïvete, to anticipate both the physical and social pleasures of sexuality. Through adolescence and Eton, his imagination was dominated by sensuous and sexual feeling. He also consciously tried on attitudes and perspectives. Told that his parents were in an accident in Mexico and likely to die, he began to dramatise several versions of 'what I thought it ought to feel like' until the next day when he heard that the accident was not serious and they certain to recover. His focus on feelings, particularly sexual ones, and on consciously adopted perspectives remained throughout Green's career. They are central to his major novels, *Living*, *Party-Going* (1939) and *Loving* (1945). They appear frequently as images, often individually effective, in his later and less metaphorically resonant fiction. The beginning of *Concluding* (1948) is full of sensuous imagery: a woman drawing curtains 'took hold on velvet, which had red lilies over a deeper red, and paused as she gently parted the twin halves, to admire her hands' whiteness against the heavy pile;' 'At this instant, like a woman letting down her mass of hair from a white towel in which she had bound it, the sun came through for a moment, and lit the azaleas on either side before fog, redescending, blanketted these off again'. *Doting* (1952), a more thematic novel about relationships within and between generations, depends on sensuously articulated differences between doting and loving. Doting, the only possibility between different generations, is represented as emotionally and morally inferior to loving.

The language of human feeling in Green's best fiction is both vibrant and decorative. In *Living*, when a character falls in love, Green writes: 'We have seen her feeling . . . had been like a tropical ocean with an infinite variety of colour. As her boat came near dry land you could see coral reefs and the seaweed where in and out went bright fishes, as her thoughts turned to him so you could see all these in her eyes. Further out, in the deep sea, in her deeper feelings about him when he was away, now and again dolphins came up to feed on the surface of that ocean'. The passage continues with 'shoals of flying fish', a marine 'orchestration of her feelings'. When this kind of prose and sensitivity is applied to a situation and given coherent focus by a limited point of view, the gerund as title becomes an appropriate and compressed metaphor. The gerund is grammatically the on-going process, the deepening continuity of the approach, *Living*, *Party-Going*, *Loving*. These situations do not conclude or resolve themselves into thematic statements. They continue, and the only summary or capsulisation of the fiction is in the achieved understanding of Green's vision of the process itself.

Not all Green's titles are gerunds. *Blindness* and *Nothing* are nouns. Yet even the 'nothing', which is what the principal character has at the end of the novel, is less a summary than the nothingness, the process of all his manipulations about love that have led to the foreseeably empty conclusion. The condition, the situation, its emotional content explored as deeply as possible, carries the principal significance in Green's fiction.

In Green's best fiction, the conditions or processes are simultaneously individual and social. The novels are compressed metaphors that resonate and expand with particular social detail. They are also the novels that span the 1930s, explorations of social conditions that illuminate the literary decade. The genesis of *Living* is slightly earlier, the late twenties when Green, after leaving Oxford, went to work making castings in the foundry his father owned in Birmingham. Aware that he was outside working-class life, that he could not entirely immerse himself in the factory or abandon his identity, Green tried to record the speech, concerns and attitudes of the Birmingham workers as faithfully as he could. He kept to the particularity of the factory and region he knew, for, as he said retrospectively in *Pack My Bag*, Britain consisted of not two or three social classes 'but hundreds well defined'. Birmingham workers, prosperous during the First World War, were crowded by returning veterans and suffered during the slump of 1923 and later, a time, Green realised, that Britain was 'fortunate to get through without some kind of upheaval'. In his autobiography, he focuses on his generation's guilts during the twenties: the feeling of uselessness because, as rich, educated young men, they did not do manual work; the question of whether they ought to inherit; guilt about having missed the war; guilt for his own immersion in the socially parasitic indolence and snobberies of Oxford in the twenties. He recalled, however, that he had not taken sides during the 1926 General Strike when 'for some time I had been unable to look a labourer in the eye'. In *Living*, one uneasy upper-class woman, upset when a chauffeur is killed in the fly-wheel of a generator, wonders what she might do: 'It was true, she said, she had enjoyed enormously the General Strike when she had carried plates from one hut to another all day, that was true enough, but what work could she do?' Green, however, focuses less on political attitudes in his depiction of working-class life than on daily life: the combinations of pride and pain in the difficult making

of castings; the conflicts between generations, which can erupt into
momentary violence because people are angry and deprived; the
language of their feelings of anger, attraction or excitement. In so
far as the working classes talk about issues, they assume their own
class perspective, as in the talk of the possibilities of emigration or
retraining at technical colleges. Other issues that characterise class
centre on the politically trivial, like the arguments and resentments
that build on whether or not a workman should be suspended
when caught smoking in the lavatory. Green's sympathy is in the
depth and complexity of depiction, revealing the processes of their
living, not one of political advocacy or perspective.

*Party-Going*, the novel in and of the thirties, is the most extensive
and astringent about divisions of class. The entire novel is set in a
London railway station. A group of upper-class characters, arriving
at the station separately, are to travel together on a continental
holiday, but all departures are delayed by fog. Commuters fill
the station as evening thickens, their trains, too, delayed until
the unknown moment when the fog may lift. The fog is the
paralysis of contemporary social experience, and it is also made
tactile, an image of the pain and isolation of inadequate vision or
knowledge:

> Fog burdened with night began to roll into this station striking
> cold through thin leather up into their feet where in thousands
> they stood and waited. Coils of it reached down like women's
> long hair reached down and caught their throats and veiled here
> and there what they could see, like lovers' glances. A hundred
> cold suns switched on above found out these coils where, before
> the night joined in, they had been smudges and looking up at
> two of them above was like she was looking down at you from
> under long strands hanging down from her forehead only that
> light was cold and these curls tore at your lungs.

Green works in terms of 'looking up' and 'looking down', for the
small, upper-class group eventually (through a texture of misapprehension, confusion, telephone calls, jealousies and changed
arrangements) find each other and, through the aid of the railway
director who is the uncle of one of the women, are sheltered
in the warm comfort of the station hotel above. The mass, the
commuters and the servants guarding or misplacing the luggage
of the upper-class characters are in the increasingly congested

station below. The classes are separated, imprisoned, by heavy steel shutters across the hotel's entrance, although a few shadowy characters, like the man who may be the hotel detective, find ways to get from one prison to the other. They all can, from various places, see each other, and each class is always sensitive to the other's existence.

The upper-class characters, concerned with their sexual alliances and jealousies, are made vapid and sterile. One woman's first reaction to the fog is to ask if 'they're really doing anything about it'. One of the men looks down at the mass below and says 'what targets for a bomb'. Another woman fears that the numbers below might lead to proletarian revolution, 'they'll come up here and be dirty and violent . . . They'll probably try to kiss us or something'. Some of the rich are wiser, recognise their insularity, although they remain sheltered because 'the less well off embarrass them'. Others see the masses below like a distant diagram, 'like those illustrations you saw in weekly papers, of corpuscles in blood, for here and there a narrow stream of people shoved and moved in lines three deep and where they did this they were like veins'. That image of the human body is also an image of life, and the masses below, although equally confused and distracted, have more moments of vitality in Green's vision. A group of Welsh miners, perhaps in London for a football match, burst into spontaneous song. One of the servants guarding luggage suddenly sees an attractive woman near by and kisses her as a friendly, gratuitous tribute. The novel represents, without ever reconciling, different forms of behaviour in groups among mutually impenetrable classes. Each can see, sometimes even understand, the two different worlds of party-going or group social relationships.

*Loving* also uses a barely penetrable door dividing the classes, here the green baize door that separates the servants' quarters from the rest of the manor house in Ireland during the Second World War. By 1945, in Green's terms, a treatment mocking the rigidities of class required removal to Ireland where the war intrudes only tangentially. The family that owns the house is English, as is the young footman promoted to butler early in the novel. The novel that begins and ends with the death of a servant, the passing of an old way of life, can sustain its extreme divisions of class only through the language of fairy tale that pervades the fiction. The family also calls the newly promoted footman 'Arthur' because they have always called their footmen 'Arthur', whatever their names. Only with difficulty can they now learn that promotion entitles him to be called by his family name, Raunce. For the other servants, particularly for the maids he fondles whenever he gets an opportunity unseen by others, he is still Charley, although he imagines an outmoded world in which he would now have been called Mr Raunce. The games of naming introduce a world of comic misapprehension in which the differences in class are superficial manners and forms of speech. Beneath, in responses to common experience, common human and particular identities emerge. When they discover that the owner's daughter-in-law has been committing adultery with a neighbouring land-owner while her husband is away fighting the war, the servants pretend shock, talk as if a pattern for responsible experience has been shattered. But they soon realise that the experience mirrors their own, is one way of handling the difficulties of human sexuality. They also, despite their ignorance about the war and politics that leads to a good deal of comic misapprehension, understand that their own combinations of patriotism and selfishness (Raunce, the Englishman, keeps inventing and contradicting reasons for leaving and not leaving peaceful Ireland) match the evasions and justifications that keep the English family owning an Irish manor house. The family's mannered evasions, their poses of aristocratic fecklessness, are made morally no different from the servants' practice of padding accounts and pocketing the difference, or their occasional retention of one of the family's casually mislaid possessions, like a valued ring, until they can reveal discovery at a moment advantageous for themselves. Particularly different, and comic in the insistence on difference, the classes in *Loving* are fundamentally closer than they seem. The novel is more one of the early forties, class differences dissolving under the threat of common danger and consequent change (although that danger is only dimly apprehended by the characters). Yet, for the comedy of trivial differences that the humane perspective of the novel overcomes, *Loving* is dependent on Green's sensitive knowledge about social divisions in the thirties, the atmosphere of his comically seen particularity. *Loving* itself, of course, is universal.

A number of significant points of focus appear in all Green's different metaphorical reconstructions of experience, consistent patterns of representation that substitute for themes in giving the fiction coherence. Dirt, for example, is omnipresent in *Living*, graphically described in the grit and oily smudge of the machinery, the industrial waste, the grungy skylights and black sand on the foundry floor. The workmen bring their dirt home with them, in locutions of 'dirty sod' and 'dirty old man', as well as in the conversations like 'You silly bleeder and 'ow does your little bit like it when you come 'ome and lay your head up against hers on the pillow and her 'as only been married to you three months and as can't be used to the dirt'. In this instance, she likes it 'all right', and, throughout the novel, Green shows beauty and value emerging through the dirt. The metal castings from the foundry, nestled in grime or black sand are admired as 'beautiful', at one point even preferred to 'the country, in summer, trees were like sheep while here men created what you could touch, wild shapes, soft like silk, which could last and would be working in great factories, they made them with their hands'. The beauty from dirt is domestic as well, connected in grime-ridden cottages to the creation of children. As a young woman hopes to become pregnant, she thinks:

> All was black with smoke, here even, by her, cows went soot-covered and the sheep grey. She saw milk taken out from them, grey the surface of it. Yes, and blackbird fled across the town flying crying and made noise like noise made by ratchet. Yes and in every house was mother with her child and that was grey . . .

Green sees, with considerable ambivalence, this dirty industrial world as changing. In the voice of the released old workman who had made the finest castings:

> "Take foundry work," he said, "the young chaps won't 'ave it now, it's too dirty for 'em and too hard, you can't get lads to start in foundries nowadays. In a few years there won't 'ardly be any moulders left and those that can do a clean job then will get any money, any amount o' money."

The same antimonies of dirt and cleanliness are central to the texture of class in *Party-Going*. The crowds in the station are described in terms of smoke and dirt, increasingly so as the black-particled fog and night combine to thicken the vision. The upper classes isolated in the hotel are light and clean, almost antiseptic in their social isolation and chatter that never connects. At one point, Green stops the chatter and jealousies for a description that covers nearly twenty pages devoted to the bath of the 'beautiful Amabel'. Amabel is the teasing, ultra-sophisticated queen bee of the group, her bath full of comic echoes of the ritual of sexual preparation never consummated in the novel. Her bath does not suggest a disabling antisepsis or sexual incapacity, for the prose is full of promising images, her eyes 'like two humming birds in the tropic airs' and her hands 'with rings still on her fingers were water-lilies done in rubies'. Rather, the bath is narcissistic love and excitement, all its energy poured back into the self, a representation of the insularity of the elevated, socially irresponsible classes.

Green's images and tropes, whether simple or elaborate, depend on the physical, on the embodiment of sensation, emotion or idea. In *Loving* much of the comedy of misappropriation depends on the servants' incapacity to see political or exterior experience in terms other than those of the body. Trying to convince the other servants that Ireland ought to fear the possibility of a German invasion, Raunce characteristically asserts that the 'panzer grenadiers' will 'come through this tight little island like a dose of Epsom salts'. In the scene in which he and the maid Edith first, despite frequent earlier kisses, realise that they love each other, Raunce, after kissing, 'put his other arm round her waist so that he had her in a hoop of himself and was obliged to lean awkwardly to do this'. She does not respond in words, only in 'her eyes which seemed now to have a curve of laughter in their brimming light'. Green's focus on the language of the physical connects to his use of animals as simile or metaphor for human beings in a texture that, whether the example is simple or complex, becomes almost Dickensian. Cows, sheep, fish, birds and dogs cluster throughout all the fiction. In *Blindness*, the stepmother can grasp the youth's blindness only when she looks at an old blind dog about whom she has been wondering if 'it would be kinder to put him out of the way'. She later does so, because she says old dogs are 'germ traps', and resolves to keep the youth clean and protected. In *Doting*, almost the only sexual energy is conveyed in a scene that recalls a rabbit hutch and mutual fascination with the 'rabbit twitching its nose at you while you got down on hands and knees to show me how it had to climb to get back'. The response involves further rabbit parallels and the language of a 'stuck pig'. Occasionally, Green's comic animal parallels seem arch, trivial, rather Disneyfied. In

*Party-Going* Amabel, after her bath, 'dried her breasts . , . with as much care as she would puppies after she had given them a bath, smiling all the time'. Without even the self-contented smile that might save that example, a character in *Back* (1946) is attracted to his new secretary with breasts that she wore 'like two soft nests of white mice'. More often, however, and particularly in the major novels, the links between animal and human being become a symbolic pattern that extends and deepens the fiction.

Green's use of symbol shows a consistency, comedy and complexity that enlivens and expands his particular visions and his fictional world. Birds, for example, suggest human attributes that develop into significant patterns. Pigeons, either kept by individual workmen or flying about industrial city-scapes on their own, crowd the foundry world of *Living*. Green sees them as emblems of the grimy dirt and the sense of community or connection among the working classes, and they are also, in their ability to find their way home, significant for the novel's sense of the comfort of locality. *Party-Going* begins with a stray pigeon in the fog flying into a balustrade in the London railway station to drop dead at the feet of Miss Fellowes, a shy unworldly woman who has come to the station to see her niece, one of the upper-class travellers, off to the Continent. Miss Fellowes is appalled by the dirty clamminess of the pigeon, as she is by the station in the fog. She takes the pigeon to the Ladies Room, washes it carefully and wraps it in a parcel of brown paper which she continues to carry. When one of the upper-class men throws the parcel in a dustbin, Miss Fellowes retrieves it. Although she feels responsible, she has no idea of what she can do with the dead pigeon, since, as a presumably clean housekeeper for Britain, she and her class cannot accommodate the lost, useless figure of working-class grime. She goes to the station bar, although unaccustomed to drink, and becomes ill. Discovered by others, she is taken to the hotel, to the insulation she has not sought. For a time she cannot speak. When others hover over her, she hears her niece's voice which 'rose and fell like a celluloid ball on the water-jet men shoot at and miss at fairs'. She also through the thick curtains of the hotel room hears or recollects other, more vital voices, sounds of summer and water, voices of birds. When, at the end of the novel, a recovered Miss Fellowes leaves the hotel, she no longer carries the parcel of dead pigeon, while others envision seagulls they expect to see on their now soon to be restored channel crossing. Pigeons and fog are ignored by the upper classes, replaced by the cleaner clarity and screech of seagulls. Not always with understanding, for the most vapid of the young women says that she had forgotten they were seagulls and thought they had been doves. In Green's complex comic world, she may not be wrong after all, for the beautiful Amabel, finally kissing the rich and elusive Max whom she may want more than she wants the others, at least temporarily, is described as 'folded up with almost imperceptible breathing like seagulls settled on the water cock over gentle waves' while, for Max, 'her hands drifted to rest like white doves drowned on peat water'.

Bird symbols are even more extensively developed in *Loving*. The Irish manor house has a large tribe of peacocks. Talked of as rare, valuable, dirty and useless, they strut about the lawns screeching with clamorously insistent voices. The owners talk of them as a nuisance and a prized possession, keeping the radiantly coloured and dried out feathers in large vases around the house. The servant girls, when unobserved, like to wear fresh peacock feathers in their hair and steal peacock eggs that they carry in gloves as a gauntlet. The children of the manor house use broken and smeared peacock's eggs to pledge secrecy. The peacocks are also vulnerable, subject to attack, sometimes violent, from dogs, visiting children and a nervous pantry boy. The peacocks change colour, screech and parade in jewelled splendour, a parade likened to the ritualistic night when the servants dance among the dust-covered furnishings of the drawing room while the family is away. A surly, sleepy Irish gardener is in charge of the peacocks, and, when shocked by evidence of the family's adultery and politics, he keeps the peacocks penned and invisible. When he acknowledges his love for one of the maids he liberates the peacocks. Children may sometimes prefer the safety of the recumbent, fat white doves, also on the lawns, but the peacocks, in all their dirt, colour, screeching and inability to protect themselves, are connected with human energy and sexuality. The sound of the peacock is audible, or the sight of the bird or his feathers visible, at almost every point of human contact or communication. For the masters, the cry of peacocks is dim, refracted, dried out or arranged in artificial parades; for the servants, especially for Raunce, who has eyes of different colours, one dark, one light, and for his Edith, the cry of peacocks is strident, exciting and immediate.

*Loving* contains symbolic patterns apart from animals, for the owner's lost ring operates significantly in both the texture and the plot of the novel. The elaborate, beautiful ring with rubies and sapphires is connected with the peacocks in a number of lines like the mixed images used to suspect the destructive son of the old housekeeper: 'After what 'e done to that peacock one or two sapphires in a ring would be mincemeat for 'im'. The symbol of the ring, in the pattern of the novel, binds love, encircles it, and makes permanent and moral the cry of the peacock. The owner of the manor and the lost ring, a 'museum piece', for a time does not even realise it is lost. Edith discovers it, is fascinated and not sure what, if anything, she wants to do with it. When she sees that the daughter-in-law has committed adultery, she throws the ring in the fire, but soon retrieves and cleans it. When the owner misses the ring, Edith is still silent during a period of time that coincides with the Irish gardener keeping the peacocks penned and invisible. Only when Raunce and Edith have acknowledged their love, formed their own connection, does she return the ring, telling the owner she has just found it. She and Raunce then leave, as the owner says, 'without a word of warning', for an England involved with the war. They have heard the peacocks screeching, and, now, given the novel's fairy tale assurance that they 'lived happily ever after', will presumably find their own ring, their own binding and richly colourful morality, both personally and socially, in England. Peacocks and rings, in a less structurally significant way, continue to convey similar meaning in Green's fiction. In *Nothing*, in the midst of the novel's conflicts about generational identities, a mother, satisfied that she has quenched her son's interest in a young woman when she has insisted he have a 'good, hot bath' to prevent his fever turning his cold to pneumonia, 'settled back like a great peacock after a dust bath'. The young lovers, later approved of, are inundated with family heirlooms, rings they don't want and refuse to accept. They, like the servants in *Loving*, must commit themselves in their own terms.

Symbolic patterns in Green's novels, interesting as they are, are not always easily visible and are often less striking than the sounds of the language. Much of all the novels consists of dialogue, Green conveying the world he observes and imagines through human speech. He seldom gives characters much physical description or probes their thoughts and interior speculation. The fiction builds from the echoes of what they say. Blindness is, in fact, the appropriate place for Green to have started, the self-imposed limitation of one form of perception in order to concentrate on what of experience can be heard or touched. In that novel, in the diary section before the boy is blinded, he concentrates on words and phrases he hears, like the metaphorical insults, 'milch cow', 'bovine goat', the schoolboys hurl at each other. He imaginatively anticipates his fate, thinking it the fashion of the other boys to 'throw stones at me as I sit at my window' because he is literary, and not very good at games. The limitation of the blindness is the conscious articulation of a perspective already there in less cohate form. The same perspective is applied when the servants in *Loving* play 'blind man's buff' to discover their loving relationship. Green himself was never blind or weak-sighted. Rather, he was slightly deaf, increasingly so as time went on. Some critics have attributed his comedy of misapprehension and miscommunication to his poor hearing, a comedy that had its genesis in what he misheard or half-heard. Perhaps so, but it seems more important to connect the faulty hearing with the conscious attempt to listen carefully, to construct his vision out of the many voices that surrounded him.

The voices Green uses are socially referential, the sounds of an occupation or locality and, most frequently, identifications of class. Most of the life of the workmen in *Living* is conveyed through their distinctive speech, their omission of almost all articles and possessive pronouns, as well as the images they draw from foundry particulars like the grime and castings. They make fun of the upper-class designation of all working-class speech as the failure to aspirate 'haitches'. Green also uses the speech of the managing classes. The son of the owner, noting the combination of dirt and beauty in the foundry, talks of 'a kind of romance' and the fact that 'the castings, they call them, were very moving'. But most of the speech in the novel is that of the working classes whose 'living', almost never in terms of profits or business, is thoroughly revealed. Their locutions often take over the narrative voice, as in a scene that begins, 'Mr Bert Jones with Mr Herbert Tomson, who smoked cigarette, walked along street'. In a later interview, Green claimed that he'd a reason more compelling than representative accuracy for omitting all the articles in the novel. He wanted to make the book 'taut and spare', which in itself would 'fit the proletarian life'. He was cautious about any claim for more reportorial representation, adding that the writer must be socially 'disengaged' and that the workmen in his factory thought the novel 'rotten'.[2] He varied the grammatical technique to make the upper-class voices of *Party-Going* equally 'taut and spare'. Instead of omitting all articles, the talk isolated in the hotel consistently uses demonstrative articles ('that' or 'those') rather than the definite articles (like 'the' or 'a'), a texture which suggests the remoteness and the disconnections of their social identities. Green continued to use socially characterising language in all his fiction. In the same interview cited above, he asserted that the language of *Back*, a novel about the middle classes in the country returning from the war, is 'soft', whereas the language of *Nothing* and *Doting*, both satirising post-war urban upper classes is 'hard and sharp'.[3] *Back*, in which descriptions of proliferating country growth, winds and flowers are connected to a world to which people return, identities and relationships changed, many uncertain about who is alive or dead, or who is whose child, is full of soft and sliding prose. The prose reflects the importance and uncertainties of survival, a world in which, as one of the characters advises, 'you must take what pleasure and comfort you can, because who is there to tell what may befall'. Soft, floral descriptions also echo through Green's next, more quietly fatigued, post-war novel, *Concluding*. In this rural world, in which generations are discontinuous and institutions like schools full of confusion and misunderstanding, few birds exist, just flowers at the end of the season in heavy, dimming sunsets, 'just time enough for lovers'. At the end, a single ominous pigeon flies by as the characters hold a large dance, perhaps a lame or partial recovery suggested when the old man named Mr Rock dances approvingly with his formerly estranged granddaughter. An earlier sense of the society in the Second World War is conveyed through the language of *Caught*, the novel of the Blitz. *Caught* is full of blood, flashes of colour, overt sexuality, for, as one of the characters, who seems to echo Rosamond Lehmann's stories, says: 'This war's been a tremendous release for most'. The war also threatens, especially at the time of Dunkirk: 'But the moon, fixed in the sky without a cloud, flooded everything with intolerance, made such a cold peace below that it did not seem possible that extermination could be so near, over to the east'.

The evocative quality of Green's prose, both socially and sensuously suggestive, was part of his literary consciousness from the start. His autobiography records an early interest in style, a recognition that this interest could lead to narcissism, and a conviction shared by those to whom he was close at school that 'art was not representation'. Although later in the autobiography Green realises

that the issue of 'representation' is more complicated, that a writer
or artist is not so adamantly closed off from his social or sensual
experience, he always maintained that his forms of representation
were neither literal nor direct. The prose required elaboration
and symbol to represent without simplifying or transcribing. A
number of critics have likened Green's prose to that of Charles
M. Doughty's *Travels in Arabia Deserta*, an attempt to counter
what Doughty thought of as the arid sterility of Victorian literal
prose with a combination of the elaborate rhythms of Spenserean
English and 'the alogical linkages of spoken language' among the
Arab illiterates he encountered.[4] For the most part absent among
his late Victorian contemporaries, interest in Doughty was strongly
revived among writers at about the time he died in 1926. Green
wrote an appreciative essay in 1941, acknowledging Doughty's
influence and asserting that travel, made necessary for many
young writers by the war, would help increase sensitivities, as they
did for Doughty, to the literary possibilities of the spoken word
in the rhythms of unfamiliar languages.[5] Although not a literary
theorist or programmatic, Green was a modernist, linked to his
avant-garde literary time by his interest in style, his appreciation
of language like Doughty's, and his confidence in the possibilities
of symbolic representation for a world outside the self. He was
the modernist as well in working through short scenes, back
and forth among characters, most often rendered without explicit
transitions. The connections between scenes emerge only through
symbols, or through a reader's interpretation of the collocation of
compressed, non-linear scenes. A plot as an ordered sequence
of events is usually buried or non-existent as meaning emerges
through symbol and situation, the process that the title or gerund
suggests. Green began experimenting with the short scenes in
*Blindness*, particularly in a section entitled 'Picture Postcardism',
a series of descriptive vignettes, some satirical, some satirising
the method itself, that comprise the youth's development of
sensuous understanding. The descriptions are full of what Ruskin
stigmatised as 'pathetic fallacy', and of other voices in different
tones. *Living* depends even more on short disconnected scenes
that depict life among the workmen. Not until more than halfway
through the novel do scenes begin to form a discernible sequence
or follow possible patterns of causation. The method continues
throughout Green's fiction, although in his later work, like *Doting*
or *Nothing*, scenes reach climaxes of revelation or disjunction

between characters and then dribble back to the stasis or banality with which they started, as if the revelation is buried or useless. In short, the plot, whether in the novel as a whole or miniaturised in a particular scene, is less than the language and the condition, whatever the subject. In those novels, like *Loving*, in which more discernible plots suggest some kind of resolution, the conclusion insists on an ambiguous silence. The language of resolution or of statement has gone as far as Green wants to take it, leaving, in all its richness and metaphor, the language of condition or situation.

Nevertheless, certain patterns in Green's prose and situations suggest statement, echo through the novels as possibilities that dramatise social and psychological meaning beyond the particular situation itself. Green's characters, for example, are determined, reflect in their nature and behaviour predictable aspects of social and psychological origin. They are not just tags or counters – they are far too complicatedly seen and elaborately described. They are also not individualised, not unpredictable and distinct examples of human character. Green frequently determines character by work or occupation – not just the workmen in the foundry in *Living*, but all Green's characters, exemplify unchanging and usually unchangeable occupations. As individuals, his characters often 'have no history',[6] they seem to have sprung full blown from the reverberations of their occupations or classes. Class, too, is unchanging and determining. Green satirises conventional simplicities about what class is in his complex and expansive depictions, but he does not question the determining force of the 'hundreds' of particular classes in Britain. Green recognises, too, the forces that have determined his own unchangeable perspectives. In his autobiography, he refers frequently to his class, to having been brought up largely by servants, to being a younger son, and to his oldest brother who died suddenly just before leaving school during the First World War. He is conscious of the fact that he may not understand his past, that part of it 'Like the wilder wild animals, lies in wait, in ambush for when one has grown up'. *Blindness* emphasises more of the social and generational forces determining the early Green, particularly the sense of deprivation experienced by his whole generation growing up in the twenties with 'the frightful war to pay for'. His characters are of their generation as well as of their class. They seldom indulge in speculation or interior debate about how they might or might not change themselves; they act out of inner imperatives they may well not understand or think about, which have psychologically determined them long since. Max in *Party-Going*, for example, is accorded a status among the upper-class characters because he is remote and, instead of talking, always pays for everything. He becomes a comically dislocated centre for the group when he insists on paying for the hotel rooms, out of some inner compulsion he is never shown to question or understand, although the railway company has offered the protection as a gift and a right. Much of the comedy in *Loving*, the texture of the servants' misapprehension of various forms, originates in their inability to sanction or imagine any perspective not their own. When the insurance company representative comes to investigate the loss of the ring, the fact that his company has initials identical to those of the IRA baffles the servants, despite all his logical explanations. They see him only as a revolutionary out of Ireland's past, and, in their limitations, invent a fantastic and paranoid politics from their attempts to explain their fears. When the owner talks to the loyal old cook and speculates that the ring may have fallen into the home's antiquated system of drains, the cook can understand drains only in terms of their stench and possible disease. She misconstrues every word the owner says, and, when the owner, still conditional, acknowledges that she has no evidence because she has not found the ring there, the cook, smug, 'profound', is sure she has won what she imagines is a debate and replies irrelevantly, 'Ah there you are'. There, determined by a history, a class, or a psyche they never question, are Green's characters.

Physically and psychologically, Green's characters seldom move very far from where they started. Even in the later fiction that reflects the world after the presumably socially and geographically liberating Second World War, Green's characters are reluctant to move or travel, and they reveal no expectations that they can make free and intelligent choices about their lives. In the best fiction, that written by 1945, the characters are frightened and sceptical of all travel. The upper-class characters in *Party-Going*, veterans of previous continental holidays, are fearful of and disoriented by travel, looking to servants to take care of the imponderable difficulties for them. In ways, they welcome the fog and the railway station hotel that isolate them in comfort. The working classes in *Living* exhibit a more desperate fear of either travel or movement. They are reluctant to train for better jobs in other factories in the same part of Birmingham. In the longest series of sequential scenes in the novel, the part that most closely approximates plot, a disillusioned workman named Bert and a young woman excited by the cinema named Lily, who have lived in the same house with little communication, recognise that they have fallen in love. They decide rationally that they can only realise their love by silently going off to Liverpool where Bert has parents he has not seen in many years and from where they can emigrate to a promising Australia. Their plans develop slowly, elaborately, but have not been thought through since Bert never tries to contact his parents or find out about emigration schemes. At first, their journey on the train makes their fears and incapacities comic, matters of the huge bouquet of tulips that Bert has bought for Lily at the cemetery, which embarrasses Lily, and Bert's compelling need to find the Gents at the station, which embarrasses Bert. When they get to Liverpool, in deepening dusk, anxieties mount. Bert is unable to find his parents who, over the years, have moved to a series of ever seedier shops. As they try to trace his parents' history, trams and their feet carry them into increasingly deprived and menacing slums. When they reach the sinister world of the docks, in the cold black of night, still unable to find his parents, Bert deserts Lily, which allows her to return to Birmingham, while he vanishes into the dockland darkness without identity. Characters in Green's fiction find survival difficult and frightening without the familiar prisons of designated names, functions, occupations, classes and places. Particularly between the two wars, an idea of home, however narrow, is socially and geographically necessary for Green's human voices.

Another consistent characteristic of Green's fiction, one that can yield the interpretive focus of general statement in a different way, is the frequent self-derogation or self-abasement, both personal and generational, in Green's narrative voice. This has been referred to by many who knew Green as extraordinary modesty and lack of pretense or ambition, but his dedication to style and his confidence in allowing his intricate metaphors to carry his novels are hardly signs of modesty as an artist. What Green undercuts in the narrative voice is its own social representation, pushing it into the background to allow other, different, social and class voices to be heard, periodically emerging to summarise or represent a situation in symbolic terms. The comedy is often in the juxtaposed differences between various voices and their consequent misunderstandings. Green also controls the narrative voice, undercutting it or subjecting it to parody whenever it seems to simplify, justify itself, or ignore its differences from other voices and the circumstances of class privilege that have determined and created it. The early diary of the youth in *Blindness* exaggerates the differences in class, the social forms of determinism, he has known almost since birth. He writes of a trip to London just before the 1922 election, when he (like Green) was seventeen and, with his friends, encountered 'Socialist working-men-God-bless-them in the Strand:' 'We each got into the centre of groups, and expected to be killed at any moment, for there is something about me that makes that type see red. However, they contained themselves very nicely while we talked nonsense at them'. The language and the expectation are made melodramatic and naïve; the sense of class guilt and permanent differences are not. Green's autobiography is full of the guilts determined by his birth and upbringing, and his responses to them. At one point, he talks of his need for praise and encouragement, but thought (not verified in the relevant text) that his housemaster hated him. He concludes that had he received the housemaster's praise he 'might be even less of a person now'. Brought up mostly by servant women, loving his mother and fearing the stern, remote father for whom he felt he could never replace the older brother who died, Green claims that he was fascinated with and inhibited about sex. He couldn't believe that women might enjoy making love, even kissing. He is acutely critical about the early colourful, elaborate, mannered prose he never quite abandoned. In the best of Green's fictions, his guilts and his confidence, his capacity to listen to and appreciate other voices while recognising that the voices could not be assimilated, and his comic sense that coherence was possible only through symbol, that social transformations were never real, combined to produce evocative fiction about the conditions of British society. His depth was not analytical or political in the sense that politics suggests possible reform or the conversion of imagination into external reality. Green, in his elaborate treatment of a class voice so different from his own (*Living*), his satire of the vapid of his own class, the sense of hierarchy, and the incommunicable differences between class (*Party-Going*), and the history and origins of contemporary class removed and displaced into fairy-tale (*Loving*), used his comic art, to create serious and searching treatments of the conditions of British society in the thirties.

Green did not sustain the depth and complexity of his social fictions much beyond 1945, although he continued to publish novels until 1952 and lived until late 1973. One symptom of the decline in the social resonance of the fiction is that occupations become more vague and shadowy, generalised satire rather than particular reconstructions. When the veteran returns from the Second World War in *Back*, although his personal life is dramatised with complexity, he works in a government ministry. Green spends pages in predictable satire of the pointless paper-passing and blame-shifting that go on at the office. *Concluding* represents its satire of bureaucracy through a school established by the government to produce government workers. The urban, formerly upper-class characters in the last two novels simply work in unspecified government offices. Their jobs are generalised as boring, financially necessary, time-consuming and endlessly wearying, and the accounts contain neither fictional life nor complexity as social representation of the post-war world. They are arid symbols of aridity. These novels, *Nothing* and *Doting*, depend on the depiction of shifting relationships and on plots that propel the shifts. Since the characters have little interior life and nothing to discover, the plots become abstracted cross-hatchings rather than instruments designed to reveal a particular quality or condition. The language is spare and comic, but reveals little beyond the insularity, disloyalty and comically seen shifting commitments of most of the characters. They, part of what once were the upper classes, are determined more by generation. The post-war young are pallid, reserved, less emotional and more moral about their sexuality and integrity. They are also seen as dull by their manipulative, teasing and disloyal parents. The parental generation (Green's own, in their forties in most of the fiction) has been decimated, many of the characters, especially in *Nothing*, widows and widowers, and they seek to transmit trivial tokens of their pasts to their children who politely accept nothing of them. Travel, literally or psychologically, is not a possibility. Green's last two novels convey a constant subtext of fatigue, perhaps itself an accurate representation of Green's version of post-war British society, but not one likely to sustain his best or most interesting fiction.

The decline in Green's fiction has been given biographical substance in memoirs recently published by his friend, Alan Ross, a poet, journalist (mostly about cricket), editor and travel writer. When Ross first knew Green well, in the late forties and early fifties, Green still worked for his father, although in the firm's London office. Ross describes Green as charming, teasing, not forthcoming with other writers or part of a literary group, and fond of women although solidly married with a son. Green loved to imitate, not reverentially, his still powerful father and, socially, he was 'most comfortable with anecdotes to do with his years on the shop floor of his father's engineering factory'.[7] A short time later, when his father finally retired, Green inherited the firm which 'unfortunately did not prosper under Henry, and it was not long before he himself withdrew, falling into a rapid physical decline which was accelerated by gin'.[8] His talk, as always, was rarely serious, except late at night over drinks. By 1954, Ross thought him no longer the amusing man of the world, but one who had become a 'tottering, unshaven recluse, hard of hearing, short of breath and teeth, who nevertheless lingered on for another twenty years'.[9] His son took over and revived the business, was interested primarily in bridge and sports cars. Green never liked to travel. Ross's account pretends no thorough causative explanation for Green's decline, and the decline in the fiction, before it stopped altogether, antedates the stages Ross chronicles by a few years. Yet the pattern and the focus Ross suggests in Green himself are consistent with the sense of Green as a writer who lost the acuity and depth of his social imagination while still in his early forties.

The early decline, in retrospect, ties Green's fictional achievement even more closely to the decade of the thirties. Whatever the story of the determinations or necessities of his life, his fiction represents an individual, searching and brilliantly achieved social portrait of the immobile British thirties. In his incorporation of the particularity of the many different voices he heard so acutely and shaped so carefully, as well as in the processes of experience, the bounded particular situations or conditions he presented so imaginatively, Green's language and grammar are a significant part of the literary decade. His visionary gerunds themselves are an important, inventive and resonant social voice.

## NOTES

1.   'Henry Green', in *Writers at Work: The Paris Review Interviews*, Second Series (London: Secker & Warburg, 1963) p. 209.
2.   Ibid., pp. 212–13.

3. Ibid., p. 212.
4. See introduction by John Updike to Henry Green's *Loving, Living, Party-Going* (London: Pan Books, 1978) p. 11.
5. Cunningham, *British Writers of the Thirties*, p. 241.
6. James Hall, *The Tragic Comedians* (Bloomington and London: Indiana University Press, 1963) p. 67.
7. Alan Ross, *Coastwise Lights* (London: Collins Harvill, 1988) p. 109.
8. Ibid.
9. Ibid., pp. 109–10.

# 8

# Nicholas Blake's 'Stake in the Social System'

In the late 1920s and 1930s, detective fiction, in so far as it represented metaphorically through crime what is wrong with society and through detection how it might be cured or restored, reached a large public. The use of the form to represent social value is at least as old as the fiction of Wilkie Collins (as in *The Moonstone*) and some of Conan Doyle's work, like *The Hound of the Baskervilles*, advocates a conservative restoration of the traditional country house against new social and commercial fractures. Within the context of the social and international strains of the 1930s, however, the use of the detective novel for a critical examination of society became widespread. In the 1920s, detective fiction was more likely to concentrate on the intellectual puzzle, the metaphor of the locked room, a formal severity that led to the publication of rules and specifications to which authentic detective fiction should conform. At the turn from the twenties to the thirties, one of the most influential and innovative writers of detective fiction was Anthony Berkeley, who, under his own name and the pseudonym of Anthony Berkeley Cox, published several locked room mysteries. In 1931, under another pseudonym, Francis Iles, Berkeley combined the intellectual puzzle with the representation of social metaphor in *Malice Aforethought*. The criminal, a doctor, is known from the first line, as the novel emphasises his use of new knowledge to poison the already corrupt society. The Great House, owned by the characterologically debased, has decayed into a septic pile of bad drains, infection and pollution. The doctor, the scientist, whose social role presumes attempts at sanitation, only magnifies the sepsis in his desire selfishly to control the house and surrounding area. *Malice Aforethought* also questions the justice visible in many earlier formulations of detective fiction. As a reflection of a thirties point of view that sees no just resolution for social infection, the doctor is exonerated in a trial for the murder he committed, although later executed for a crime he did not commit. Berkeley recognised that the pollution of the Great House, the infectious decay in the condition of England, was psychological as well as chemical. As early as 1930, he wrote: 'The detective story is in the process of developing into the novel . . . holding its readers less by mathematical than by psychological ties. The puzzle element will no doubt remain, but it will become a puzzle of character rather than a puzzle of time, place, motive, and opportunity'.[1]

Berkeley wrote only three novels as Francis Iles, the criminal always the social climber feeding on endemic corruption and the ending a violation of justice. More socially committed reformers also used the popular form, as Christopher Caudwell, in addition to his Marxist appraisals of the literary and popular culture, wrote eight simplistic detective novels between 1933 and 1937. A more cogent and prolific representative of the literary social critic working with the conflicts of the thirties in the form of detective fiction is Cecil Day Lewis, part of MacSpaunday, of the Auden Generation, who wanted to be known as a poet, translator of Virgil, and an essayist formulating the social and literary values of his generation in works from the thirties like the once highly-praised 'A Hope for Poetry' and 'Revolution in Writing'. Always committed to both social reform and poetry, and Poet Laureate from 1968 until his death in 1972, Day Lewis' reputation as a poet faded quickly after his initial successes in the early and mid-thirties, although he continued to write. His poetry never could sustain comparison with Auden's, and over the years the verse of Spender and of MacNeice has been more highly regarded. Sensitive to the contradictory snobberies of publishing and literary reputation, Day Lewis wrote all his detective fiction under the pseudonym – never a secret – of Nicholas Blake. Nevertheless, his talents, his sense of plot and his capacity to convey intelligently the social world around him make the writings of Nicholas Blake not only more popular but also more likely to endure than the writings of Cecil Day Lewis. Even his close friend Stephen Spender said in 1982 that he had recently read through all the work of his old friend in a mood of fond recall and found 'the best of Cecil' in the detective fiction.[2] Many would agree: the critic John Strachey had praised the work of Nicholas Blake as more searching and important as far back as 1942.[3]

Although Blake's novels of the thirties are more likely to take place in institutions like a boys' school or in a small country retreat than in a Great House, the setting as representative of a larger Britain is always apparent. The literal Great House is gone by the 1930s, a figment of the past or a borrowed and artificially constructed ruse, as in *Thou Shell of Death* (1936). In one that uses a small country house and family to illustrate the larger society, *The Case of the Abominable Snowman* (1941 – the American title is *The Corpse in the Snowman*), the divided house resembles a 'battlefield' in a 'war' about drugs and psychiatry: 'But, like the war that was convulsing Europe, it would be an affair of long boredoms, broken by sudden brief spasms of violent action'. By the time of a later novel, *Head of a Traveller* (1949), the country house is introduced as an echo of legendary fiction: 'glancing in at the drawing-room windows, one might have expected to see a group of brocaded figures arrested in courtiers' attitudes around a Sleeping Beauty, the stems of roses twining through their ceremonious fingers'. The woman who is proud of her house and would do anything to maintain it is told 'you carry your centuries very well'. The house is a 'brick-and-mortar' charmer, appealing in its frailty, its calm aloofness, or its fragments of treasure 'ticketed already for the auctioneer's hammer'. Yet its legendary improbability, complete with the genetic anomaly of a dwarf who needs protection as the only legitimate heir, operates strongly enough on the characters' imagination to provide the origin and motive for crime.

The texture of Blake's 1930s world uses the Great House as only occasional legend or memory. Most of his sense of Britain is conveyed in a prose thick with contemporary reference, exuding a topical ambience. Blake's first novel, *A Question of Proof* (1935), set in the boys' school, contains haystacks as part of a ritual to connect with the surrounding farming community, cricket, and the innovator who would 'teach boys to think in English instead of Latin', even though, on most issues, there's 'the kind of silence that obtained in the Common Room when someone had the bad taste to bring Russia or religion into the conversation'. In *Thou Shell of Death*, the Home Secretary has 'suddenly developed Communist-phobia; thinks they're going to put a bomb under his bed'. Scholars debate 'the comparative merits of Greta Garbo and Elizabeth Bergner', and one of them, an Oxford don, in talking of the horrors of College food, describes his 'colleagues' as 'so wrapt up in the Higher Criticism or Buchmanism or some other equally squalid form of intellectual suicide that they are quite blind to the importance of creature comforts'. *There's Trouble Brewing* (1937) begins with the death of a dog dissolved in a huge vat in a brewery: 'His pusillanimous and shifty-looking terrier face appeared in every illustrated newspaper in the United Kingdom, ousting from the front page the not altogether dissimilar features of Hitler, the neurotic-bulldog expression of Mussolini, the sealed lips of Mr. Baldwin, and the unconcealed charms of bathing beauties'. As the international scene becomes more sinister and threatening, in the 1938 novel, *The Beast Must Die*, an apparently scatter-brained actress interrupts her story to say 'but of course all these Jews are in league I must say we could do with a bit a Hitler here though I do rather bar rubber truncheons and sterilisation. Well, now, as I was saying . . . '. With no connection to the plot, 'the radio in the hotel was repeating unemotionally the Japanese claim that their bombing of open towns in China was pure self-defense'. In several novels, Henry Luce is mocked as dense, specious authority. The holiday camp devoted to 'Organised Recreation' is satirised in 1940's *Malice in Wonderland* (the American title is *Murder with Malice*):

> Within that massive fun-factory (so a careful study of the brochure issued by Wonderland Ltd. Holiday Camp had informed him) were vast dining halls where ravenous visitors could partake of epicurean meals cooked by London chefs in hygienic kitchens and served on spotless napery by cheerful waitresses to the accompaniment of a string band: there was also a ballroom, whose sprung maple floor positively incited you to the light fantastic; to say nothing of bars, an indoor swimming-bath equipped with Aerofilter and coloured fountains, a concert hall . . .

The impending war (the novel is set in 1939) is foreshadowed in the metaphorical links between the order and discipline of the holiday camp and that of Nazi Youth movements. The war is central in *The Case of the Abominable Snowman*, set crucially in the frozen, static winter of 1939–40, the winter of the 'phony war' (Blake frequently used actual historical weather conditions, as he made another unusually severe winter, the post-Christmas blizzards of 1962–3 crucial to the metaphors and plots of two later novels). In 1939, however, people still compare the elegant hostess to the 'stately, arch, sorely put-upon hostess of *Animal Crackers*'. Blake's use of food as historical reference continues, as in *Minute for Murder* (1947), set in a government ministry at the end of the Second World War, he comically captures austerity with an account of the coffee as 'an almost colorless liquid which might have been brewed from a compound of acorns, dishcloths and wormwood' – a reference that later became almost a genre in the fiction of Kingsley Amis and John Wain.

Blake's thirties world, however, is more concerned with technology than with food or creature comforts. Like his contemporaries of the Auden Generation, he saw knowledgeable accommodation to modern technology as central to in the thirties. Collecting evidence in *A Question of Proof* is contingent on driving a car fast and skilfully. The heroine is just as good a driver as the hero, to his surprise, except at rare moments of emotional distraction. Their car is fast and manoeuverable, able to catch the criminal's pretentious Daimler which, wrecked, disgorges its contents 'as though vomited out of a volcano'. In *Thou Shell of Death*, the hero (who is also the victim who stages his own death to implicate men guilty of deeper social crimes) is a First World War flying ace who also designs new planes that may function as interceptors in the bombing raids of the next war. The novel ends in an air chase, the criminal falling from a plane's wing in a comic and futile attempt to escape from the technologically proficient. Deduction itself is scientific and technological. The detective in *There's Trouble Brewing* must learn the techniques of brewing beer in order to solve the crime. Day Lewis' son reported that his father, in preparation for writing the novel, made several visits to the Cheltenham Original Brewery.[4] The process of sailing a boat is elaborately described and necessary for the plot in *The Beast Must Die*. This focus on technical process has become standard in many detective novels since, but few current writers have such confidence in technology, create a world in which travel, movement and process, like rational deduction itself, are the equipment necessary for understanding the causes and attempting the cures in the insular and deeply corrupted modern world. The confidence extends to theoretical science, as, in *Malice in Wonderland*, the decade's intellectual popularisers of science, Eddington and Jeans, are read as illustrating 'part of the cosmic dance' rather than as showing inevitable limits on scientific method and discovery.

Nicholas Blake began his detective fiction with a gesture against the encrusted literary past in the name of a healthy modernity.

At the beginning of *A Question of Proof*, his hero, the lover and iconoclastic schoolmaster, tells his mistress, the headmaster's wife, that even if banned from teaching, he can always do something in the modern world: 'I might even degrade myself to writing novels'. Initially, literature, past and present, is seen as the abstraction and degradation of actual experience. But this brave simplicity cannot last, just as the schoolmaster cannot solve the crime without the help of the detective who is more rational and interested in an accumulated past. After the first novel, the texture of Blake's fiction is literary, full of references that depict character and provide crucial understanding of plot or theme. *Thou Shell of Death* lists the flyer's books as an index to his character and modernity: Kafka, C. M. Doughty, Donne, Dorothy Sayers and Yeats (the last in an inscribed first edition). The text is full of references to Shakespeare, even from a passing tramp who provides helpful information. But Shakespeare is insufficient, for the scholar must track a reference left by the flyer/hero/victim through the darkening Jacobean social and psychological echoes of Webster to Tourneur's *The Revenger's Tragedy* before the complicated and causative social crimes can be understood. *There's Trouble Brewing* and *The Beast Must Die* use *Hamlet* crucially, not with the arcane dependence on reference that makes a Shakespeare quiz part of the puzzle, visible in the detective fiction of Michael Innes (the pseudonym for J. I. M. Stewart) written at the same time, but in a way that is part of a traditional and popularly apprehensible past. *The Beast Must Die*, with a writer as the central character who is both the hero and the killer, is constantly literary. The first page of the writer's diary refers to appropriate lines by both Meredith and T. S. Eliot, and references to Shakespeare, Wordsworth, Aldous Huxley and other Nicholas Blake novels follow before the central self-definition in terms of Hamlet's combination of procrastination and conscience allow him to act out his justifiable revenge. Shakespeare is again crucial in *The Case of the Abominable Snowman*, although here, in another suicide rigged to look like murder, the locus shifts from *Hamlet* to *Macbeth* to illustrate a less self-reflexive revenge. In between these novels, in *Malice in Wonderland*, a novel of 'mad hatter' pranks that turn increasingly malicious, the references to Lewis Carroll's *Alice in Wonderland* signal a psychological evasion and obfuscation that Blake, before the Second World War, associated with the Victorians. His sense of literary history altered and expanded during the war itself.

By *Minute for Murder*, the victim/heroine reads Victorian novels and poets, detective fiction and novels by E. M. Forster, D. H. Lawrence and Henry Green. The principal and appropriate clue, the statement of the emotional and psychological relationship that has determined the murder, comes through the poetry of Arthur Hugh Clough. Reliance on Shakespeare and Jacobean drama in the fiction of the thirties is replaced by a wider sense of literary tradition, and later novels continue the use of T. S. Eliot, Meredith and Donne, and contain random or structurally crucial references to Hardy, Housman, Arnold, Greek tragedy, Elinor Glyn, Dylan Thomas, Cocteau and Dostoyevsky. But for Blake, the world after the Second World War is less coherent than that of the thirties. He makes frequent reference to a world of 'degraded culture' (in *End of Chapter*, 1957) and one that had 'had an overdose of history during the last twenty years' (in *The Whisper in the Gloom*, 1954). Despite all its fractures and pains, Blake's thirties world is more coherently conveyed through a literary culture. The popular and the traditionally literary are closer together, the tradition itself more apprehensible within the popular culture. Much of the force and applicability of his detective fiction inheres in Blake's capacity to make his literary knowledge and tradition appropriate in topical terms.

Not all literary and cultural critics, especially forty or fifty years ago, have been willing to grant so much to detective fiction. Edmund Wilson was perhaps the most acerbic. In a 1940s essay, 'Who Cares Who Killed Roger Ackroyd?' (in response to critics of an essay he wrote for *The New Yorker*), Wilson declared that he found all detective fiction, except for that of Raymond Chandler, dull, hackneyed, full of useless information, and 'the explanation of mysteries, when it comes, . . . neither interesting nor plausible enough'. He thought social issues depicted only on a superficial level. He likened his friends' addiction to detective fiction to a 'vice that, for silliness and minor harmfulness ranks somewhere between smoking and crossword puzzles', and thought it 'degrading to the intellect' and a wasteful 'squandering' of paper.[5] Many writers were quick to defend detective fiction. Auden, in 'The Guilty Vicarage', while confessing himself an addict, diagrammed the form convincingly in terms close to those of Aristotle's definition of Greek tragedy and saw the society presented as consisting of 'apparently innocent individuals': 'The murder is the act of disruption by which innocence is lost'. After classifying crimes by their degree of seriousness (blackmail is always a lesser crime propelled by the fear of discovery of a trivial sin), Auden explained his addiction as a product of his own social and ethical 'guilt'. Auden's guilt worked in a psychologically complex way:

> It is sometimes said that detective stories are read by respectable law-abiding citizens in order to gratify in fantasy the violent or murderous wishes they dare not, or are ashamed to, translate into action. This may be true for the readers of thrillers (which I rarely enjoy), but it is quite false for the reader of detective stories . . . the magical satisfaction the latter provide . . . is the illusion of being dissociated from the murderer. The magic formula is an innocence which is discovered to contain guilt; then a suspicion of being the guilty other has been expelled, a cure effected, not by me or my neighbors, but by the miraculous intervention of a genius from outside who removes guilt by giving knowledge of guilt.[6]

For others, like Joseph Wood Krutch, the essential element was 'dread' rather than 'guilt', a fear of social collapse and a miraculous reprieve. Later detective writers have connected the 'guilt' and the 'dread' in ways that generate more complex forms of catharsis. Day Lewis as writer and Auden as reader propelled response to a form that could connect 'guilt' and 'dread', could bring together a response to contemporary experience that was simultaneously ethical, social and psychological.

Day Lewis was guardedly unpretentious about detective fiction. In his autobiography, he stated that, teaching at Cheltenham College on a small salary, with a wife and two children, he wrote his first detective novel because he needed 100 pounds to repair the stone-tiled roof of his cottage: 'it nearly got me sacked from the College staff, and then enabled me to give up teaching'.[7] He had, however, read many detective novels beforehand. He also adduced a homespun and unconvincing version of 'guilt' and an 'unconscious need for punishment', when he attributed his to having, at the age of eight, pilfered candy money from the funds he collected, as a chore for his father, for the Church of England Missionary Society.[8] His ambivalence about the form is reflected in bits of satire throughout the fiction, as when the hero of *The Beast Must Die* is apologetic about writing detective fiction for money and says he'll tell inquisitive, stuffy neighbours he's working on a life of Wordsworth. At other times, Day Lewis claimed more for detective fiction. He once, in an essay, imagined that a future anthropologist like Frazer might call the detective story 'The Folk Myth of the Twentieth Century'.[9] His public comments about detective fiction emphasised its social function, like the preface he wrote in 1942 for Howard Haycraft's *Murder for Pleasure: The Life and Times of the Detective Story*, the first serious extended critical appraisal of the form. Day Lewis wrote that detective fiction served those 'who have a stake in the social system and must, therefore, even in fantasy, see the ultimate triumph of their social values ensured'. He contrasted this 'stake' to the absence of one in those to whom thrillers appealed, and he underlined a sharp, rather condescending difference in class between responsible readers of detective fiction and the irresponsible or indifferent readers of thrillers: 'the detective-novel proper is read almost exclusively by the upper and professional classes. The so-called "lower-middle" and "working" classes tend to read "bloods", thrillers'.[10] Sean Day-Lewis thought his father's motives more ethical and psychological than social. He claimed his father wrote detective fiction to make money, to introduce others to his own addiction, and, because of his own guilt for his lost belief in God, as a 'substitute religious ritual with the detective and murderer representing the light and dark ˙side of man's nature, two sides which could both be identified with by both reader and writer'.[11] In the fiction, whenever 'light' and 'dark' are so easily separated, 'light' is an ethical version of stratified social responsibility, with confidence in science and technology, while 'dark' contains the insoluble dilemmas of politics, region and class. The 'light' is also the voice, as Sean Day-Lewis implicitly suggests, of the popular, progressive, upper-class secular minister or schoolmaster.

Much of the voice of the 'light' in the fiction emerges through the discoveries of the brilliant, eccentric and humane Nigel Strangeways, the single series detective. Named for Strangeways, a famous Manchester prison, Nigel looks like 'one of the less successful busts' of T. E. Lawrence in the first novel. As many have commented, the resemblance soon switches to the young Auden with his ungainly 'ostrich-like strides', his voracious appetite for tea, and his insistence on sleeping under mounds of blankets. The second novel adds the 'lock of sandy-coloured hair drooping over his forehead'. Amiable satire of Auden continues, as in *Malice in Wonderland*, in which a young man looks forward to the sleek, modern machines of the holiday camp 'with all deference to the early Auden, whose weakness for rusting metal and escaping steam was a notorious instance of the foibles of genius'. The emphasis in all the fiction is on Strangeways' unique combination of rationality, concern for society and genius. He is also impeccably upper class. He is introduced as having, after Cambridge, 'travelled about for a bit, learning languages': 'Then settled down to investigate crime; said it was the only career left which offered scope to good manners and scientific curiosity'. A full account of his upper-class heritage is given in the second novel. Nigel, changed to an Oxford graduate, 'where he had neglected Demosthenes in favour of Freud', is the nephew of the Assistant Commissioner of Police at Scotland Yard. Another uncle and aunt, Lord and Lady Marlinworth, are on the surface less in touch with the modern world, although they provide important insights into the crime. At the beginning of the novel, they offer Nigel a lift to the country site in their Daimler, 'as draughtless and dustless as a hospital ward', Lady Marlinworth with her 'thick motoring veil, several layers of petticoat, and a bottle of smelling salts for any journey of more than twenty miles. Her husband, in an enormous check ulster, cloth cap and goggles, looked like a cross between Edward the Seventh and Guy Fawkes'. Nigel, as jovially eccentric as his forbears, adds 'psychological knowledge' to his inherited combination of 'analytical intelligence, common sense and imagination'. Most settings, like the boys' school in *A Question of Proof*, deny the validity of psychological conclusions, likening them to the 'washing of dirty linen' or consultation with a medium. But Nigel, in each of the novels, teaches society that psychology is significant in apprehending the criminal, in analysing what has gone wrong. From the point of view of the more terminologically sophisticated 1990s, the diagnoses seem simplistic: 'inferiority complex', 'schizophrenic' as synonymous with 'split personality', the labelling of nervous or truculent people as 'neurotic'. Yet Blake is consistent in having Nigel work carefully through the social and personal backgrounds of his suspects to construct a pattern of plausible response, a psychosocial analysis necessary in apprehending the crime. Sometimes, as in *Thou Shell of Death*, the victim is also psychologically acute, as the hero/flyer can stage his own death in a way he knows will exact revenge by counting on the reactions of the villains from the past (the arrogant instigators of social crimes against Ireland twenty years earlier) and on Nigel's education and deductive capacity.

In *Thou Shell of Death* Nigel acquires an indispensable aid in Georgia Cavendish, the equally well-born woman (a relative had been one of the 'first blue-stockings – a don at Girton', an historian who became a shrewdly elegant representative of the eighteenth century she studied) who has been an intrepid explorer in Africa and, 'monkey-faced', once the mistress of the hero/flyer/victim, who had rescued her on an earlier disastrous expedition. While working out the case, Nigel falls in love with her. They marry, and on subsequent cases she provides insight Nigel lacks into varieties of lovers, a necessary area of psychological examination. In *The Case of the Abominable Snowman*, she is quicker to spot a drug-dealing doctor posing as a trendy psychoanalyst than Nigel is. In *The Smiler with the Knife* (1939), the most overtly political of Blake's thirties novels in that the enemy is an organisation of British Nazis smuggling arms into England to fuel a potential revolt, Georgia and Nigel must split for nearly a year to apprehend the leaders who are deeply embedded in the conventional fabric of British life. They each play roles in the complicated detection, Georgia, less well known, able to mask herself to infiltrate the organisation and risk the perils of unmasking as the more identifiable Nigel never could. In later novels, after Georgia has been killed driving an ambulance in the London Blitz, Nigel feels that he has absorbed her insight, although he is ambivalent about his capacity to regard 'human behavior with absolute detachment'. This isolation does not last, for he becomes the lover of the sculptress Clare Massinger, who provides a more physical relationship, other forms of psychological insight, and emotionally extends the range of Nigel's capacities as he becomes less an Audenesque figure and more modestly and covertly a surrogate for the author himself.

In the thirties and forties, much of Blake's psychological probing concerns sibling relationships. At first the relationship is simple, as in *Thou Shell of Death*, Georgia Cavendish tries to protect her guilty brother, impeding the solution of the crime. Nigel recognises that Georgia will not lie and, when her brother tries to throw suspicion on her, Nigel sees that the violation of an expected familial relationship (two of the earlier Irish victims had been a mutually protective brother and sister) is an accurate index of guilt. Siblings interlock more in subsequent novels. In *There's Trouble Brewing*, the identity of the two brothers is masked, then switched, in the death by drowning and decomposing in a beer vat. The apparent victim, the mercenary capitalistic evil brother, is finally the killer who has disposed of his feckless and humane brother who was the principal suspect. The theme is economic and social, the rich capitalist destroying communal unity, and the psychological identities and distances of brothers are parallel to social crime. The psychological pattern conforms to sibling identities locked in guilt, the murderer impersonating the victim or the victim collaborating in his own death. Such psychic interlocking also pervades *The Beast Must Die*, in which a writer's diary, the first half of the novel, details his plan to get to know and kill the loathsome bully who had accidentally killed the writer's son. The plan misfires; the bully is nevertheless killed, throwing suspicion on others. But Nigel discovers that the writer is in fact the murderer, and then allows him to commit suicide and write a confession designed to save the son of the bully he'd killed who'd killed his son. The intricacies of family relationships both propel and resolve crime as they intensify the identities and guilts upon which, for Blake as for Auden, detective fiction depends. Brothers running the holiday camp are paired as contrasting suspects throughout *Malice in Wonderland*, although only one of them, the one vulnerable to economic and fascistic means of control, is guilty. The house in *The Case of the Abominable Snowman* is riddled with the identities shared between a young puritanical brother and his beautiful 'neurotic' sister. The sister is found dead, thought to be murdered by the doctor on whom she is dependent for drugs. Nigel and Georgia recognise as they delve into the past that the sister's drug dependency was the brother's 'rape of his own innocence'. The sister had killed herself, wrapping a rope 'twined double around her neck' to suggest her brother's complicity. She had left her brother a suicide note, which he burned. In his notion of revenge, he murdered the sleazy doctor (the corpse hidden in the snowman, its discovery delayed by the long frozen winter) who was guilty only of blackmail and supplying drugs, not of murder. The incapacity of brother and sister to separate from each other is the septic introversion that tears down the house, as symbolic incest represents the atrophy of a once healthy social class. In the post-war *Minute for Murder*, the closeness of a twin brother and sister has prevented either from loving anyone else and leads directly to the crime; although neither is the victim or the murderer, each must share the guilt.

The legendary Great House of *Head of a Traveller* is permeated and destroyed by the rivalry between brothers, the good one, the poet, finally killing the parasitic one in his attempt to preserve the fiction of the Great House. In all these novels the close identity of siblings creates crime, and emphasises, in plot and theme, introversion and insularity that destroys the social fabric.

In Blake's fictional world, health or social resurrection requires breaking from the isolation his siblings represent. From the first novel, health requires open and adventurous sexuality. The antisepsis of the boys' school, 'the airy, green-washed, ostentatiously hygienic dormitories so reassuring to the science-ridden mind of modern parenthood', is, like puritanism, no antidote to social crime. The lovers in the novel conquer convention and class, while the criminal is the repressed puritan who hates and tries to implicate the lovers. Similar themes run through the early novels, although the priggish puritan becomes, as in *Malice in Wonderland*, more salvageable through experience. The fiction of the thirties generally sustains Sean Day-Lewis' statement that, in 1936, his father's views were 'an amalgam of D. H. Lawrence and Karl Marx that blamed capitalism for inhibiting the relationship between the sexes'.[12] The version of D. H. Lawrence, in the fiction of the thirties, is abstracted and the liberation from puritanism asexual. Georgia Cavendish, the ideal woman, is 'monkey-faced', thin and brittle. She, the explorer, has an 'odd craving for the most solitary and uncomfortable parts of the world'. Even when they first marry, she and Nigel sleep in separate beds, he finding it hard to get 'used to waking up and finding a woman in the room'. Their relationship is more that of pals, mates, and wise, witty intellectual cohorts than of lovers. In the first novel in which Georgia appears, she is contrasted to the flyer hero's other mistress, the opulently sexual and selfish Lucilla whose 'face was launching too many overdrafts among the undergraduates' and who is described as 'tall for a woman, blonde as a Nazi's dream, full-figured'. In *There's Trouble Brewing*, the overtly sexual young woman, the daughter of the foreman of the brewery, emulates Greta Garbo and has irresponsibly caused the death of the dog in the vat of beer. Extenuation begins in *The Beast Must Die*, in which the explicitly sexual woman is all right 'even if she is vulgar, she's not unhealthy, not unclean, she doesn't infect the room with a stink of camphor and stale proprieties and rotting power'. By the 1940 *Malice in Wonderland* she is the heroine able to liberate or convert the prig. By the end of the war, in the 1947 *Minute for Murder*, the beautiful, opulent Nita Prince is the victim, murdered by her gentle establishment lover Jimmy, because he is unable to tolerate her change from the superficially free and irresponsible party girl to the woman of closeness, sexuality and Victorian domesticity. Jimmy, the genial and accomplished public man, is the consummate egotist, 'not capable of sustaining a deep, whole-hearted emotional relationship'. The change in Blake's perspective is also represented by the fictional killing off-stage of Georgia Cavendish, because, according to Sean Day-Lewis, his father said he was 'bored' with her.[13] The subsequent ideal, Clare Massinger, is more explicitly and devotedly sexual. From that point on, in the fiction, heads are often severed from bodies, as crimes and as clues, as if complete humanity requires full acknowledgment of the physical.

The change in Blake's perspective is visible in Day Lewis' own relationships, for as he increasingly recognised, his detective fiction reflected his experience directly. His accounts of his first marriage to Mary King underline its physical distances, despite the creation of two sons, although he and his wife were close intellectually and politically. Georgia Cavendish contains much of Mary King who also had a deeply devoted brother with whom Day Lewis remained close long after the divorce. In late 1938, Day Lewis moved himself and his family to a cottage in Devon in order to write uninterruptedly. Less interested in Marx than he had been just a short time earlier, he acted out his reverence for D. H. Lawrence, about which he had felt he had to be more circumspect at Cheltenham than he did about his politics. He began an affair with Billie Currall, the beautiful wife of a man who had moved to Devon to farm. In his autobiography, he describes it as a 'shameless, half-savage, inordinate affair which taught me a great deal about women and about myself . . . as I look back, all of a piece with the desperate irresponsibility and fatalism which had been in the air since Munich'.[14] He did not depict Billie Currall until his last detective novel, *The Private Wound* (1968), and he wrote her in 1971 that it was 'her book'.[15] Billie Currall and Day Lewis had a son, William, born in 1940, who is hardly mentioned in biographical or autobiographical accounts (an illegitimate son does kill his father in *The Worm of Death*, published in 1961). After 1940, however, Day Lewis spent most of his time in London working as the editor for publications in the Ministry of Information, while

Mary and their two sons remained in Devon. The Blitz of April 1941, in which Georgia Cavendish is killed, marks the meeting and beginning of the affair between Day Lewis and Rosamond Lehmann (they had known each other slightly before and Day Lewis had reviewed *The Weather in the Streets*). The affair lasted for nine years, as they lived together mostly in London during the war. After the war, Day Lewis divided his time unevenly between living with Lehmann in London or at her country house in Essex and living with his wife and children in Devon. Rosamond Lehmann is suggested in the character of Nita Prince, the victim who is both brilliant and beautiful in 1947's *Minute for Murder*. Content to be only the mistress while the war lasts, she is, as the war ends, committed to abandoning her earlier liberated life for a single, domestic, intense relationship. The criminality of Jimmy, who kills what he cannot sustain and realises afterwards that he was wrong, is Day Lewis' treatment of his own guilt. The affair lingered for several years more, Day Lewis at one point resolving to leave his wife and marry Lehmann. When he divorced his wife in 1951, he married Jill Balcon, a younger actress. Rosamond Lehmann's *The Echoing Grove* of 1952 is her most full and searching account of female sibling rivalry turning into the shared recognition of male inadequacy, of the genial, charming, intelligent man who is emotionally shallow and undependable. While Day Lewis had earlier internalised this theme, he followed with something of a defence in *The Dreadful Hollow* (1953), long and pointed reflections through Nigel Strangeways about the 'opportunistic' attitude to the 'truth' on the part of some beautiful, brilliant and compelling women.

In Blake's fiction of the thirties, themes of social and communal life, the legacy of the interest in Marx, are just as significant as Lawrentian liberation. The early fiction, however, although aimed at a popular audience and irreverent about middle-class conventions, is hardly populist in tone or sentiment. Nigel Strangeways' attitudes are as aristocratic as his origins. The proletarian villagers in *A Question of Proof* are depicted as stupid and mercenary, ready to do anything for five shillings; most of the boys at the school would willingly submit themselves to fascistic control. The capitalistic brewer in the Midlands town who is the murderer in *There's Trouble Brewing* is excoriated more for the unsanitary and unsafe conditions of his brewery (his principal opponent is the local doctor) than for his contempt for the populace. For

Blake, totalitarian control is the enemy – not that its victims are sanctified, or even worthy, but that human beings have no right to prey brutally upon the weaknesses and diseases of others. Nigel is the guardian of a past he sees as particularly British, a tradition that leaves others alone and is sensitive to the others' humanity, however flawed. He values cricket, the game that can accommodate itself to changing patterns of weather and rewards the watchful patience necessary to stave off aggression. This British tradition needs to be distinguished from other British traditions, as in *The Beast Must Die*, perhaps the most searching of the thirties treatments of psychological totalitarianism, in which the corrupt British tradition is the military and imperialistic one that developed in the late nineteenth century through the Boer War. Nigel would expunge this and defend the sensitivity and concern of the traditionally solitary and independent writer, a tradition just as British and bourgeois, but is willing to sacrifice itself to preserve the health and eccentricity of the next generation. Blake first shows a veneration for the proletariat in *The Smiler with the Knife*, the novel about the 'English Banner', the fascistic military organisation that would take over Britain. Here, militant trade unionists, crude lorry drivers, chirruping vicars' wives, and a troupe of performing 'young ladies in magenta knickers' who call themselves 'The Radiance Girls' and go in for 'Psycho-physical Irradiation' are all soundly anti-fascistic and aid Georgia's escape. The evil is in the 'English Banner', its insistence on order and control, its network of social and economic 'co-operatives' (which, when described, sound equally communistic and fascistic), and its charismatic leader who, Georgia recognises, exhibits underneath the 'profound indifference of the egoist'. Another who, in addition to Georgia, infiltrates the organisation is the watchful professional cricketer, willing, at a crucial point, to sacrifice himself in blowing up a munitions cache in Nottingham. Britain, for the first time seemingly classless, is united only in defence against totalitarianism. The proletarian novelist in *The Case of the Abominable Snowman* is virile and honest, combining 'imaginative understanding with sturdy common sense and a code of morality'. By the time of the 'phony war' in which the novel takes place, he has lost his earlier allegiance to Marxism and cultural dissidence: 'respectability's a thing you fight to keep because you've had to fight to achieve it'. As the 'phony war' turns into a hot one, the aristocratic, priggish murderer brother of the suicide sister he could not separate himself from can expiate his guilt by escaping into Germany to 'do as much damage as I can before they find me out'. After the war, priggishness is the vice of the bureaucrat or public person, from whatever class, examples in both a climbing lower-middle-class functionary and the aristocratic Jimmy in *Minute for Murder*. Language, too, mixes class counters. By the time of *Head of a Traveller*, Inspector Blount of Scotland Yard, Nigel's literal-minded, linguistically fastidious and factual assistant, is able to exchange 'elephantine badinage' with a 'slatterny' young woman in the village and the timetable of the murder is called a 'shocking schlemazel'.

The changes in Blake's treatment of issues of class and politics through the thirties and into the Second World War are neither consistently populist nor Marxist. Rather, the uses of Marx, like those of D. H. Lawrence, change in ways more explicable through biography than through ideology. In the early thirties, not long out of Oxford and teaching at public schools and then Cheltenham, Day Lewis' Marxism seems vague, innocent and abstracted, a repository for the need for social and communal reform and a gesture against an establishment, as in 'A Hope for Poetry'. The only articulate locus for the ideas is the poetry, and one senses, in Day Lewis, little recognition of classes other than his own. In 1932, his first year at Cheltenham, in a meeting with the headmaster, Day Lewis was reprimanded for his 'intellectual superiority', visible in his dress, his taste and the fact that his poems used sexual imagery.[16] Yet his skill and popularity as a teacher were acknowledged. In 1934, a boy charged that Day Lewis had insulted the King. But he had, in fact, said that 'Henry VIII was a bad man', and the boy had mistakenly applied the statement to the current monarch. All this says more about the culture of Cheltenham College than it does of Day Lewis, although the Cheltenham hearing with the headmaster in 1935, after *A Question of Proof* was published, was more serious. The specific objection was that Day Lewis had written a novel with an affair between a young master and the headmaster's wife, and that this might be read as literally true at Cheltenham. The school's board of governors knew of Day Lewis' vague left-wing sympathies, but they did not object because, by all accounts, he did not mention politics in the classroom. Although not dismissed, only reprimanded, Day Lewis, armed with a contract for further novels, resigned from Cheltenham anyway. He continued to live in the town and, in mid–1936, joined the British Communist party. In his 1960 autobiography, his sympathies are clearer than his precise reasons. Guilt seems to have played as large a part as theory, for he writes of his rejection of Christian faith as connected with his feeling that, given the atrophy of parliament and the death of English liberalism, communism 'had a religious quality . . . also romantic',[17] his version of the love that animated so many of the Auden Generation. By 1960, he saw this as generous and absurd. In 1936, he thought that only the Communists would confront the greater danger of the Fascists. Joining the party was a way to work actively: he spoke at meetings, wrote committed works (two novels and, particularly, a play called *Noah and the Waters* were popular and critical disasters), and did journalistic reports. A series of reports on a group called 'English Mystery' that established local militia units for defence in Gloucestershire was possibly a source for *The Smiler with the Knife*.[18] In the summer of 1938, quite suddenly as Day Lewis chronicled the change, while giving a speech to a large audience at the Queen's Hall in London, he heard, as if detached, his own pronouncements as insincere, removed and mistaken.[19] He quit the party. Stephen Spender, who like Auden never joined the Communist party, has attributed Day Lewis's break to his rejection of Stalin and what he represented.[20] But Day Lewis always had reservations about Stalin, and the one consistent theme of the detective fiction is the objection to totalitarianism. Communism, even at best, seems to have been defensible only as a form of pragmatic opposition to a far greater totalitarianism, Nazism. The theoretical 'hope' of the first half of the decade had been lost to a sense of choice between far from perfect alternatives. Only late in the thirties, perhaps in a few of his contacts during his two years of working for the Communist party, perhaps not until late 1938 when he moved to Devon and wrote of his friendships with rural proletarians in Devon pubs, had he respect for the thoughts and voices of ordinary people. The ordinary voices he began to chronicle, in his first celebrations of classes other than his own, were not Marxist or theoretical, not connected to the Communists at all, were simply resistant to any form of political imposition from the outside. Defensive, even insular, and in some ways a retreat from the modern world, the people in the pub were the more authentic creations of Day Lewis' expanding class sympathies, as they were more central to his writing, than were alien theories. His leaving the Communist party enabled Day Lewis to continue and expand what he did best, reconstruct in popular fiction a British tradition that under threat of extinction was able to assimilate more of island geography and class divisions than it had before. Unlike many of his contemporaries, he feared chaos less than he feared certainty.

Application of a term like insularity to Day Lewis' social attitudes is an equivocal judgement. In one sense, like his contemporaries in the 1920s and early thirties who were so committed to influence from a wider technological and international world, he was not insular at all. Georgia Cavendish is first introduced as modern woman, a heroic international explorer both physically and intellectually. The major theme of the novel is both the flyer/hero/victim's and Nigel's recovery of a past and tradition in Ireland that reveals the English addiction to locality and class as criminal. But the suggested healthy assimilation is neither worldwide nor extended to all classes. It is, including Blount, Nigel's Scots assistant, only the shift from an outworn and restrictive English insularity to a larger, more humane British one. A similar extension takes place as a minor theme within the characters of the Second World War ministry in *Minute for Murder*. In the novels in between, those of the thirties, a fully British society is seen as value threatened by raging continental abstractions and forms of universal order. Although Blake refers to international issues, like the war in China, the major theme and the valid or impossible reconstruction of tradition is always a uniquely British phenomenon. According to his son, Day Lewis at Oxford, in contrast to his more widely travelled friends, was regarded as insular, talked of as something of a 'provincial' despite the fact that he had lived and gone to school in London.[21] Before 1947, he never left the British Isles except for a weekend Communist meeting in Paris in July, 1938. He found the French communist intellectuals, grouped in a clique, both 'shallow and pretentious'.[22] Day Lewis was not as judgementally insular as Priestley, more English than British, was. In the early days of the Second World War, Priestley publicly attacked Auden and Isherwood for remaining in the United States, as Day Lewis obviously would not have done.[23] In the detective fiction written after the war, although characters travel the world quite easily, the social and geographical locus remains British. In one of these novels, *The Whisper in the Gloom*, suspect international politics are a matter of vague 'negotiation', unlike the straightforward British, and the millionaire kingpin of crime is 'cosmopolitan'. The Great House in this novel, a derelict hiding place for criminals, burns appropriately to the ground, but significant action and the eradication of crime are achieved in the public, classless, but British structure of the Albert Hall.

In Blake's British fictional world, the social implications of the two world wars in the twentieth century were entirely different. As the old commissionaire who guards the ministry tells Nigel Strangeways at the beginning of *Minute for Murder*, all wars produce and lead to 'chay-oh' [chaos]. His war, the First, lead only to chaos: 'All killed off we was. What come back, we'd 'ad enough; anything for a quiet life'. But the Second, accidentally, with its low, defensive expectations and its episodes of eccentric heroism, produced out of chaos a healthier social Britain, one less constricted and desperate for order, less permeated with class. The old man, however, is not sentimental. He tells Nigel that maybe 'this war hasn't killed off enough, not on your bleedin' life it ain't'. As Nigel knows and the novel demonstrates, psychological fractures, evasions and inadequacies still exist in British life on personal and historical levels within what seems like a moment of public triumph. These fractures are deep and traditional enough to be just as destructive as the social ones. Day Lewis continued to write detective fiction, but, after 1950 or so, gradually and unevenly the fiction lost its force, comedy and intensity. Some of the later novels contain effective scenes of social commentary and satire, like the ludicrous 1954 'Peace Meeting' and the revelation that the thug posing as a commercial traveller is an unreconstructed old Mosleyite in *The Whisper in the Gloom*, but they generally depend less on social or communal crime or reconstruction and the 'stake in the social system' that the novels radiate is often attenuated. He also, at times, backed into fictional legends attached to traditions he had earlier excoriated. *The Whisper in the Gloom*, *The Sad Variety* and some other novels had impossibly glorified British children, innovative and steadfast to the national interest under the most terrifying conditions, sometimes heroically adventurous as well in the tradition of *Boys' Own* fiction or Ballantyne's *Coral Island*. Blake's detective fiction of the thirties and forties remains as both a representation and a comment in popular terms of a time when many felt impending chaos survivable only through forms of potentially restrictive and destructive order. Like Blake, many felt the 1940 social release and survival in resistance to the most humanly debilitating forms of order a fortunate accident, although not without pain, deprivation and psychological cost. In particular, Blake's representation of the thirties remains a forceful fictional re-creation. Day Lewis did not see the thirties as Auden's 'low, dishonest decade, although they shared the common thirties metaphor of 'bad weather of the times'. Ethical, judgemental and didactic like Auden, although also softer and less searching, Day Lewis saw a decade that began in 'hope', the 'hope' that a relatively small group of the educated and sensitive could lead others to a more humane social recognition. But, he commented retrospectively, his generation 'had not vision equal to desire' in the 'tricky, darkening decade'[24], and could express their 'stake' only in resistance, sometimes itself chaotic and eccentric, to the powerful forms of order that destroy.

## NOTES

1.  Melvyn Barnes, entry on Anthony Berkeley, in John M. Reilly (ed.) *Twentieth Century Crime and Mystery Writers* (London and New York: Macmillan and St. Martin's Press, 1980) p. 118.
2.  Conversation with author, 20 April 1982.
3.  Sean Day-Lewis, *C. Day-Lewis: An English Literary Life* (London: Weidenfield & Nicolson, 1980) p. 147.
4.  Ibid., p. 102.
5.  Edmund Wilson, 'Who Cares Who Killed Roger Ackroyd?', reprinted in Robin W. Winks (ed.) *Detective Fiction: A Collection of Critical Essays* (Woodstock, Vermont: The Countryman Press, 1988) pp. 38–40.
6.  W. H. Auden, 'The Guilty Vicarage', reprinted in Winks (ed.), *Detective Fiction*, pp. 20, 23–4.
7.  C. Day Lewis, *The Buried Day* (London: Chatto & Windus, 1960) p. 202.
8.  Ibid., p. 47.
9.  Julian Symons, *Bloody Murder: From the Detective Story to the Crime Novel* (New York: Viking Penguin, 1985) p. 19.
10.  Nicholas Blake, introduction to Howard Haycraft, *Murder for Pleasure: The Life and Times of the Detective Story*, 1st edn (London: Peter Davies, 1942) p. xxii.
11.  Day-Lewis, *C. Day-Lewis*, p. 86.
12.  Ibid., p. 95.
13.  Ibid., pp. 168–9.
14.  Day Lewis, *The Buried Day*, p. 230.
15.  Day-Lewis, *C. Day-Lewis*, p. 134.
16.  Ibid., p. 66.

17. Day Lewis, *The Buried Day*, pp. 209–10.
18. Day-Lewis, *C. Day Lewis*, p. 101.
19. Day Lewis, *The Buried Day*, pp. 222–3.
20. Day-Lewis, *C. Day-Lewis*, p. 116.
21. Ibid., pp. 32–3, 36.
22. Ibid., p. 116.
23. Ibid., p. 145.
24. Day Lewis, *The Buried Day*, p. 217.

# 9

# L. P. Hartley and the Reverberations of Absence

To scan the fiction of L. P. Hartley for explicit reference to the world of the 1930s is to confront absence. He neither published fiction during the thirties, nor used the substance of the thirties in the historically located fiction he began to publish in 1944. Biographically as well, Hartley's thirties are routine and silence. Discharged from the army in the First World War because of a weak heart before his regiment went to France, he finished his degree at Oxford and began to write fiction in the 1920s. He published only a few stories, then a Jamesian novella set in Venice, *Simonetta Perkins* (1925). Living on an income from his father's investments, he spent the thirties reviewing others' fiction for periodicals. He had a house on the Avon near Bath; he also spent five months in Venice every year (the social months for the expatriate community, April, May, June, October and November). Although he apparently never wavered in his ambition to write fiction, he did not publicly articulate his world until after he was forced back to England by the Second World War. In his life, as in his fiction, the thirties, in fact the whole period between the wars, seems on the surface to have been one long evasion of experience.

In Hartley's later fiction, explicit historical reference is likely to be a generalisation that seems to stereotype or excoriate the modern world. In *The Betrayal* (1966), the principal character and point of view, Richard Mardick, introduces the subject of class divisions with 'a romantic feeling that amounted to reverence for such vestiges of the past as had survived the Great Divide of 1939' and sees younger people, those born in the twenties and thirties, 'reared on Freud', as all-knowing 'about inordinate affections between parents and children'. In *Eustace and Hilda* (1947), the prize-winning last novel of the trilogy that began Hartley's searching fiction, a friend of Eustace, the protagonist, writing

178

between the wars, tells him not to worry about his old allegiance to 'Moral Law: Marx undermined it and Freud has exploded it'. In Hartley's best-known novel, *The Go-Between* (1953), the narrator, Leo Colston, sixty-five in 1952, finds his diary of 1900, 'confidently heralded, the first year of the century, winged with hope', to recall the events of the crucial days surrounding his thirteenth birthday, events that have led to what another character calls this 'hideous century we live in, which has denatured humanity and planted death and hate where love and living were'. Leo recognises that 'the past is a foreign country: they do things differently there', and he leaps over the distance between 1952 and 1900, a narrative go-between now, as he was a naïve messenger between the different classes and loves of 1900. But the terrain under the leap, the crowded and disastrous years between, is empty. It is as if, for Leo Colston (typical of Hartley's principal characters), the events of 1900 established immutable consequences that were lived through the years, but never recognised and thus never voiced until long after. The whole period between the wars, the period of change itself, is silent.

The issue is not that Leo and other central Hartleyan fig-ures are committed to resisting change or necessarily regard the claims of the past to a more humane morality as valid. Rather, as James Hall has shown, in what is still the most discerning critical view of Hartley's fiction, the central figures in the later fiction demonstrate, in different ways, futile attempts to change or an accidental inflexibility that prevents them from being other than their long determined selves, fixed in patterns socially and historically locatable before the First World War. They can vary, in the comedy of different fictions, through the 'cycle of minor frustration to sense of persecution to absurd outbreak'.[1] These accidentally unaccommodating characters end by evading con-temporary experience or definitive choices as thoroughly as they can. The texture of the experience itself is left vague or trivialised, suspended outside time as only the characters' belated response is detailed. Historical context that might refer to change between the wars is a vast absence, but one that inferentially communicates. As Hartley's voice declares in another context in *The Betrayal*, when a dying man's wife abandons him, and someone complains that her abandonment shows a total absence of concern: 'But it *could* argue the presence rather than the absence of affection, don't you think so?' Hartley never resolves the argument. Throughout his fiction, in recognitions that find voice for characters moulded before the First World War only after the Second, the world between signifies primarily through its reverberatingly silent absence.

*The Go-Between* is historically the most precise and explicit of Hartley's novels. As Leo re-creates his diary from 1900, Hartley establishes a mock conflict between the two Leos, the naïve adolescent and the old man. The old man is tempted to charge the younger: 'you who let me down . . . you flew too near the sun, and you were scorched. This cindery creature is what you made me'. To which the younger, in imagination, 'might reply:' 'But you have had half a century to get over it! . . . half the twentieth century, that glorious epoch, that golden age that I bequeathed to you!' Yet there is only one Leo, one identity, fixed permanently in the hot July days of 1900. The language, point of view and metaphors, as the older Leo reads and recalls, are those of the young Leo, the adolescent seeking to control intensities of experience he cannot understand. Leo, staying at the manor house his schoolfriend's wealthy family rents, carefully chronicles the temperature several times each day, losing his initial confidence in the fact that 1900 will not be as hot a summer as 1899 during which Leo's father had died. As the mercury mounts, Leo tries to believe that his magic tricks (accidentally successful at school), might influence the heat, 'my dread of which was at least as much moral and hypochondriacal as physical'. Leo, poorer and lower in class than his friend, wears a heavy Norfolk jacket and knickerbockers, his only suit. His friend's older sister, the family beauty Marian, takes him to Norfolk, a distance he carefully measures by chronometer, to buy him a comfortable green summer suit. Leo becomes her 'Mercury', carrying her messages to establish clandestine meetings with the neighbouring local farmer, Ted Burgess, and also conveying messages from the owner of the manor, the ninth Viscount Trimingham, disfigured in the Boer War (Viscount Trimingham is a guest in the house he owns), to Marian to whom his engagement is shortly to be announced. Leo understands little of the implications of his messages (he asks Ted to explain what 'spooning' is), although as the heat escalates he wonders whether his careful measurements and his assignment of people to conventional characteristics of the zodiac, or his fantasy that he is Robin Hood in green devoted to the pure maid Marian, have little to do with adult experience. In weaving his magic spell to exercise control over a sexuality he cannot understand in either himself or in others, Leo rips up the plant of deadly nightshade that has concealed the lovers' meeting place, which, in addition to Leo's lies about time and his foolishly inept cover story to Marian's mother, leads to the disastrous discovery of the lovers. Leo never understands what he is doing and thinks of passion as a 'parasite of the emotions'.

Always conscious of class divisions and the clothes that represent them, convinced that 'what causes wars, what makes them drag on so interminably [is] the fear of losing face', Leo is also the messenger between classes, the go-between in the novel as metaphor for society. He is attracted to Ted's physical energy and instinctive knowledge, especially when he sees him naked after a swim. He also approves of Marian and her family's conviction that she must marry the kind, physically impaired Viscount Trimingham to create the unity of her money and his lineage. Leo tries to deny the influence of his own background, his late father's opposition to the Boer War and his unfamiliarity with family prayers, in his allegiance to his hosts. Accidentally, in the Hall versus Tenants cricket match, Leo makes the crucial catch of Ted's powerful drive that saves victory for the Hall. The servants regard Leo as a hero upholding society. But the social controls represented in cricket have little to do with social or sexual experience in a world about to be inundated in the Great War by the fissures in its fabric. Leo, the adolescent go-between, who has wondered about the nature of 'sin' and 'right and wrong', cannot handle his feeling, on his thirteenth birthday, that he has betrayed something significant. He suffers a serious breakdown. Before his mother is able to collect him from the Hall, he hears that Ted Burgess has killed himself in the aftermath of discovery.

Fifty-two years later, Leo is still emotionally as he was. He has never married or experienced passion, has held himself in a suspended adolescence apart from classes or emotions. Meditating on the 1900 diary, Leo revisits the town around the manor house to learn what had happened to the family, although he had known that his friend had been killed in the First World War. By accident, he meets the eleventh Viscount, Marian's grandson, and, looking at tombs and working out dates, he recognises that Marian married the ninth Viscount, although pregnant with Ted's child (she had, Leo realises in retrospect, communicated this to him, but he had not understood it). That child, the tenth Viscount, had been killed in the Second World War, his wife killed before him in a 1941 air raid. Leo visits Marian, the only survivor, who tells him that her marriage to the ninth Viscount had worked, that she could, had Ted only lived, have held sexual love, class and the lineage of the manor house together by the force of her being. But the wars and the half-century have dissolved that love and left nothing. Marian still wants Leo as her go-between, wants him to explain her intense physical love for Ted to her removed and evasive grandson, to tell him that he has 'nothing to be ashamed of . . . nothing mean or sordid in it . . . nothing that could possibly hurt anyone'. Leo understands for the first time. In a 1957 lecture, Hartley claimed that his 'original intention' in this epilogue had been 'to reveal Marian as an evildoer who had utterly demoralized Leo and ruined at least seven lives'.[2] But he knew that he had not done that, and that the epilogue, with its conclusively understated affect on Leo, reveals Marian, however arrogant and unconventional, as the only force of love or emotion left in the world after Ted was destroyed. Leo has learned about the half-century without love through which he has lived. The middle generation, the generation between the wars, is written off as entirely silent, uncommunicative, victims like Marian's son and daughter-in-law.

The metaphors that characterise Eustace, the figure of Leo-like stasis at the centre of the trilogy, indicate even less sense of control over identity than do Leo's adolescent forms of factual measurement. At the beginning of the first novel, *The Shrimp and the Anemone* (1944), nine-year-old Eustace, playing with his older sister Hilda in the rock pools along the beach, sees an anemone devouring a shrimp. He wonders what to do and calls the dominant Hilda, who pulls out and separates the creatures. By the time she rescues them, the shrimp is dead and the anemone has been disembowelled by the forcible separation. Eustace wishes they had let the creatures alone; Hilda is convinced they had to 'do something'. The episode itself is a metaphor for the disastrous symbiosis between the two children, in which the anemone, the vehement and decisive Hilda, consumes the passive floating shrimp. References to the metaphor dominate the first volume and continue, as brother and sister grow up, through *The Sixth Heaven* (1946) and *Eustace and Hilda*. In *The Shrimp and the Anemone*, the episodes are protracted simple incidents with every emotion between the two articulated, as in the one in which Hilda forces Eustace to be polite to an old invalid woman in a bath chair, who then invites him to tea frequently and, fond of the exquisitely polite boy, leaves him a fortune when she dies. This encourages their accountant father (their mother is dead) to send Eustace to a good school, to enable his rise in class, although in a link between the first two volumes called 'Hilda's Letter', Hilda attempts to keep Eustace from going to school to stay with her until she discovers plans to send her to school as well.

In the later two volumes, more crowded with incident, others try to adopt Eustace, to convert this amiable, passive being to some active course of life, but he is invariably drawn back into Hilda's protective orbit. He joins the army during the First World War, but Hilda arranges for his discharge, on grounds of a weak heart, before he is sent to France. Even though military routine had 'gone against his nature', Eustace had 'first consciously cultivated the stoicism of outlook, the mental habit of enduring rather than experiencing, of standing outside what was happening, which had seemed at the time not only helpful but noble'. The process of assigning himself virtue through passivity, evasion and self-effacement continues. At one point, when he is coming to meet Hilda (she has become the efficient administrator of a clinic, a 'Half-Way House' for those shell-shocked or emotionally impaired by the war, willingly financed by part of Eustace's inheritance), Eustace laboriously climbs a steep hill:

> the successive stages were like purifications of his personality; other associations were dismissed, competing preoccupations were sloughed off, and he would bring to the encounter a mind like a clean slate, charged with expectancy – if a slate could be. The interest of seeing whether he was before or behind his schedule – for Eustace, like many unpunctual people, was exceedingly time-conscious – also helped, in its humble way, the process of perlustration'.

Language like 'purification' and 'perlustration', as well as Eustace's childhood incantations to himself borrowed from the Anglican burial service, have led some critics to read the novel as 'the eternal conflict of puritan and hedonist revealed against a background of mysterious spiritual forces' and Hartley as using 'the story of Eustace to express his vision of the spiritual laws governing human existence'.[3] But no spiritual pattern of language or concept runs through the novel. Rather, such language and religious references are, like other tokens from the worlds of Oxford, society in Venice

or commercial activity, like the control over time itself, means for
Eustace to empty himself, to underline his absence of all except
the symbolic return to the childhood symbiosis with Hilda.

Neither Eustace nor Hilda achieves any mature form of sexual
relationship. Eustace is happiest in the social expatriate world of
literary Venice, a tepid, parasitic, superficially Jamesian enclosure,
in which, as Hartley describes it, gossip and malicious schemes for
pairing others substitute for any direct encounter. At one point
he meets a woman leaving an unhappy marriage, whom he had
known and liked as a child, with whom he had been lost in the
woods on a paper-chase, a rebellion which led to serious illness and
a rigidified return to Hilda's domination. His sympathy now elicits
the woman's confession and expression of her need for connection.
He, without understanding, offers to send her a cheque when she
had asked for help in sexual terms, and she leaves angry at the
rejection. Hilda, almost forced by Eustace to spend a weekend at
the country house of his most aristocratic friend – a reversal of the
pattern in which Hilda forces Eustace to reject experience – falls
in love with the aristocrat who plays a fierce game of billiards
and takes her up in his new flying machine (an example of the
post-war world that horrifies Eustace). The aristocrat is fond and
inconstant, as he always knows he will be. When he jilts Hilda,
she collapses into the safety of silent depression, cared for in a
bath chair by Eustace until he tricks and frightens her into mobility
and speech by staging what is almost an accident on the edge of a
cliff. Both Hilda and Eustace are contrasted to their younger sister,
more independent, active and not at all central to the novel. She
enjoys social life and friends, marries and has a child, and plays
no part in the deadening symbiosis.

The younger sister and her husband are the modern world after
the war. The husband is 'not at all like a character in Henry James,
definitely a representative of the Better Sort rather than the Finer
Grain'. He is interested in the 'engine room or the garage, a
creative messiness inseparable from energy and movement, in the
busy stir of which Eustace sometimes felt static and functionless
and outmoded, but he did not mind that'. Eustace's friends
from Oxford are also active in the modern world, but Eustace
evades the opportunity to work at criticism or scholarship on his
postgraduate fellowship by retreating to Venice, a world outside
contemporary time. He cultivates his reputation as an 'un-terrible
enfant terrible'. Nevertheless, he begins a few tentative gestures

toward autonomy. He writes a slight novel, to be published, and is pleased when his first nephew may be named 'Eustace' until he is recalled to care for Hilda in her depression. He can rescue her, but then sinks into weakness and vapid dream. In fantasy, he has even been part of Hilda's love affair, as in reality he has chosen her clothes. Whether the final dream of the shrimp and anemone from which 'he did not wake' is to be read as his literal death or as the triumph of the childhood metaphor hardly matters, for Eustace, asexual, can never emerge from the symbiosis or the evasion, never psychologically or historically participate in contemporary life.

The world after the First World War is more visible in *The Hireling* (1957) than in any of Hartley's other novels. The titular and principal character is Leadbitter, who, through the war and longer service rising to sergeant in the army, is now, some number of unspecified years later (Hartley is uncharacteristically imprecise in his only novel set between the wars), a skilful car-hire owner-driver. Whereas Ted Burgess in 1900, in *The Go-Between*, was physical energy without mind or mental courage (Marian later said 'if he'd had more brains he wouldn't have blown them out'), the urban working-class Leadbitter has the same energy and more courage held under the control of mind. He is described as 'formidable' and 'impassive', as a man and as a driver, using his skill and precise knowledge to convey his upper-class passengers through the shoals of the modern world: 'His figure looked as if it had been shaved. Aiming at correctness, he somehow achieved style; if the material was plebian, it had a patrician cut'. Described as if he were architecture, tangible form, he is punctual, unlike Hartley's upper-class characters, and is able to deal with all the messages, arrangements and re-arrangements of his business through the telephone. He is a 'staunch Conservative and voted for the very people he made fun of, not only because they were his bread and butter but because with all their faults they represented something that he himself was striving to attain'. He had liked the army which had liberated him from lower-class chaos into system and discipline. He also represents increasing mobility in the post-war class system. He saw 'life as a campaign' and 'opposition whetted his nature': 'Wherever he might be he wanted to take the next position, he had no interest in the terrain for itself, only in its possibilities for advance'. As he and Lady Franklin, his principal customer, begin to communicate on their long drives, she says that 'class-distinctions add richness to life . . . but there aren't any now'. Leadbitter silently thinks class distinctions still exist, and later, when she rejects the sexual advance that he thinks that she, in her sympathy, has invited, he explains to himself: 'She had pinned his ears back for him, she had wrapped the rolling pin round him, and all because he wasn't her class', despite her talking 'a lot of blah about classlessness'. As Hartley depicts the two, muted desire to transgress class through sexual contact is latent, although each is fixed in class attitudes. The sympathy between them is genuine. Lady Franklin, deeply depressed after the death of her husband, wants some kind of intimacy outside of class, which Leadbitter provides by inventing a wife (strangely like Lady Franklin, apart from class) and three children about whom he tells stories: 'He had no scruples in doing this because it was his principle to give his customers what they wanted'.

Lady Franklin also represents a cultural past. She has Leadbitter drive her to visit cathedrals, her attempts to displace sexuality and restore vitality through a nourishment of the spirit. She explains Henry Adams' *Mont St. Michel and Chartres*, the figure of the Virgin and the tenderness it incorporated into a 'vaguely masculine' Trinity. When she tells Leadbitter that the cult of the Virgin became 'a craze, a universal film-star, or pin-up girl, if that doesn't sound blasphemous', he replies, 'I'd like to know which film-star'. Despite this unbridgeable difference in specific referents, Leadbitter wants 'a spiritual affinity' with Lady Franklin, 'to be spiritually for a moment in her class', just as she wants a spiritual connection with his vitality, eventually asking him to visit the cathedral with her instead of estimating the length or height of architectural spans and collecting her punctually with the car. Symbolically, they strain toward each other, but she is still the creature of aesthetic apprehensions of a spiritual past and he still invests his emotions in the controls of contemporary mechanism. She gives him money to extend his prospering business with a new limousine, a 'gleaming symphony of black and chrome': 'It would be his friend, his wife, his mistress; he could lavish all his love on it without the fear that it would turn against him'. When events propel each away from contact with people, they respond to their isolation in characteristically different language. Lady Franklin regards 'Madness' as her 'friend' and 'Life' as her 'enemy', the betrayal of trying to reach outside the self. Leadbitter thinks of himself as a mechanism, his body undergoing a sort of metal fatigue: 'With his physical ear alert for noises that shouldn't be there – a creak, a rattle, a knocking – his inner ear couldn't quite disregard those warning symptoms in himself, much as his conscious mind might discount them'.

Events in the novel become dramatic as the pace accelerates. Encouraged toward active life by Leadbitter and his lies, despite her rejection of his sexual advance, Lady Franklin resumes social life and plans to marry an artist. Leadbitter has been driving the artist and his mistress to trysts at an inn in Richmond, and learns that the artist will use marriage to Lady Franklin, whom he sees as naïve and archaic, only for her money while he continues to see his mistress. Leadbitter, out of the web of his jealousy, his honesty, his continuing affection and 'spiritual affinity' for Lady Franklin, and his anger, writes her an anonymous warning letter. Since she believed his lies and rejected his honest sexual advance, he expects that she will never believe the truth. But she does and cancels the wedding. Leadbitter, learning this as he drives the artist and his mistress in his new car to another Richmond tryst, cannot handle the combination of guilt, anger, tense fatigue and love. He smashes the car, killing both the artist and himself. Lady Franklin, in despair, learns the story from the surviving mistress, and opening her wedding presents to return them, finds the St Christopher medal from his old car that Leadbitter had sent her. Although she recognises the tawdriness of the symbol in comparison to her cathedrals, she values it and kisses it, as Leadbitter had kissed it when he sent it to her. They communicate only through symbols, but the symbol may restore her to a kind of truncated life. In this novel, the present and the working classes have sacrificed themselves to enable the outmoded, sensitive and tenuous upper classes to survive a little longer. Hartley has provided by implication a searching, complicated description of the English class structure between the wars, the ways in which irremediably different classes use, abuse, understand and misunderstand each other. In regard to the period between the wars, socially and historically, despite or perhaps because of the melodrama of its last third, *The Hireling* is Hartley's most significant novel.

Lady Franklin, in her passivity, her mannered depression, and her inevitable adherence to a past, is much closer to central characters like Leo or Eustace than she is to other Hartleyan upper-class women. Or rather, Hartley's central upper-class males, in terms of the suggestions of gender description in his own language, are feminised, whereas only the central lower-class males like Leadbitter and Ted Burgess are Hartley's version of potent masculine figures. In most of the later fiction, the central consciousness is that of the aging, feminised, self-excoriating male, the Leo or Eustace, like Richard Mardick who moves through both *The Brickfield* (1964) and *The Betrayal*. Trapped well after the Second World War in a genteel and isolated posture that has existed since his youth before the First, Richard hires a parasitic younger man (whose pretensions to an old family and class position turn out to be false – in the new world, for Hartley, people lie about class which they never did in the old) to write his story. Although social life in the new world is more articulate and revealing than it used to be, the always weak-hearted Richard can only refer to the seminal incident in his own life, which took place when he was seventeen, in vague terms like sin, betrayal, or the 'shame of public exposure'. The story is his childish love affair with a girl who, frightened and thinking mistakenly that she was pregnant (neither even knew how conception takes place), committed suicide. Richard discovered the body in the brickfield his family owned and from which he has derived a considerable income for half a century. In fear, guilt and self-induced shame, he has been emotionally paralysed ever since. Even when, in *The Betrayal*, he meets the only woman who has since attracted him, who turns out to be the now fortyish half-sister of the girl dead before her half-sister was born, Richard cannot even tell the story. The story is a reticent, often concealed framework. The substance of most of the novel is egregiously comic description of all the various parasites and servants who psychologically assault, blackmail or manipulate Richard under the guise of caring for him in his aging weakness. Richard mixes appeals from his own dependency with comic versions of petulant, compulsive domestic protest and grumbles against the decline of class values and the Welfare State. Even in his moments of recognition, as in his realisation that his long evasion, impotence and generalised sense of sin and shame have always been based on a fear of sexual definition as male, Richard trivialises everything into what his principal parasite calls 'kitchen metaphor'. Richard's recognitions are conveyed in language like: 'Perhaps it's just today the lid has been taken off a saucepan that was always simmering'.

The modern world's chaos of servants and classes, misunderstandings and misappropriations, sexual roles and choices, and lies and deceptions is not restricted to the world after the Second World War. The same confusions, which can only intensify the isolation of Hartley's central figures, are conveyed in *The Boat* (1949), in which the aging and ludicrously naïve writer, Timothy Casson, forced to return to England in 1940 after eighteen years of genteel evasion in Italy, settles in the mock-typical English village of Upton-on-Swirrel. He tries to make himself the village lord that his economic and social position would warrant, to become a multiple 'go-between' and unify the village through a journey on his boat kept in his mock-Gothic boathouse with a stained glass window. The journey, as it ventures into a world that suggests insanity and incest, becomes comically ludicrous, as are Timothy's efforts to propel (efforts described with sexual imagery) or immolate the boat in a ceremony of sacrifice. He retreats from the dangers of contact with villagers into his essential passive isolation. The central isolate, the Hartley male figure of the middle or upper class, is always asexual, determined by vaguely seen adolescent or pre-adolescent experience in which heterosexual impulse leads to disaster. This produces a sad, ineffectual feminisation of the male figure and the displacement of all sexual impulse from males to females, as if only women have interest in or need for sexual contact. Only in fiction of his last decade does Hartley demonstrate homosexuality in his central figures. Richard, toward the end of *The Betrayal*, begins to see (and the narrator begins to direct attention towards) the genesis of his dependence on parasites as homosexual impulse, the desire to connect himself with others in the only way he can. The connections can't reproduce and they propel disaster; only fundamental isolation enables a survival that is quiet, slow suspiration eventually shocked into death from a weakened heart. A later novel, *The Harness Room* (1971), is more explicit in depicting a relationship between men that is both directly physical and an important contact between representatives of different classes. The prose of the attraction is fulsome and heavy, devoid of Hartley's characteristic comic stringency, self-castigation and complexity. Evasion seems to have been both Hartley's story and his particular literary grace.

Historically, the centre of Hartley's evasion was the period between the two world wars during which he published little and set few of his fictional re-creations. Mostly by implication, this period for Hartley represents changes in conceptions of sexuality and class structure of which his figures are aware and to which they are unable, despite intention and desire, to accommodate. Almost the only resolution is silence, a silence that cannot find voice until it is surrounded by a texture of lies, deception and misapprehension that characterise the sounds of a post–1940 world looking back. Yet the post–1940 cacophony enables the recognition of what the twenties and thirties were, enables Hartley's brilliant articulation of silence and isolation, of those human beings unable to accommodate change or history, or love for that matter. James Hall sees Hartley's work concentrated into 'the comedy of a particular despair . . . – the wish to be someone else'.[4] It is also the despair of a particular period in history that, for Hartley, could have no voice. The centre of the changes of all contact with society, both individual or physical and social, the period reverberated in silence in Hartley's literary world. At the centre of the silence, like Lady Franklin at the end of *The Hireling* without the tawdry and aleatory St Christopher's medal that Leadbitter sends, lies a deeper and unassuageable despair. Whereas for other of Hartley's literary contemporaries, writers like Rosamond Lehmann, Nicholas Blake, Elizabeth Bowen and Henry Green, 1940 signified a release from despair, a release into sexuality or other forms of social commitment under the most terrifying circumstances, for Hartley the release of 1940 was release into writing, into creating fictions, the discovery of the capacity to understand and articulate his personal and public historical silence.

## NOTES

1. Hall, *The Tragic Comedians*, p. 114.
2. Edward T. Jones, *L. P. Hartley* (Boston: G. K. Hall, Twayne Publishers, 1978) p. 108.
3. David Cecil, 'Introduction' to *Eustace and Hilda: A Trilogy* (London: Putnam, 1958) pp. 8–9.
4. Hall, *The Tragic Comedians*, p. 112.

# 10

# Essays, Chronicles and Fiction: Alternatives to Despair

As some of the foregoing discussion has indicated, mutually exclusive distinctions between fact and fiction, or between the essay and the novel, can narrow the significance of reference to the literary and social climate. The essay and that form of fiction sometimes close to the essay, the chronicle, emphasise the tangible, direct, socially referential language that novelists sought to bring into fiction. Some writers of the period go further in blurring conventional distinctions between essay and fiction, in formal terms, in their own definitions of their careers, and in the acknowledgement, implicit or explicit, that essays and novels both mix fact and fiction in the author's attempt to communicate her or his version of experience. The blurring of distinctions between literary forms is also, for some in the thirties, an anti-modernistic gesture, a deliberate counter-movement to what they, accurately or not, saw as a modernistic tendency to separate art from life, or artist from audience. The range and diversity of this literary representation of experience might best be seen through the language and concerns of three women influential during the 1930s: Rose Macaulay, Rebecca West and Storm Jameson. All wrote novels, essays, reports and chronicles throughout long careers; none was as great a novelist, as probing and intense in her representations of language, as were Elizabeth Bowen or Rosamond Lehmann. All were also slightly older than Bowen or Lehmann, were women who never connected their sense of sexual liberation with the First World War and its aftermath. Macaulay, West and Jameson, each advanced or accepted a designation of herself as the 'new' woman before or during the First World War. Each advocated, for herself and

191

others, the right to independent careers, aversion to a definition
of woman dependent on domesticity, and the freedom to choose
lovers without the sanctions of marriage (whatever the guilts
and ambivalences involved). Although sexual relationships and
definitions dependent on gender comprise much of the material
of their literary work, these are seen as changing less than did the
meanings of the larger society, the representations of class and
nation. As commentators on intelligent and autonomous women
within a context of a fractured and dangerous social and political
world, Macaulay, West and Jameson were both representative and
influential parts of the literary culture.

The oldest of the three, Rose Macaulay had published fiction
and poetry before the First World War. Daughter of a well-known
medieval scholar (with seven children, none of whom married),
she wrote learned Anglo-Catholic novels and was friendly with
Rupert Brooke. The First World War, in which so many of her
friends were killed (and a brother had, before the war, been
murdered while serving in India), transformed her entirely. She
began a love affair with a novelist and former priest, who had left
the Church to marry (and never divorced his wife), that lasted until
his death in 1942; still fascinated with High Church learning and
lore, she became what she called an 'Anglo-agnostic'.[1] Her fiction
became sharply satirical and quick, as she achieved a reputation
as representing the generation of young women disenchanted by
the war. She wrote a three-generation family chronicle called *Told
by an Idiot* (1923), which runs from 1879 to 1920. Every few years,
the mild, benign, prelatical head of the family changes his religion,
back and forth between High Church, Low Church and no church,
the chronicle beginning with the announcement that 'Poor papa
has lost his faith again'. Within this context, the children represent
different religious and aesthetic positions in response to historical
change, although Macaulay concentrates on the women and the
meanings of 'new' women. The perspective is always distant, from
the accounts of 'solemn', 'earnest', university-educated young
women of the eighties to the principal daughter, named Rome:

> fastidious, *mondaine*, urbane, lettered, critical, amused, scep-
> tical, and what was called in 1890 *fin-de-siecle*, . . . It is not a
> type which, so to speak, makes the world go round; it does
> not assist movements nor join in crusades; it coolly distrusts
> enthusiasm and eschews the heat and ardour of the day. It

is to be found among both sexes equally, and is the stuff of which the urbane bachelor and spinster, rather than the spouse and parent, are made. For mating and producing (as a career, not as an occasional encounter) are apt to destroy the type, by forcing it to too continuous and ardent intercourse with life; that graceful and dilettante aloofness can scarcely survive such prolonged heat.

Other women follow, equally distant from, evasive about, or disillusioned by sexuality, witheringly avoiding domesticity or maternity.

Macaulay's attitudes toward female experience change less over time than does the manner in which history is conveyed through language. In *Told by an Idiot*, in a style reminiscent of Defoe's, history is the light, rapid survey, full of quick references to entities like the concentration camps during the Boer War. Religions are described by tag: 'Ethicist', 'Irvingite'. The distance and framework invite comedy, although the language itself is often not comic. History is distilled into simple or absurd cause, like attributing the origins of the First World War to 'an attack of megalomania on the part of Servia in 1909' abetted by the 'inefficiency' of the Liberal government in England between 1910 and 1914:

> Those were inefficient years; silly years, full of sound and fury, signifying nothing . . . by Welsh churchmen, who marched through London declaring that on no account would they have their church either disestablished or disendowed . . . by Liberals and Conservatives, who, for some reason, suddenly . . . took on to dislike each other, even leaving dinner parties to which members of the opposition party had been carelessly invited.

The war itself is 'too desperate' a folly. After the war, the peace is 'horrid', the treaty 'patchwork, violent, militarist, manufactured, makeshift, frail, silly, uneconomic, unstatesmanlike; and all the names except the last may be true'. The novel ends with a jibe at those pretentious enough to talk of recent events as 'the wreckage of civilisation, as if it mattered much, as if civilisations had not been wrecked and wrecked all down human history'. Macaulay's language has been described as an influence on Virginia Woolf's method of writing history in *Orlando*(1928)[2], although Woolf's style is thicker with referential and symbolic meaning as well as more comically outrageous and absurd, characters who live for over three hundred years, undergoing a change in sex halfway through. Macaulay's version of the technique is thinner, more conventional as in the eighteenth-century comic novel. Macaulay and Woolf were close and respected one another's fiction.[3]

The pace of Macaulay's comedy slows, the absurdity intensifies, and the focus is more topical and particular in Macaulay's well-respected novel of the thirties, *Going Abroad* (1934). Macaulay's view had never been insular, for the English in *Told by an Idiot* had looked at the European world, even if only to deplore the 'violent attack of Fascismo' in Italy. As part of the 1930s' greater recognition that Europe is important, that England can no longer be insular, tourism is both a social necessity and an object of ridicule in *Going Abroad*. History is represented, not surveyed. The central characters, a bishop and his wife, are travellers who hope, in the wake of the barbarism of the First World War, to extend knowable geography to distinguish barbarism from civilisation. The bishop's scholarly wife dreams of reconstructing Eden in her 'dry Mesopotamian imagination', but they can only manage a trip to the Basque country where she thinks she may find the Basques Edenic because they eat fruit all day. They begin, too, with a slightly modified version of the difference between Spain and France in Hemingway's earlier representation in *The Sun Also Rises*, the corrupt materialism, without soul, that in France as well as in the rest of a superficially civilised Europe is the legacy of the First World War contrasted to an elemental human purity, in which money is irrelevant, in a medieval Spain fortunately exempted from both the war and the growing bourgeois industrial civilisation of several centuries. Macaulay's version is more complicated than Hemingway's (although still different from that of the Auden Generation only a few years later which saw Spain as the crucible of the political struggles of modern Europe). In Macaulay's satire, corruption has reached the tourist-clogged beaches of Spain, creating a 'Spanish Blackpool', and, with bad roads, it is difficult to reach the interior which distinguishes the 'wild medieval Spain from safe, cheerful, twentieth-century France'. The Basques are divided and corrupt, represented by a couple (originally from warring factions within the Basque culture) who have made a fortune by establishing beauty salons all over Europe. The plot is propelled into absurdity when a whole busload of English tourists is kidnapped and held hostage because of rival Basque claims to the fortune of the beauty salon operators. Religious history is represented in the satire of other tourists, a large convention of young Buchmanites with their international visions of Moral Rearmament. Depicted as even more fatuous and ignorant than the solemn, earnest young university women of the 1880s, the Buchmanites 'flourish in Geneva' for the Swiss are 'more successful than the League of Nations'. They can work immediate 'change' and conversion: 'Communists, Fascists, everyone, melting the barriers between black and white, Swede and Dane, Frenchman and German, Russian and Pole, Aryan and non-Aryan, Oxford and Cambridge'. The young in the thirties, with no memory of a world before 1914, are far more easily swayed by communism, fascism or Buchmanism, than is the older generation.

Although references and attitudes changed in Macaulay's later fiction, the comic historical style she developed in the 1930s remained. So did the sense of experience as an irresolvable conflict between the barbarous and the civilised. Like many others after the Second World War, she saw, with self-undercutting humour, a little England representing a small repository of civilisation. In *The World My Wilderness* (1950), she wrote from the point of view of a young English woman raised amidst the cosmopolitan fractures of class, divorce and religious division under the 'barbarous sun' of France who finally locates more significant meaning for herself, which involves surprising images of domesticity, under cold cloudiness among the ruins that circled St Paul's. Macaulay is again less insular in her last, and, for most readers, her best novel, *The Towers of Trebizond* (1956), set in the framework of a contemporary Anglican mission to convert Islamic women to Christianity. The picaresque novel begins with an account of church history, a comedy of the misunderstandings and absurdities of religious colonial impositions of Europe on the Middle East, of missionary cannibalism and of the cultural recognitions broadened by travel. Ridiculous details sustain serious themes; carefully developed arguments, on preposterous premises, are reduced by final trivia.[4] Politics and religious sects mix in the world of the 1950s, as commandoes are seen as a Roman Catholic underworld, remnants of storm troopers as militantly Protestant, and Yugoslavs as atheists. One woman's missionary husband had been killed in Africa and she made part of a tribal chief's harem. When asked how she escaped, she replies: 'One of the wives who didn't want me to wait till the chief came back, bribed one of the tribe to take me away into the jungle and kill me. But he was afraid to do this, as I was a goddess, so he showed me a path out of the forest that led to a Baptist missionary settlement'. Later, she and an Anglican priest wander into Russian territory to fish and are assumed to be spying, held for months until their political irrelevance is realised. This allows Macaulay to expand on the Christian significance of fish, their connection with the souls of human beings, as well as on the tradition of eighteenth-century hunting/fishing parsons. The woman's niece, recalls the history of 'the broad Anglican river' when 'we persecuted Papists, conventiclers and Quakers with great impartiality'. She draws the strands of her random thought together: 'It is not, therefore, strange that we should have inherited a firm and tenacious adherence to the Church of our country. With it has come down to most of us a great enthusiasm for catching fish . . . perhaps . . . a slight confusion between the words Anglican and angling'. The niece conflates forms of being as well as religious sects. She empathises with the neurotic camel who carries her over desert territory in the Middle East. Back in 'spoilt' England, she teaches her ape to drive and to play chess, croquet and tennis. Her ape is a better driver than she, for, at the end of the novel, she causes an accident that kills her lover. She concludes by recalling the dimly seen, never assimilated or converted, grandeur of the towers of Trebizond, the representation of Islam valued and never understood that is suspended over the historical, religious and feeble human activity of the novel. For Macaulay, civilisation is futile and irrelevant, an often kind-hearted imposition on less knowable and controllable forms of being. The thirties is the point of extreme fatuity, that at which the presumably civilised were unaware of their hypocrisies and assumed they could exercise knowledgeable control over their world. Later Macaulay characters are no wiser, but at least they and their comically respected religions acknowledge how little truth and meaning their generously intended institutions contain. Pain, darkness and beauty remain just beneath the civilised, detailed and ritualistic surface on which Macaulay's characters live.

Rebecca West could never have so thoroughly undercut a sense of mission she invented for herself. A suffragist, a literary journalist interested in social and political ideas, and a consciously liberated woman, all before she was twenty, West early demonstrated a committed interest in all forms of literature. Her first published book, *Henry James* (1916), was literary criticism which combined a discerning view of James as a modernist artist (a view that her lover, H. G. Wells, did not always share, as had been evident in his long exchanges with James on distances between life and art) with objections to what she saw as James's sympathetic condescension to women, as if they were imprisoned within their sexual sensitivities. She published a novel, *The Return of the Soldier* (1918), a woman's view of the war. The persona is that of a young woman whose cousin is a soldier and who is living, during the war, with the soldier's wife. At first, the persona and the wife are almost identical: 'Disregarding the national interest and everything except the keen prehensile gesture of our hearts toward him, I wanted to snatch my cousin Christopher from the wars and seal him in this green pleasantness his wife and I now looked upon'. The persona is more vividly imaginative: 'By night I saw Chris running across the brown rottenness of No Man's Land, starting back because he had trod upon a hand'. The difference between the women is magnified when the soldier returns maimed not in body, but in mind. In amnesia, he forgets his wife entirely and recalls an earlier attraction to the daughter of a pub-keeper he had known before he married, a woman who might be seen as 'not so much a person as an implication of dreary poverty like an open door in a mean house that lets out the smell of cooking cabbage and the screams of children' The book becomes the contrast between the persona who can understand personally and socially what the war has done to England and the conventional wife mystified in both emotional and class-bound terms by what the war has done to her husband. The characterisations never deepen, and one feels as if one is reading an interesting essay about a perceptive woman's view of the war's affect on English men and society. The novel as form is never exploited.

West wrote fiction and literary journalism throughout the twenties and into the thirties. She wrote of art, people and places, political ideas and events. In her essays, she mixed art, history and politics, as an early 1936 obituary of Kipling combined astringent literary and social criticism with recall of the dead glories of Empire that stretched back to the international panoply and parades she watched, as a child, at Queen Victoria's Diamond Jubilee in 1897. Although arguing for democratic self-determination, and at times strongly attracted to British socialism, she regarded the monarchy as significantly representative. She was publicly furious with Edward VIII's abdication in 1936, not because of moral disapproval

of Mrs Simpson, divorces or Americans, but because of the King's
'paucity of being', his mind so like 'a telephone exchange with
not enough subscribers' that he had abdicated all responsibility.[5]
According to her biographer, Victoria Glendinning, she always had
'an addiction to exotic genealogy', a legacy from her father, and
even in old age 'would trace' her family's 'exiguous connections
with noble families all over the British Isles'.[6] Throughout the
twenties, she had written discerningly and sympathetically about
old Fabians in London, expatriates in France and intellectual Jews
in the literary, theatrical and commercial worlds of New York. She
never followed the stereotypes that seem to separate Bohemian
artists from the respectable and prominent, and in 1930 married
a wealthy, international business man, Henry Andrews. They
began, propelled by both his business affairs and her interest in
social and political organisation, to travel frequently to Germany
and Switzerland, to move towards Central and Eastern Europe,
which she saw as both the locus of impending conflict and the
origin of a world of conflict, the First World War.

Rebecca West was simultaneously engaged in writing stories
and novels. Her most ambitious attempt to fit her experiences
and observations into fiction was *The Thinking Reed* (1936). The
novel establishes a Jamesian situation through the perspective
of Isabel, a young American widow living in Paris. The first
half is crowded with Parisian detail, touristic jaunts, restaurants,
salons and furnishings that protect Isabel from contemporary life
around her. Even when out of doors, waiting to meet a lover, she
chooses 'a table on the terrace, for she knew he would want to
eat out there where the trellis wall shut out all the urban lower
part of the landscape, with its babies and nurses and seats and
gravel walks, and admitted only the full-foliaged tree-tops and the
bright crest of the fountain spray'. Bohemians and conventionally
seen Parisians are also satirised: expatriates, bored and wealthy
women filled with fashionable *anomie*, international playboys,
corrupt financial speculators. Isabel is initially a voice of 'reason',
which propels withdrawal instead of encouraging the desire of
Jamesian female protagonists to participate more fully in life. As
the novel moves from the late twenties into the thirties, Isabel
recognises that 'reason' cannot control experience, and that she
is moved by deeper imperatives like a desire to have a child,
her attraction to men and violence, her descents into what she
thinks of as a kind of madness. She marries a wealthy Jew and

begins to understand social antagonism and jealousy for the first time. When she and her husband recognise their responsibility for their child's death, she experiences unassuageable pain and loss. Simultaneously, the impinging world becomes more crowded with conflicting politics, organised violence, the moral decay of the French, the pious hypocrisy of the English, economic conflict, and organisations that depend solely on national or tribal loyalties. Self-pity generates most emotions. Only a painter looks for meaningful coherence in experience, yet he remains focused on photographs and artifacts, pale and derivative substitutes for what once might have been the Jamesian art that represented the whole experience. Although symptomatic of the same disorder, the social and political observations never connect with the theme of Isabel's disillusion with sensitivity and 'reason'. Stacked with or against each other, both seem interesting simplifications of novelistic form. The novel becomes, as novel, thesis-ridden and crowded with the excessive detail it excoriates. It is a critical use of James that seems, inadvertently, to violate or render useless the Jamesian form of the novel, not the parody that qualifies and extends, but the relentlessly forced adaptation that reads as if it is not a novel at all. Rebecca West was far more a later, female version of H. G. Wells than a later James.

West herself recognised the inadequacy of her attempt in *The Thinking Reed*. She referred to it as her 'French novel' after she had come to think that France, much as she loved it, was bloated and arid, showing only the deleterious influences of money and of men on women.[7] Later, in an epilogue to her next book, she thought of it as superficial, without empathy for her characters, and entirely exterior, 'a novel about rich people to find out why they seemed to me as dangerous as wild boars and pythons'.[8] That next book was *Black Lamb and Grey Falcon* (1941), an extended account of her journeys through Yugoslavia in 1936 and 1937, her best, most searching and most influential work in and of the 1930s. Within the framework of the journey, the attempt to live within another culture, she found room for a coherent transformation of her personal, social and political sensitivities, her facts and fictions, into her own form of art that both expressed herself and represented a form particularly meaningful for the decade. Casting herself as the 'thinking reed' (quoted from Pascal in a passage that defines the human being as a 'reed, the most feeble thing in nature, but . . . a thinking reed'), West begins, in the prologue, with a long history of the Balkans. Much of the history, especially of the nineteenth century, is royal history, royalty as a representation that tries either to assimilate or separate the regional, ethnic and religious strains in Balkan culture. Since the subject intrinsically is the clash between civilisation and barbarism, she focuses on royal assassinations, especially those of the Empress Elizabeth in 1898 and the Austrian Archduke Franz Ferdinand in Serbia in 1914. The pattern did not end with the First World War, and she spends many pages on the ethnic and political conflicts that led to the murder of King Alexander I of Yugoslavia while on a visit to France in 1934. She is constantly interested in leadership and national or ethnic representation, seeing it in the faces or gestures of world figures as she watches them in newsreels. She describes the religious, national and social conflicts, past and present, of Serbs, Croats, Hungarians and Czechs. She often works through her guides, educated men who themselves represent the strains in Yugoslav society and take her on difficult tours to the mountainous interiors as well as the cathedrals. Her relations with her guides are variously personal as well, attractions and long talks reported. She is interested in how they see a knowable and presumably civilised West in contrast to Turks or Arabs, or a hegemony of the unknowable East where 'some were still candid in their enjoyment of murder'. One guide is a poet, a Serbian Jew with a German wife; another is a Croat, a Slav member of the Roman Catholic Church; a third is another Croat, loyal to Croatia, a critic who is both agnostic and attracted to the Orthodox Church. West is constantly interested in religion both as doctrine and as the sociology of various sects and churches connects to politics and attitudes towards violence. Her own religious attitudes emerge throughout the book, and are represented in its title. She is horrified by animal sacrifice, the sight of a black lamb sacrificed in the bloody ritual of a Muslim fertility rite, a symbol of violence and cruelty. At the same time, like D. H. Lawrence, she objects to the concept of self-sacrifice built into modern Christianity, the images that cluster around Christ's willing sacrifice for others, the sanctity of Christians 'bleating' about the blood of the lamb. Her image of the grey falcon comes from a Serbian poem about a fourteenth-century battle the Serbs lost to the Turks. Given a choice of reigning on earth or in heaven, the Serbian prince chooses heaven and his forces are destroyed by the Turks, civilisation sacrificing itself in sanctity. Black lamb and grey falcon represent traditions opposed to each other, and they both, as visible in contemporary Yugoslavia, are destructive.

West also, throughout the book, sees Yugoslavia as a metaphor for the current European crisis. Black lambs represent Nazis, destructive, barbaric (West began writing fiercely critical articles about the Nazis and their forms of order before Hitler came to power); grey falcons are the ambivalently civilised West, its gods of self-defeat, and fears that the West may sacrifice itself rather than oppose and eradicate the Nazis. Yugoslavia also signifies in other ways. The omnipresence of its ethnic strains, its difficult terrain and its legacy of violence are a naked assertion of the problems of twentieth-century Europe. Unlike England or France, encrusted with monuments to past triumphs, with furniture of the civilised, Yugoslavia has few monuments, few demonstrations of the triumphs of civilisation. Yugoslavian cities show 'the appalling lack of accumulation observable in history, the perpetual cancellation of human achievement, which is the work of a careless and violent nature'. Through her growing historical and contemporary knowledge of the horrors and violence of one culture imposing itself on another, Rebecca West also learned more surely the limitations of Empire, became less insular than she had thought herself:

> I became newly doubtful of empires. Since childhood I had been consciously and unconsciously debating their value, because I had been born a citizen of one of the greatest empires the world has ever seen, and grew up as its exasperated critic. Never at any time was I fool enough to condemn man for conceiving the imperial theory, or to deny that it had often proved magnificent in practice. In the days when there were striking inequalities among the peoples of the earth . . .

She defends the knowledge of agriculture, industry, social organisation and justice that the British, at their best, introduced into more barbaric societies. Although 'the theory of the British Empire that it existed to bring order into the disordered parts of the earth was more than half humbug', it lead to actions against plagues, floods and cruelties that sometimes helped subject peoples. Still, Yugoslavia and the 1930s taught West that the benefits of Empire were no longer, if they had ever been, worth the imposition:

But I saw in British imperialism room for roguery and stupidity as well as magnificence. A conquered people is a helpless people; and if they are of different physical type and another culture from their conquerors they cannot avail themselves of anything like the protection which would otherwise be given them by the current conceptions of justice and humanity.

British civilisation must defend itself against other barbarisms, like the one represented by the Nazis, but not risk becoming itself barbaric by imposing on others.

When it was published in 1941, *Black Lamb and Grey Falcon* became highly controversial within both the British press and the foreign policy establishment. By that time, the war had begun and Hitler was invading Balkan territory. The controversies centred on deciding which factions or leaders deserved aid because they were honestly anti-Nazi, and many knowledgeable people did not agree with West's definitions and formulations.[9] Nevertheless, few in the literary or political worlds challenged West's axiom that an understanding of Yugoslavia and the Balkans was central to an understanding of the European conflict that had begun in 1914 and, as seen increasingly throughout the thirties, was not over yet. Those of the Auden Generation, younger, only in their own thirties when the decade ended, might see the necessary locus of the decade in Spain, in a war that they, to some extent, knew they were fabricating into the necessary struggle between fascism and communism, and for which some honest intellectuals sacrificed their lives. But those just slightly older, with a sentient and conscious memory of the First World War, like Rebecca West and Storm Jameson, still in their forties when the 1930s ended, whatever their politics or attraction to ideology, recognised that the significant locus for unresolved and perhaps unresolvable European conflict was the Balkans, the origin and the continuation of European anguish. Travel was important for all British writers of the thirties, recognition of the necessity, mental and physical, to avoid the insularity of England. But the motives and impulses toward Spain, that country mercifully or mercilessly exempt from the pain and problems of the First World War, seem an ideological abstraction in comparison to the conflicts, cultural fractures, violence and ambivalence about the connections between ideology and social fact visible in the Balkans.[10] Some of the Auden Generation did describe the Balkans, as John Lehmann wrote biographically of his travels with his eldest sister, Helen, around Bratislava, through the Slovakian hills and the Hungarian Plain to Budapest and Belgrade.[11] Elizabeth Bowen also saw the phenomenon of Balkan travel as sufficiently significant to treat it satirically as the enterprise of her off-beat, incompetent travel agency. Members of the Auden Generation, too, early recognised the importance of learning about Germany and Austria, looking sometimes toward the East. But, for the most part, a recognition of the singular importance of the Balkans in the 1930s, a theme and focus that interested a large segment of the literate and politically concerned audience, was left to writers slightly older than the Auden Generation who had an older concept of Spain and did not see it as the crucible of the decade's issues.

Using the same techniques, the mixture of fact and fiction, the public detail and the private relationship, and the framework of an actual event, West's other major work, based on the Nuremberg trials, was *The Meaning of Treason* (published in 1947 in the US, 1949 in Britain, and updated in 1952 and 1964). The work attempted to explore the meanings of treason or political betrayal of a democratic state or a concept of humanity. The updates treated the violations of humanity by communists as well as by Nazis, and, again, her work generated public and private controversy. The references were consciously placed in the immediate worlds of the late forties and fifties, but the terms, the sense of the human and individual betrayal involved in active commitment to political ideology, arose from the 1930s, as did the form of the extensive report enhanced by the inclusions of fiction, history, personal experiences and perspectives, the human and vulnerable material that deepens meaning and avoids apocalypse. The form itself, in its mixtures and qualifications, in both *Black Lamb and Grey Falcon* and in *The Meaning of Treason*, becomes a defence of humanity and survival, is axiomatically non-apocalyptic, itself a counter to hope and despair, as West herself, in the thirties, shared neither the extravagant hopes nor the total despair of some of her contemporaries. She continued to write fiction, essays and reminiscences to the end of her long life. Some of the fiction, influenced by *The Meaning of Treason*, sustains considerable interest. *The Birds Fall Down* (1966), uses meanings of treachery and betrayal, public and private, that she had developed to create a comprehensive history, through royalty and others, of what led to the 1917 Russian revolution. In a sense, she gives communism a particular and historical locus. The

Cousin Rosamund novels, projected as a trilogy but never finished
(*The Fountain Overflows* was published in 1957, the second novel,
*This Real Night*, posthumously in 1984), were similar comprehensive records of public and private worlds, focused on justice and
community, that traced the history of England from late in the
nineteenth century through the First World War. In these, the
furniture seems to overwhelm the form of the novel, the record,
fascinating as it is, to inundate the complexity and shape of the
novel. Anachronistic intrusions needlessly break down the art, as
in *This Real Night* a narrative voice interrupts a scene describing
influences of the First World War on a middle-class family to
say 'The First World War did not suddenly turn on civil life
and strangle it as the. Second did' and then immediately return
to the description. The interest in the history, the details, the facts
and the fiction remain; so does the conviction that West's most
significant form and commentary came through the framework of
the extensive historical report.

   Almost an exact contemporary – and equally committed to writing
that combined the personal and the sociopolitical – Storm Jameson
also worked out her own different version of non-apocalyptic
form. For Jameson, as well as West, the 1930s was the most
significant decade, in terms of her audience, her skill and the
attitudes central to her work. Like West, Jameson began in literary
journalism before the First World War (her academic thesis on the
Romantic poets was never published and her first publication was
an attack on Shaw as already dated in Orage's *The New Age* in
1913), and she wrote and published fiction from the beginning.
In her constantly rigid self-appraisal, she placed little value on
her novels of the century's teens and early twenties. Only in the
later twenties did she begin the form in which she wrote best, the
vast chronicle or series of novels through which a set of characters,
seen through a single narrative voice, replicate nearly contemporary
experience. In a form like that in which John Galsworthy was
working in the twenties, Jameson developed a series of seven
novels, none of them conclusive, through the persona of Mary
Hervey Russell, a young woman making her way in the literary
and commercial worlds of contemporary London who is always
conscious of her inheritance as the descendant of her grandmother,
a strong, tyrannical head of the family ship-building firm in the
north-east of England. Jameson developed her non-apocalyptic
form through the early thirties, calling the whole series *The*

*Mirror in Darkness*. At her confident moments, she thought her
aims like those of Balzac, recording a continuous human comedy.
The chronicle is, formally, infinitely expandable. Immersed in the
details of experience, both the individual and the world outside, the
chronicle could logically end only in the death of the persona, when
another persona or another generation can take over the narration.
In her autobiography, Jameson claimed that only fatigue stopped
the series, 'that Balzacian monster I abandoned in 1935, and my
shadow'.[12]

Although beginning to write for *The New Age*, Jameson thought
her work anti-modernist, as following older forms of fiction and
avoiding the arcane and metaphorical prose she thought modernism involved. She was pleased when, in 1920, Galsworthy called
her second novel, *The Happy Highways*, the best new fiction of
the past decade, even though she was retrospectively not very
well pleased by the novel itself.[13] Almost half a century later, she
still saw Joyce as 'uprooting established forms to create a waste
land, a great anti-humanist . . . writers who give themselves up to
the disintegration of language are, so far as they know, innocent
of the impulse to destroy civilisation'.[14] The language of Storm
Jameson's autobiography is virtually identical with the language
of her novels. This is not to say that there is no difference between
fact and fiction, for she always signals awareness of her own
and her personas' vulnerability to distortion, their reticence about
events and attitudes that may embarrass friends and relatives, and
their texture of guilts and denials that infuse both fiction and
autobiography. Both forms, however, avoid relentlessly whatever
might be interpreted as a sign of high or self-conscious art. Jameson
was dedicated to the conviction that artistic gestures and shapes,
like human language, require a directness, a distance from the self
and a lack of pretense. As the persona Hervey explains, in *Love
in Winter* (1935), when she recalls the falsities and inadequacies
of her earlier writing:

> There is only one book worth writing – not to cheat, but to record
> every item in the tale of mistakes, jobs, cruelties, and simple
> meannesses that make up our dealings one with others, then to
> write down the total, hand it in, and clear off without making a
> fuss. She knew that she had not the head for this. Even the book
> she was now writing was false. She kept at it from obstinacy and
> a sort of pride. And to have something to show her mother.

One of the items chronicled throughout Jameson's work is women's literary life itself, the journals, the editorial decisions, the novels everyone is writing, the connections with literary men and the advertising agencies in which they work to support their talent. Storm Jameson and Rebecca West saw themselves as rivals in the small literary-journalistic world before the First World War. Jameson apparently turned down the offer of a minor part-time editorial job that West gratefully accepted. But West's early concept of a Jamesian art was alien to Jameson, and she wrote that Jameson's third novel, in the early twenties, had no taste, which 'is incurable'.[15] Jameson, at least retrospectively, thought West was right at the time, although she had 'painfully' cured it. Issues of class and the sexuality of the liberated woman also crowd the fiction. Jameson's young literary women are always conscious of their origin in the grim, repressed, middle-class North, attracted to men who are wealthier, softer, more wandering and aimless, likely to squander talent or pose as more involved than they are. Hervey's crucial and representative mistake, before the First World War, is to fall in love with and marry Penn (duplicitous, content to linger for years in his wartime job as an equipment officer who never leaves England until his wealthy parents decide they might finally send him to Oxford), a version of her mother's mistake, more than twenty-five years earlier, in marrying a feckless sea-captain just because he sails around the world. Hervey has the strength to rectify her mistake, although she makes others and is often almost paralysed by guilt; her mother, in the grim northern world of a slightly earlier time, never does and is never reconciled to her own mother who fiercely disapproved all along. Less guilty, less responsible, more entirely free women writers are, as in a novella called *Delicate Monster* (1937), likely to be satirised as 'vulgar': 'the first female novelist to have a public career equaling in interest the career of a Ziegfield Follies girl'. The issues of women's attempts at responsibility and independence are always seen in the context of class, class as what women require socially and economically to raise the next generation, class as what irresponsible men can neglect or play with because they have always known its security. The irresponsible, falsely or superficially classless men are most sexually attractive to the responsible women. The attraction of classlessness, of getting outside the self, is sometimes extended nationally and geographically. Although unhappy with her aimless husband throughout the First World War (she has a child, so feels she cannot leave her husband, although they seldom live together), Jameson wrote in her autobiography that the only man she loved at the time, a love never consummated because of her guilts, was an energetic Texan in the American forces stationed in England. She reported his appeal to her before he left England in 1919 to live in a 'real country' because England is finished. Jameson reports herself 'amused' by his 'grotesque arrogance' and says she later 'realised the crude truth in his boasts'. Of course, for Jameson, what the Texan had said was never *the* truth, but it was the social challenge, the assault on her own class and culture, and the immolation of her insularity that was sexually attractive. Another version of the theme is developed as fiction in the best of Jameson's novellas of the thirties, *The Single Heart* (1932)[16] In this novella, a ship-owner's daughter initiates and continues a long adulterous affair with one of her family firm's energetic, working-class clerks during the First World War. When her kind, complacent upper-class husband dies of fatigue shortly after the war, she marries the clerk (by whom she has already had two children) and begins to shepherd his career in Labour Party politics. On a trip to Vienna in the early twenties, they see depravity, genteel poverty and despair. Both return dedicated to change England, 'its complacence, its rising tide of unemployed, its pointless extravagance'. The former clerk does well, becomes a member of the Labour-controlled Parliament of 1929–31. A political success, he is often unfaithful to his wife, and Jameson connects the collapse of the vitality of the marriage, the assimilation of divergent classes, with the collapse of the Labour government, the attempt to assimilate classes nationally, and the defection of Ramsay Macdonald to the Tory-controlled National Government. The woman accepts defeat and feels herself responsible for it, knowing that the affair, representing her own attempts to break out of classbound conventions, has been the only love of her life. Sexuality is the woman's attraction to a wider social and political world, seen as possible before and during the First World War, but betrayed by public events and indifference through the twenties and into the thirties.

For Jameson, the thirties was the decade of full recognition of herself as a writer and of her version of the world she depicted in such tangible social and political detail. She had begun, before the war, thinking of herself as the sea-captain's daughter, fascinated by the geographical, social and artistic possibilities of a world outside her narrow North, and she often wrote of the 'idealism' before 1914. But the war brought pain and cruelty, publicly and privately, the cruelties of infidelity and the pains of childbirth (her son was born in 1915), which she later connected with Nazi forms of torture and the horrors of war. She wrote in her autobiography that she thought mankind *damned* because of an endemic love of giving pain, visible in private affairs, more massively in wars. The war had maimed men far more deeply than it had maimed women. Male survivors were pallid, a theme frequent in *Love in Winter* where Hervey realises 'that the War had taken the fullness of his life and energy. Less than a whole man survived'. The theme is repeated with other men, physical and psychological impotence, women in despair sometimes sacrificing themselves to a gentle asexuality. Donne's poems are less the discovery of the new strident complexities, more laments for vanished physical and spiritual energy. Sexuality and energy seemed possible, from Jameson's point of view, only in new places with new classes, only with those substantially unmaimed by the war. For a short time, in the early twenties, Jameson thought some public rebirth might just be possible, an 'illusion of freedom'. Yet, as she wrote in *Company Parade* (1934), she and others were convinced by 1923 that Versailles was a 'dirty Peace' and another war inevitable. She began to characterise the period between the wars as an 'interregnum', economically, socially and nationally. As she wrote in her autobiography, by the thirties everyone sentient knew that the war was not over and that new forms of political organisation threatened human decency. She linked the 'moral stench' of the unemployed to Dachau, knowable from the mid-thirties onward. Although she never supported communism, she retrospectively wrote that, in the thirties: 'Put to it, I might have said that if my throat was cut I had sooner it were done on behalf of Communism than by a Fascist (This state of mind shows how little faith I had then in the triumph of that liberal humanism under whose banner I had enlisted)'.[17] Although active in support of what she saw as 'liberal humanism', decency, or survival, a pacifistic avoidance of pain was also attractive to her. Feelings of despair escalated. She wrote of the pacifist's cry 'Submit, submit' and their conviction that war 'was impossible and cruel'. She responded to the pacifists she respected: 'The price was too high, the smell from the concentration camps, from cells where men tortured men, from trains crammed to suffocation with human cattle, choked the words back into my throat. My despair was such that I could only let myself cry over the last war'. War, for Jameson, had become endemic, and despair, although warranted, a luxury or an artifact that humanity could not afford. Her background and the period of the 'interregnum' brought her close, but Storm Jameson, like many of her audience, did not succumb to the representation of the 'grey falcon' Rebecca West so strongly feared.

Words, travel and political activity were, for Storm Jameson, the only possible, sometimes dimly or faithlessly perceived, antidotes to despair. Travel had been important, since childhood when she stood on the rocky Whitby seacoast, in the mild or grim 'savagery of winter', thinking of the 'exotic products and creatures from Mexico, Japan, Africa'.[18] When she began to travel herself, after the First World War, she went most often to France, living there for a time, but also to Germany. She saw the incessant antagonism between the two, not just different 'climates, architecture, language, manners, customs, wines, but . . . a different state of soul'.[19] Through the twenties, she claimed that she did not dislike or fear Germany, but felt 'a cold passion of curiosity' as she watched, with growing aversion, a 'romantic distaste' for tolerance, compromise, individual freedom, which tolls through German history . . . the defeated despairing Germany of the twenties turns itself by an immense effort of cunning, tenacity, hypocrisy, moral and physical energy, shameless brutality into the Reich'.[20] By 1932, she saw that 'angry young men and women stripped themselves of conventional ideas and emotions, practising total evacuation as a moral hygiene'.[21] Jameson used Alsace, the point at which the France she loved intersected with the Germany she increasingly feared and hated, as the locus for her best known novel about Europe, *Cousin Honore* (1940). As war approached, she, like Rebecca West, turned towards the Balkans, took trips through Austria to Hungary, Czechoslovakia and Romania, feeling estranged by the nationalist bigotry everywhere she went (she found the anti-semitism in Hungary particularly appalling). She listened sympathetically to the dispossessed voices, the Jews, the Czechs, the Slovaks. In 1938, she became the president of the English PEN, following Wells and Priestley, and increased the organisation's activities in securing passage and homes for dispossessed writers, particularly Jews and Czechs, from Central Europe. Rebecca West, too, was indefatigable in getting writers and intellectuals out of Austria and Central Europe, as well as finding them jobs when they reached France or England. No longer rivals, the two women represented an active rescue mission from the lands of the totalitarian and the bigoted.

In her autobiography, full of words and torments from Central and Eastern Europe, Jameson says little about Spain. She never talks of it as the forecast of impending conflict; rather, like Rose Macaulay's, her Spain is close to Hemingway's of the twenties: 'the Spanish myth – or metaphor – in which even before the civil war, before Guernica, Spain began to be identified with contempt for luxury and death, and the instinct to revolt'.[22] In so far as her attention went toward the Mediterranean, travel took her to Italy rather than to Spain, and to another discovery not uncommon in the thirties. In a later novel, *A Cup of Tea for Mr Thorgill* (1957), a set of Oxford intellectuals is still replaying the political issues of the thirties. One of the characters muses: 'Why haven't I the courage to cut loose, to take the little money I could raise, and spend the rest of my life in mortal poverty and peace in a Greek or Turkish village, at that end of the Mediterranean?' This wish is seen as just beyond the fringe, outside the knowable and political world of Europe. Other characters talk of the thirties' discovery of Venice, a city that faces East and looks away from Europe. Jameson explains essayistically:

> Venice is, too, only partly a European capital: the Adriatic leads directly to Istanbul and the honey of the East, by-passing Greece; the slowness of movement along the canals or on foot in the labyrinth of stone-flagged passages and narrow streets; the vast empty squares you stumble into by accident, enclosed by shuttered houses, a wine shop, and a deserted half-ruined church, not a living soul, not so much as a cat, in sight; the walls of palaces on the smaller canals, with their windows eaten away by an inner shadow and their decaying steps, all share something, some knowledge, which owes nothing to Europe.

This account is far from the still-Jamesian Venice of L. P. Hartley, the Venice of princesses, gondolas, palazzi and elaborate social arrangements. It is a Venice, only half known in the thirties (in contrast to the Anglo-French intimate knowledge of Florence as the repository of Western culture), with a view toward the East, toward a wider and more mysterious world, although without the texture, the dense and clotted social detail, of Jameson's re-creation of more knowable parts of Europe.

Jameson saw clearly the echoes of both fascism and communism that emerged in England from the First World War. *Love in Winter*, set in 1924, gives voice to the language of both ideologies, language that Hervey finds repulsive and objects to explicitly. A proto-fascist says 'I declare war on all spineless snickering intellectuals, blind-at-birth, liberals, pacifists, shopkeepers . . . the white-faced black-coated shopkeepers for whom carefulness and liberalism were invented, have ruled the world long enough! . . . all that the sneering lying half-men have invented we restore, we, the whole men, the captains in armour'. He specifies further that the 'modern intellect is only a morbid growth . . . the invention of Jews and liberals. One of these days there will be a rush of clean blood through society driving them out'. When a foolish young woman is fascinated by his talk, and responds about the need for 'authority' and 'obedience' in the valueless world, he agrees, but he refuses to share the sensual excitement she offers. The voice of the narrator comments: 'It was not caution that restrained him so much as the streak of cruelty in his nature'. Fascism, for Jameson, involves both militant political order and the gratuitous cruelty of one who cares nothing for others. Communism in England in 1924 is seen as less indigenous, conveyed primarily through some characters' objections to the first Labour government:

> Sentiment is no use . . . you can have sane readjustments or you can have a bloody revolution. The Labour party thinks you can have a revolution without blood. That's one good rea-son I despise them. They're woolly-minded. A logical Socialist would be a Communist . . . no Englishman who is worth any-thing wants to splitarse about the streets in a uniform, bawling *Giovinezza* and administering castor oil to Ramsay Macdonald.

Yet those on the left looking to Moscow for stronger ideology, greater commitment, are betrayed by the fraud of the Zinoviev letter – and, from Jameson's point of view, whatever the motives of various leftists, connection with communism in ideology or its Soviet practice is suspect from 1924 on. From the 1957 point of view of *A Cup of Tea for Mr Thorgill*, the professions of communists from the thirties sound more ideologically narrow. The deracinated Oxford intellectuals who visit each other in a series of bizarre private coffee clatches that resemble the form for exchanges of confidence in Iris Murdoch's novels make statements seen as vague or ludicrous: 'the triumph of Communism is what *must* happen' or 'the one single road to an united world and the end of history'. Another calls communism the necessary and up-to-date form of his parents' Christianity, a system of belief that requires sacrifice, and holds his 'Calvinist childhood' responsible for his continued allegiance to the Party. A saner voice is that of a young woman, the ward of one of the academics, an orphan whose father was killed in Spain. She acknowledges that class judgements have become less intractable over the last twenty years, but refuses to follow allegiance to her father's dogma that others think she owes. She is both less sentimental and less addicted to a version of singular historical cause that impels her elders: 'Any action, however cruel and sordid, becomes noble when you baptize it in the name of the class struggle'. The novel also depicts intellectuals of both the thirties and the fifties whose belief in abstract principle or the necessities of history allows them to 'go on applauding executions in Eastern Europe while living safely in Oxford'. To them, and to those who nostalgically rhapsodise the 'courage, devotion, and, yes, humility poured out in the name of Communism', Jameson has a Czech, a refugee from the Nazis, respond simply: 'You don't know what you are and have'. Communism, for Jameson, represented an ideology and a cruel deception almost as lethal to civilisation as the combination of ideology and gratuitous cruelty in Nazism. Both were apocalyptic. In a world which seemed frightened and distorted by their unevenly competing strengths, Jameson sometimes expressed the climate of despair so painful to her for more than a quarter of a century. But she never succumbed to false hope or apocalypticism of her own, saw always her work and her effort with words as a gesture towards continuity, towards survival, never towards inhuman transformation. Life was never triumph, but the only defeat was death, which the language and texture of the chronicle manages to forestall for a considerable time, personally and historically.

The values implicit in the chronicle can also be incorporated into more compressed and modernistic forms of fiction, as they were by the great British novelist of the decade, Virginia Woolf.[23] Woolf had always written essays and fiction, often using the essay for a more public and simplified version of what she complicated, expanded and transformed into modernistic art in the fiction. In the twenties, she had articulated, in her precisely and metaphorically resonant style, public arguments about modernistic fiction in 'Mr Bennett and Mrs Brown' (an earlier, less fully developed version was called 'Modern Fiction' in 1919) and about her feminist convictions applied to literature in *A Room of One's Own* (1929). She had also expanded literary historical essays, at which she had become so skilful, into the form of *Orlando*, a unique form that combines the parody survey of English literature since the Elizabethans (far beyond the range of Rose Macaulay's *Told by an Idiot*) with her themes of gender, sexuality and the identities of art. To distinguish essay from novel in regard to *Orlando*, with all its versions of subjective historical time, seems futile or meaningless, especially in a context in which her earlier essays had accepted, sometimes preposterously, the boundaries of linear historical time and her fiction of the twenties had, in both narrative and dialogue, relied on subjective time. In the thirties, however, more securely committed to the relevance of public history than she had ever been (in common with many of her contemporaries), Woolf attempted the conjunction of essay and novel, of the perspectives of linear, public time and change combined with the determining subjectivities of a number of different characters. From the evidence in her letters and diaries, the project that led to *The Years* (1937) was technically, artistically, the most difficult of her life, her attempt to write her 'Arnold Bennett novel', her chronicle, to combine her own forms of fiction with the tactile demonstration of change through historical time that she had rejected as pre-modern, superficial, excessively materialistic and inconclusive in 'Mr Bennett and Mrs Brown'. She wrote a series of essays in the early thirties designed to merge with the novelistic development of character in *The Years*.[24] She eventually scrapped the essays as unworkable, and began to filter essayistic kinds of historical continuity into the framework of her fiction, her characters' perspectives. The problem was not in the attempt to mix what others might call fact with fiction, for she had always mixed the two, combined direct reference to tangible detail outside the self with the created perspective of the self. Nor was it a new attempt to bring political, social and historical reference into her fiction, for she had been doing that, in various unique ways, ever since *Jacob's Room* in 1923 incorporated the pains and losses of the unknown Edwardian young male in the First World War.[25] Rather, *The Years* established a complicated, metaphorical Woolfian sense of identity and perception within the framework of the chronicle, within a form of non-apocalyptic and historical continuity. Her earlier modernistic fiction had not been historically apocalyptic either, but its conclusions had established painfully won epiphanies, personal transformations, simple identity for Clarissa Dalloway, moments of art and vision for Lily Briscoe and others in *To the Lighthouse*, a metaphorical and momentary triumph over death in the midst of the continuous waves for the artist. These transformations were understated yet genuine. What was different for Woolf's fiction of the thirties was that, within the pains and continuities of history, transformation, in form and in content, was neither useful nor necessary in avoiding despair.

*The Years*, chronicling the children of Abel Pargiter, and others, from 1880 to the mid–1930s, uses public events and finalities, the death of Parnell in 1891 or that of Edward VII in 1910, to toll changes in time, like the function of Big Ben in *Mrs Dalloway*. Within that context, wind scourges and scrapes, much as the rainstorm destroyed in the 'Time Passes' section of *To the Lighthouse*. Characters, both individually and socially or publicly, however, change and survive, are not contingent on the identities they establish. One of Abel Pargiter's daughters, Eleanor, the principal voice of the novel, is seen as 'philanthropic; well-nourished; a spinster; a virgin; like all the women of her class, cold' in 1891, as fearing she might 'turn into a grey-haired lady cutting flowers with a pair of scissors and tapping at cottage doors' in 1910, as suddenly an active educator welcoming bombs and diminutions of class structures in 1917, and as feeling, in the midst of what she thinks of as her ignorance, that she is just beginning to understand and appreciate her academic brother (pompous as she's known he is) and her niece, the new professional woman, the doctor, in the 1930s. Similarly, a younger sister, frightened when she sees a sinister man expose himself on the street in 1880, shuttles back and forth, depending on the time, between militant advocacy of public causes (she is imprisoned when she throws a brick at the police during a suffragist demonstration) and retreat from the dirt of the poor she loves, by taking baths and growing fat. The sexually relating daughter of an Oxford master, expected to pour tea graciously for a lifetime, rebels in her desire to live on a farm, yet, after years of content, in accommodation to the world after the war, becomes a patroness of culture and the arts in a new, cosmopolitan London she sees as exciting. The Pargiter men change less, as do men in the upper classes generally. But lower-class men, or Africans or Poles, acquire energy and insight, in the context of established English society, in the world after the war. Hyde Park oratory is seen as excitingly diverse, different religious and class representations, in 1914, as grim and sordid, dirty and suggestive, after the war. The changes are good and bad, the characters never ultimately triumphant or defeated, and the surrounding worlds offer more possibility for some, less for others. The novel is itself history, a tactile movement of a half-century of British life, an artistically conceived and rendered chronicle that conveys both inner and outer lives. Woolf's most popular novel during her lifetime, and thoroughly modernistic in its uses of compression and metaphor, *The Years* is her accommodation to the tactility of Bennett's fictional England, as it is also, in the varieties of wetly symbolic weather, her accommodation to another chronicler she dismissed as Edwardian, Galsworthy, or to that side of Galsworthy that always resisted finality and called one of his trilogies *A Modern Comedy* because 'Tragedy's dry and England's damp'. Woolf never overcame the dread of water, the fear and attraction of drowning or immersion that would dissolve hard-won identity, which, in different forms, pervades the fiction from *Jacob's Room* through *Orlando*. In its sexual connotations, Woolf's need for an individual and self-enclosed dryness in order to survive is the opposite of Rosamond Lehmann's metaphor of the intense, willing and necessary immersion in water. Yet, in the fiction of her final decade, beginning with suggestions in the ambivalences of *The Waves*, Woolf focused on a recognition that the artistic voice also needed to include, whatever the individual cost, public and social life, required alternations of wet and dry, the inconstant rhythms, the conjunctions and disjunctions of public weather. Identity, more difficult than ever to achieve, could not be isolated to the dry sufficiency of the solely individual.

Woolf's final novel, *Between the Acts* (1941), preserves the tactility and extends the historical continuity through the metaphor of a pageant held on the lawn of a decaying Great House in the threatening summer of 1939. The house itself is a now seedy repository of civilisation, built in a hollow facing north to protect it from weather and barbarism. The inhabitants represent politely managed fractures within English society. The old owner is an apostle of reason, knowledgeable about the relics of Roman order and early British agriculture; his sister is religious and dreams of the days when, according to Wells's *Outline of History*, no water separated England from the Continent and mastodon roamed the valley that now includes London. The owner's son, Giles, is a stockbroker who looks toward a 'hedgehog' Europe, 'bristling with guns', and is strongly attracted to the Jewish Mrs Manresa, seen as brassy, exciting, warm-hearted, not as the vulgar outsider the society once had regarded her. Giles's wife, Isa, the age of the century, is discontent in her full library of books, angry at her husband because of their mutual infidelities, and in love, for the moment, with a handsome gentleman farmer she has met at a tennis party whose wife is 'goosefaced'. Isa also feels herself 'in her webbed feet entangled by her husband, the stockbroker'. Giles's attention is held by what he stumbles on and sees as a metaphor for Europe, a snake 'choked with a toad in its mouth', the snake unable to swallow, the toad unable to die. Within this context, the pageant takes place involving the whole village. The weather, subject of constant speculation beforehand, is variously dry and wet, sunshine interrupted by thick showers. Villagers enact the various parts, written and directed by the lonely, dispirited, artistic, homosexual Miss LaTrobe, anxious to give England a meaning she cannot see. Various scenes depict the rollicking, pastoral Elizabethans, the rationality of the Restoration which is primarily sexual intrigue and class division and which the old owner praises as 'God's truth'. The Victorians are castigated through satires of 'sweet lavender' combined with poverty, political uncertainty inflicted on others through the panoply and injustice of Empire, foggy disorder with 'muffin bells ringing and church bells pealing' presided over by the images of a Victorian constable and a piously canting minister. The staged scenes dissolve into the chaos of the final line listed on the programme, 'Present Time. Ourselves'. The audience is puzzled about the meaning or relevance of the statement, and the empty stage defies the unity and harmony both the villagers and inhabitants of the House seek. Comment is random, disconnected, gossip about Europe or leadership, speculations about whether or not old Queen Mary has met her errant son, the abdicated King, on England's south coast. Yet, almost contradictorily, as part of the weather, with no chain of historical causation, the bizarre pageant in its incompleteness has had an effect. Miss LaTrobe, initially disappointed, walks into the local pub for a solitary drink: 'She raised her glass to her lips. And drank. And listened. Words of one syllable sank down into the mud. She drowsed; she nodded. The mud became fertile. Words rose above the intolerably laden dumb oxen plodding through the mud. Words without meaning – wonderful words'. Her imperfect art allows others to speak for themselves. People talk. Giles and Isa, at the end, alone for the first time in the space of the novel, face each other without their customary evasive politeness: 'Alone, enmity was bared; also love. Before they slept, they must fight; after they fought, they would embrace. From that embrace another life might be born. But first they must fight, as the dog fox fights with the vixen, in the heart of darkness, in the fields of night'. They recognise how threatened an England they represent, how contemporary, continuous and permanent: 'The house had lost its shelter. It was night before roads were made, or houses. It was night that dwellers in caves had watched from some high place among rocks . . . .Then the curtain rose. They spoke'.

*Between the Acts*, in its conclusion, becomes history, the continuous attempt to survive that is the chronicle. It is the reverse of apocalypse, and the reverse of the heroism the Auden Generation sought. In her metaphors and language, Virginia Woolf, never more relentlessly than in her last two novels, avoided, undercut and opposed the heroic. Language itself, art, what could be spoken, was deliberately, assiduously, anti-heroic. It says something about the thirties that Auden himself, from honest, thoughtful intentions, desperately wanting some form of salvation from intractable problems, seems most inadequate in his late-thirties heroic popular mode, the empty fustian and rhetoric, for example, of the play *The Ascent of F6*. Woolf, in contrast, equally of the thirties, always the incipient artist, became more and more unheroic, more sympathetic with others, more interested in the mundane continuities that the decade, within the changes of history, represented. The unheroic, like the chronicle, like mere and ordinary words and their representation, was finally the counter to despair.

Perhaps his recognition of the failure and the emptiness of the heroic or wishes for apocalypse led to Auden's calling the decade of the thirties 'dishonest', a statement he later found inaccurate or too personal and expunged from his poem. Certainly, Auden himself, in retrospect, invested the heroic or the apocalyptic, in form or in content, with none of the value he had given it when young in the thirties. One of his greatest later poems, 'In Praise of Limestone' (1951) praises the equivocal, absorptive, pedestrian and unheroic qualities of limestone as a metaphor that is historical, geographical and sexual, that represents personal and political experience. In the work of other writers, too, many growing up in the thirties and interested in national and political issues, as well as in art, the thirties as represented in these different chronicles signify more than does any wish for heroic transformation. Stevie Smith objects to a later extension of the heroic, its application to the British in 1940. In her novel *The Holiday* she inserted a short essay on the Blitz: 'People say people were heroic in the raids. They were certainly good humoured and plucky and uncomplaining, but is it heroic to endure the unavoidable? Is not heroism rather to seek an end through danger? There was no end thought of or sought'. Iris Murdoch, in *The Book and the Brotherhood*, follows a 'brotherhood' of old Oxford friends from the thirties, once virtually all Marxist in their fear that the only alternative was certain destruction and paralysis. They still support the most committed among them, a man whose charismatic qualities have led them to anticipate the emergence of the great Marxist work that will transform their lives, even though most of them have long since lost faith in the ideas. Murdoch's novel becomes a treatment of the dangers of charisma, of emotional addiction to the certainties of leadership, both in the working out of plot and in the recognition that the now old Marxist, in defiance of years of history, is still committed to seeing 'history as slaughterhouse . . . something that *has to be*, even if it's terrible' or the rigidities of the determinism that insists 'we must purify our ideas with visions of utopia during a collapse of civilisation, which is inevitable'. The others recognise, in their own pains and defeats, that the Marxist is 'a black determinist, that's the most dangerous and attractive kind', that Marxism itself is an ideology of despair that forbids alternatives, forbids words. A more explicit social chronicler, Angus Wilson, in retrospect, came to share Woolf's attitudes toward the thirties, although he had earlier thought himself different from Woolf because of what he saw as social snobbery in her earlier fiction, as well as differences in attitude toward the potentially transformative power of art. In his most ambitious chronicle, *No Laughing Matter*, Wilson follows six children of a family from the hot, complacent summer of 1911 through to the perplexing social changes of the 1960s. The centre of the novel is the thirties, the decade during which the 'liberal humanism' in which Wilson, like Storm Jameson, strongly believes is most threatened by dogmas, religions and political experience. Through books, plays, dramatic re-enactments, and tangible social facts, Wilson establishes psychological and sexual profiles that might justify each of his characters becoming Nazi or communist, embracing a form of apocalyptic dogma. None of them do; all hold defensively, unheroically, out of vanity or accident or no knowable historical cause, to anti-dogmatic allegiance. It is not a matter of principle, and not at any time seen as heroic. Rather, it is seen as the language of individual and social identity, as simply as what people, in the midst of their follies and contradictions, are. In that sense, Virginia Woolf's version of the 1930s and what might have been learned through the decade's pain, betrayals and disillusions, has had the strongest literary influence.

## NOTES

1. A. N. Wilson, introduction to Rose Macaulay, *Told by an Idiot* (London: Virago, 1983) p. xiv.
2. Ibid., p. ix.
3. A far more interesting influence of this novel on Woolf's later fiction is advocated in Gloria G. Fromm's 'Re-inscribing *The Years*: Virginia Woolf, Rose Macaulay, and the Critics', *Journal of Modern Literature* XIII (July 1986), 2. Fromm argues that Woolf's method of incorporating essay into fiction in *The Years* owes something to Macaulay's earlier and cruder version. Fromm also speculates that, both as technique and as a version of history, Woolf's work can be seen as a rebuttal of Macaulay's.
4. The rhetoric of this novel, with its mixture of historical detail and universal absurdity, provides the closest parallel to that of Virginia Woolf's *Orlando*, a fact which leads one to speculate about the reciprocity of literary influence between Macaulay and Woolf.
5. Victoria Glendinning, *Rebecca West: A Life* (New York: Alfred A. Knopf, 1987) p. 180.
6. Ibid., p. 11.
7. Ibid., pp. 158–9.
8. Epilogue to Rebecca West, *Black Lamb and Grey Falcon*, reprinted in Samuel Hynes (ed.) *Rebecca West: A Celebration* (New York: Viking Press, 1977) p. 741.
9. For a full account of these controversies, see Glendinning, *Rebecca West: A Life*, pp. 170–79.
10. Recent criticism that has centred on writers in the thirties has over-emphasised the importance of Spain, both as fact and as symbol. For Valentine Cunningham in *British Writers of the Thirties* Spain is the singularly significant locus for travel outside the British Isles. When Cunningham does not use Spain, he locates travel in the visionary, as in a chapter entitled 'Somewhere the Good Place?', in which he discusses writers attempting to find venues for utopian or dystopian visions. Evelyn Waugh's Africa, in his

1930s fiction, is clearly a dystopic version of England and British colonialism, although his later retrospective versions of Yugoslavia during the Second World War are quite different. Given the theme of the book, the virtual omission of significant travel to the Balkans is more surprising in Paul Fussell's *Abroad: British Literary Traveling Between the Wars* (New York: Oxford University Press, 1980).

11.  John Lehmann, *I Am My Brother* (New York: Reynal & Company, 1960).

12.  Margaret Storm Jameson, *Journey from the North* vol. II (2 vols, London: Collins, 1969; Harvill Press, 1970) p. 135.

13.  Ibid., p. 158.

14.  Ibid., p. 245.

15.  Ibid., p. 55.

16.  This novella, as well as *Delicate Monster* and *A Day Off* (1933) were published in a volume entitled *Women Against Men* by Virago Press, London, in 1982.

17.  Margaret Storm Jameson, *Journey from the North*, vol. I, pp. 294–5.

18.  Ibid., p. 27.

19.  Ibid., p. 260.

20.  Ibid., p. 281.

21.  Ibid., p. 267.

22.  Ibid., p. 316.

23.  This statement is not intended to suggest comparative measuring of Woolf against other great modernists in fiction. James died in 1916, Lawrence in early 1930. I cannot pretend the capacity to deconstruct, post-deconstruct, or discuss suggestively Joyce's *Finnegan's Wake* in terms of these social details or perspectives relevant for the thirties. Woolf remains the only one of the greatest modernists in British fiction in whose work I can demonstrate significant and locatable changes through the particularity of the decade.

24.  These essays, part of an initial plan Woolf called *The Pargiters: A Novel-Essay*, have been collected and published in a volume called *The Pargiters by Virginia Woolf* edited, with an introduction, by Mitchell A. Leaska (New York: The New York Public Library & Readex Books, 1977). Woolf retained the name of Pargiter for her family in the final version of *The Years*.

25.  The appraisals of literary critics have frequently misunderstood Woolf's intentions and achievements in *The Years*. Mitchell Leaska, whose editorial work in assembling and publishing *The Pargiters* has been revealing, wrote that the combination of essay and fiction demonstrates Woolf's attempt to combine the rhetoric of 'granite' with that of 'rainbow' (p. vii) in the terms she used in a later essay, the 'granite' as the hard tangibility of fact and the 'rainbow' as the evanescence of fiction. But such a combination was consciously part of Woolf's attempts throughout the twenties, easily translatable into terms like art's necessary combination of 'bolts of iron' or the arches of the cathedral with the evanescence of the colours on butterfly wings repeated in *To the Lighthouse*.

Alex Zwerdling in *Virginia Woolf and the Real World* (Berkeley, Los Angeles and London: University of California Press, 1986) although effectively recalling and working with some little known social and political essays by Woolf in the thirties, assumed, in both his title and his consistent inflation that Woolf's writings rest on 'a previously unknown foundation' (p. 2) that only in the thirties did she discover a 'real' world in contrast to some entirely imaginary projection in the work of the twenties. Still, Zwerdling has some appreciation for *The Years*, in contrast with earlier critics. Even one so acute on *Mrs Dalloway*, *To the Lighthouse*, and *The Waves* as Phyllis Rose (in *Woman of Letters: A Life of Virginia Woolf*, New York: Oxford University Press, 1978) dismissed the novel with the claim that '*The Years* pass, but go nowhere', a severely reductive conflation of time with teleology. Rather, Woolf's fictional combinations of subjective and historical time, of what might be referred to as fiction and fact, took place earlier and were part of her conscious formulation of her own modernism, her experimental work. A more accurate line of commentary on Woolf's mixtures seems represented in an earlier letter written by her friend and rival Katherine Mansfield. Asked to review Woolf's 1919 novel, *Night and Day*, by John Middleton Murry, Mansfield's husband and the editor of *The Athenaeum*, Mansfield wrote, on 10 November 1919: 'I am doing Virginia for this week's novel. I don't like it, Boge. My private opinion is that it is a lie in the soul. The war never has been: that is what its message is. I don't want G. forbid mobilisation and the violation of Belgium – but the novel can't just leave the war out. There *must* have been a change of heart. It is really fearful to see the "settling down" of human beings. I feel In the *profoundest* sense that nothing can ever be the same that as artists we are traitors if we feel otherwise – we have to take it into account and find new expressions new moulds for our new thoughts & feelings . . . There is a trifling scene in Virginia's book where a charming young creature in a light fantastic attitude plays the flute: it positively frightens me – to realise this *utter coldness* & indifference. But I will be very careful and do my best to be dignified and sober. Inwardly I despise them all for a set of *cowards*. We have to face our war'. [Cherry A. Hankin (ed.) *Letters Between Katherine Mansfield and John Middleton Murry* (London: Virago, 1988) pp. 204–5.] The review itself was a more moderate and anonymous version of Mansfield's thought. From Woolf's letters and diaries, it is clear that Mansfield then influenced the experimental fiction of the sketches of *Kew Gardens* and *Monday or Tuesday* on which Woolf was already at work. The significant public and historical world was always, from that point on, part of Woolf's fiction, part of 'new moulds for our new thought'.

# Index